JUST YOU AND ME

BY WESLEY HARPER

Book two in the Three Rocks series

ISBN- 979-8-9943033-2-0 (paperback)

ISBN- 979-8-9943033-3-7 (e-book)

2026 Second Edition.

Cover design by: Juniper Hartmann of The Red Fox Creative
Photographer: A. McKay
Editor: Pace A.

For my roadtrip partners. Thousands of miles and I'm grateful for every single one.

Hello.

I can't believe you're here, holding my book in your hands! This book. The book that never was. The one that was supposed to be a short story, an exercise as I found my voice in writing.

Well, turns out, I needed a lot of pages to find my voice. Or, more likely, I just loved Gramps. And Dane.

After my first book, I had so many people in my real life ask who my characters were, if they were real people, if I'd ever put them in a book. The answer was no.

Well, I lied. The answer is yes.

I sprinkled names from my real life everywhere. Are the names true to the character? Oftentimes, absolutely not. But there are a few special characters that are.

Real or not, I hope you enjoy all of them.

Chapter One
Zoe

The wind whips my hair as I stand in the meadow at the end of the trail, looking out over the endless whitecaps of the Pacific Ocean. The knot of tension that lives in my chest loosens as I inhale the salty sea air. I close my eyes, listening to the waves crashing against the cliff far below. This is what I've been missing. Hiking, fresh air, and mud on my boots.

"Okay, now put your arms out and slowly spin in a circle," Abby directs, jolting me out of my Zen moment. "Wait, take your hat off first."

I look over to see her pointing her phone at me. I obediently toss my favorite Portland Trail Blazers hat to her and run my fingers through my long, tangled hair. I tip my head up toward the sky and spin in a circle, making sure to flex my quads by subtly raising onto my toes. Then, before she even asks, I move through a few yoga sequences, ending with a dancer pose, which seems to be an Instagram favorite.

"Perfect! Want me to post?" she asks, tossing my hat back.

"Sure," I say evenly over my shoulder, my back to her, Kristen, and Casey.

My vision blurs as I stare at the horizon and I hurriedly blink away the tears. How did I end up here? I should be #grateful for my #blessed life as a fitness #influencer, and I am, I really am, but I'm also mentally and emotionally exhausted.

I started ZoeSaysSoFitness as a creative outlet, a way to share my love of fitness with other college students. How it went from me making smoothies in the shared dorm kitchen and doing yoga in my tiny room to *this*, this monster that's taken over my life, I don't really know. I mean, a lot of hard work has gone into it, but still. All I know is I needed to get away and Abby huffed in annoyance as she scrambled to adjust my schedule.

I honestly hadn't planned on taking a couple days away, but when I saw the perky and beautiful teenager with the massive dog and hilarious little boy touting a girls' weekend at "Breakers Bliss," a cute rental cottage in a little beach town, I had a vision of the four of us getting back to our roots. Playing cards and sharing stories around a fire, not thinking about the next photoshoot or if another influencer was gaining traction with my target audience.

I got Abby to agree when she saw that the first guests would do a social media takeover for the up-and-coming rental account, and Kristen and Casey are always up for a girls' night if they can get away from work. Abby rescheduled with the yoga studio while I pulled up my AllTrails app to find us a hike.

I wander over to a large, flat rock and sit down. After three failed attempts to stuff my tangled hair back under my hat, I accept defeat. It's that windblown covergirl look from here on out I guess.

Kristen sits down beside me a few seconds later and leans her head on my shoulder. "So freaking breathtaking," she says quietly, staring out at the horizon.

I hum my agreement. It really is.

"Was that a whale?!" Kristen jumps up from our rock excitedly, nearly knocking me sideways. She points and I follow her finger, seeing nothing but rolling waves.

"There!" Casey exclaims excitedly from a few feet away. "Whales! Oh my god! This is amazing!"

Kristen squeals and jumps up and down like a little kid. Without a word, all four of us move to stand together, shoulder to shoulder, watching and waiting.

"A spout! There!" Abby is so excited she actually drops her phone. I thought it had been permanently attached to her hand. "Holy shit you guys, whales!"

Abby grabs my hand, and I take Kristen's hand with my other, who holds Casey's hand. This. This is what I pictured with this last-minute trip. Instead of looking for whale spouts, I look to my right and to my left, at the happy, excited smiles on my friends' faces. They radiate joy. I squeeze Abby and Kristen's hands, close my eyes, and soak in the moment.

Our hike back to the car is a completely different experience than our hike to the meadow over the ocean. I win the ongoing dad jokes war that started ages ago, we sing old 90's and early 2000's country songs, chat with the few other hikers we pass, and no one takes a single picture. Why haven't we hiked lately? There are tons of parks and trails all around Portland. This is what I need in my life.

***

A winding drive down Highway 101 brings us to Three Rocks, a blink-and-you'll-miss-it town. I slowly turn onto the narrow road just past a garage-sized fire station and pull into a parking space in front of what appears to be the only business here, The Town Mercantile. The store has a covered porch with a few small tables and chairs, each with what looks like driftwood and wildflowers centerpieces. Bundles of firewood are stacked next to the door and I can already picture a beach bonfire with s'mores and wine.

"Oh, shit," Abby says from the backseat.

"Uh, everything okay? Because this place is adorable," Kristen asks, peering out the windshield at the store. She unbuckles her seat belt and turns to face Abby and Casey in the back. Abby is frowning at her phone as she scrolls.

"Yeah, but our host messaged us. She says there was a family emergency this morning. Okay, we have a code to get in the front door of the house, but not for maybe an hour or so, and she says she will personally be at..." Abby looks up at The Town Mercantile, "this store most of the day. She's just going to trust us with the social media takeover because Kelsey, the teenager that convinced us to come here, is at the hospital. That doesn't sound good. But I guess we just go in and ask for Tex?"

With a shrug, I hop out and start across the parking lot. Casey jogs to catch up. The sweet, sugary scent of pastries hits me as soon as she pulls open the front door and my mouth instantly waters. What I wouldn't give to eat an actual cinnamon roll instead of drinking a cinnamon-roll-flavored protein shake. As soon as my eyes land on the pastry case, it's decided. A cinnamon roll will be eaten. Maybe two. Hashtag fitness.

Once I drag my eyes away from the rows of pastries, I'm immediately charmed by the rest of the store. There's Mercantile branded apparel displayed in a corner, tons of local soaps, candles, and trinkets, a wine selection that Kristen is already perusing, and Casey is trying on a bracelet. I hear Abby asking an older woman if Tex is in, so I go to the coffee counter.

"Can I help you?" a guy about my age asks.

He's tall with wavy, dark brown hair falling into his bright green eyes. When he smiles, a dimple winks at me. He is *cute* in a way that tells me he doesn't even know that he's just one more smile away from making me swoon.

"Are the cinnamon rolls as amazing as they look?" I ask him, remembering to turn on my ZoeSays personality. It may be a night away, but my entire life is tied to my work, which means I am always bubbly, happy, and outgoing.

He motions me forward, leaning slightly over the counter toward me. I give him a questioning look and he gives me another smile and waits. That damn dimple does me in. There's no need for a ZoeSays smile anymore, I can't help but grin as I lean in, trying not to lose myself in his green eyes.

"They're even better," he whispers.

"Why are we whispering? Is it a secret they're so good?" I whisper back, amused by his playful antics. "That seems like bad marketing."

"I don't want Marabelle to know she could use them as a weapon against me," he stage-whispers, tipping his head toward the older woman that's talking to Abby.

"Lucas Henry Stark, I already know you're the one hiding a cinnamon roll in the back every day to keep for yourself *and* that you have Kelsey saving you one when you don't have a shift," Marabelle calls down the counter.

"Ouch, did she just full-name you?" I ask with a laugh.

"If I had a dollar for every time she full-named me, I'd have a lot of dollars."

4

"Well, Lucas Henry Stark, I'm sold on the cinnamon rolls. Can I get two, please?" I ask. "Ooh! And two almond croissants." If I'm going to have a cheat meal, I might as well *really* make it worth it.

"I like it better when you full-name me, although it's a little unfair you know my full name and I don't even know your first name," he says, sounding casual, as he carefully places my cinnamon rolls in a white pastry box.

"I'm Zoe, it's nice to meet you." I hope he's casually flirting and not just being casually friendly. God, he's cute. "We're staying at a rental here tonight, any suggestions on where to eat? We didn't plan ahead or stop at a grocery store."

"Yeah, for sure, welcome to town. The cafe next door is opening right about now, they have a big menu for such a small restaurant. If you're into pizza, you can order pizza for dinner now and pick it up later. Sarah, the owner, is great. The cafe is the one and only restaurant here in the sprawling metropolis of Three Rocks, but there's quite a few in Rock Beach, which is about fifteen minutes away. And Pelican Pub in the other direction is always a win, especially if you like beer," he recites like he's been asked this question every day, most likely multiple times. His voice drops and he looks me in the eye. "Definitely make sure you're on the beach at sunset though, it's always amazing."

I want to ask if he'll be on the beach at sunset. Instead, I stare mutely at him as he walks around the counter and holds out my box of pastries.

"Your cinnamon rolls," he says, flashing that damn dimple again.

I swoon.

"Thanks," I say, blinking up at him before I finally remember to take the box. Our hands brush and tingles race up my arm.

I must swoon again because I'm suddenly closer to him. A lot closer. He smells like fresh air, clean laundry, and sunshine.

"Hi, I'm Abby!" Abby's hand is suddenly in my peripheral vision. "And this is Kristen and Casey."

I take a step back and un-swoon myself as Kristen shoots me a knowing smirk.

"Hi, it's nice to meet you all, welcome to our town." Lucas graces them with his smile as he shakes hands with Abby. I'm more than

5

a little pleased to see his dimple doesn't make an appearance for them. "Hey, boss," he adds, looking over my shoulder.

"Hi! You must be Zoe! I'm Harper, known around here as Tex," Lucas's boss says as she reaches her hand out toward me.

She looks a little stressed but her smile is genuine. I love her "Beach Please" hat and I think I see a flash of a tattoo on her hand. Maybe it's just ink from the pen that's tucked under her hat.

"Tex, it's so nice to meet you. I know we're here a little early, we absolutely don't expect to get in the house yet," I say, shaking her hand. I give her my real smile, because something about her just makes me feel at ease. Like she doesn't expect ZoeSaysSoFitness, just Zoe. "Lucas was just telling us about the cafe next door. We'll grab lunch first. This is Kristen, Abby, and Casey."

I nod my head in turn to each of my friends as I make the introduction. They say hello and Kristen asks Lucas a question about the wine display and they all walk that direction. I notice a small paperback book peeking out from Lucas's back pocket as I watch him walk away. A perfect dimple and he reads? Ugh.

"I'm happy you guys are here. This morning went a little sideways but I'll go make sure everything is set for you at the house now. Kelsey is our social media manager but will not be available, so even though I joke that I only trust two people and my dog, I'll trust you with the account takeover," Tex says with a wry grin.

Kelsey is the teenager, the dog is a doberman with a Z name, I remind myself. I make an effort to remember personal details about all of my social media contacts and collaborators, even though these days there's an alarming number of them.

I do remember looking through their socials with Abby, though. "I was blown away when I saw how quickly Kelsey had grown your accounts, is she really only eighteen years old?" I ask curiously. Kelsey's enthusiasm was only eclipsed by the dog's, at least in their reels.

"She is about to turn nineteen and then abandon me for Oregon State. You actually helped her win free books and class supplies from Avery, our boss slash my childhood best friend," Tex tells me, looking and sounding like a proud employee slash best friend.

This is the opening I was really hoping to get. I glimpsed Avery in a few of their pictures when they were celebrating the opening of the rental and, thanks to some light-to-moderate internet stalking and burner accounts used just to follow the A.Marino fan accounts, I have to know if my theory is correct. I'm bouncing with excitement at the prospect.

Leaning toward Tex, I drop my voice to a whisper. "Is Avery really A.Marino, the author? I thought I recognized her in one of the stories Kelsey posted, but I know how private she is so I didn't even tell my friends. We all love her books!"

I don't think "love" quite covers it. From the time I found them in high school until right this second, I have been *obsessed* with her books. And the fact she wrote them when she was a teenager? Blown away.

Tex just smiles at me. I try to hide my squeal. I fail. I also try not to do my happy dance. I fail at that, too. Tex laughs. I think I've won her over with my borderline obsession with her "boss slash best friend."

After we work through the access to the rental Instagram and TikTok accounts, I reassure Tex that Abby and I have been doing this for years and we can easily put together exactly what they're looking for. She looks both nervous and relieved; her distraction is evident. I hope that whatever emergency has taken Kelsey to the hospital is short-lived and not as serious as the word "hospital" makes it seem. Since I can't do anything else to help, I plan on crushing this social media takeover. My followers are going to be lining up to stay with them.

With my arms laden with mouth-watering pastries, cute matching bracelets, and all the ingredients for the s'mores I've been picturing, I approach Lucas at the register. My friends are trying on hoodies in the corner, taking outrageous mirror selfies that Abby will add to our stories, I'm sure. I can already picture what she'll put together and while I'm glad I'm being allowed to stay out of the pics right now, I know the end product is going to be just what Tex and Kelsey are looking for.

"So, Zoe, whose middle and last name are unknown, I don't want to ruin any surprises, but I also don't want to sell you these s'mores ingredients," Lucas says, smiling at me as he starts scanning my purchases.

7

"Well, Lucas Henry Stark, I love surprises, so say no more, I'll just leave them here," I reply, biting my lip. I really do love surprises.

I manage to pay and take the reusable bag from his hands without swooning, but it takes a lot of focus. A *lot*.

"I hope you enjoy your cinnamon rolls, Zoe, and maybe I'll see you around town. Don't forget sunset," he says, his voice slightly quieter, like it's just for me.

"Thanks," I say a little breathily, feeling my cheeks heat up.

How long has it been since I've felt this? Definitely not since Aiden.

I can feel his eyes on me as I'm swept out the door by my friends. I try to resist the urge to look back but can't. With a hand on the doorframe, I glance back. His bright green eyes meet mine. I get one more smile before I let the door fall closed behind me. That damn dimple.

Chapter Two
Lucas

Who was *that*? Really, who *was* that?

Marabelle gives me a knowing smile as I glance out the window toward the cafe. If I'm going to be dealing with tourists daily for the foreseeable future, I can't let one get to me like this at the beginning of the season or I'm in for a longass summer. I grab a box of tee shirts to add to the displays. It's mindless work, folding and refolding, and I try to lose myself in the task. Instead, I keep seeing Zoe's dark eyes, bright smile, and flushed cheeks.

Folding shirts is definitely not what I saw myself doing at twenty-three years old, but sometimes real life isn't quite what we expect it to be. The photography thing was a pipe dream anyway, a brief fantasy fueled by my summer working for the National Parks Service. Very few people make it as a travel photographer and they're usually either self-funded to start or have a connection in the industry. Social media has changed things as well, but it's not a route I know anything about or have the time or money to pursue.

It was hard enough to find this job, not because I'm terrible at folding shirts, but because I was looking for an employer that had some, okay a lot, of flexibility with my schedule. Tex listened to my worries, brought Avery, who owns the store, in, and they both gave their word that if anything came up with Gramps, no matter the time of day, I could leave immediately, even if it meant closing the store until someone else could come in. Luckily that hasn't come up yet but I'm sure it's just a matter of time.

"How's Henry doing?" Marabelle asks after her customers walk out. I swear she can read my mind some days. Maybe most days.

"He's holding his own, we've found a good routine," I tell her. "Thanks for those recipes, I've been getting pretty sick of spaghetti and meatballs."

That's an understatement. I have grown to despise spaghetti and meatballs, but it's an easy meal to make and one that Gramps loves. Grandma is the one that did all the cooking when I was young, while Gramps worked long hours down in Newport. Without her, we have spaghetti and meatballs three times a week.

I didn't even realize how much Gramps was struggling until Jake, a childhood friend, called me. He's now Officer Jake Jung of the Rock Beach Police Department.

"Hey, man, I just got a call about an elderly man at the park who seemed lost," he had started as my stomach immediately dropped. "It's Henry; I've got him in the front seat of my patrol car. I'll take him home, but is anyone there?"

That phone call changed my life. I had worked my ass off and was a year shy of getting my business degree from Western Oregon University (chosen for its proximity to Rock Beach) with a minor in art and design. By that night, I was a college drop out.

"I have a pot roast recipe for you next. You can start it in the morning and it'll be ready when you get home," Marabelle says, pulling me back into the present. "I have an extra crock pot, I'll run home and grab it for you during my break."

"You're a lifesaver, Mar, I really appreciate it," I reply.

Another understatement.

"You just let me know when you're willing to let Nancy or I give you a night off, maybe so you can hang out with people your own age for once," Marabelle says, with a slight head tilt toward the cafe.

"You both do more than enough for me," I tell her, folding the empty tee shirt box and stopping to give her a hug before I take it through the back door to the recycling bin.

Marabelle is the one who suggested this job for me, after seeing Gramps and I struggling to find our way. She had offered me a job when she was the overwhelmed and unhappy manager, before Tex came to town, but I declined, needing more hours. I promptly lost the job with more hours after having to leave twice mid-shift in the same week for Gramps.

The Mercantile is further from home and less hours, but a fifteen-minute drive for a job that doesn't put pressure on me is what is best for Gramps at this point. I just need to get my feet under me and figure out what we're going to do this fall when the tourists stop coming to the coast and my hours inevitably get cut.

My phone buzzes in my pocket as I push the recycling into the bin and that familiar fear takes hold until I realize it's a text, not a call. Gramps only calls. Same for the police.

Kelsey:
avery said you covered me, thx.

Lucas:
No prob, you ok?

Kelsey:
ok-ish. worried. glad brian convinced mom to come in. bummed i'm missing zoe.

Of course right as I've pushed Zoe out of my mind and come back down to reality, I'm reminded of her bright smile, quick wit, and rich caramel eyes.

Lucas:
Do you know her? She just stopped in.

Kelsey:
you got to meet her?? is she as cool as she seems? so jealous. girl crush.

Lucas:
Nothing you said makes sense. You don't know her?

Kelsey:
ok mr no social media. shes famous and seems super cool.

Lucas:
She didn't seem famous, but she did seem cool.

Kelsey:
she has millions of followers on insta, tiktok, youtube.

Kelsey:
you know all the things you avoid.

Kelsey:
its a big deal she rented from us. her takeover could be huge for team merc.

Kelsey: *(link) shes awesome.*

Lucas: *Well I hope your mom is ok. I'll cover for you as much as I can. I could use the hours. And I'm sorry you didn't get to meet your girl crush. She was nice.*

"Nice" is definitely not how I'd describe Zoe although I suppose that's what I just did. I mean, she did seem nice, but there are so many better adjectives out there for her. Beautiful, funny, alluring, stunning, bright, charismatic, beautiful, captivating, witty, charming, breathtaking, jaw-dropping, and out of my league. I'm a little bummed to hear she's some sort of social media star, but I click on the link Kelsey sent anyway and find myself on Zoe's Instagram page. ZoeSaysSoFitness.

Kelsey was right, she has a shit ton of followers. An overwhelming amount. A quick scroll shows a lot of yoga, mason jars filled with smoothies of every color, her stunning smile, more yoga, impressive handstands, and more smoothies. No wonder why she looked so longingly at the cinnamon rolls if green smoothies are her usual. Cinnamon rolls beat smoothies every time, it's just a fact of life.

I click on a picture of her leading a yoga class. While the picture shows her lean muscles gently stretching and a happy smile on her face, the comments are not so happy and gentle. Don't get me wrong, many of them are, but there's also quite a few that completely objectify her with sexual innuendos that come off as thinly veiled threats. I don't know if the men suggesting other positions they'd like her in or the women making snarky comments on her body are worse. Half point out a tiny, possibly imaginary roll of fat and the other half are shaming her for being too skinny. When did the internet get so mean?

I click on the red circle around her profile picture and find a photo journal of her day, which starts with a coffee stop at Dutch Bros, four drinks held up with a red 4Runner in the background. Next is the start of a hike; it looks like the Cascade Head trail, one I know well, with tall trees on either side of the trail. A picture with four pairs of hiking boots squished in mud. Then Zoe's joyfully spinning in a circle in the meadow at the end of the trail, head tipped back, arms stretched wide, looking completely carefree, the Pacific Ocean stretching to the blue horizon in the background.

She's already shared some of the pictures her friends took trying on clothes here at the store, a link to the account Kelsey made for The Mercantile flashing in the corner. I wonder if she ever worries about sharing her location, the comments on her post still have me slightly alarmed. Zoe even has a couple pictures from the cafe, sitting on the deck with Rejection Rock, the biggest of the three sea stack rock islands this town is named for, just peeking over her shoulder in the background, one of Sarah's gigantic, colorful salads in front of her. It feels weird watching her from my phone, solidifying the fact that social media is not my thing. I take one more look at her bright smile and then shove my phone back in my pocket.

Even if I was interested in the girl that walked into the store this morning, I have no interest in the job that comes with the girl.

That's a lie. I was, and am, absolutely interested in the girl, no matter what comes with her.

14

Chapter Three
Zoe

After devouring our lunches at the cute cafe overlooking the creek, we pile back into my 4Runner and drive over a narrow bridge toward our rental. The roads are barely big enough to accommodate two-way traffic, flowers are in bloom in every single yard, and there are handmade "go slow" signs posted on most fences.

"How does this town keep getting more adorable?!" Casey exclaims from the backseat. "Did you see that crab sign?"

"And the little library on the corner?" Kristen adds. "So freaking adorable."

"We're home!" I sing out as I pull into a small rocky driveway in front of a white cottage with a covered front porch.

A small pink sign on the porch railing welcomes us with the name of the cottage: Breakers Bliss.

Casey's right. It's adorable. The cottage, the town, the boy back at the store.

"There's a porch swing! I love porch swings!" Abby scrambles out of the car and runs toward the cottage.

I shut the engine off and am the last one up the steps. Casey has taken the spot next to Abby on the pink swing and Kristen is happily on camera duty. I stick my tongue out at her as she points it toward me. During lunch, between stuffing our faces and staring in awe at the giant rocks rising out of the sea in the distance, we decided to share media duties for the trip so it wasn't always Abby and I with a phone in hand. Kristen is already having a field day wielding her new power.

"Okay, Zoe, you're going to open the door and I'll just keep the video running as we check the place out, so keep up a commentary for me," Kristen says.

"Geez, give Kristen a camera and she turns into a dictator instead of a director," Abby jokes. "We should have done this ages ago."

"Quiet on the set!" Kristen snaps. She holds character for about three seconds then bursts into laughter. "Okay, I'm done. Want me to go live on Insta as we walk in?"

"Great idea," I nod excitedly. "Let's do it. This whole mini trip, let's do less editing, more real. Obviously we'll pull some polished content together for the rental accounts, but anything on ZoeSays, let's make it a little more *me*." Maybe I can use this getaway as not only a reset for me personally, but for ZoeSays as well. Get back to my roots.

"I love it, but as your friend and dedicated employee, I have to ask, are you ready for that? The comments might be brutal." Abby winces as she looks up at me from the swing.

My excitement fades, turning into something darker. Heavier. I hate that she's right. Our ZoeSays content is always carefully curated, even the "candid" moments, and when it's not, it can be brutal.

When did I start letting comments get to me so much? Why? It didn't used to feel like this.

It didn't used to *be* this.

"Also, we try not to post your location until after the fact when it's not a studio, gym, or restaurant. I don't know why I didn't think about that until right now, I think I was just excited to get away," Abby says, biting the corner of her lip. That's her guilty tell, which immediately triggers my own guilt. I'm not the only one that needs a break.

"Abby, that's not on you," I tell her. "I should have thought of it."

I *did* think of it, for about thirty seconds before our hike. But I wasn't willing to give up our hike. Our night away.

My guilt grows. Am I putting my friends at risk?

16

"There haven't been any weirdos lately, right? Like, more than usual?" Kristen asks, looking at Abby.

Abby shakes her head.

"You're not alone, you've got us!" Casey chimes in.

"And this town feels safe, you know?" Kristen says.

I look at my friends, who all smile and nod. If any of them looked nervous, I'd call the whole thing off. Or at least call Dane.

"Want to call Dane?" Abby asks, reading my mind.

No. I want to have a normal girls' weekend with wine on this freaking adorable porch swing and s'mores by a fire that I might or might not be able to build. I want the reset that both Abby and I need.

I shake my head as my determination builds. "Nope. This is for us." I look at each of my friends again. There can be middle ground, right? "And let's do our usual content for Tex's accounts but let's at least add *some* of the messy stuff to mine," I say.

Two minutes later I'm smiling at Abby's phone in Kristen's hand, welcoming my followers to our cottage. I don't have to fake anything, as soon as I swing the door open I'm back to literally bouncing with excitement. The cottage has bright, natural light spilling in from windows on all sides, there's a huge gift basket sitting on the counter that I can't wait to dig into, and in the corner are plants and plants and more plants. Hanging baskets with vines spilling over, cute mismatched pots of all sizes on shelves, and a prickly cactus wearing a pink Santa hat of all things.

In fact, pink accents are everywhere. The pots the plants are residing in are a kaleidoscope of pink, a few of the shelves are streaked with a very light, bright pink, the pillows on the couch are a soft blush, and the coffee maker on the counter is the brightest pink I've ever seen. Barbie, but less. Or more? And it works. I love it.

"Sand dollar!" Abby shrieks from another room, interrupting my train of thought. "I found a sand dollar!"

She bursts back into the living room holding a shell the size of her palm. She has a huge smile and does a ridiculous, overexaggerated version of my happy dance.

"I found one, too!" Casey hollers from the small bathroom. She slides back into the room with socked-feet like Tom Cruise in Risky

17

Business. "It's pink! Oooh! Look at the back, there's writing! It says 'Breakers Bliss 3 of 7' on it. So there must be seven hidden."

There's a moment where you could hear a pin drop, then we all scatter, scrambling to find the hidden shells. My heart is racing, beating against my chest, adrenaline pounding through my veins. I feel like a little kid. I'm opening dresser drawers when I hear Kristen in the kitchen call for us.

"Guys! Check this out!"

When I slide back into the kitchen, I'm happy to see I'm not the only one out of breath. Kristen waves her hand at a cabinet and we all stare at her, unsure what we are supposed to be looking at. She opens the door slowly and there's a pink chalkboard on the inside.

"Welcome, Breakers!" is written in swirly handwriting. She then turns and opens another cupboard with another pink chalkboard. "Be Fucking Unstoppable" is written on this one. There's a little mason jar of chalk with a note encouraging guests to leave notes for the next renters.

"I love this place," Kristen announces. "So much."

She no longer has Abby's phone in hand. Shit. I hope she remembered to turn off the live feed before she discarded it in our race to find sand dollars. I mean, it is my source of income.

"Uh, Kris, where's my phone?" Abby asks, reading my mind.

"Oh, I stopped our live when I realized we were racing," she shrugs.

Abby eyes me for my reaction. I let my eyes wander between my friends. They all look uncertain. The only thing I'm certain about is there's at least three sand dollars left to find. Abby has two in one hand, Casey has one, Kristen has one, and I have zero.

"Three shells left!" I exclaim and run out the back door.

Laughter sounds behind me but I pull the door closed, hoping to slow down anyone that gives chase. I find a sand dollar in the fire pit and collapse on a chair, content with my single find. This is just what we need, carefree fun.

***

"When and why did we stop doing random shit like this?" Casey asks, ducking as the 4Runner liftgate opens. "We used to take off for a night all the time, even when we were dumb eighteen-year-old freshmen with no money, just wanting to have fun."

"Yeah, now we're just dumb twenty-four year olds with money but without fun," Kristen snorts, leaning in to grab her overnight bag.

"Remember when we thought about getting tattoos?" I add, remembering our spur-of-the-moment trip to San Francisco. "We really should have done that." I shoulder my duffel as well as Abby's backpack and start back up the walkway.

"Maybe this trip we will! Why the hell not?" Casey asks, her eyes sparkling as she looks at me.

Okay, now that's tempting. Casey is obviously in, Kristen is nodding along as well.

"Abs!" I holler in the open front door. "You in for tattoos this trip?"

"I swear I heard you ask if I wanted to get a tattoo," Abby says, walking out of the bedroom she and I are sharing, phone in hand. I bet in the time it took us to grab the bags, she's already smoothed over the abandoned Instagram live with pictures of our rental.

"So is that a yes?" Casey asks with a grin.

Abby gives a little sigh and Casey's expression falters. She drops her bag on the floor and makes a pouty face at Abby.

"It would be a 'hell yes!' but the only tattoo parlor in the area is closed on Mondays and most Tuesdays, including tomorrow," Abby says. She holds out her phone so we can see the website. "Rock Beach Tattoo, open every other freaking day but the two we are here."

"That's a bummer, I got all excited," I say, looking down to my wrist where I've already decided my first tattoo will go.

"Stay excited," Kristen demands. "Gift basket time!"

"Oooh!" Abby and Casey squeal and clap. Easy to stay excited with friends like these.

We dump our bags in the bedrooms and reconvene in the kitchen, all of us eyeing the gift basket on the kitchen island. We find pink champagne hidden under bright pink hats, cookies and shower scrub, candles and sparkling cider. When I see s'mores ingredients packaged together with a neon pink bow, I bite back my smile. They're not just any marshmallows either, they're strawberry-flavored homemade

19

marshmallows that are, of course, pink. While I love the pink theme, it's the coffee-flavored marshmallows that catch my eye. "Great with dark chocolate!" reads a tiny tag attached to the package. I can't freaking wait.

***

"No, 'stroke' is definitely a golf term," Casey argues, crossing her arms.

"Lamest use of the word," I mutter.

"We saw a sign for a golf course, that's gotta be it," Abby says, flipping the card back over.

"I mean, we're not going to find the next clue just sitting here," Kristen says. "Let's go!"

Three minutes later, we've made it halfway down the block. While I've gotten pretty good at multitasking, I will always feel ridiculous walking down a street while taking a video. But I also freaking love this idea of a scavenger hunt so I gotta give Tex props on this one.

"Okay, internet friends and strangers," I begin, giving a ZoeSays smile. "We found a cryptic clue in that amazing gift basket we showed you, so we are off on a scavenger hunt. The first clue reads:

'welcome to our tiny town, a great place to slow down.
we've left a trail of hints, that might only make a little sense.
where can you count your strokes? no, it's not one of my dirty jokes.
go and find the next clue, maybe it will tell you what to do.'

so we think the next clue is at the golf course, let's go!"

As soon as I have the story up, our competitive sides come out (as well as my real smile) and we are off to the races.

Casey was right about the golf course and we find a tiny map of the town, pirate x-marks-the-spot style, hidden on the back of a three-wheel golf cart which has, of course, a pink steering wheel.

"I think that's a tsunami evacuation route," Abby says, tilting her head and squinting.

"It's north, because that's the beach, so probably up that road." Casey nods toward the road that parallels the golf course.

"Uh, don't tsunami routes go uphill?" Kristen asks, looking across the golf course to the houses dotting the hillside. The very steep hillside.

"Hey guys, why do these mountains make people laugh?" I wave toward the hills. "Because they're hill-areas. Get it? Hilarious?"

"Zoe!" Kristen and Casey groan.

"So glad you didn't get that one on video," Abby says. "Come on, we've got clues to find!"

We find the narrow pedestrian evacuation route about a quarter-mile past the golf course and follow the path through the trees. Luckily the next clue is sidewalk-chalked on a small bridge over a creek, not at the top of the hill like I feared. Note to self: in case of a tsunami, you better be fit!

I snap a few pictures of salmon berries ripening along the trail before we jog back to the cafe we had lunch at earlier. Sarah, the owner, is happy to see us again and after we recite a poem, she hands over the next cryptic clue. Of course it sends us in the opposite direction and we trek all the way back across town to yet another beach path, this one along a falling-down split rail fence. We check nearly every fence post before we find the hidden pink card.

"Okay, people of the internet, this is the last one. Well, I think. We have a list of pictures to take, including two with bonus points. What are the bonus points for, you ask? I have no clue. Get it, clue? Like a scavenger hunt clue?" I ask the camera, before snapping a picture of our photo list and posting both, quite pleased with my pun.

"Oh my god, Zoe, stop with the bad jokes," Casey admonishes, laughing at me. "You're not funny!"

Kristen snatches the list from me and scans it.

- ☐ Rejection Rock
- ☐ Sea anemone
- ☐ Flying kite
- ☐ Someone golfing
- ☐ A seagull
- ☐ A house with pink flowers
- ☐ Frisbee game

☐ Starfish

☐ Dog on the beach (bonus points for Zero)

☐ A stranger in a "BREAKERS" hat (bonus points for Betty)

"Some of these will be easy, others not so much. Zero is Tex's dog from the videos, right?" Kristen asks. "But who the hell is Betty? And Rejection Rock is just the biggest of the three rocks, the one with the trees that you can climb? Oh! The kids and I just read a book about an anemone family!" She gets that sappy look on her face that she always gets when she talks about the three kids she nannies for. They're pretty fun kids, I'll give her that, *and* they laugh at my jokes. Should have brought them along.

"We got this, no problem," Abby says confidently. She looks down at her phone. "And your followers are going crazy for this!"

***

"Okay, we're walking down the path to the beach and we think we see Zero," I whisper as I film much, much later. Despite Abby's confidence, the list has taken us quite a while. "There's a cute little boy with her so we won't film until we get permission, but there's only this hot, older, lumberjack guy on the beach with them. Please hold for more."

"Definitely hot lumberjack," Casey agrees, eyeing the man in flannel.

"Excuse me," I say with my ZoeSays smile as we approach the bearded man. "Is that dog named Zero?"

Hot Lumberjack looks at me, clearly on guard, and I don't really blame him. His eyes dart between the four of us.

"Sorry, we're staying at Breakers Bliss, and we get bonus points on a scavenger hunt if the dog we take a picture with is Zero," Abby adds, trying to explain that we aren't stalkers.

"We don't know what the bonus points will get us, but we are fully invested in this scavenger hunt," I say, laughing at how ridiculous we are.

"Oh, yeah, sorry, it's been a weird day," Hot Lumberjack says, standing up to greet us. My eyes widen slightly, he's a *lot* bigger than he

22

looked when he was sitting in the sand. Dane's got nothing on this guy. "I'm West, and yes, that's the famous Zero."

West, West, remember his name is West. West coast, best coast. I really need new ways to remember names.

"And Cutie Colt?" Kristen asks. "Okay, this must be weird, strangers asking you about your dog and your kid."

"Well, neither are technically mine, I'm just the lucky babysitter I guess," Hot Lumberjack West says with a laugh. No. Just West.

"I'm Zoe, and this is Abby, Casey, and Kristen. If you know Zero and Colt then you must know Kelsey and Tex. They crushed it with this rental, we are having so much fun with the scavenger hunt! I feel like we are running around like kids. We love your town, the house, the store, everything. You're so lucky to live here!" I can't help but gush.

"Besides babysitting, what do you do for work?" Abby asks him. "Because I am ready to move here. But, you know, money. Adulting. Bills."

Same, Abby, same. I'm guessing there's not a yoga studio in this tiny town.

"I own the tattoo shop in the next town, bigger town, over. Rock Beach Tattoo. I also do carpentry work. And," he nods at Colt and Zero who are chasing seagulls, "babysitting. But that doesn't pay well, or at all."

"No fucking way," I breathe, my eyes immediately tracing the tattoos on his muscular forearm.

"Uh, yes fucking way?" he replies, sounding confused but his smile shows he's at least slightly amused.

"We looked you up earlier but it said you don't have hours on Mondays and Tuesdays. We wanted to get tattoos this trip," I explain quickly.

"Well, as long as my two charges have a different babysitter tomorrow, I can do that. I know Harper told you about the family emergency today, so let me check on the plan for these two," he says, whistling for Zero who obediently trots over, Colt trailing along. "Hey bud, remember Tex's scavenger hunt? These ladies are hoping for a picture with Zero, can you share her for a minute?"

"I love your hat!" Casey tells him, tapping the bill of his hat.

23

"Miss Betty has one, too, you're supposed to find her," Colt informs us. "But that's a secret."

"Your secret is safe with us," I tell him, giving him a grin. "Thanks for sharing Zero with us! Looks like you were having a lot of fun together."

After making sure Colt is comfortable with us, West takes a few steps away and pulls out his phone. Colt is freaking adorable and Zero loves our attention nearly as much as he does, rolling around on her back in the sand as Colt shows us the rocks and shells he's been collecting.

"I didn't know Dobermans were so goofy," Casey says, laughing as Zero takes off and runs enthusiastic zoomies around us. "She's so fast!"

"I'm really fast, too," Colt announces.

"I bet you are," I tell him.

"I'll race you to the ocean," he challenges.

I'm pretty sure I shouldn't run off with a stranger's kid. I look over at Hot Lumberjack, no, West, and he's overheard Colt's challenge. He gives me a nod.

"You're on," I tell Colt.

I make a show of jumping up and down, stretching. He isn't intimidated in the slightest.

"3-2-1-Go!" he yells without warning. Little cheater.

All four of us and the dog take off after him. Running in dry sand is hard, not even going to lie. Colt pumps his little arms hard and I make sure to stay half a step behind him. I can hear Abby, Kristen, and Casey on my heels.

"I won!" Colt cries, flinging his arms up as soon as his feet splash in the receding waves.

"Oh man, it wasn't even close, you are really fast," I tell him, holding my hand out for a high five.

After high fives all around, we walk back toward West. Colt really has the good life. It must be amazing to grow up here.

"I can get you guys in at 1 p.m., does that work?" West asks, looking between the four of us as we approach.

"Perfect! We're supposed to check out by 11 a.m., but I think I'm going to text Tex and ask if we can book another night. I need to make sure we have enough time to get all the selfies for the scavenger hunt," I tell him, laughing once again at how invested in this scavenger hunt I am.

West gives me his number in case anything comes up, then after a quick stop at the house to get the rest of the matching pink hats, we go in search of Betty.

Betty is everything I didn't know I needed in my life. She goes from a super sweet old lady to a freaking riot in about seven seconds flat. I mean, she must be nearly eighty years old, but she has me blushing within the first two minutes.

"Well now, dear, back in my day, if I would have had this fancy Instabook, I would have had *all* the boys looking at my pictures, if you know what I mean," Betty says as Kristen takes video, waggling her eyebrows suggestively at the camera. "Tex says you're famous on The Gram, so let's make me famous, too. I got rid of my last husband, good riddance, but I'm not looking to marry, I just like the attention."

I almost ask how she got rid of her last husband, but I decide it's one of those things that maybe should remain a mystery. The last thing I need is a police investigation or Dateline special. We give Betty all the attention we can, Abby picking up our pizza from the cafe to share with her, only leaving when the sky hints at sunset. My cheeks hurt from smiling as we walk back toward the beach and it's not from the selfies, although giving Betty the phone was another of Abby's genius ideas.

"I want to be Betty when I grow up," Kristen declares as we hustle back toward the beach trail closest to Breakers Bliss.

"I want to be Betty right now," Casey says.

"Guys," I say, stopping short at the top of the trail, just before it drops down onto the beach. "I found our tattoo."

The sky is streaked with pink, purple, and yellow as the sun slowly sinks into the ocean. A slight twinge of disappointment hits when I scan the beach and don't see cute, dimpled Lucas Henry Stark anywhere, but the sunset is absolutely breathtaking. We stand in a line, just like we did this morning on the hike, holding hands as we stare in wonder, and I count this as one of my favorite days.

Chapter Four
Lucas

"Good morning, Gramps, how'd you sleep?" I call as I quickly chop carrots and potatoes to add to the crock pot. "Are you going to the library today?"

"Nancy really had me working yesterday," Gramps replies as he shuffles into the kitchen. "We moved some of the shelves around in the children' s section. I told her I'd help her finish today."

Jake's great-aunt Nancy, who I knew as my grandma's best friend when I was a kid, is the one that suggested Gramps volunteer at the library. She's been the head librarian in Rock Beach forever, and three days a week she picks Gramps up from our house and he spends all afternoon at the library. Even if he's having a bad day, shelving books is an easy task. I do wonder on days like today if she creates extra work just to help keep him busy. I only hope that she'll tell me if it's ever too much for her.

"Sounds like you'll work up an appetite. Marabelle sent me home yesterday with a new recipe and a crock pot, think this roast is going to work out?" I ask, nodding at the red crock pot on the cluttered kitchen counter.

"You told me last night about the damn crock pot," Gramps grumbles.

"So is that a no on thinking it's going to work?" I ask, smiling to myself as I dump the carrots in with the roast.

I try to give him little reminders, especially when he seems more tired than usual, and when he complains about it, I know it means he's feeling sharp. Sharp mornings are good mornings. It's a good morning.

I take a coffee mug out of the cupboard in front of me and hand it to him before double checking the recipe. I watch him out of the corner of my eye. His hand is steady as he pours, another good sign.

"Roast sounds good, but when did you have time to get one?" Gramps asks after filling his mug.

"I couldn't sleep. I went to the grocery store after you went to bed," I reply, only slightly guilty about the white lie.

I could sleep, I just couldn't find another time to get groceries. I had really hoped to make it back to Three Rocks for sunset, in case Zoe happened to be on the beach, but my days all seem to go the same. Morning coffee with Gramps, work, pick Gramps up from the library, start laundry, make dinner, move laundry, eat dinner with Gramps, do the dishes, stare at the bills that I don't know how we're going to pay, fold laundry, then pick up my book until Gramps shuffles off to bed. After making sure he's settled, I head to the grocery store. I have yet to master planning ahead for our meals.

I glance at my watch as I put the lid on the crock pot. Marabelle might be onto something. That didn't take long at all and if I don't have to make dinner later, I'll have time to…do something else? Look for a second job is probably what I'll end up doing. How I'll juggle a second job and Gramps, I don't know.

"I have to go in early, I don't have time for backyard coffee this morning, I'm sorry. Kelsey had that family emergency yesterday so I don't know what time I'm getting off tonight either. Dinner should be done by 5 p.m. though," I tell him. I make a mental note to text Nancy, letting her know as well. She already told me she could bring Gramps home tonight.

"No apologies, Luke, ever. I should be the one apologizing to you, what kind of twenty-three-year-old wants to take care of their old grandpa?"

I stop gathering my things and turn to look him in the eye. "This kind of twenty-three-year-old, Gramps," I tell him. "This is where I want to be."

***

"You just missed your girl!" Marabelle greets me with a sly smile as soon as I open the front door.

"Zero?" I ask, confused.

I try to sneak Zero a treat every day but I didn't realize that classified her as my girl, especially because she's the boss's dog and Colt, my little five-year-old buddy, has won Zero's heart more than anyone.

"No, your pretty friend from yesterday," Marabelle says. "She left something for you. It's in the case."

Marabelle laughs when I freeze in shock halfway to the counter. My heart pounds in my chest as I dart behind the coffee counter and duck to look in the pastry case. There's a small pastry box with "Lucas Henry Stark" written in neat block letters. I open the box and inside sits a single cinnamon roll.

It's definitely a good day.

I spend the rest of the morning and early afternoon bantering with the locals, advising tourists on fun places to check out, and trying to help stressed-out Tex however I can. She checks her phone approximately every seven seconds, waiting to hear from Kelsey or Avery, who are back at the hospital with Kelsey's mom. Every time she looks at her phone, I feel a little stab of guilt. How can I be on a cinnamon roll high when Mrs. G is in the hospital? I should feel lucky it's not Gramps. I discreetly check his location on my phone. Still at the library.

Marabelle finally pushes Tex into the back office and directs her to work on The To-Do List, which is just a bunch of sticky notes lining the wall above her desk that we all try to pitch in on if the store is slow. When I peek around the corner to check on her after an hour's silence, she's laughing at her phone. I raise my eyebrows at her, wondering if she's officially lost it, but she shows me a picture of Zoe, arm raised to show off a blur of ink on her wrist, with West almost smiling beside her. My heart rate jumps.

Zoe hasn't left the coast yet.

I'm still pondering this development when Tex hollers that she's cutting out early and races out the front door. Barely two minutes later I feel my phone buzz. I check to make sure the store is empty before pulling it out of my pocket.

Kelsey:
on our way home!

Relief washes over me. Kelsey has gone from an annoying little sister-type to a cool little sister-type.

Kelsey:
thx again for covering.

Lucas:
No problem, glad your mom is better.

Kelsey:
she's better and i get to hang w girl crush tonight!

Zoe? She's staying another night?

Kelsey:
she invited the 3 of us and i'm going to learn her ways. team merc is going next level

Lucas:
Is it going to be awkward when you slip up and call her "Girl Crush" in person?

Kelsey:
lucas!

Kelsey:
now when i do, i'm blaming you

I put my phone away with a smile. Zoe is still in town. It's a very good day.

***

My stomach drops as soon as I pull into the driveway and see Nancy's sedan parked close to the front steps. Don't panic, don't panic, don't panic. She's probably just being nice and keeping Gramps company. Gramps is fine. Nancy would have called if she needed me.

"Nancy! I didn't know you'd still be here," I say, keeping my voice even as I pull open the front door. "Hi, Gramps."

"Hi hon, I just wanted to chat, thought I'd hang out a few minutes until you got home," Nancy says, rising from her seat to give me a hug.

A chat. That doesn't sound good. My stomach tightens again.

"I'm sorry I couldn't get over there to pick him up," I tell her quietly as she gives me a squeeze.

"Oh, no, Lucas, no problem whatsoever. I might have taken a little taste of the roast, must be Mar's recipe," she says with a smile. "You're learning!"

Gramps hasn't replied to my greeting so I peer behind Nancy into the dining room. He's eating methodically, staring at his plate. My heart sinks.

"Hi, Gramps, I'll be in to eat with you in a few minutes," I call. "I'm just going to walk Nancy out to her car."

No reply. Nancy gives me a sympathetic smile and tips her head toward the door. I hold it open for her and follow her out. We sink into the beat-up chairs on the front porch and sit in silence for a few seconds, each of us gathering our thoughts.

"He's just tired tonight; I think my little project at the library backfired. I wanted him to have a reason to come in, Marabelle told me about Rebekah and I knew you'd be working longer hours. I think I overdid it," Nancy says, breaking the silence. It takes me a second to realize Rebekah is Mrs. G.

"I'm sorry, Nancy. I really appreciate everything you do for us. I know I need to find a more permanent solution, but I can't bear the thought of moving him into a retirement center. I also don't think we can afford it. This trailer might not be much, but he worked so hard to keep the roof over our heads for all those years," I tell her. "It's home, the only home he knows." I lean forward, elbows on my knees, and bury my face in my hands. What am I going to do now?

"Lucas. Lucas, look at me," Nancy says in her no-nonsense voice.

I take a deep breath and sit back, repositioning my chair so it's angled toward her.

"You are not alone in this," she says. "I promised Elle that I'd look out for both of you, not because I loved her, but because I loved all three of you. Still do."

A wave of grief knocks me sideways. I blink back tears. Of course Grandma made sure that Gramps and I would still be taken care of. I rub my hands down my face and stare at my boots. Nancy gives me a minute to pull myself together.

"So what do we do?" I finally ask when I'm sure my voice will be steady.

"Well, right now you go in and eat that delicious pot roast you made. Tomorrow is a new day. I'll have Jakey drive by the house a few times during his patrol tomorrow while you're at work. It'll be okay," she says.

"This isn't sustainable, we both know it," I say miserably. I am failing the only family member I have left and I'm dragging Nancy down with us.

"Tomorrow is a new day," she repeats. She reaches out and puts her hand on my arm, giving it a reassuring squeeze. "And that isn't actually why I wanted to chat. I was hoping I could convince you to help me with the book sale that Tex is planning during the Fourth of July Festival in Three Rocks. Don't tell your boss, I told her I had it taken care of, but I'm still working on the plans for it. I'm just so pleased they chose an event to benefit the library."

"Of course I'll help," I tell her. "Just tell me what you need. Your library got me through my childhood, you know that, right?"

Free books were a free escape for me. Still are. Back then, I could forget about the mom I never knew, the dad that walked out on me, the way Gramps's shoulders slouched more each week, how Grandma paid for school supplies in loose change, and get lost in a story instead.

32

Much like Gramps does now, some afternoons I'd help Nancy shelve books, just to have something to do.

"I knew I could count on you," Nancy says. "Now, go eat that pot roast. We'll go over the plans soon. Henry will be fine after a good night's sleep. Call me if you need anything, day or night."

She gives me another hug before walking down the steps to her car. I take one more deep breath and walk back inside, ready to spend time with Gramps, to reassure myself that he's okay.

Nancy was right, the pot roast is pretty damn good. The cinnamon roll Gramps and I share for dessert is even better.

***

"Go out front," Marabelle hisses as she hurries around the corner into the kitchen the next morning.

"Are you okay?" I ask, worried she's cut herself again.

"Hurry!" she says, physically pushing me toward the door.

"Good morning, Lucas Henry Stark," Zoe says.

She's here. Actually here. My heart rate speeds up when she smiles brightly at me. I'm pretty sure I'd do anything to have it flashed at me just one more time. She looks both happy and a little shy this morning, as well as breathtakingly beautiful, but that seems to be her normal.

"Good morning, ZoeSaysSo," I reply, mentally thanking Marabelle for pushing me out here.

"Ah, so you did know who I was the other morning," she says, dropping her eyes to the floor.

"Well, no, but my coworker happens to have what she calls a 'girl crush' on you, so she texted me approximately fifty-seven times when she thought she wasn't going to get to meet you," I tell her. "One of those texts happened to be a link to your Instagram."

"Oh, well, after spending last night with three of your coworkers, I think I have a girl crush on every single one of them." Zoe brings her gaze back up to meet mine. "They are all so fun, smart, and hilarious."

"I'll agree with you there." I lean my elbows on the counter between us, drawn in by her dark eyes. "Also, they're a little scary. They're basically an unstoppable force when they're together."

"I'm also a little in love with your town," she says, placing her elbows on the counter as well. "And Betty."

It's hard to focus with her so close. There's a little sprinkle of freckles across her nose that I didn't notice before. She licks her lips and I can't help but glance at her mouth, which turns up into a small smile when she catches me. I bring my eyes back to hers and have to remind myself we're in a conversation, not a staring contest.

"You survived Betty? That's impressive," I tell her. "So, am I boxing up a few of those cinnamon rolls for you? I had one last night for second dinner, so thank you for that."

"Second dinner, huh?" she asks, her cheeks turning pink.

"It's my third favorite meal of the day, after breakfast and second breakfast," I tell her seriously.

"Yes, please, on the cinnamon rolls. Let's go crazy with four. We're all sad to be leaving so we can just eat our feelings," she tells me with a light laugh.

"Anything else?" I ask, not quite ready to step back to get a pastry box.

She sinks her teeth into her bottom lip as she pulls away from the counter to glance at the pastry case and I'm once again staring at her mouth. She moves her hands into the universal "I don't know" gesture and something flashes on her wrist.

"Wait, Tex might have quickly shown me a picture yesterday afternoon when I caught her giggling at her phone, what's that?" I lift my chin toward her extended left arm.

"You like?" she asks, holding her arm over the counter for me to inspect.

I reach for her hand and as soon as I touch her soft skin, just like yesterday when our hands brushed, fire licks up my arm, spreading through my veins. Her cheeks turn pink again and I think she feels it, too. I hope she feels it. I smile as I drop my eyes back to her tattoo, holding her hand still as I inspect the small sunset on her inner wrist. It's wrapped in a transparent film but it's obvious West did an amazing job. I bring my gaze back up to hers and find her staring at me, lips slightly parted and her cheeks now fully red.

34

"I really like it," I tell her, getting a little lost in her eyes before pulling myself back again. "Sunset is my favorite time of the day." As soon as I say it, I hope she doesn't mention the other night when I basically told her I'd be on the beach...and then wasn't.

"Thanks," she replies, slowly sliding her hand out of mine. "West did a really good job."

"I'll box up the cinnamon rolls, Zoe No Last Name," I tell her.

"Can I get an americano as well?" she requests. At my nod, she wanders toward the apparel section.

I have an internal argument with myself as I box up her cinnamon rolls and start on her coffee. In the end, the optimistic side of me that apparently doesn't live in the real world wins, and when Zoe walks out of the store, I'm hopeful I'll see her again.

Chapter Five
Zoe

What the hell? I thought for sure we had some spark between us. I felt a spark, that's for damn sure. But here I am, walking out of the store. I was obvious, right? I mean, I attempted to flirt on Monday, I had sweet Marabelle set aside the cinnamon roll yesterday, and I swear he felt the same thing I did just now when he held my hand to admire my tattoo. An electric jolt, burning hot. But no. Of course the first guy I'm interested in since Asshole Aiden isn't interested in me. And also lives two hours away.

"You don't look like someone who's about to eat a cinnamon roll," Abby says as I storm back in our cottage.

"But you do look like someone that didn't bring coffee for everyone," Kristen says with a fake (I hope) glare. Since she's already sipping coffee, I'm pretty sure she's not really mad.

"Remember the cute guy at the store? With the dimple? Lucas? Well, I basically gave him all the signs, other than climbing over the counter and up his body, and he didn't even ask for my number, where I live, anything," I moan. "I'm doomed to be alone forever."

"Well that's dramatic, even for you." Casey rolls her eyes as she walks past. "Especially since he wrote his number on that coffee cup you're holding."

She snatches the pastry box from my hands as I stand there, utterly dumbfounded. I slowly turn my cup around, holding my breath.

Lucas Henry Stark.

503-981-6215

I squeal and do a little happy dance.

"No one show her this box," Kristen says in a stage whisper, licking frosting off her fingers.

Casey and Abby look inside the pastry box and then back to me. They have matching Cheshire cat grins.

"What?" I ask. "Just tell me!"

Kristen spins the box around with a flourish, lid open.

"Zoe No Last Name, this is my favorite hike that's not really between Portland and Three Rocks, but it's beautiful. I have Monday off, see if you can find it," she reads. "And there's a hand-drawn map, which might take a hot second to decipher."

Best date invitation ever.

"Oh my god, you're blushing!" Casey crows.

If only she knew how many times I've blushed in front of Lucas the two times I've talked to him.

"Does this mean you're finally over Asshole Aiden?" Kristen asks. "I know you were creeping closer to the rage stage of the breakup, but did you ever get fully into rage?"

"Ugh, don't even mention that asshole," Casey says, wrinkling her nose in disgust.

"I skipped the rage stage, went straight to making out with his best friend," I tell them. "Not worth it. Bad kisser."

I should backtrack and find my rage, he really messed a lot of things up for me.

"Zoe! You little secret-keeping slut!" Kristen exclaims, clapping. I give a little bow, making all three of them laugh.

"Zoe and Lucas, sitting in a tree," Abby sings.

"I'd like to do a lot more than k-i-s-s-i-n-g," I say, blushing even more. My cheeks are on actual fire.

"Zoe!" Kristen says between coughs.

"No cinnamon roll deaths," Abby says sternly. "But, guys, we gotta get out of here. I promised YogaFit Newberg that Zoe would teach their 2 p.m. class this afternoon."

Exhibit A of Things Aiden Messed Up. It seemed sweet when he wanted to help me with my job, lending me his expertise to free up more

38

time to spend together. But I put my trust in the wrong person and now Abby and I are still working on getting out of contracts I didn't even know existed. Do I love teaching? Yes. Do I love YogaFit Newberg? Also yes. Do I love getting emails about me being in breach of a contract I didn't know I was under? Absolutely not. I'm scared to know how many more are out there. And that's just Exhibit A.

We quickly clean up the rest of the house, double check the check-out list that Tex left, and load up my 4Runner. I take pictures of both my coffee cup and the inside lid of the box before reluctantly putting them in recycling. I give The Town Mercantile one last look as we drive out of town. Lucas Henry Stark, why can't you live closer to Portland?

***

"Zoe," Abby whispers right as I'm about to go into the studio. "I think you're viral again. But like, *really* viral."

"If it's bad, I don't want to know," I tell her, my heart rate speeding up, metallic taste filling my mouth. "Do your thing, I'll teach, then we'll talk."

I walk into the studio with a ZoeSays smile, which turns into a real smile after I shake off the nerves. I don't know why I always get nervous, I've taught hundreds and hundreds of classes, but the first few minutes are always nerve-wracking for me.

Every studio has a different vibe and each class has its own personality. Most early classes, the 5 a.m. and 6 a.m. groups, are quiet and focused. Or maybe just tired. If it's a 9 a.m. or 10 a.m. class, it's most likely moms, already frazzled after dropping kids off at school. The noon crew is usually laid back, happy to be away from the office for an hour. Evening classes are an interesting mix. You have the people that are happy to be done with work for the day, but also the ones that are pretty exhausted from working all day.

This 2 p.m. class definitely has noon vibes. I push them through a power series and they work hard but they joke with each other as well. They're a tight-knit group, a little chatty, but also respectful when I ask for a few minutes of quiet contemplation at the end. It's obvious that most of them have been taking this class for a long time. This is why I'll fulfill the contracts Aiden hid, this sense of community, fitness bringing people together, making everyone stronger together.

Once we clean up our spaces, I offer time to chat and pose for pictures. I'm asked about my tattoo multiple times, which is covered by my sleeves and the first indication of which reel went viral. The second indication is when half of the women ask if Hot Lumberjack and I are a thing, had a thing, or might someday have a thing.

"But your chemistry!" moans a girl about my age when I shut that rumor down.

While West was great, I think what she was seeing was my genuine happiness, something that hasn't exactly been showcased recently.

"God, he's just so gentle, but *big*," her friend adds. "So, so big."

I mean, fair.

"His hands," sighs the third girl in the trio.

Oops, sorry West (and Tex).

Abby hands me my phone when I climb into the passenger seat. I am shocked by the number of notifications. I have all my social media platforms set up without push notifications, there's no way I'd be able to keep up, but the number of texts and even missed calls I have is insane.

"It's both the tattoo one and the rental story," Abby says before I can question her. "I've talked to Tex and Kelsey and they're pumped, if a little overwhelmed. Rentals are filling up fast, so we did our job well! Tex said West is getting an insane amount of appointment requests, so you crushed it for all of them."

"*We* crushed it, Abs," I immediately correct her. "We'll have to tell Kristen that her dictator debut took off."

Abby snorts at that. I would have hired Kristen ages ago but she loves her job as a nanny. Luckily the dad is a firefighter and his days off coincided with our last-minute trip. Now that I think about it, herding three kids must be almost as hard as herding the three of us the last few days, no wonder why she was so good at it.

"Okay, so the bad part," Abby says with a wince, pulling out of the parking lot.

"Just get it over with," I tell her. I'm sure it has to do with the lack of editing, the on-the-fly stories, basically the real me.

"I know you tell me to leave the mean comments up, but there were some pretty bad ones, and a few were about Kelsey, so those got deleted," she says. "It was mainly the soaking tub with the four of us. I'll keep deleting and reporting as necessary."

There was nothing sexual about the picture of Kelsey, Tex, Abby, and I fully clothed, laughing hysterically, in the (empty) soaking tub on the back deck of The Glass House rental that Tex's team is opening soon, but I'm sure the internet found a way to make it weird.

"Creeper assholes," I mutter, clenching my jaw in frustration. "Well, business as usual I guess. We'll tag team it."

I'm definitely not immune to hurtful comments but dragging Kelsey into it makes my blood boil. Reason number one I keep my little sister off my public accounts. I make sure to send Kelsey a text, telling her she crushed her portion of the story. The girl really is going places.

After a quick stop at Trader Joes, we pull back into our apartment complex. Abby and Casey share a two bedroom unit in the next building over from mine. Kristen's job is live-in due to the dad's shift schedule or she'd still live with me. I keep her room as a guest room and when we have sleepovers, like the night before our getaway, we all crash at my place. I should probably use some of my ZoeSays money to buy a house, invest in real estate, be a real adult, but I haven't pulled the trigger yet. I just don't know where I want to end up. For now, this feels right.

I balance my groceries in one arm, barely managing not to spill them as I unlock the front door. Egg greets me as soon as I step inside, winding around my feet as he purrs. He was not pleased when I stopped home for a few minutes before rushing off to teach earlier. As soon as I set my groceries on the counter and squat down to give him attention, he swats at me and stalks off, tail twitching. Little brat. I know for a fact that Maia, my neighbor's ten-year-old daughter, was over here giving him attention the last few days. I swear he likes pets from everyone but me.

I busy myself unloading groceries, sorting my beach clothes into laundry piles, and try to convince myself to wait longer to text Lucas. Then I picture his dimple and flop down on my couch, dirty laundry at my feet, Egg glaring from the arm rest, and pull out my phone. I do a

41

quick search on social media for him and come up empty. I should be able to find him, I have his full name. Odd.

I pull up the picture of my coffee cup and add his number to my phone. Then I look at the picture of the map and try to figure out his clues.

Zoe:
i wish i had a cinnamon roll right now.

Zoe:
it's zoe, if that wasn't obvious.

LucasHenryStark:
Hi, Zoe No Last Name.

Zoe No Last Name:
hi, lucas henry stark

LucasHenryStark:
How're your map skills?

Zoe No Last Name:
terrible.

LucasHenryStark:
You have time. I have faith.

I take another look. I'm impressed with the drawing, I wasn't looking at the sweatshirts for that long while he made my coffee and drew a whole dang map.

Zoe No Last Name:
Rose-pdx. 3 rocks-obv. pine trees-bend. rubber duck-eugene. man-??

Zoe No Last Name:
google says it's the dude on top of the capitol building. man-salem.

LucasHenryStark:
Shit. I made it too easy. In all fairness, I had about two minutes.

After figuring out the cities, I'm almost certain the hike is the Trail of Ten Falls in Silver Falls State Park, where I've always wanted to go. The pictures I've seen make it look absolutely breathtaking. I cannot freaking wait.

Zoe No Last Name:
trail of ten falls.

Zoe No Last Name:
(Spotify Link: Waterfalls)

LucasHenryStark:
TLC. Nice. Nailed it. Noon?

Zoe No Last Name:
if i survive the weekend, i'll be there.

Chapter Six
Zoe

"You look fucking hot," Kristen says, nodding approvingly as I walk out of my bedroom on Saturday evening, nervously tugging the short dress down my thighs. "Your quads, Zoe, damn!"

"That green on you, a-freaking-mazing," Casey confirms. "Egg agrees."

Egg yawns from his spot in her lap and doesn't look at me.

"Your date might actually ditch his boyfriend for you," Abby adds.

"I definitely might," Dane says, rising from the couch to walk over and hold my hand above my head, motioning me to twirl.

"I wouldn't blame you, babe, she looks stunning." Dane's boyfriend Chase gives a wolf whistle as I spin.

"Thank you so much for agreeing to go with me," I tell Dane, tugging the dress down again. "And thank you for sharing, Chase."

"He's the best date, he'll dote on you all night *and* he's way hotter than Asshole Aiden," Chase says. "But stop trying to cover more, you work hard for those legs, show them off!"

I panicked earlier when I saw Aiden's name on the guest list that Abby got ahold of. Luckily Dane happily agreed to join me. Both Dane and Chase are regulars to the Monday/Wednesday/Friday 8 a.m. class that I've been teaching forever. We struck up an easy friendship after we realized we all went to the same coffee shop after class and now Dane is my go-to for both security and date events.

45

"Everyone approves?" I ask nervously.

I should be used to events like this; I've been invited to so many in the last few years, but I always feel like a fraud. I lucked my way into this fame and now I'm just kinda here, existing on the internet. The World Wide Web, as my dad says.

"Zoe, you are amazing, you earned this invite, and nothing he says matters," Casey says, an edge to her voice. "You were you before him. He didn't build you, you did."

"We did," I immediately reply.

"We did, without him." She holds my stare, unwavering in her support, as usual.

I know this is true, I do. But I also know that when Aiden showed up in my life, a lot happened, some really good, and some really stressful.

"Okay, I'm fine, this is fine." I blow out a breath.

"Babe, all he did was make you think you always have to be perfect, which you absolutely are perfect in all ways, but you can also be messy and fun and just Zoe, not ZoeSays," Chase chimes in.

I bite my lip and nod, fanning my face. Now is not the time to cry. I take a deep breath, make sure my boobs are going to stay covered (shout out to sticky boob adhesive bras), and give my friends a shaky smile. I'm as ready as I'll ever be.

"Let's fucking do this," Dane says, taking my hand. He leads me to the town car that's waiting outside, the driver opening the door as we approach. Dane helps me in before walking around to his side, the best date as promised.

"Stop fidgeting," Dane says the second he slides in next to me, covering my hands with his. "All you need to do is follow my lead, I was born for this. Do you even see me in this suit?"

With a snort, I roll my eyes. "You're ridiculous."

I can't believe I'm letting Aiden get to me like this. I haven't even seen him, just his name on a list. He might not even show. It'd be just like him, make sure his name is on the donor list, then not show up to actually support the organization.

I take a few deep breaths, mentally preparing myself to stand tall and be the bigger person. I cannot control his actions, only my reaction to them, and sometimes the best reaction is no reaction. I repeat that in my head again. And again. And again.

When we pull up to the curb, I need to repeat it once more. But I still can't make a move to get out. Dane watches me, waiting patiently.

"Give us a minute," I tell our driver.

He nods in the rearview mirror at me.

"Just remember, my left side is my good side," Dane tells me, turning his face slightly and rubbing his stubbled jaw, trying to make me smile. "But really, how are we playing this? Am I your hot boyfriend, hot friend, or hot new date?"

"Uh…date?"

I have not thought this through. I just knew I didn't want to go alone. Dane does look insanely handsome in a suit and Adain doesn't know him, but now that we're here, I think this is a bad idea. A really bad idea. I should have bailed as soon as I saw Aiden's name.

"Hey, why are you scared, Zoe? You do *not* have to do this. We can go right back to the apartment or we can duck into that dive bar half a block down," Dane says gently when he sees the tears in my eyes.

"No, I'm doing this. I just haven't seen him since the breakup and in that time I've realized what an asshole of epic proportions he really was. Is. He really stomped on my self confidence, which I'm just now realizing right at this exact moment. Right now. It freaks me out that I let him treat me that way. Just stay with me and I'll be okay," I tell him.

He gives me a long look, unconvinced, and still doesn't move to step out of the car.

"I did make out with his best friend though, like a few weeks after we broke up," I whisper. The only good thing about that experience was Noah telling me that Aiden never deserved me. A line? Maybe. Still felt good.

With a laugh, Dane steps out and circles behind the car. Our driver hurries around the front and opens my door as Dane steps in, shielding me from view. He leans down and winks at me. I step out as gracefully as I can and Dane immediately takes my hand, even threading our fingers together. Best date, indeed.

I smile at our driver and let Dane lead me to the ridiculous red carpet where we pose for pictures. Left side, right side, Dane has all good

47

sides. He wraps his hand around my waist, pulls me close and whispers in my ear to place my hand on his chest. He's a natural and makes me feel a lot less like a fraud.

"Who's your date, Zoe?" the photographer asks.

"This is Dane," I say with a ZoeSays smile, not giving any hints about who he is to me.

After the Aiden debacle, I'm not sharing anything about my dating life, or current lack thereof, with anyone other than my tight-knit group. After a few more pictures, I let Dane guide me through the doors, his hand on my low back. I take a deep breath when we're out of sight of the cameras. It was supposed to just be event photographers but there were a couple news cameras out there, too. Whoever did the PR for this fundraiser must have a lot of pull.

"You were perfect," Dane reassures me. "I have the hottest date here, besides your date, I mean." I snort at that. No one loves Dane as much as Dane loves Dane. Or at least that's what he wants everyone to think.

"I'm sorry if they figure out who you are," I tell him. "I obviously did not think this through."

"Lucky for you, I love attention," he says with a grin.

I give him a playful nudge with my shoulder and he leads me into the ballroom. We bid on a few silent auction items, I nibble on whatever food Dane hands me, and he happily leads the conversations. He really was born to do this.

"How are you so good at this?" I ask after listening to him charm Molly, the principal of the middle school I volunteer at twice a week.

"I'm in sales, bullshit is my life," he says.

"So my life is the fake reality that is social media, that's why I suck at the real world?" I ask as I shake my head at the waiter that offers us a tray of champagne. I don't normally drink at events, especially when I'm already on edge.

Dane grabs a flute though. He dumps half the champagne in a fake plant before handing it to me. "Here, carry this. Now you don't have to answer questions about not drinking. And you don't suck at the real world. You're just not good at this *part* of the real world." He shrugs. "You're better in small groups."

"This just feels-"

"Incoming," Dane warns, his voice steely, eyes over my shoulder. I slowly turn.

"Zoe, I thought you didn't like green," Aiden says, eyes sweeping my body. They linger on my legs and I fight the urge to fidget.

False, I love green. Aiden hates green.

Dane doesn't miss my slight shudder. He puts his left hand on my low back and reaches his right hand out.

"You must be Aaron, I'm Dane," he says confidently.

I hide my smirk behind my glass as Aiden glowers at Dane, doing that thing I always hated where he puffs his chest out. It's a little ridiculous right now because Dane is 6'3" and looks like a bodybuilder, not the kind that would be intimidated by anyone. Plus he's the one with his hand on my back.

"Aiden," he replies, shaking Dane's hand before turning back to me. "Can we talk in private?"

"No," I tell him firmly. "I'm not interested."

"I can say it here, then," Aiden says, raising his eyebrows in a challenge.

"No, we're done, I have nothing to say to you," I reply, my confidence finally showing up.

A few people look at us curiously. Dane shifts us slightly so I'm nearly hidden in front of his large frame, my back to his broad chest.

"I actually wanted to apologize," Aiden says, softening his voice, his eyes darting to the people around us. He was always good at reading his audience and telling them what they wanted to hear. Including me.

"I do not want to hear anything you have to say," I say, reaching my right hand down to take Dane's. "Dane, want to take me for a spin around the dance floor?"

"I've been waiting all night," Dane tells me, bringing my hand to his lips and kissing it gently, his eyes burning into mine. Damn, he's good. He turns to Aiden. "Nice to meet you, Adam."

We turn in unison away from Aiden and weave our way through the room to the dance floor. Dane gathers me in his arms and lets me stew in silence.

"I'm sorry," I tell him after a few minutes.

49

"No way, I know what he did. I'm proud of you for standing your ground," Dane reassures me.

"I can't believe he apologized," I say. "That was weird."

"Technically, he said he wanted to apologize, he didn't actually apologize," Dane corrects.

"True, I'm also guessing it was just for anyone watching," I add, chewing my lip.

"He absolutely should apologize. He basically preyed upon a young girl, used you for your mild fame, no offense, and then went internet rage troll when you dumped him," Dane says, dropping his voice so no one else can hear. "Can I punch him? Just once?"

"I don't know where to start: young girl, mild fame, internet rage troll, or your threats of violence," I say through laughter as Dane gently spins me.

"I'd go punch him right now if you told me to," Dane says, making a show of looking around the room for Aiden.

I'm actually tempted. Dane doesn't even know half of it.

"Well, thank you. You're a good friend and you sure do clean up nice," I tell him. "Will it crush your extroverted, salesman heart if I ask that we sneak out of here after this song?"

"How about we get the rest of the crew to meet us at that dive bar? The night is young, Zoe, as are you, let's have some fun!"

He really is the perfect date. Too bad he's taken. Also too bad he doesn't have a dimple.

***

Zoe No Last Name:
good morning.

LucasHenryStark:
I'm assuming you survived and I'll see you tomorrow?

Zoe No Last Name:
it was a close call. my asshole ex was at the fundraiser. luckily i had a professional date.

50

Zoe No Last Name:
wait.

Zoe No Last Name:
to clarify, i did not hire an escort. dane's just a friend who is an amazing date.

LucasHenryStark:
I'm glad your escort helped.

Zoe No Last Name:
not an escort.

LucasHenryStark:
I'm glad your professional date helped.

Zoe No Last Name:
maybe i'll bring him to our date tomorrow.

Zoe No Last Name:
wait.

Zoe No Last Name:
our hike. i didn't mean to call it a date. that's weird. i just made things weird.

LucasHenryStark:
Store is about to get busy so I have to go. I'm looking forward to our date tomorrow. With or without your professional escort.

Okay, I guess it's a date. And, no offense to Professional Date Dane, but I'm much more excited about this one.

Chapter Seven
Lucas

"Hi," I say with a smile as I step out of my old, rusted, single cab truck that looks truly dilapidated next to Zoe's new, red, fully-loaded 4Runner. "Sorry I'm late."

"You had a lot longer to drive," Zoe replies with a shrug. She bites her lip and smiles at me, her dark eyes turning golden as they catch the sunlight streaming through the towering trees.

"But that's not why I was late," I say, hoping this doesn't backfire. I decided on the drive here that I might as well be honest. I can't hide my life from her when hers is out there for the whole world to see.

She tilts her head to the right, a slightly guarded look crossing her face as she raises her eyebrows in question.

"Gramps was having a bad morning so I drove him to the library instead of Nancy coming to pick him up," I say, hoping that she doesn't get back in her fancy 4Runner at this next part. "I live with my grandfather. I'm his caretaker and Nancy was my grandma's best friend. Now I think Nancy might be *my* best friend."

I'm actually sure she is my best friend. This is great, really great. Zoe's a freaking social media celebrity who goes to fancy fundraisers and I hang out with Gramps, Nancy, and the women of Team Merc. Sometimes Officer Jakey, who hates when anyone besides Nancy calls him Jakey, when he's not working, working out, or sleeping, which is rare.

"Is he okay? Are you sure we should be doing this?" she immediately asks. "I could have met you somewhere closer."

"This is one of my favorite trails, I want to be here," I tell her, trying to erase her obvious concern, which was not at all my intention. "I absolutely would not have left Gramps if I shouldn't have."

"Okay, I just, I don't know. Now I'm worried," she says, eyes darting around the parking lot.

"I didn't mean to make you worry, I just wanted to be honest about what my life is and what it isn't." At those words, her eyes land on mine.

"I like honesty," she says, smiling up at me. "I like honesty a lot."

"I also know you like surprises, so I have two."

Her dark eyes light up. "I can't believe you remembered," she says.

I remember everything about our short interactions last week, from her freckles to her laugh. "Big surprise or small surprise first?"

"Small," she answers without hesitation.

"Close your eyes, please," I request.

She tilts her head once again, deciding if she trusts me, then closes her eyes. I quickly dig in my pocket and pull out the necklace that we just got at The Mercantile yesterday. I untangle it and hold it in my palm.

"Open," I say, suddenly hit with nerves. Who the hell brings jewelry on a first date? Not cool.

"Lucas Henry Stark," Zoe breathes, gently taking the delicate chain out of my hand. "I love it."

"It's made from recycled metal. The artist lives a few miles inland and we just started carrying them at The Mercantile," I tell her. "It reminded me of your tattoo."

"Help me put it on?" she asks, handing it back to me. She turns and gathers her hair, holding it out of the way.

Thankful for the reason to move closer, I manage to only fumble with the tiny clasp once, right when my fingers brush against her skin. I hear her take a quick inhale at the contact and hope that means she's feeling the same thing I am.

54

"There," I say softly.

She spins back around, bringing her hand up to touch the pendant. It's a simple circle with jagged silver mountain silhouettes, bronze sun rising or setting over the peaks. I'm sure there are better ways to describe it, but I don't know shit about jewelry, only how to sell it to tourists.

"Thank you," she says, smiling up at me. "I really love it, I can't even imagine what the other surprise is."

"It's not quite as tangible," I tell her, reaching into my backpack to bring out my most prized possession: my camera. "I brought my camera, and I thought I'd be your ZoeSaysSoFitness photographer for the day."

Zoe freezes. I can't quite read her expression. I don't think it's a good one though.

"Okay," she says, licking her lips nervously, her eyes anywhere but on mine. "In the name of honesty, here goes."

Oh, shit. This is not good.

"I would love pictures from today, especially ones you take, but I had a bad experience with my ex and my social media." She stops and takes a deep breath, like she's bracing herself. "I want today for just you and me, not for the fake reality that lives in my phone."

She looks up at me, uncertainty in her eyes.

"Zoe, that's the best thing I've heard today," I tell her honestly. Hell yes, it's the best thing. I have no interest in being on social media in any way, shape, or form. I was just trying to be thoughtful, supportive.

"Wait, really?" she asks hopefully.

"Again, honesty happening here. I have not looked at your social media since the very first day Kelsey sent me your link. I felt weird seeing pictures of you at the cafe when I had just met you. So the last I saw of your fake-but-real reality, you were eating a salad at the cafe, less than an hour after I met you. I think it's amazing that you've made it into your job, if it's something you love, but I just wanted to do something for you," I tell her. "I like you in the real world, not the fake reality that lives in your phone. Or my phone. I mean I do, but I like you here, now."

She grins at me and my heart leaps in my chest. There's a beat of silence where we just smile at each other, then she reaches up and

55

touches the necklace again. Her cheeks turn pink and she turns to grab a small backpack from the backseat of her car.

"Let's hike!" she says, taking off across the parking lot without looking back to make sure I follow.

Does she already realize that I'd follow her anywhere?

***

The full hike is over seven miles long. The waterfalls are breathtaking, but watching Zoe experience this hike is even better. You can see the happiness radiating off her. She bounces, she oohs and aahs, she tells me which trees are her favorite, she chats with other hikers, even posing for a few pictures when a group of teenage girls recognize her. I thought it would be awkward, but she seemed excited to meet the girls.

"Sorry," she tells me with a little shrug. "I know that can be weird, but I love my followers, they make this life possible for me. Even when I get frustrated by always being 'on' some days, I'm very thankful. And if I take pictures *with* them, it's less likely they will take pictures *of* me."

"I think it's great," I tell her honestly. "You've connected with a lot of people and you definitely just made those girls' day. That's pretty awesome."

Zoe convinces me to take selfies on her phone and lets me play with my camera whenever we stop. Her pictures start with her making funny faces and me looking like a deer in headlights, but soon she has me laughing along with her. She snaps one as she kisses my cheek and as we both look at the picture, her cheeks turn bright red. I think her blush is my new favorite thing.

"Are you sure we still have time?" she asks every time we stop. "I don't want you to be late for your grandpa."

"Well, Marabelle got it out of me at work yesterday where I was going, she's friends with Nancy, and they both told me they didn't want to see me until dark," I finally tell her sheepishly.

She does a little shoulder shimmy dance and steals half of my granola bar before taking off down the trail again.

"Zoe, wait!" I call after her.

She turns and tilts her head questioningly. I think her head tilt is my second favorite thing.

56

"The light through the trees right there, don't move," I instruct, fumbling with the lens cap.

Of course she doesn't listen and she moves. She's rarely still. She looks up through the trees, trying to read the light. She turns in a full circle and then shifts slightly further down the trail and to the right. Now I can see the waterfall behind her and still catch the light I wanted. She has a good eye for this.

I take my time capturing the light spilling through the tangled branches, watching Zoe through the lens. She's obviously used to getting her picture taken; she lets me play with the angles and doesn't bat an eye when I move in close or ask her to turn. I can already tell my favorite will be the one where she bites her lip and looks past the camera to me, her cheeks turning pink. I don't think she knows I caught it, my eyes were on hers, not through the lens.

"Those are so good!" she squeals as she looks over my shoulder a few minutes later.

"I wanted to be a travel writer and photographer," I admit to her when we start hiking again.

"From what little I've seen, you have talent," she says. Now my cheeks might be red. "I can't wait to see them all."

"Travel isn't in the cards for me any time soon," I tell her. "And I'm okay with it. Gramps and Grandma raised me. Gramps comes first."

"I like that," Zoe says. "I like that he's your priority."

I can only hope she still thinks that when she realizes how little time I have for anyone or anything else. That's assuming I make it past this first date.

***

The miles fly by. As our feet hit the parking lot pavement, I can't believe our hike is over, it feels like we just started. I want to keep hiking, take more pictures of Zoe, laugh at more of her bad jokes, see more of her genuine joy as she bounces down the trail. I knew she was different the moment I met her, but I didn't know it'd be like this. I'm already in deep with this girl, I only hope she feels a fraction of what I do.

"So, I believe you were told you can't show your face at home for another four hours, give or take," Zoe says with a playful grin as we walk toward our cars. "Does that mean I can buy you dinner?"

57

"I'll have dinner with you, but why do you get to buy?" I ask. I don't care if I can't afford to buy her dinner, I'll eat ramen all next week if I need to.

I put my backpack in the passenger seat of my truck and take hers from her shoulder. I walk to the back of her SUV and she hits a button. Automatic liftgate, not something my old truck has. In fact, it has old crank windows and a radio that doesn't work. Neither does the tape deck. I gently set her backpack inside. She hops up and swings her feet, smiling at me.

She's been smiling all afternoon. At me, at the people we meet, at the waterfalls and the trees. She smiled as she told me about her family, the classes she teaches, and the kids she volunteers with. She smiled as I told her about my photography hobby, Gramps's obsession with Top Gun, and how I finally got Colt's approval of my special hot chocolate by doubling the sprinkles. I'm officially addicted to her smile.

"Because I said so," she answers with a shrug.

"ZoeSaysSo, huh?" I ask, leaning back next to her.

"I might like to get my way, or so I've been told," she says.

"I'm not sure I like you buying me dinner," I tell her. Why am I arguing? She's asking me to spend more time with her, which is exactly what I want.

"What if I can convince you?" she asks.

I look over at her and see her cheeks are slightly pink, her head tilted. I turn my body toward her and she reaches for my hand. She pulls me in and next thing I know, I'm standing between her legs as she looks up at me through long eyelashes.

"Zoe, I'm pretty sure you could convince me to do a lot of things, especially when you give me that look," I admit softly.

Her cheeks turn from pink to red as she blinks up at me. I set my hands on the outsides of her thighs and lean down slightly. I can hear her take a quick inhale and her lips slowly part. I let her decide, but as soon as she reaches up and lets her lips touch mine, I move my hand to her jaw, tipping her chin slightly and deepening our kiss before pushing my hand back into her hair.

I thought holding her hand in the store the other day sent waves of electricity through me, but that moment has nothing on this. All I feel

58

is Zoe. All I taste is Zoe. She's soft and sweet with a hint of vanilla chapstick, and I never want to come up for air.

More, I need more.

She's just as desperate as I am, her hands fisting my tee shirt as she pulls me closer, wiggling her hips to the edge of the cargo space at the same time. I squeeze her warm thigh before running my hand up to her hip, pulling her flush against me. I dart my tongue into her mouth and her grip on my shirt tightens. When her knuckles brush against my abs, my entire body feels the contact. She moans softly and hooks her leg around the back of my thigh. Her teeth find my lower lip and any control I thought I had shatters. I dip my hand under her shirt, gripping her waist, relishing the feel of her soft skin beneath my hand.

In the distance, hundreds of miles away, I hear a wolf whistle. Okay, maybe from across the parking lot. Zoe pulls back slowly, unfisting my shirt and unhooking her foot from behind my leg, her eyes wide.

"Lucas. Henry. Stark." She bites down on her lower lip and my brain short circuits.

"Zoe. No. Last. Name."

"Why didn't we start the day with that?" she asks, starting to giggle.

"Because I'm an idiot," I tell her ruefully.

Her giggles turn into full laughter. It's my new favorite sound. Everything about her is my new favorite.

"Campbell. My last name is Campbell," she says when she stops laughing.

"Zoe Last Name Campbell, I believe you promised me dinner," I tell her, grimacing and trying to discreetly adjust myself as I step away from her. That escalated *very* quickly.

"I know just the place, follow me," she says, sliding down from her perch.

Her hand goes to her necklace and I smile. I really would follow her anywhere. Well, as long as I can be home by dark.

"Hey, Zoe, wait," I say.

She turns, looking at me expectantly, a small head tilt, hand still on her necklace. I reach for her free hand and gently tug her closer. I lean down and give her a soft, slow, totally PG kiss.

***

Our kiss after dinner, also in a parking lot, is not PG. I barely make it home before dark.

Chapter Eight
Zoe

Holy shit, it's been three days since our hiking date and I still feel that goodnight kiss. Lucas comes off as laid-back, sweet, and playful, which he is, but the guy can *kiss*. If we would have had more time, I would have tried to find out what else he can do that well. I'm guessing a lot. A. Lot.

I'm blaming that kiss for the way I've thrown caution to the wind. I texted him as soon as I got home and we've been texting nonstop ever since. It's embarrassing how often I check my phone, hoping to see his name. Like right now.

LucasHenryStark:
Ready to see the pics from our hike?

Zoe Last Name Campbell:
yes please!

LucasHenryStark:
(link)

LucasHenryStark:
I hope you like them.

Holy shit again. Lucas is an amazing photographer. Tall trees, cascading waterfalls, moss-covered rocks, the beauty of the Pacific Northwest that I've always been spoiled by, but with a whole new layer to it. I can feel the breeze, the slight chill of the mist hanging in the air as I click through the gallery. I'm obviously biased, but these are breathtaking.

I gasp out loud when I see the first picture of me, of the way he captured me through his lens. I've had my picture taken more times than I'd like to admit, but never quite like this. The light, color, and texture come together in a way I've never seen, conveying the exact emotions of these moments in time. From the flicker of nerves during our first mile together, caught in my dark eyes as I smile at the camera, to the balance between my twirling movement and the stoic old-growth forest surrounding me as we grew more comfortable, more playful together. But my favorite? I'm not looking at the camera, I'm looking at Lucas, biting my lip, cheeks pink, happy and hopeful, just like I am right now.

I glance at the time. I've gotten to know his schedule over the last few days and he's probably folding laundry right now or fixing something around the house. I want to see his face and hear his voice. We've never talked on the phone, only texted, but I once again throw caution to the wind.

"Hi, Zoe Last Name Campbell," he answers my FaceTime call on the first ring.

He's in a small living room and I think I can hear a TV in the background.

"Lucas Henry Stark, those pictures are amazing! I might have to change my mind about using them for work," I gush. "Actually I already did, can I use them?"

I'm rewarded with his dimple. How can I spend only one day with him and miss him so much?

"Of course you can, they're yours. But you never sent me the ones you took…" he trails off the end of his sentence and I see him looking past his phone before speaking to someone off camera. "No, I'm going to put this away and go grocery shopping."

"Is that the girl that has you all twitterpated?" a gruff voice asks, seemingly moving closer. "Trying to hide her from me, Luke?"

"Want to meet Gramps?" Lucas whispers. "Actually I don't think you have a choice."

"Absolutely," I say, nodding eagerly.

62

Besides getting to know his schedule, I've also gotten to know more about Lucas over the past few days. He was raised by his grandparents in the same small home he lives in now. His mom left right after he was born and his dad only made it until Lucas was three before leaving him to be raised by Henry and Elle. They didn't always have a lot of money but it sounds like it was a home full of love. And now Lucas takes care of his grandpa, aka Gramps, who I'm already dying to meet.

"Gramps, this is Zoe," Lucas says and stands to move toward his grandpa. "Zoe, this is Gramps, the best man I know."

Suddenly my screen is filled with a smiling man who has the same bright green eyes as Lucas. His dimple is on his right cheek though.

"Hi, Mr. Stark, I can see where Lucas got his good looks," I say, smiling back at the older man who means so much to Lucas.

"Miss Zoe, I can see why Luke is so captivated by you," Gramps says. "I hope I get to meet you in person one day."

"I hope so, too," I reply. "I'll work on my schedule and see what I can do."

"I'd like that," he says, his voice a little quieter.

"Me, too."

"He's a good boy, a good man, my Luke. I hope you know that, Miss Zoe," Gramps says, his eyes showing an emotion I can't quite pin down, but I can feel it nonetheless.

"I do know that, Mr. Stark," I tell him, hoping he can hear the honesty in my voice. "I could tell the very first time I met him. And he's a very talented photographer, from what little I've seen."

"Ah, yes, he is talented. I wish he'd spend less time worrying about me and more time with his camera."

"Can I talk to her again, Gramps?" Lucas asks from somewhere offscreen.

"Goodnight, Miss Zoe," Gramps tells me.

I blow him a kiss and tell him I hope to meet him in person soon.

"She's too pretty for the likes of you," he tells Lucas as he hands the phone back.

"I think he's a fan," Lucas tells me with a grin. "And you just made his night. He was a little quiet earlier."

63

"I'm glad," I say. "You have his eyes, bright green and kind."

"He'd really like to meet you, is that weird? Too soon?" he asks, looking nervous for the first time.

"I'd love to meet him, get to spend time with both of you," I tell him honestly. Caution. To. The. Wind. Who am I?

"I'd like that," Lucas replies. "I'd like that a lot."

When he smiles at me, that dimple makes the decision for me: I'm taking time off and going to the beach.

***

"Surprise!" I call as West and I approach the group standing near the bonfire.

"Zoe!" Kelsey shrieks, darting out from under an older man's arm slung around her shoulder.

She runs down the beach toward me and I hug her tight. Although we text often, I haven't been able to congratulate Kelsey in person on what she's done with the rental accounts. I can feel her enthusiasm through every text exchange though; she's brimming with ideas, energy, and creativity. I'm like a proud big sister.

"You didn't tell me you were coming!" she says, linking her arm through mine.

I smile and search the group for Lucas. He told me he'd be at the community bonfire but I don't see him anywhere. My heart falls. I was really hoping to surprise him as well as my new Team Merc friends. I hope Gramps is okay.

"Zoe wanted to surprise Team Merc with a visit," West says, smiling down at Tex, aka Harper. I'm still not sure who calls her by which name. "I know it's not really what we're supposed to do, but she rented The Garden using her friend's account. Sorry."

He shrugs, not looking at all sorry. I'm also not sorry. I knew Avery and Tex would try to comp my stay, so I reached out to West to get his opinion. He agreed that using Dane's account was the way to go. It also assured me that Lucas wouldn't catch wind of my visit. My love of surprises runs deep.

"You helped with this?" Kelsey asks West, a note of disbelief in her voice.

"He did," I confirm. I also knew my friends would be more comfortable with my solo trip if they knew West was involved. "He offered to let me stay at his house, or yours, Harper, but I wanted to support your business."

Kelsey grins at West, who tries and fails to maintain his stoic, grouchy demeanor. It seems like Tex is quickly turning him into a teddy bear.

I let Kelsey pull me away to introduce me to her mom, who thanks me for mentoring her daughter before pulling me into a hug that makes me feel like I've known her my whole life. I meet Brian, the man who just had his arm around Kelsey, and his wife Rachel, who Kelsey explains are like second parents to her. Marabelle comes over and gives me a quick hug, whispering in my ear that Lucas had to go home early. I guess that answers two questions. One: Gramps had a bad day. Two: she thinks we're a secret. Are we?

I sink into the chair offered to me by Nate, one of Brian's fellow firefighters who must be around my age, maybe a little older. Kelsey nudges me when Nate shows obvious interest. He's funny, charming, and objectively super hot, but I have zero interest. None.

I chat with the group, flashing my ZoeSays smile, but I'm really wondering, worrying actually, over just what Lucas and I really are. We've texted, talked, and FaceTimed daily since I "met" his grandpa a week ago. We've shared links to different hikes we've done or want to do, sent book recommendations back and forth, and challenged each other to endless word games.

One night we shared a recipe and then talked while we both went grocery shopping. Wandering the deserted aisles of Safeway late at night with Lucas's voice in my ear was a completely different experience than my usual rushed stops into Trader Joe's, ducking to avoid being recognized. The next night, Gramps gave the pasta primavera two thumbs up when we FaceTimed.

I've also helped Lucas with the digital advertising for the upcoming book sale he's helping plan, spent more time than I should admit daydreaming about that life-changing goodnight kiss, and I haven't taken my necklace off since our hike.

When I shared a few of Lucas's pictures from our hike, not only did my followers start tagging me in their own Silver Falls adventures, but they went a little crazy over my necklace. I reached out to the artist and I'm hoping to meet her tomorrow at the Fourth Fest Farmer's Market.

Despite how real all of this feels to me, I don't know what Lucas and I are. My phone is oddly silent, making me question why I thought this surprise trip was a good idea at all. Marabelle squeezes my shoulder as she walks past, bringing me out of my thoughts and back into the moment. I give her a smile, thankful for her quiet reassurance, and focus on my surroundings.

The fire crackles before me, warming my toes, and Kelsey's laugh is infectious. Ever since my stay at Breakers Bliss, I've been working on really enjoying each moment for what it is, not for what picture or story comes out of it. I snap a single picture of the bonfire and post it, pocket my phone, then lose myself in the conversation with Kelsey and her amazing community.

***

LucasHenryStark:
That firefighter across the bonfire looks familiar.

Zoe Last Name Campbell:
LHS, does that mean you're following me on social media?

LucasHenryStark:
I might have created an account just to follow you. But in a nice way, not a stalker way. I want to support you. And also see more of your life.

LucasHenryStark:
I'm butchering this aren't I? Call me when you have time.

I immediately bail on the bonfire, claiming my early yoga class this morning has me needing sleep. I give hugs to all of my new friends, decline an offer to be walked home by both Nate (Kelsey covers a snicker from her chair) and West (who scowls at Nate), and call Lucas as soon as I'm on the street.

"Surprise?" I say, my voice rising in a question, as soon as Lucas answers.

"I am surprised, I'm just in the wrong place I guess," he says. "Nancy gave me a call around lunch time and said Gramps was pretty tired. Tex and Avery told me to cut out early, so I did."

"It's more than okay, I understand," I tell him, stopping to let a car pass by on the narrow street. His dejected tone makes my heart twinge.

"How long are you in town?" Lucas asks. "Please say more than one night."

"More than one night." I hope he can hear my smile in my voice.

That gets me a small laugh. "I'm glad," he says quietly.

I can hear him gathering his keys. I pull the phone away from my ear and check the time. Grocery shopping time. I've realized that Lucas's nightly shopping trip might be partly an inability to plan ahead, but days like today it's also a short escape from reality. Time to clear his mind before bed.

"Is Henry okay?" I ask, worry still tugging at my heart.

"We had minestrone soup and grilled cheese for dinner, then watched Top Gun for the 700th time, so he's much better now," Lucas reassures me. I hear a door close, he must be walking out to his truck.

"Well, I'm just walking up to the rental, so I should get settled," I tell him. "I'll be at the farmer's market tomorrow, so I guess I'll get to see you then?"

"See you then, Zoe Last Name Campbell," Lucas says softly.

"G'night, Lucas Henry Stark."

Liar, liar, pants on fire. I grab my keys from the kitchen counter and jog back out the door. Sixteen minutes later, I'm parking next to a familiar single cab pickup truck in the parking lot of the only grocery store in Rock Beach. I take a picture of our cars next to each other and then try to creep between vehicles to stay hidden; it's nearly 11 p.m. so there's only a handful to hide behind. I'm sure someone is calling security on me right now.

"Excuse me, do you know where the cinnamon rolls are?" I ask, sidling up beside Lucas as he looks between his phone and the rice selection in front of him.

Lucas startles before quickly recovering. His shopping basket hits the floor and he pulls me into his chest in a crushing hug. I breathe him in, happy to be in his arms. When he releases me, I stand on my toes to quickly press my lips on his. His hand finds its way into my hair, tipping my head back to kiss me more thoroughly.

"What are you doing here?" Lucas asks, smiling down at me when we pull apart.

"You sounded stressed, a little sad," I tell him with a shrug. "So I came to see you. Grocery shop together, this time in person."

"It appears you forgot a shopping cart," he says, dimple on full display. That dimple really is going to be the end of me.

"I was kind of hoping we could cook together tomorrow?" I ask hesitantly.

I'm just realizing I showed up out of nowhere, stalked him to the grocery store, and kissed him with no warning. Now I'm assuming he wants to make dinner with me on a Saturday night. I have a flash of all the other tourist girls that probably parade through The Town Mercantile, earning his dimpled smile. I take a step back to put some space between us.

"Whoa, hey, what's that look?" he asks. He scans my face and reaches for my hand. He tugs me close again and as soon as I look up at him, he drops a quick kiss on my lips.

"Do I have to be honest?" I ask, remembering our honesty talk on our hiking date.

"I'd prefer it," he says slowly. His green eyes look worried. He has enough worry in his life, I don't need to add to the list.

"I just realized that you joked about stalking me on Instagram but I'm the one that just showed up here without warning. Not just to your little town but like, full stalker'ed you to your grocery store, and maybe you had plans this weekend, like with someone else..." I trail off, embarrassed for so many reasons.

"Zoe, I'm so happy you're here. When I turned and you were there, I think my heart actually skipped a beat. I'm not making plans with anyone except the senior citizens I find myself surrounded by. If I didn't have plans or work or this messy life, my plan would have been to find a way to see you," he tells me. "Now that you *are* here, my plan is to finish grocery shopping as quickly as possible so I can make out with you in the parking lot. So please tell me if veggie fried rice and some sort of chicken stir fry is an acceptable dinner tomorrow night."

"I love veggie fried rice and chicken stir fry," I quickly reply, my mood immediately lifting.

I grab a bag of rice and drop it in his shopping basket that's still on the floor. He threads his fingers through mine and picks up the basket with his other hand and pulls me down the aisle. I nearly have to run to keep up with his long strides. We're both laughing as we split up in the produce section, attempting to divide and conquer the grocery list as quickly as possible.

"What was that for?" he asks when I take a picture of him holding up a bag of carrots.

"I'll show you later," I promise. "Hurry up."

I push him toward the self checkout and sneak another picture as he scans the groceries. I tap a few buttons, shove my phone in the side pocket of my leggings, and start bagging as he scans.

He takes my hand again as we walk out of the store and my body buzzes with anticipation. He leads me between our cars and opens the passenger door of his truck to load the groceries. Then he turns with a grin and backs me against the driver's side door of my 4Runner, his hand gentle on my hip. The parking lot is empty and we are tucked between our vehicles but there's still the threat of being caught adding to my adrenaline.

His eyes, barely visible in the dark, hold mine and my heart pounds, beating against my chest, racing faster with each shaky breath. I've never had this kind of reaction to anyone, ever. I stare up at him in the darkness, both of us still, waiting to see who makes the first move.

I can't wait another second, another heartbeat, without touching him. I reach my hands up at the same time he grabs my waist with both hands. As I wrap my arms around his neck, he lifts me up off my feet and presses my back against the side of my car. I wrap my legs around his waist as he moves his hands to grip under my thighs, holding me steady. When his mouth lands on mine, all I know is that I need more. More Lucas. Desperate to feel every part of him, I move my hands into his hair then down to his shoulders. I wrap one arm around his neck and let the other drift down his chest as I arch into him.

"Lucas," I whisper as he trails kisses down my neck. "I missed you."

"I missed you, too," he whispers in my ear, his breath making me shudder, before he finds my lips once again.

I tug on the bottom of his shirt and finally have his skin beneath my fingertips. His grip under my thighs tightens as I lightly scrape my fingernails up his ribcage. I bite back a moan when he presses his hips forward at the same time his teeth find my bottom lip.

"Zoe," he groans as I tighten my legs around him, tugging his shirt up further with my free hand.

Headlights flash across us as a car pulls into the parking lot and I gasp. We break apart, both of us breathless and wide-eyed. Lucas leans his forehead against mine and takes a steadying breath before slowly lowering me to the ground. My legs shake but he keeps his hands on my waist, my back still pressed against my car, until I can stand on my own again.

"Wow," is all I can think to say. But also, *wow*. What the hell was that?

"Yeah, wow," he agrees, looking as dazed as I feel. He runs his hand through his wavy hair and shakes his head.

"I love parking lots," I say, trying to keep a straight face.

"They're pretty fucking awesome," Lucas agrees, grinning down at me. That freaking dimple. "So…"

There's a pause where we just stare at each other. I wonder if I look as shell-shocked as he does. My bet is that I'm even more disheveled than him.

"So, I'll see you tomorrow morning?" I ask. I'm pretty sure if I don't get in my car right now, I might propose marriage and ask to have his babies.

Fucking *wow*.

"Tomorrow morning," he confirms.

I step sideways and try to open my door before unlocking it. It takes me three tries to get it right. I can hear Lucas laughing behind me. I turn to playfully glare at him.

70

"Goodnight, Zoe Last Name Campbell," he says, holding my finally-unlocked door open for me.

I step back into his space and give him a soft, quick kiss.

"Goodnight, Lucas Henry Stark."

Chapter Nine
Lucas

I don't notice the notification until I'm in bed. When I accept the invitation and open the shared album Zoe sent me, I smile in the darkness. It's a timeline of us. I don't know what "us" really means, but it starts with a picture of The Town Mercantile, then Zoe licking cinnamon roll frosting off her fingers while sitting in the Breakers Bliss rental, pink potted plants behind her. A selfie of her holding the box she left me a cinnamon roll in, fingers awkwardly crossed, a sharpie between her teeth. The coffee cup I left my number on. My hand-drawn map. A selfie of Zoe in her 4Runner, I think in the parking lot while she waited for me before our hike, she has a nervous smile. All the funny pics she took from the hike. I quickly change her contact photo to the one of her kissing my cheek, her own cheeks flaming. A screenshot of a FaceTime call. Bonfire. Our cars in the dark parking lot. Grocery store.

LucasHenryStark:
While I enjoy ZoeSaysSo, I really like the album you shared.

Zoe Last Name Campbell:
i'm such a picture nerd. i have so many that no one sees just bc i like looking back. they make me happy. i guess i'm a visual person.

LucasHenryStark:
Real Picture Nerd Zoe Last Name Campbell makes me happy.

Zoe Last Name Campbell:
you mean this nerd?

She sends a picture of her in bed, glasses on, hair piled on top of her head, comforter tucked around her, book in hand. Holy fuck.

LucasHenryStark:
I honestly did not think you could get any hotter. Glasses+book really doing it for me though.

Zoe Last Name Campbell:
it's nonfiction.

LucasHenryStark:
You're killing me.

Zoe Last Name Campbell:
and a hardcover.

I'm just about to reply when she sends another picture. She's no longer under the comforter. She's lying on her side, hand tucked under her chin. Her hair is loose around her face and her tank top strap is falling off her shoulder. She still has her glasses on and her book is laying on the bed in front of her.

LucasHenryStark:
Damn Zoe. Killing me.

Zoe Last Name Campbell:
it'd probably be a better pic if i had a photographer...

LucasHenryStark:
I volunteer as tribute.

LucasHenryStark:
But also, that's my new favorite photo

74

Zoe Last Name Campbell:
selfies as my job for the win

Zoe No Last Name:
g'night, LHS.

***

I think I get an hour of sleep. I toss and turn, wishing I was wrapped up in Zoe. When I do sleep, I dream of her. What is wrong with me? I barely know her. I've only spent one full afternoon with her, that's it. That's all. A handful of hours. Nothing more.

Of course, I've spent the time since that afternoon getting to know her from afar. I know that she might complain about her alarm but she loves mornings. She also loves teaching yoga but gets nervous every time. She hates big parties and events but always tells me about meeting her followers. She has a love/hate relationship with her social media job. She has a love/love relationship with cinnamon rolls. Her cat is an asshole. She only recently started to love cooking. Her parents live close and she has a little sister that's still in high school. She already wants another tattoo.

I groan, realizing I'm in way too deep with this girl, and roll over. It's finally 6 a.m. Gramps will be up soon for coffee. I'm still not sure what I'm going to do with him all day if it's an off morning. With the farmer's market, I'm supposed to be in Three Rocks from 8 a.m. until at least 4 p.m. today, probably later. Then tomorrow is another early morning for the book sale. I scrub my hand down my face and stretch. Unlike Zoe, I am not a morning person but the thought of seeing her within a few hours has me up and moving. And also needing a cold shower.

"Good morning, Gramps," I say when he slowly shuffles his way into the kitchen.

"You're chipper this morning," he replies, eyeing me suspiciously as I pour him a cup of coffee.

He takes the steaming coffee mug I hand him, his hand steady, and looks me up and down. I can't help but smile. I am chipper. I follow him out the back door to the small deck and we silently share a cinnamon roll, taking sips of coffee as we enjoy the rare morning sun.

75

"I'm guessing Miss Zoe is coming to town," he finally says.

"She got in last night to see friends in Three Rocks. She wants to have dinner with us tonight, is that okay?" I ask, already knowing his answer.

The man asks me about her daily. Any time my phone vibrates, he asks if it's her. He's also in too deep and he hasn't even met her in person yet.

"That'd be alright I suppose," he nods. "Guess I better tidy up some things around here today."

"I'm going to be gone a little longer than usual today, I think you'll have plenty of time," I say. "Also, I don't think she expects you to clean for her."

"Hrmph, how many times do I have to tell you, put in the effort when you find the one," Gramps scolds.

"Slow down, hot shot, I've only known her a couple weeks," I tell him, trying to rein in his, and perhaps my, expectations. "And I don't think you've ever told me that. But it's noted."

I finish my coffee and set the empty mug on the table between us, thinking about what he said. I have been putting in effort, more than I ever have, but it doesn't feel like effort. The map, the necklace, hiking, all the texts and calls, it all felt effortless. But what if the effort she's used to is so much more than I have the time and money for? She's fairly well-known, especially in Portland, she goes to fancy fundraisers with Professional Date Dane and has free shit thrown at her left and right. I gave her a $23 necklace and some free pictures. Maybe I need to rethink my efforts.

"Luke, I'll be fine today, go see your girl," Gramps says. He looks pointedly at my knee, which is bouncing.

"Are you sure you're okay today?" I ask one last time. I hate days after bad days, I never know how things will pan out. It feels like a gamble every time.

"Luke, if you don't leave this house within five minutes, I'm checking myself into that retirement home down the way, the one with the fake flowers out front," Gramps threatens.

It's a good threat. That is the exact place I'm trying to keep him out of, not just because of the fake flowers. I pat his shoulder and take

76

our mugs inside, then bring him the newspaper that was tossed onto the driveway. I leave the house with thirty seconds to spare.

***

Marabelle gives me a knowing smirk when I duck into The Mercantile nearly forty-five minutes early and quickly make an americano. I snag a cinnamon roll and dart back out. Leaving my truck where it is, I walk toward the bridge that leads to the village area of town. When I see the sun shining on Rejection Rock in the distance, I set the pastry box and coffee cup on the bridge railing and snap a picture. I quickly add it to the shared album, hoping Zoe will get a notification. I'm still not totally sure how this shared album works, but I do see she put in the crazy hot selfies from last night.

"I was hoping you weren't teasing me," Zoe's voice floats toward me as I walk up the stone pathway to The Green Door Garden cottage that Team Merc manages.

Jessie, Colt's mom and West's sister, has really taken this rental up a notch with her green thumb. Flowers are bursting from their planters, vines crawl along the fence, and hanging baskets frame the front porch. It's basically an explosion of color.

Zoe fits right in. She's in a pink pullover and her smile is just as bright. Even the cover of the book sitting beside her has a splash of color. And is about astrophysics. That's unexpected.

"Astrophysics, huh?" I hand her the coffee cup and sit down beside her, stretching my legs out and leaning back on my hands after I put the cinnamon roll box between us.

"Yep," Zoe says as she sips her americano. She closes her eyes and hums her appreciation for the hot drink. "This is amazing, thank you. How long until you have to be at work?"

"I've got about half an hour," I reply after checking the time.

She moves the cinnamon roll to her other side and scoots closer to me. She nudges me to sit up. As soon as I sit forward and place my feet back on the steps, she sets her hand that's loosely holding her coffee cup on my thigh. She leans into me, resting her head on my shoulder.

"I'm glad I'm here, and that you're here," she says quietly.

"Hey Zoe," I say softly, and as soon as she looks up toward me, her dark eyes on mine, I snap a pic. "Am I getting the hang of this?"

77

She laughs and grabs my phone from me to look at the picture before I can. She quickly adds the picture to our shared album before holding my phone out toward me. When I reach for it, she pulls it back. The next thing I know, her lips are on mine. She's soft and sweet, a hint of coffee along with that vanilla chapstick, and she pulls back way too soon.

"Is that our first non-public kiss?" she asks with a laugh.

"Let's see, we have a trailhead parking lot, after dinner parking lot, rice aisle grocery store, and grocery store parking lot. So, yes. Although we are on a front porch, so maybe not."

"Will you kiss me on the beach?" she asks.

"Absolutely," I say, standing up and reaching my hand down to pull her up.

I softly kiss her temple and tuck her under my arm, loving how perfectly she fits against me. I quickly kiss her cheek as we walk along the path before racing her to the water's edge. I slowly kiss her lips on the beach when she leaps into my arms, wrapping herself around me like a koala.

"One more," she requests, standing on the porch steps before I go. No chance I say no.

I have to jog over the bridge so I'm not late for work.

***

"How long have you been making jewelry?" Zoe asks as I use Kelsey's phone to film.

"Since I was a teenager, which was many, many moons ago," Mary laughs. "It's always been a hobby, something I do for fun, just for me. But I just recently started my Etsy shop, thanks to the encouragement of my family, then The Town Mercantile started carrying some of my pieces, and now here I am at my first ever farmer's market!"

"Well, I absolutely love my necklace, I haven't taken it off since I got it," Zoe tells her, reaching her hand up and touching the delicate chain as she looks over at me. "I can't wait to see more of your creations."

"Perfect!" Kelsey calls. "I'll go talk to Heritage Farms next and see if they want a clip."

I stop recording on the phone and bring my real camera up to get some candid pictures of Zoe with Mary, as well as better shots of Mary's display. Somehow I lucked out and Tex assigned me to media duty today, meaning I'm following Kelsey and Zoe around like some sort of low-budget paparazzi. Apparently Kelsey and Zoe came up with this idea last night at the bonfire.

"The energy on that one," Mary says, watching Kelsey walk to the next vendor, a small, local farm with a wide variety of vibrant flowers in buckets, vases, and jars.

"Isn't she great? I meant what I said about my necklace, it's my favorite," Zoe says, making my chest twinge.

I love watching Zoe immerse herself in my life. She keeps sending small smiles my way and I've had to stop myself from reaching for her multiple times. I'm trying to follow her lead on what happens between us in public. She's already had multiple people approach her, it feels weird calling them her fans or followers, but I guess that's what they are. I know she had something happen with her ex and social media so I don't want to push her boundaries, but it's killing me not to pull her in to steal a kiss.

"Well, thank you, that means a lot to me. Before you go, I brought you something as a thank you," Mary says as she pulls a little pouch out from her cash box.

I watch Zoe carefully untie the drawstring and her face lights up when she finds two bracelets inside. Both are delicate string bracelets with metal charms, one is a wave and the other nearly matches her mountain sunset necklace. She touches the pendant and shoots another look my way. This one I capture on my camera. Zoe pulls Mary into a hug before the startled artist knows what's happening.

"Sorry, I'm a hugger and you just gave me an amazing present. I love them both," she tells Mary as she releases her from her hug. Zoe does her happy dance, eyes shining, and quickly puts both bracelets on.

"Thank you for helping my business," Mary says, squeezing Zoe's arm before ducking back under her canopy to reorganize her inventory.

"I love this," Zoe whispers to me. "Like, why did I get so caught up in the other side of whatever my job is?"

"I don't know what that means, but you look really happy," I tell her. It's true. She's absolutely glowing.

Kelsey waves Zoe over to meet Amy, the flower vendor from Heritage Farms. Just as I lift my camera to capture Kelsey and Zoe happily burying their faces in bouquets of bright flowers, I feel my phone vibrate in my pocket.

It's Gramps.

Chapter Ten
Zoe

I see Lucas's whole demeanor, from his body language to his facial expression, change in an instant. His hand grips his phone tightly as he brings it to his ear.

"One sec, Kels," I say.

Kelsey gives me a thumbs up between sneezes. I have a feeling she's allergic to something in the amazing bouquets Amy has displayed under her canopy. I walk toward Lucas, not wanting to overstep but also needing to know that he's alright.

"Hey, everything okay?" I ask, touching his arm lightly when he ends the call.

When he turns to me, I can see the worry in his eyes.

"Gramps called to say he can't find his lunch, which I know for a fact that I left in the middle of the fridge. Nancy is busy, obviously Marabelle is, too. I don't know what to do. I left early from work yesterday, I can't afford to leave today as well," he says in a rush. He looks down and types on his phone. "I'm texting Jake but I'm sure the police are busy this weekend since it's a holiday."

"But I'm here," I tell him. "I've never been a barista and I'm obviously not on payroll so I probably can't do your job, but what if you let me go check on him? I can eat lunch with him and make sure he's okay. Or, we can ask Tex if I can help out here while you go home. I can at least do a mediocre job of taking over your camera duties. I'm happy to do either."

Lucas blows out an unsteady breath as he thinks it over, his eyes darting between his phone and the crowd at the farmer's market. "I can't ask you to do either of those things, you're on vacation," he says, shaking his head.

"You didn't ask, I offered. I'm here to see you, get to know the real Lucas Henry Stark," I tell him softly. I can't imagine the worry he goes through on a daily basis. This completely trumps my daily worries about mild fame and internet rage trolls. "What better way to get to know you than spend time with the most important person in your life?"

"It would make Gramps happy if you showed up on the doorstep," Lucas admits. "He's asked about you daily since he first met you on FaceTime."

"That just made my day," I say, smiling as I think of that first FaceTime call. "But I'm also happy to continue helping out here. Whatever is best for you."

Lucas closes his eyes and sighs. When he opens his eyes again, he reaches for my hand. He glances around and then pulls back, shoving his hand in his pocket. I'm unsure what that's about, I thought I had made it clear that I'm interested in more than a weekend fling, but now isn't the time to focus on that.

"I'll text you the address," he says. "Call me if you get there and he doesn't answer and I'll call Jake. Also, the spare key is under the flower pot to the right of the door."

"I'm on it," I tell him. "Send me the address and Jake's number as well, just in case. Tell Kelsey whatever you want, I'll make it up to her tomorrow."

"Zoe!" he calls as I'm walking away. I turn to face him. "Please, just don't…nevermind. Thank you."

I tilt my head and frown, confused. But he smiles at me so I turn again and jog back toward my rental, trying to remember where I left my car key.

***

"Mr. Stark? It's Zoe, Lucas's friend!" I call, as I knock on the door once again.

82

I recheck the address that Lucas sent. I'm definitely at the right place. There's a flower pot to the right of the door, just like he said. What should I do? Do I let myself in? Call Lucas? Call Jake?

Tires crunching on gravel makes me turn and I see a Rock Beach Police cruiser pulling in next to my 4Runner. A tall, blonde, and honestly gigantic man in a police uniform unfolds himself from the driver's seat. His bicep strains his uniform when he raises his hand in greeting. I'd say he needs a bigger shirt but I doubt they even make them that big. He starts my way, his eyes scanning the house before settling on me. GymBro, incoming.

"Miss Zoe? What are you doing here?" A gruff voice behind me makes me whirl around.

"Mr. Stark! Hi! Nice to meet you in person," I say, smiling at Lucas's adorable grandpa.

"Officer Jake, what are you doing here?" Mr. Stark asks the man that's now towering over me. "Did Lucas call in the cavalry?"

Officer Jake and I quickly look at each other and then back at the elderly man standing in the doorway.

"You both look guilty," he grouches.

"Hi, I'm Lucas's..." I start, turning to Officer Jake and holding out my hand.

Well, what am I? Both men raise their eyebrows at my pause. Jake takes my hand and I can feel his barbell calluses, just like Dane's, as he shakes it slowly, still waiting for me to continue.

"I'm Zoe," I offer to an amused-looking Officer Jake.

"Jake," he replies, lip twitching as he fights a smile.

"Which one of you is supposed to be my babysitter?" Mr. Stark asks, looking between us again.

Jake and I eye each other. He's obviously trying to work out just who the hell I am and why I'm here, while I'm just trying to make this less awkward for all three of us. Possibly an impossible task. I glance at Jake's arms. I hope this GymBro is as awesome as my favorite GymBro, Professional Date Dane.

"I'll arm wrestle you for it," I tell Jake, flexing my biceps. "Winner gets a lunch date with the green-eyed grumbly one. Loser goes back to work patrolling the streets in their too-small cruiser."

Both men bark out laughs at that. I smile, quite pleased with myself, and do my shoulder shimmy happy dance. I think I just won both men over.

"You two have a nice lunch date, then," Jake says, backing away with his hands up in surrender. He crosses the yard before turning back, giving me a long, assessing look, before smiling and ducking into his cruiser.

"So, Mr. Stark, now that I've won a lunch date with you, are we eating here or can I take you out to Mo's for some clam chowder?" I ask, smiling at Lucas's grandfather, whose eyes are even more green in person than they are over FaceTime.

"Enough of this Mr. Stark nonsense, call me Henry," Henry says. "I like your spunk. I can see why Luke is so enamored with you."

I feel my cheeks heat at that. First twitterpated, now enamored.

"Well, Henry, can I treat you to Mo's?" I ask. "I haven't been in years."

"That sounds nice, Miss Zoe," Henry tells me. "Why don't you come in and give me a few minutes to get ready."

I step inside and immediately recognize the living room from our FaceTimes. I perch on the worn couch as I wait for Henry to gather his things. I can see the small dining area where we chatted after the recipe trial and beyond that is a tidy kitchen. A black and white photograph from a long ago wedding day catches my eye, I stand to get a closer look. The groom is smiling at his stunning bride, the dimple on his right cheek telling me it's Henry. He must be so lost without her by his side. My heart hurts for him, as well as for Lucas.

Lucas, who is probably still worried.

Zoe Last Name Campbell:
gramps ok and i get a lunch date out of this

LucasHenryStark:
I heard you won an arm wrestling contest.

Zoe Last Name Campbell:
i def would have but my opponent was too intimidated to take me on

84

"That's the same look Luke has when you're on the other end of the phone," Henry says as he walks back in.

I can't help but smile. I know I'm a smitten fool. I do my full happy dance. Henry guffaws at my shimmy. I've never thought "guffaws" as a description of laughter until this moment. Lucas is great but I think I'm already in love with Henry.

***

A couple hours later, our bellies full of clam chowder, Henry and I sit at a table in the public library, sorting the last few boxes of books for the sale tomorrow. Henry is tired but he looks happy, which makes me happy.

"I bet you didn't think this was how you'd be spending your weekend beach getaway," Nancy says from beside me.

Nancy is probably in her seventies but has the energy of someone much younger. She doesn't stop moving. Ever. She's shelving books, answering questions from patrons, and telling me all about her favorite local hikes. She even pulls up AllTrails on her phone to show me her profile with pictures from past hikes.

"Maybe not, but I really think the best things in life come as a surprise," I reply.

"So where else does your job take you?" Nancy asks interestedly. "I think it's so neat that you can document your life and make a living. Your generation just astounds me."

"Well, I haven't really taken advantage of that," I admit. "I think I'm just now realizing how much more I could do with this weird job I have. I started sharing my life through pictures and it grew so fast, it was fun to share and learn and help people find fitness in their own life. During Covid, that's when we really took off. It was more like a community then, staying healthy while isolated, trying new things. Since then, I've partnered with a lot of yoga studios, gyms, nutrition companies, apparel, you name it." I don't add that those partnerships didn't start until Aiden was in my life and now I'm not really sure why I've kept them up. Or really, why I even did half of them in the first place.

"Well, what are your favorite parts of your job and is there something else that you want to do with it?" Nancy asks, getting right to the point.

"I'm still figuring that out. I love helping people find the best kind of fitness for them, for their lifestyle, because it's not the same for everyone. During Covid I did a series of YouTube yoga classes for kids and teens and the response was amazing! Parents were busy, working and homeschooling, lives were messy. It felt good to see how I helped real people. Real families. Now I volunteer at an underserved middle school a couple days a week during the school year. I call it a fitness program but really we just play games. It's so fun," I tell her enthusiastically. There really is so much to love about my work. How did I ever let it get away from me like this?

"That's amazing," Nancy says. "It sounds like you have a lot of directions you could take if you so choose."

"Yeah..." I trail off. But could I? It feels like I've cornered myself in this one section, this one particular brand. "It feels like I put on a persona some days, even if we're just filming in my living room or at a park, I feel like I have to be perfect, exactly what everyone has already seen and therefore expects. But changing that, showing the real me, could result in losing my followers and views, which means my income, which affects Abby, my best friend who works for me, as well."

"What does the real you want to do?" Nancy asks. "I understand not wanting to let people down, especially your best friend, but happy counts."

She really isn't one to small talk I guess. I like that she's pushing me, making me think. Did I ever want to look perfect and sell bullshit? Not really. Do I know what I want to do? Not really.

Today has been a weird day.

"I'm not totally sure. I just know that it feels like change is coming, it's just out of my grasp but I'm almost there. I've been out of college for a couple years and it seems like I should have a little more direction in life than just showing off on the internet."

"Direction is overrated," Henry breaks in suddenly. "When Luke was wandering that summer, it was the happiest I've seen the boy. If you

86

have the opportunity to wander your way to happiness, you take that opportunity. Nancy is right. Happy counts."

"That sounds like really good advice, Henry," I say slowly. I can feel excitement building, but also trepidation. "I do have the opportunity, I should make the most of it, shouldn't I? Why does that thought scare me though?"

Nancy gives me an encouraging smile.

"Change should scare you," Henry says firmly.

"I think I'd like to find a way to try new things, but also to use what I've built, what Abby and I have built, I'm just not sure how," I tell both of them.

"Where there's a will, there's a way," Henry states, a note of finality in his voice. I guess he's done with this conversation. I just don't know if I am.

Chapter Eleven
Lucas

When I walk in the house and see Gramps, Zoe, Jake, and Nancy all standing in the middle of our tiny living room, furniture pushed to the side, arms raised to the ceiling, I wonder if I'm in some alternate reality. None of them notice my arrival so I just stand and stare. Seeing Jake's cruiser out front nearly sent me into a panic, but instead of an emergency, I walked in the house to this.

"And now let's gently stretch forward. Henry, make sure you use your chair," Zoe says in a calm, even tone. "Deep inhale, find that focal point, roll down nice and slow."

All four of them slowly tuck their chins and roll their shoulders, letting their arms hang toward the floor. Gramps rests his hands on the back of a folding chair that I didn't notice at first glance; his forward stretch isn't very pronounced but his feet are planted firmly in the dirty beige carpet with no signs of faltering.

Jake and Nancy are following Zoe's lead, stretching down to reach their toes. Jake looks like he might snap in half at any moment. It's amusing that Nancy is better at this than Jake. He spends hours in the gym, I'm guessing none of that time is spent doing yoga.

Zoe is bent in half, completely folded in two, head to her knees, perfect ass in the air. Her hands are flat on the floor and she's absolutely relaxed, talking quietly to Gramps who is next to her. I blink a couple times to make sure this is reality.

"Well, Luke, are you gonna just stand there and oggle our instructor or are you going to join us?" Gramps says, the first to notice me.

Zoe's head whips in my direction but she stays in her position. Her cheeks are red, but that might just be because she's upside down. Jake snorts and looks at me, then Zoe, then back at me. Nancy just gives me a knowing, but upside down, smile.

"And let's slowly roll back to mountain pose, one vertebrae at a time," Zoe says as she very slowly, tortuously rises. "Let's take four deep, slow, intentional breaths here…"

All four of them stand tall, arms at their sides, palms facing forward. I can see their chests rise and lower with each breath. Zoe looks radiant in our dingy living room, sharing what she loves with those I love.

"Thank you for spending time with me, I hope we can do this again soon," Zoe says before reaching to squeeze Gramps's arm. He smiles back at her and she makes sure he settles back into his recliner as Nancy moves the folding chair to the corner.

"We're on furniture and cooking duty," Jake says, greeting me with a handshake and clap on my shoulder.

"What the hell is happening right now?" I ask under my breath.

"If she's not your girlfriend, I'm going to do everything I can to make her mine," Jake replies. He gives me a grin that tells me he's joking.

"Not happening," I tell him. "Put your muscles to good use and let's move this couch back."

We make quick work of the couch and coffee table then Jake retreats to the kitchen. I can hear him washing his hands and opening the refrigerator.

"Hi, I didn't mean for this whole life takeover thing to happen," Zoe says, looking worried. "But lunch turned into stopping by the library which then led to finalizing the book sale details. Then we-"

I stop her with a quick kiss to her lips. She sighs and melts into me but her eyes widen and cut to Gramps and Nancy across the room when I pull away.

90

"While I did wonder if I accidentally walked in on some weird cult ritual, I like this life takeover," I whisper. "I've spent every day since I met you wishing you were here. And now you are."

Her cheeks turn pink and she bites her lower lip. "Are you saying that because I helped your Gramps or because you got to stare at my ass?"

"Yes, that," I tell her. "Both. All of it."

She smiles up at me and I really wish we didn't have a senior citizen audience of two.

"Want help with dinner?" she asks me, glancing toward the kitchen. "I know we were supposed to cook together, but Jake said since I got lunch duty, he was on dinner."

"Nah," I say and then raise my voice so Jake will be able to hear. "The meathead is actually a good cook. I only keep him around for manual labor and his cooking."

"Abs are made in the kitchen, bro!" Jake calls back. "And I thought it was my squat you liked."

Gramps and Zoe both nearly cry tears of laughter at that. I haven't seen Gramps this happy in ages. I don't know if I've been this happy in ages either.

***

"You're amazing," I say, setting an americano on the corner of Zoe's yoga mat.

"Well, thank you, both for the compliment and the coffee, but how or why am I amazing this morning?" Zoe asks, not moving from her position.

"I mean, you look like this," I wave my hand up and down her body which is stretched into some yoga pose, clad in blue and green leggings that remind me of a mermaid tail, with a matching sports bra. Her abs flex as she straightens. "But mainly because Gramps is walking on water this morning after spending yesterday with you."

"It was the best day since our waterfall hike," she replies, cheeks turning pink as she smiles at me.

The morning definitely was, I'll agree there. And the evening was pretty amazing as well. After I walked in on living room yoga, Jake and I made the dinner that Zoe and I had shopped for the night before.

91

Gramps was happy to have the kitchen quite literally bursting at the seams and after Zoe soundly kicked our asses at cards, Jake offered to help his great-aunt load up his truck for the book sale, giving Zoe and I a chance to sit out back together while Gramps went to bed. We talk nearly every night but having her there in person, being able to reach over and hold her hand, was a thousand times better than talking over FaceTime. Of course our goodnight kiss, once again with her pressed up against her 4Runner, was also a highlight of my night.

"Should I leave you to your morning?" I ask, watching as she shifts her weight forward, folding in half.

"Want to put my coffee inside for me?"

"Of course."

I swear I try really hard not to stare at her ass as I walk past her and open the front door, it's just an impossible task. I set her coffee cup down and brace my hands on the counter, leaning forward and bowing my head. I give myself the opposite of a pep talk. A calm the fuck down talk. She's doing her morning yoga. We spent all evening together. I showed up unannounced at 7:30 in the damn morning. Let her do her thing.

"Wanna make out?"

I startle, not having heard Zoe walk in the front door. I turn around and she's smiling at me from the middle of the living room, her cheeks now bright pink.

"Sorry, I just wasn't sure if I should blurt out that question on the front porch. I don't live here, but you work here, I'm not sure how you're feeling about this," she gestures between us. "And then the whole ZoeSays issue, which sucks and I'm sorry."

"I'm feeling really good about this," I say, mimicking her gesture. "And really good about your question."

She practically runs across the room, closing the distance between us in a flash, then she throws her arms around my neck. I lift her up, spinning so I can set her on the counter. She wraps her legs around my waist and I kiss her like I haven't seen her for weeks, which I realize is probably our reality.

"Luke," she whispers, pulling back. "Where'd you go?"

"Luke?" I chase her lips, needing more.

"Lucas Henry Stark, where did you go?" she asks again, putting her hand on my chest to create space between us. She keeps her legs wrapped around me though, keeping me close, and I run my hands along the outside of her thighs.

"Mmmm...I think I like the way you say 'Luke' though," I tell her. I think I really fucking like it.

"Answer. The. Question." I'd think she was really upset, but her legs tighten around me.

"I felt like I was kissing you after weeks apart, instead of just a night." I shrug, glancing sideways to avoid her gaze. "Then I realized that we're always going to have weeks apart."

"And?" she prompts.

"I really like you, Zoe. Please let me kiss you again."

Her hand that's on my chest fists my shirt and pulls me in. Her lips crash into mine and as soon as they part, I sweep my tongue inside. She gives a breathy moan as I move my hands from her thighs up her hips to her waist, finding warm skin between her leggings and sports bra. That moan nearly does me in. I want to find every place on her body that makes her moan at my touch.

Zoe runs her fingers through my hair, grasping at the long ends at the base of my neck. I have a flash of a very different scenario with her fingers in my hair and I tighten my grip around her waist, trying to anchor myself to this moment. She slides to the edge of the counter, rocking her hips into mine. It takes everything in me to not turn and carry her to the bedroom. She nips my lower lip, then sucks it gently, making me groan, my willpower barely hanging by a thread. With one last lingering kiss, she pulls away, both of us breathless. She rests her forehead on mine and brings a hand to cup my jaw.

"Luke, I really like you, too," she says quietly, making my heart soar. "But-"

"Please no but," I whisper, cutting her off. 'But' can only mean one thing. And it's a thing I don't want to hear.

"But we have a book sale to get set up for, so I'm going to need you to take your talented mouth to the other side of the house while I get ready. I promised Jake I wouldn't be late," she finishes her sentence with a smile.

I laugh at that. Jake must have looked Zoe up right after he left last night because he had texted me asking me if I knew who my girl was. I had tilted my phone for Zoe to see and she adorably blushed.

"Your girl?" she questioned.

"That's what has your cheeks turning pink, not the fact that my meathead friend figured out you're fitness famous?"

The best part of this exchange was when she got on her phone and texted Jake, whose number I had given her earlier. She tilted her phone toward me a minute later and this time I was the one blushing.

Zoe:
he knows who his girl is

Zoe:
spoiler alert: it's me

Officer Jake:
ZoeSaysSoFitness, I presume?

Zoe (Lucas's Girl):
officer jake, loser of arm wrestling

Officer Jake:
AKA the guy that let you steal his lunch date AND who took over book duty so my bro could have time with his girl tonight

Zoe (Lucas's Girl):
true. i owe you. meet you at 8 to help unload.

Officer Jake:
Don't be late.

Zoe (Lucas's Girl):
10-4. copy. over and out.

Seeing her call herself my girl felt really good. Jake texting me three seconds later telling me that my girl is awesome, also good. He's been a loyal friend, even when I spent years attempting to hold most people at arm's length, having learned at an early age that people always leave in the end. Or in the case of my mom, in the beginning. Luckily Jake is stubborn.

Zoe returns from the bedroom within minutes, a different pair of leggings on, her crop tank leaving a sliver of stomach showing. Her long hair is in a messy braid over her shoulder and she's carrying a small tube of sunscreen in one hand. I can see her vanilla chapstick peeking out from her waistband.

"One last kiss?" Zoe asks, standing just inside the front door.

"Not the last, but the last for right now," I tell her, leaning down to kiss her softly.

Chapter Twelve
Zoe

Story time at the book sale is freaking adorable. Nancy and Kelsey have coloring pages and craft stations set up to keep kids busy and I park myself at the table with beads and string, helping little ones tie bracelets around their tiny wrists. Lucas comes to sit next to me, his thigh pressed against mine, and makes a colorful bracelet with Colt.

"We match!" Colt says happily, admiring his wrist after I tie the bracelet loosely.

Lucas holds his arm out to me and I carefully tie his bracelet as well, which does indeed match Colt's. I try not to be distracted by the way Lucas watches me or the feel of his skin under my fingers.

"Great bracelets, guys," I tell them. Colt beams at me and Lucas knocks his knee into mine under the table.

"Wait! I need to make one for Tex!" Colt exclaims when West walks over.

"She's been working hard all day, I bet she'll love it, bud," West tells him.

"Hey, are there any events happening tomorrow?" I ask.

"No, thank god," West says, crossing his arms. "Colt, when you're done with Tex's bracelet, go sit with Mrs. G, she's about to start reading."

"Okay!" Colt says happily, his attention still focused on the beads in his hand.

West's eyes lock on Tex, who is standing across the lawn, and he stalks toward her without saying goodbye. Grouchy lumberjack today. I don't think he's much for crowds. Or really anything other than Colt and Tex.

"Why'd you ask about tomorrow?" Lucas asks as I watch West snake an arm around Tex, tucking his hand under her shirt to squeeze her waist as she smiles up at him. God, they're cute together.

I pull my attention back to Lucas. "I bailed on Kelsey yesterday; I was thinking of seeing if the Team Merc girls could go for an early hike," I tell him, watching his hands fumble with tiny beads. "Wait, what does that say?"

Lucas holds his bracelet up triumphantly. L-U-K-E-S-G-I-R-L is spelled out in beads. My heart melts and I laugh out loud. I hold out my wrist and suck in a breath when Lucas's fingers brush against the inside of my wrist, right over my sunset tattoo.

"Thanks, Lucas," I whisper.

"Thanks, Lucas," Colt parrots, making me jump. He holds Tex's bracelet out to Lucas, who ties the end. After inspecting the knot, Colt climbs down from the bench and runs to join the kids gathered around Mrs. G.

"No more 'Luke' then? Because I definitely liked that," Lucas says quietly as he leans a little closer to me.

Everyone is focused on Mrs. G, who is introducing the book she's about to read. I drop my hand to his, making sure the beads are facing the right direction, and adjust my farmer's market bracelets from Mary on either side. I link our fingers and give his hand a squeeze. I quickly take a picture before pulling away. Another pic to add to our album. I have a quick flash of Aiden and his fancy watch, his exasperation if I wore anything that wasn't designer or sponsored in some way. I shake my head, trying to rid myself of the heavy weight that always settles over me like a dark cloud when I think of him.

"You should definitely hike tomorrow morning. I'll take Tex's early morning shift," Luke says, nudging my shoulder.

"Thanks, Luke." I lean into his warm shoulder and bring my hand up to my necklace. I immediately feel calm.

"You're welcome, Zoe Last Name Campbell."

I lean my back against Luke's solid chest as he wraps his arms around my shoulders, keeping the blanket snug around both of us. I tip my head back and he leans down to give me a soft kiss. I want to stay wrapped up with him all night.

"I've wanted to watch the sunset with you since the first time I met you," he whispers before kissing just below my ear. Warmth spreads through my body, I'm unsure if it's from his words or the way he trails kisses down to my neck.

"I looked for you that night," I admit. "I was hoping you'd be there."

"I was hoping I'd be there, too, but Gramps, dinner, grocery shopping, the night got away from me. I really did mean to make it back in time for sunset," he says, tightening his arms around me. "I thought I had missed my chance after that."

"Well, we're here now." I turn in his arms so I'm facing him. "And I can't decide between begging you to kiss me senseless or taking a picture for our album."

"Both?" he asks, bringing his mouth down to mine.

He's so playful and sweet, the heat behind his kisses surprises me every single time. I forget the sunset and my wish for a picture as soon as his tongue tangles with mine. I slip my hands under his shirt, needing to feel his skin beneath my fingers. I let my hands roam his abs and up to his chest as he nips my bottom lip. He pulls back slowly, like he has to convince himself to put space between us.

"Why are we always in a public place?" Luke whispers, resting his forehead on mine.

"It's probably a good thing. You're too easy to get lost in, Lucas Henry Stark," I say, sighing and leaning further into him, wrapping my hands around his waist.

That's definitely the truth. I don't know if it's because we've spent so much time getting to know each other through the phone, or if it's just him, but two days with Luke and I might be in over my head. No, I'm definitely in over my head. It's like everything else just fades when I'm with him. It might also be this life, this town, this community, how easy it is to slip into Luke's world and the peace I feel here.

After the book sale today, when Luke had to go back to work, I spent a couple hours on the beach playing frisbee and sand volleyball with other beachgoers. I met and talked to a few of my followers, taking pictures and even doing a little yoga with them. Colt and his mom, Jessie, found me and we raced up and down the beach and splashed in the freezing cold water before sinking into the sand to build a very crooked sand castle. After a shower back at my cottage, I finally checked ZoeSays after going radio silent since leaving Portland on Friday, probably a mistake.

"Trying to get back on track by showing more skin? Your minion should have edited this one more."

Instead of sending me into a tailspin, I just rolled my eyes and texted Abby.

Zoe:
i knew he was full of shit

Abs:
lucas?! what'd i miss?

Zoe:
no. asshole DM'ed about friday's zssf post

Abs:
1. that's def less skin than we've shown. 2. you have more new followers now so i don't know wtf back on track means 3. we didn't photoshop/edit that at all?? like you're literally just sitting on the counter with your smoothie.

Abs:
fucker. now i'm pissed. want me to block him?

Zoe:
honestly i don't really care.

I didn't. For the first time in a long time, I just Did. Not. Care. I texted Abby as a heads up, an FYI as she watches my accounts. Since I was the one to open the DM, she probably wouldn't have seen it, but I wanted her to be aware. She seemed to care a hell of a lot more than me, which is why she's my best friend.

Abs:
your last two virals were when you said F it at the beach and we didn't polish anything

Abs:
i love the real you and the zssf you, which is actually still you. and i'm not just saying that bc i'm your minion.

Abs:
you should post something "real" and he'll see how it takes off

Zoe:
nah, i'm just gonna go have dinner with a cute old man and his cute in a different way grandson

Abs:
YOU are so cute with this one

Zoe:
(pic)

Abs:
does that say luke's girl? omg you two are adorable. gag.

Abs:
love how happy you are.

My minion was right, I am happy. I made dinner for Henry and Luke in their tidy kitchen and then after Luke did the dishes, Henry basically kicked us out of the house. Luke brought me to this little beach, just a couple minutes from their house.

"Zoe?" Luke pulls me back into the moment. "You say that like it's a bad thing."

"Not a bad thing, I really like getting lost in you," I say, pulling him back in for another kiss. But didn't I get lost in Aiden, too? And look what that did.

"I really want to kiss you all night long but I need you to turn around," Luke says, using his hands that are on my waist to turn me, pulling my back to his chest once again.

I suck in a breath. The sun is just starting to sink into the ocean, pink and orange streaks fill the sky. For some reason tears prick my eyes. Luke ducks to lean his chin on my shoulder, snapping a pic of us. I tilt my head to rest against his and just enjoy this moment. The spectacular sunset, the feeling of Luke's chest rising and falling against my back, his hands snug around my middle. This feeling, the warmth that spreads through my veins when I'm in Luke's arms, is completely different than anything I ever felt with Aiden. A different lost. A better lost. There's really no comparison.

When the sun fully disappears into the water, Luke takes my hand and leads me down the small beach to a large log that the ocean has tossed onto the sand. Leaving the blanket around my shoulders, he drops into the sand, using the log as a backrest. Then he tugs my hand until I sit down between his legs and lean into him again.

We sit in silence, each lost in our own thoughts, as the light fades.

***

"Holy shit you guys, this is insanely beautiful!" I exclaim, staring out over the ocean.

"Now you know why I live at the top of a hill," Avery tells me. "The view never gets old."

"This is my favorite hike," Kelsey says as she takes pictures of Zero standing on a rock. Somehow Kelsey must have taught the massive Doberman to pose, because she stands perfectly still and stares out at the view while Kelsey snaps away.

"Thank you for agreeing to be my tour guides, I know you have a crazy busy day tomorrow," I tell all three of them.

"That's even more reason to run away this morning," Tex says. She checks the time. "But that also means we only have about ten minutes to enjoy this view."

"One minute of pictures, then nine minutes of staring in awe," Kelsey decides.

"If Abby ever quits on me, I'm hiring you," I tell her with a laugh.

I happily pose with my new friends and then enjoy every single second of my nine minutes of staring in awe. What is it about this place that makes me ache for more? More time away from large studios, more time with living room yoga, more time playing, more time expanding my circle. I close my eyes and take a deep breath, remembering my library conversation with Nancy and Henry. Whatever idea wiggled its way into my brain that afternoon is still there, not quite fully formed, just out of my reach.

Zero must sense the shift in my mood, because she's suddenly at my side, nudging my hand. I scratch her ears, eyes still on the horizon. What is it that I'm trying to figure out?

"Not going to lie, I think running away was my best decision," Tex says suddenly. "This is fucking awesome."

"Agreed," Avery says.

"Definitely agree," Kelsey nods. "So glad you ended up here when you did."

"I'm unsure what we're talking about, but I agree, too," I tell her with a shrug.

"Oh, yeah, so I dumped my live-in boyfriend and an hour later I got in my car with my dog and drove two thousand miles, now I'm here," Tex tells me. "Luckily I have a badass best friend to catch me when I fall. Or in this case, corral me when I run away."

"Anything and everything, always," Avery says. She raises a single eyebrow at Tex and Tex winks back at her.

"When was that?" I question Tex. "I'm a little unclear on your job description but you're all killing it with the rentals. And I've seen you multiple times with Hot Lumberjack and you're obviously in deep there."

"Ummm, yeah, so West kinda snuck up on me," Tex says with a grin. "I moved here less than two months ago."

"Shutup!" I exclaim. Kelsey snickers at my reaction.

Tex shrugs at me. "The best ones sneak up on you when you least expect it."

A-freaking-men to that. I might have had a moment or two of overthinking last night on the beach, but feeling Luke's arms wrapped tight around me as darkness fell, his breath tickling my neck as he whispered how perfect I felt in his arms, brought me right back to what I've been focusing on: enjoying each moment. I sank further in the comforting cocoon of Luke's warmth until the night sky was inky black above us and let that feeling carry me through the night.

"Huh, well, you picked a breathtakingly beautiful place to run to, not gonna lie, a little jealous this is your guys' real life," I tell the trio.

"Okay, ZoeSaysSo." Kelsey rolls her eyes at me. "You're famous, living in a big city that has like, real places to go and things to do, and I saw those pictures of you and that Dane guy from the fundraiser. He's almost as hot as Lucas's cop friend."

Since I'm still unclear on Luke and I's relationship status, I don't blurt out that Lucas is way hotter than both Jake and Dane. But I definitely think it.

"Portland is a great city, obviously my job is pretty amazing, it brought me here, and my friend Dane is the best arm candy, I'm definitely very lucky," I tell them.

"You know, my one concern when I moved to Three Rocks was that I'd miss city living, it'd be too quiet, too isolated. I know I haven't spent a winter here yet, but right now, I have everything I need," Tex says as we start to hike back down to my 4Runner, Zero leading the way. "I love this community."

"It's definitely a community again, thanks to you," Avery says. She turns to me. "When Tex showed up on my doorstep, I pulled a little bit of a bait and switch on her. She thought she was coming here to manage The Town Mercantile, which she is, but I also dumped six

104

houses on her to remodel and get ready to rent, and asked her to save my entire town."

"Yeah, I kinda freaked out," Tex admits. "But I had already driven nearly three days, it would have been a huge pain in the ass to drive back. Plus, Zero loves the beach."

"Well, I'm looking forward to getting out of here," Kelsey says.

"As you should be," I tell her. "College is super fun, time to stretch your wings, see what's out there. You're going to have a blast."

"I bet you end up back here," Avery says with a smile.

"I'll come back if Officer Jake handcuffs me and drags me back," Kelsey says, wiggling her eyebrows.

I burst out laughing, then I remember that I'm not sure if I'm supposed to admit I know Officer Jake, loser of arm wrestling. Tex gives me a knowing look. Does she think I'm the one being handcuffed by Officer Jake?

"Handcuffs? He better be really hot for that," I say quickly.

"No joke, he's super hot," Kelsey tells me, fanning herself.

"Oh my god, you're going to have the best time at college," Tex laughs. "Just remember, if you need bail money or an attorney, call Aves."

"I'm changing my phone number," Avery mutters.

Chapter Thirteen

Luke

"Americano?" I ask with a smile when Zoe follows the Team Merc girls into the store.

"Your dimple is what did me in," she whispers, leaning over the counter toward me. She raises her voice. "Yes, please, on the americano."

Note to self: smile more. Not hard to do when Zoe's around.

"You guys have fun?" I direct my question to Kelsey, who has already washed her hands and is making a mocha for Brian, who I've realized over the last weeks is a father figure to her.

"So fun!" she chirps, then gives Zoe a secret grin.

Did Zoe spill our maybe-secret relationship?

"Kelsey says you have a super hot cop friend," Zoe says, raising her eyebrows at me.

Ah, yes, Kelsey's not-so-secret crush on Jake. She saw the guy one time when he stopped in to say hi, and she was a goner. Now that I think about it, that was me with Zoe, a total goner. Perhaps I shouldn't judge.

"Yeah, Jake is super dreamy," I reply, keeping a straight face.

"Are you talking about Officer Hot Cop?" Brian cuts in. "With the biceps? And the quads?"

"Oh my god, not you, too," Kelsey groans, burying her face in her hands.

"He can help me on a fire call *any* day," Brian says.

"Guys! I know he's like a decade older than me, just let a small town girl have a small town cop fantasy, geez," Kelsey whines. "Age gap romances are a whole freaking sub-genre, anyway."

"Lucas, can you bring him to the fireworks tomorrow? I really think I need to meet him," Tex chimes in.

"You have West, I don't have anyone," Avery, who I've rarely heard joke around, joins in.

"Worst pretend sisters, ever." Kelsey stomps around the counter to hand Brian his usual, an extra hot mocha with extra whipped cream. He pulls her under his arm and gives her shoulders an affectionate squeeze and she smiles despite her words.

"Wait, I want pretend sisters," Zoe says, looking around the group.

"You can have them," Kelsey says. "And take Brian, too, while you're at it. Just for that, you have to pay for your mocha this morning." She shrugs out from under his arm and glares at him.

"Ouch, kiddo, ouch." Brian puts a hand over his heart like he's wounded.

"I think it was my comment that started all of this, so how about I pay for the mocha and maybe some cinnamon rolls for Nate and the other guys, too," Zoe offers.

Freaking Nate. Of course he was at the bonfire. I'm sure he made a move on her, too.

"Ugh, famous, beautiful, and nice. You're the worst," Kelsey says loudly. "Lucas, do not bring Jake to the fireworks, he'd probably just fall in love with her."

"Not interested," Zoe says immediately. Her eyes meet mine. "Officer Jake is all yours, Kelsey."

"He's only six or seven years older than you, Kels, that's not much, but he's married to the squat rack," I tell her.

"Don't I know it, those glutes," Brian says loudly, making all of the girls crack up, even shy Katie, my new coworker, who has made her way down the counter to our group.

"Go away, Brian," Kelsey says, stomping her foot.

"I did not know my comment would turn into this, I swear," Zoe tells Kelsey, her eyes wide.

"I hate all of you," Kelsey mutters and flounces out of the store, flipping her hair over her shoulder as she goes.

"Did she just ditch work?" Tex asks, looking at Avery.

"I mean…yes? I'll go chase her down," Avery says.

The door flies back open.

"Just so you know, I'm not leaving work, I'm going to clean the North House," Kelsey calls. "But I am slamming the door again because I'm still a teenager."

The door slams to our laughter. Zoe looks at me, her eyes shining. I love how much fun she's having here.

***

"Dude, that so was her," a teenage boy says as the door shuts behind him.

"No way, why would she be in this shit town?" his friend replies. They head toward the snack aisle.

"I'm telling you, it was her. My sister said she came here a few weeks ago, too," the first kid insists.

"I dunno man," the other kid sticks to his guns. "The girl was fucking hot though. So was her friend."

"No, look, this is the guy she was with just now, the lumberjack," the first kid shoves his phone in front of his friend. "He did her tattoo and they're like dating now. But she's also dating this guy in Portland." He scrolls and then shows his friend his phone again. "I swear I saw her with a different guy the other day though. She gets around. Figures."

I grit my teeth. Today might be the day I punch a customer. A teenage customer, at that. Shit. I turn my back to the counter and wipe down the espresso machine with a little more vigor than necessary, trying to calm my rage.

"You better bulk up if you want a shot with her, those dudes are monsters."

"I'd like more than a shot with her," he snickers.

I suddenly get why so many women would choose the bear. I turn to take over the register, wondering how quiet Katie is handling this, but she subtly shakes her head at me, looking calm as can be as the boys walk toward us, candy and soda stacked in their arms.

109

"Hey, have you seen anyone sorta famous here?" the first kid asks Katie. "I thought I just saw this fitness girl on the beach."

I look over my shoulder and see that he has his phone under Katie's nose.

"Nope, sorry," she chirps. "That'd be super cool though."

"I told you it wasn't her," the kid says, hitting his friend as they walk out.

"Teenage boys are idiots," Katie says, shaking her head in disgust. "Like, when do you males stop being terrible?"

"Sorry, Katie," I tell her. "You've got a few more years."

"Figures," she mutters.

Now I understand a little more why Zoe is cautious about whatever we have going. I've seen her interact with people that recognize her and she's always happy and engaging, but I haven't seen this side of it in person. I've only seen this side in her comments section. I'm sure these kids are harmless, they'd probably freeze and stammer if Zoe so much as looked their way, but it's a reminder of the darker side of her job. And also that she's way more well known that she lets on.

I'm still contemplating all of this an hour later when I choose to drive my truck across the bridge to her rental instead of walk. We're driving back to my house together to cook and eat dinner with Gramps, then I'll drive her back home. Almost like a date, but we have to cook and it's with my elderly grandfather. So also not at all like a date.

"Hi! I'm running late, give me five minutes, sorry!" Zoe answers her door in just a towel, dark hair dripping water droplets down her shoulders.

I have what feels like heart palpitations as I slowly take her in. Not only is she wet and naked under that cream towel, but she's smiling at me like she's been waiting all day to see me. I've never had anyone smile at me like that.

"No rush," I reassure her, willing my body and heart to calm the fuck down. "Want me to wait on the porch?"

"Uh, no," she looks up at me, confused. "I'd prefer it if you'd come in."

I step inside and pull the door shut behind me. "I just didn't want-"

110

She stops me with a kiss as soon as the door latches. She stands on her toes and her hands land lightly on my chest, right over my heart. My hands automatically wrap around her waist and I try to forget the fact that she's nearly naked. Obviously I don't forget. My heart palpitations return as her hands slowly lower and then wrap around my waist. She burrows into my chest, hugging me tight. When was the last time I was hugged like this? Like I was needed? I drop my chin to the top of her head and just hold her, wondering if she can hear the pounding of my heart.

"Okay, five minutes from now," she says when she pulls away from me.

True to her word, five minutes later she's bouncing back out of the bedroom. She's in charcoal gray leggings with a matching sports bra showing under a pink off-the-shoulder sweatshirt. Her dark hair is still damp and she's barefoot. There's no way she had time to put makeup on. She's breathtakingly beautiful, as always.

"How was the rest of your day?" I ask once we're in the truck and headed over the bridge toward 101.

"My whole day was amazing," she says and I can actually hear the happiness in her voice. "I woke up to a really sweet good morning text that made me feel all warm and fuzzy, then I got to go on an insanely beautiful hike with new friends. After that, I saw a really cute guy at the store who made me coffee. I got to hear Brian call Jake 'Officer Hot Cop' and, I mean, how does everyone resist calling him that all the time? He must hate it." I glance over and she's grinning at me from the passenger seat. She's also fiddling with a bluetooth speaker and soon country music fills the radio-less cab of my truck.

"If I had a dollar for every time I heard about how hot Jake is, from about the time we were fifteen until right now, I'd have a lot of dollars," I say with an exaggerated groan.

"I felt bad about that escalating like that, so I took Kelsey lunch at the rental she was cleaning. I helped her finish up early so we could hang out on the beach for a couple hours."

"Ah, yeah, you were spotted by a couple teenage boys, they came into the store and asked Katie if she'd seen you. They weren't the most...polite," I tell her. "That's why I brought the truck over to pick you up, I figured they would be the kind to post pictures of you. It seems like you're trying to keep this separate." I wave my hand between us, unsure how else to get my point across.

"That was thoughtful but usually teenage boys talk a big game and then as soon as I ask them their names, they melt into a puddle. As for this," she copies me, waving her hand between us, "I want it separate so it's just for us, not because I want to hide you. Just so you know."

"I like that," I tell her, reaching over to rest my hand on her thigh.

"Oh! I love this song!" She turns the volume up on the speaker. "Cole Swindell is one of my favorites, and now that I'm sitting in your truck, these lyrics are even better."

She cranks her window down and puts her hand out the window, letting it rise and fall in the wind. For someone used to attending black tie fundraisers and driving her brand new vehicle, she sure looks comfortable in my old truck.

"*Come pick me up in your truck, I wanna drive,*" she sings along to the lyrics.

My chest aches. I only have one more day with her until she goes home, that's not nearly enough time. I squeeze her thigh before rubbing my thumb in lazy circles over her leggings. She smiles over at me, her hair blowing in the wind.

"*Makin' out in the parking lot,*" she sings, before starting to giggle. "That one really fits for us, huh?"

"That is quite fitting," I reply, looking over to see her pink cheeks turn red.

She sets her hand down on top of mine and links our fingers when I flip my hand over. "I'm guessing the grocery store will be a little more crowded at 4:30 p.m. so probably not going to happen this time. Bummer."

I laugh at that and squeeze her hand. This girl. She's perfect. Why does she have to live in Portland?

***

"I can't believe he kicked us out again," Zoe fumes from her seat in the truck. "I thought you said he liked me. And he asked for living room

112

yoga again. Which we did. *And* he agreed that I could pick him up for the parade in the morning."

"Uh, Zoe," I interrupt her rant. "He wanted us to have time alone together."

"Oh, okay, well in that case, where are you taking me?" She gives me a head tilt and raises her eyebrows.

"You have three options. One: we go back to the beach I took you to last night and watch the sunset, then I take you home. Two: I take you home so you can rest up for your big race in the morning. Three: whatever you tell me to do." I really wish I could add Four: spend the night with me. Five: never go back to Portland.

"Hmmm," she hums, eyeing me as I pull out of the driveway.

"You have about one minute until I need to know which way to turn," I warn, slowly inching down the trailer park drive toward 101.

"Option two, please," she says.

My heart sinks. Tomorrow is the Fourth of July and it's going to be a really fucking busy day where we barely have any time together, alone or otherwise. She's running the 5k at 8 a.m. with Team Merc (plus Zero) while I man the aid station and take pictures. Then she's going to drive back here and pick up Gramps so he can come to the parade. Luckily the route goes right by Zoe's rental so Gramps will be comfortable on the front porch.

Zoe will take Gramps home and have lunch with him before returning for the sandcastle contest while I work at the store. I already ordered pizza from Sarah at the cafe, so dinner will be easy. As long as Gramps feels okay, we're hoping to watch fireworks in Three Rocks and then I'll have to say goodbye to her until next time.

Every day I spend with her, every hour, every minute, I want her to stay even more. When I moved back to care for Gramps, I accepted that this was my life. Me and Gramps. And I like my life, despite the hard parts. I like my life a lot. But then Zoe walked into The Town Mercantile. And now here we are.

"Better get some rest, those Team Merc girls are ruthless," I tell her, swallowing down my disappointment.

Zoe reaches over and takes my hand, setting our linked hands on the bench seat between us. I smile when I see her take a picture of our

113

clasped hands. She sings along to her Spotify playlist and we don't talk on the drive back to Three Rocks.

I try not to let the heaviness known as reality settle over me. What did I expect to happen? She's probably realized that this is fun for a weekend, an escape from the city, but why would she throw herself in further when our lives will never overlap more than this? More than a couple days here and there?

"Walk me up?" she asks when I pull into the driveway.

"Of course," I reply, squeezing her hand before letting go.

I hurry around the truck and open her door, trying not to flinch when she smiles at me. I re-thread our fingers together and walk slowly toward the front door, drawing out our time. Drawing out the disappointment flooding my veins, buying just a little more time with her hand in mine, silently promising myself that if I have any chance with her, I'll take it.

When she turns to take out her key, I see it. A tiny flicker in her dark eyes, a hint of a smirk on her lips. Hope rises in my chest. I shove my hands in my pockets so I don't do something stupid and hold my breath, hoping against hope.

Chapter Fourteen
Zoe

I feel slightly guilty for telling Luke that I just wanted to go home. I mean, technically I did want to go home, just not to rest up for the fun run like he thought.

"Thanks for another fun evening," I tell him when we reach the front door. I take the key out of my waistband pocket and slowly unlock the door, trying not to smile.

He stays quiet, putting his hands in his pockets. I open the front door and then, with a grin, I grab his arm and pull him inside, kicking the door closed behind us.

He was hesitant earlier when I was in my towel, which was sweet, but that hesitation is nowhere to be seen now. My back hits the door and his arms rise above me, caging me in. I reach behind my back and blindly fumble with the deadbolt. As soon as the lock clicks, his mouth slants over mine.

If this is a preview of what's to come, holy shit, I will not survive this man. When he starts kissing down my neck, my legs actually shake.

I don't know if I can do this. I don't know if I can *not* do this.

I have to know how bad this is going to hurt.

It only takes my hand over his heart for him to pull back, his bright green eyes searching mine.

"Luke," I whisper, my heart in my throat. "I'm only with you. The bracelet is right, I'm Luke's girl. Or I definitely want to be. If this is just a weekend thing for you, I need you to tell me." My voice hitches, betraying my emotions, and I swallow hard.

If this is just this weekend, I'm going to be wrecked. It will still be worth it, but I. Will. Be. Wrecked.

Luke's expression softens and relief floods my veins. I need to hear his words, hear him say it though. He cups my face, his thumb brushing my cheek before he lowers his forehead to mine.

"It's only you for me," he whispers against my lips before kissing me again softly, gently.

At his words, the little piece of me that was holding back is unleashed. Our kiss turns into something else, something deeper, more frantic. He groans as I work my hands under his shirt, tugging it up as I explore his abs. He pulls back, reaching a single hand behind his neck and yanking it off, the other hand still on the door above me. All I see are lean muscles and hard lines.

Unable to bear another second without him kissing me, I slide my hands over his shoulders and into his hair, pulling his lips right back to mine again. Without losing contact, he leans down and boosts me up. I wrap my legs around his waist, our tongues still tangling, mouths fused together. He keeps a firm hold on me as he maneuvers around the room, bumping into a table, still kissing me, always kissing me, before dropping slowly on the couch as I unwind my legs. I stay straddling him, arching my back and rolling my hips against him as we finally come up for air, foreheads pressed together, breaths mingling.

"Holy shit," I whisper, not moving my eyes from his.

"Yeah, that," he breathes. His eyes are darkened with lust and he looks as overwhelmed as I feel.

Thank god.

I sit back, placing my hands on his bare chest and I'm instantly steadied by his pounding heart and his choppy, uneven breaths that somehow match mine. Luke's hands find their way under my shirt and up to my waist, gripping gently, anchoring me to this moment.

"Slower?" he asks, thumbs faintly tracing circles on my skin.

I shake my head, my eyes still glued to his. With a dimpled smile, he pulls me closer. He kisses me with both a tenderness and an urgency that sends a shudder throughout my entire body. I lose my fingers in his hair, pushing the longer strands from his face, twirling the ends at the base of his neck. And I lose my mind in the next scorching kiss before he takes mercy on me, pulling his mouth from mine as I gasp.

Slowly, ever so slowly, he trails kisses down my neck, licking at my pulse point, scraping his teeth along my exposed collarbone, patiently working me into even more of a frenzy. His hands explore my body and I curse my sports bra. Reading my mind, he pulls my shirt over my head and half a second later I'm on my back, his gaze taking me in from above.

"Fuck, Zoe," he whispers. "You're perfect."

I moan as I writhe beneath him, desperately seeking friction, anything to ease the delicious ache continuously building from deep within. Heat spreads from every kiss he places on my skin and I crave him in a way I didn't know was humanly possible.

"Please, Luke," I beg breathlessly.

"Please what, Zoe?" he whispers in my ear, his teeth finding my earlobe.

"More, please more," I moan, closing my eyes, tilting my head back, inviting him to find the spot on my neck that makes me shake.

Instead, I get less. I open my eyes and he's sitting up. He scoops me up with ease and carefully carries me into the bedroom. He gently drops me on the bed and I barely sink into the plush comforter before he's hovering over me.

"If you want more, I need more space," he whispers, before his lips crash back to mine.

My hands roam wildly as he continues kissing me into tomorrow, possibly next week. His abs bunch and flex under my fingertips as I work my way down, tracing between each shifting muscle. He lets me unbuckle his belt and work the button on his jeans, but then he's once again taking charge, pushing my hands above my head. His hands skim my body, always just missing where I want him the most.

Just when I'm on the verge of begging, his hands dip into the waistband of my leggings. He freezes.

"Zoe Last Name Campbell, have you been without underwear all fucking day?" His voice is deep and commanding, nothing like his usual playful tone.

117

His voice, his question, the way he's looking at me, it's all so much. Every single part of my body reacts to him, from the tightening deep in my core to my toes curling and my thighs clenching. I bite my lip and grin.

"I've probably been without underwear every time you've seen me," I whisper.

His head falls back and I see him take a deep inhale. "Holy fucking shit," he breathes, exhaling loudly.

I widen my eyes, loving his reaction to the real me. The me that hates underwear under leggings, that wears sports bras and athletic clothes every day, that needs his words to reassure me. He likes the playful side of me, the messy side, and definitely the greedy side that is pulling him back down. He makes me feel good without even touching me, but right now I need the touching part.

His mouth finds the sensitive spot on my neck and I dig my fingernails into his back. "More," I pant.

Not to ruin the mood, but I've definitely been stuck in a sports bra before. Like, hasn't every woman that's ever worked out? I am definitely not stuck in this one today. Luke has it off and flung across the room in record time.

"Luke," I whimper as his mouth kisses a circle around my breast, avoiding the pebbled tip that tightens even more, aching for his attention. "This is torture."

It's the best kind of torture imaginable.

"I'm memorizing every inch of you," he whispers, his breath a caress over my skin. "So next time I close my eyes, when you're not here, all I see is you."

His words are the best kind of torture imaginable.

He is the best kind of everything imaginable.

His whispered words, his gentle hands, the combination of soft lips and biting teeth on my skin, I'm near the edge and I'm still partially clothed.

When he finally peels my leggings off, I'm pretty sure he could touch me once and I'd fall apart. He must sense this, because he takes his time, slowly kissing from the inside of my ankle up my leg, only lightly running his thumb over the apex of my trembling legs.

Hovering over me, with his hair disheveled from my greedy hands and his green eyes locked on mine, I see my own hunger mirrored in his gaze. I bite my lip and he brings his hand up, gently running the pad of his thumb over my bottom lip, tugging it loose. I wrap my legs around his waist and pull him onto me, savoring his weight pressing me into the mattress, the way he devours my mouth. When he has me thoroughly dazed once again, he pulls back just enough to give me a questioning look.

"Please," I whisper, my entire body quivering, knowing that if he can kiss like this, he's going to have me undone in no time.

My theory proves correct, my hips jumping off the bed when he hums his appreciation with his first taste. My writhing only spurs him on, he seems intent on finding every way possible to make me buck in pleasure. He's not in a rush, but in what feels like a matter of seconds, I'm crying out his name as the best orgasm of my life tears through my body. When he rests his head on my stomach, I can only shake my head. I thought this would only happen if this was the end, but he managed to ruin me anyway.

"I think you just wrecked me, Luke," I tell him, running my fingers through his messy hair. "And you look quite smug about it."

"I feel quite smug about it," he admits, shooting me a dirty grin. "Those noises you make, they're going to haunt my dreams." He kisses my stomach and then moves to lay on his side next to me.

"Haunt you, hmm?" I ask, rolling to face him. I push my weight into him until he's on his back, partially propped up on the pillows. I tug his jeans down and straddle him, only his briefs between us.

"No snuggling?" he asks, his eyes darkening further as they roam my body. The greedy glint in his gaze fuels my confidence and I roll my hips against him.

"We could snuggle," I lean forward to whisper in his ear. "But please don't make me beg to have my way with you."

"Fuck, Zoe," Lucas groans.

"Pretty please?" I whisper as I kiss down his chest, keeping my eyes on his.

All I get in response is another groan as I tug his briefs off. He's everything I thought he would be and I can't help but slowly take him in,

119

admire every part of his body as I run my hands down his lickable abs. I trace each one with my lips, memorizing every crevice as I go.

When I finally make my way lower, he gently winds his hands through my hair, pushing it aside, his eyes locked on mine. Seeing what I'm doing to him, his green eyes heating until they're blazing with fire, is unlike anything I've experienced. I've never felt such an intense connection in my life. He only closes his eyes when I finally push him over the edge, my name just a whisper on his lips.

"You're so fucking amazing," Luke says when I settle next to him, my head on his chest, leg thrown over his.

We're both breathing hard, Luke's heart pounding beneath my ear. He has one arm wrapped around me, hand splayed across my hip, the other over my hand that's resting on his chest. He lightly runs his fingers over mine, then plays with my bracelets. All I can think about is that I wasn't lying, he wrecked me, but not in the way I thought. That orgasm might have ruined me, but watching him as I brought him to the brink absolutely decimated me in a way I didn't think was possible.

"I really don't want to leave," he says, breaking our silence.

"I don't want you to leave, but I know you need to," I tell him. "I promise it's okay, I get it."

He doesn't make any move to get up. I prop myself up on my elbow and look down at him. He smiles and I cover his mouth with my hand.

"No dimples allowed, I have to kick you out," I tell him sternly. He gently bites my hand and as soon as I pull away, he rolls us together and he ends up hovering over me once again, this time without any clothing between us. I can feel his body reacting between my thighs.

"Kicking me out? We'll see about that."

His lips are on mine, the taste of me on his tongue, and I'm lost in him once again. He kisses my neck and inches lower. His teeth graze my nipple as his nimble fingers find the other, making me gasp. He kisses lower. And lower.

"Luke, I have to kick you out," I whisper, arching toward him. I do not want to kick him out at all. Not one single bit.

"Mmm, is that why you're squirming like this?"

"Please don't stop," I whisper, my hips rising.

120

I moan his name, sinking my fingers into his hair as he brings me to the edge once again. He lets me hover with my orgasm just out of grasp, deliciously building, until I grip the sheets and beg him to let me go. With one swirl of his tongue, I fall.

When I open my eyes, my body still pulsing and humming, his green eyes are the first thing I see.

"You're beautiful," Luke whispers.

What I am is ruined. I am wrecked, devastated, shattered, obliterated, annihilated, decimated. I am all of these, in the best way.

Ten minutes later, I lean against the back of the door to catch my breath as Luke drives away. Kelsey and her small-town romance books might be onto something. I really, *really* like cute, sweet, dimpled, unassuming, small-town Lucas Henry Stark.

***

I do not like him quite as much the next morning when he's taking pictures of me as I attempt to keep up with the Team Merc girls in the Fourth of July 5k. Tex was not joking when she said Avery was A Real Runner. Avery and Kelsey hold a conversation the whole time with Tex and I only (breathlessly) chiming in occasionally. All of the runners and most of the spectators are decked out in red, white, and blue. I'm thankful for my wide variety of leggings and sports bras because, when you add in the sparkly tutu Kelsey tossed at me this morning, I fit right in.

At the finish, Jessie takes pictures for us while Colt bounces around, already on a sugar high. Marabelle has individually wrapped American flag cookies set out on a table and I'm guessing Colt has had more than the "just one" he told his mom he had. I'm also guessing Jessie realizes this. Colt challenges me to a race, which is something he does basically every time he sees me now, and then he innocently tells me that since he won, he gets half my cookie. If I would have known that, I would have run a little faster.

I keep my eyes on the road that leads north, hoping Luke will appear, but he must still be manning the aid station and taking pictures. Tex had stopped running abruptly in front of a house about a mile back to ask a guy named Tom, who I think I saw the other day with a metal detector on the beach, if he was seriously handing out beers at 8:15 a.m.

He seriously was. It seems the rest of the 5k participants might be slow to trickle across the finish line.

I accept that I'm not going to sneak in any time with Luke right now and head back over the bridge to get in a quick shower before I need to leave to get Henry. When I see I have four extra minutes, I add a few of the pictures Jessie took to my Instagram story, tagging the Team Merc accounts. I don't love broadcasting my location but I'm going to be with friends or in public all day and I leave first thing tomorrow morning. I add a quick video challenging my followers to have fun with their fitness today and to tag me in whatever fun they find. Abby will help me stay on top of adding their pictures to my stories.

I drive back across the bridge and slowly creep my way through the crowd that's gathered at the finish line in The Town Mercantile's parking lot. Two teenage boys gape at me when I stop to run inside and get a cinnamon roll for Henry. They must be the boys Luke was talking about. I give them a smile and a wave, calling out good morning. Their eyes are the size of saucers and one of them nudges the other.

Fifteen minutes later, cinnamon roll in hand, I rap on Henry's front door with my knuckles. I should have gotten coffee, too.

"Good morning, Henry," I tell him when he opens the door. "Don't you look festive."

He's wearing blue suspenders with a crisp white shirt and a red bow tie, along with a newsboy cap. He's adorable.

"Back at you, Miss Zoe," he says.

I give him a curtsy, feeling quite plain in my jean shorts, white tee, and red hat.

"Have time for a cup of coffee?" he asks me.

"I was just thinking I should have brought you a cup," I reply, stepping inside.

"Nonsense, we have coffee here," he grumbles, leading me to the kitchen.

I let him pour our coffees and we carry them to the small back deck.

"You seem to be enjoying your time here," Henry says after a few minutes of silently sharing our cinnamon roll.

"I really am, it's a nice break," I tell him honestly. "I've been thinking about our conversation the other day with Nancy and the more time I spend here, the more I see opportunities to change what I'm doing."

I've already made little changes. I try to imagine posting the 5k pictures months ago. I might have on a cute outfit, but I'm a sweaty mess in every picture, thanks to chasing Avery and Kelsey for three miles. Aiden would have been horrified. But it feels good to show a little slice of my real life.

"I know I'm the one that told you to wander your way to happiness, Miss Zoe, but I do have to say that if you wander too far, I'm going to miss our yoga. Getting this old body moving these few days has helped me sleep better," Henry says, sipping his coffee and looking out over their tiny backyard.

His comment makes me pause. Once again something, some small idea, is wiggling around in my brain, still out of my grasp.

"I'm going to miss our yoga, too, when I go back home," I tell him. "But I hope to visit again soon."

"Visit me or my grandson?" he asks. I have to smile at the protective tone in his gruff voice.

"I hope both, but even if Luke gets sick of me, I'd like to see you," I reply. I glance at the time. "But, for now, we need to go see about a parade."

Chapter Fifteen
Luke

"Are you sure you're okay? You don't want us to stay, or take you to watch the fireworks with us?" Zoe asks Gramps for the third time since we sat down to dinner.

"Miss Zoe, don't make me kick you out again," Gramps threatens her. "You're going to tell me goodbye until next time and march right out of this house."

Zoe lets out an exaggerated sigh. "But I don't *want* to say goodbye. Why don't you just come to Portland with me? We can do yoga, drink coffee, my cat would probably like you more than me, seeing as how he likes everyone more than me, ungrateful little jerk."

"Too many people in that city," Gramps immediately shakes his head. "But for you, I'd at least consider it."

That makes Zoe beam. She's told me that a lot of the time she hides behind her ZoeSaysSo persona with a fake smile, but every time I've seen her, she wears her emotions on her sleeve. Unfortunately this means she's sniffling and fighting tears when we walk out to my truck.

"Did you really teach him to use FaceTime while I was cleaning up?" I ask, nudging her shoulder. "It took me weeks to teach him how to call me."

"We'll find out in a couple days if my lesson stuck," she sniffles, giving me a watery smile. "And I really hope it does."

I open her truck door and she climbs up into the seat. Instead of closing the door, I step closer to her. "As much as I love how much you enjoy spending time with Gramps, I'm really looking forward to tonight," I tell her. I use my thumb to gently wipe a tear from her freckled cheek.

She leans forward and presses a chaste kiss to my lips. "Me, too."

It takes a few more minutes of sniffling but then she once again plays DJ, choosing a quieter, acoustic playlist and humming along until we pull into Three Rocks. After a moment's hesitation, I park at The Mercantile instead of her rental. When she questions me, I tell her the teenagers were back in the store earlier and had eagerly told Katie that she was wrong, Zoe was indeed in town.

"Oh, yeah, I think I saw them this morning. I waved to them before I went to pick up Henry. I also posted sweaty 5k pics this morning." She shrugs, unconcerned. "Then I judged the sandcastle contest, ran around on the beach in my Fourth of July bikini with the girls, and did some yoga with a group in front of the big rock. I'm sure word is definitely out that I'm here, I haven't checked. Abby is in charge now, she'd tell me if something alarming came up. It's normal."

I contemplate this as I get out of the truck and round the hood. Her normal definitely feels abnormal to me. I open her door and she hops down, barely giving me time to grab the blanket that's folded under her seat before she's tugging me toward the beach path. But then she stops so suddenly that I almost crash into her.

"Will it be weird if we hang out alone?" she asks. "I spent the afternoon on the beach with the girls, I'm happy to spend time with them again, but I like time with just you, too."

"I'm sorry, I'm still back on the fact that you were in a Fourth of July bikini and I missed it," I tell her, grinning down at her.

"After last night I don't think you will have any trouble picturing it, but if you do, check the shared album," she whispers, cheeks turning red, as she winds her arms around my neck.

"Mmm, I can't wait. And to answer your question, yes, just you and me." I press my lips to hers. I honestly hadn't even considered hanging out with the group, call me selfish, but I want time with just Zoe.

I lead her to a little crevice in the rocks that provide erosion protection to the houses above, knowing they will give us at least a little privacy. Zoe settles in beside me, her head on my shoulder, her small hand in mine. The beach is crowded, excited kids with sparklers, more bonfires than I've ever seen, happy revelers everywhere, but with her tucked in next to me, the blanket our cocoon, it feels like only us. We watch the sun sink toward the ocean, not saying much. I think we're both a little overwhelmed by the last few days.

I knew I liked her the very first time I met her. I liked her a hell of a lot more after our Silver Falls hike. And now, after getting to know her, having her thrown into my world only to fit so perfectly? I really fucking like her. She's funny and smart, beautiful and kind. She charmed both my grandfather and my best friend, as well as every single other person she met in town.

But what happens when she goes home? When she remembers how much bigger her world is than mine? How many more stolen weekends will we get before reality finds us? Before she leaves me behind?

"What are you thinking about?" Zoe asks quietly, keeping her eyes on the setting sun.

I weigh my words, trying to find the line between honesty and self-preservation. I want her to know the truth, the conflict raging inside, but I can't quite lay it all out there. It's only been a few days, but I know I'm falling for her, and I also know that no one falls that quickly, right?

"On paper, we don't fit. Our normals are very different. Your normal is getting recognized on the street, attending fundraisers, and having so many sponsorships you probably have to turn some down. Mine is working in a tiny store for barely minimum wage, trips to the local library, and taking care of my elderly grandfather. I'm just a little worried that even though this feels so right when you're here, when you're not here, you're going to realize how much more is out there for you," I reply. "I don't want to hold you back."

"Lucas Henry Stark," she says. She shifts slightly and tips her chin up to meet my gaze, her dark eyes defiant in the fading light. "Maybe there is a lot out there, but I'm not interested in any of it, and it's not *more*. I want this with you. This feels like *more* to me. I want to see where this goes. I know our lives are different, but I still want to be Luke's girl. We'll figure it out as we go along. I just want us."

127

"Us," I repeat. She makes it seem so simple, so easy.

"Just you and me," she says softly.

I lean down and kiss her, tasting her vanilla chapstick, committing her soft lips to memory.

***

"I should buy Brian mochas every day for the rest of the year, that was amazing; he and the guys did a great job," Zoe says as the smoke from the fireworks show starts to clear.

She stands and reaches down to pull me up. I fold our blanket and tuck it under one arm, her under the other, and we start for the path, dodging the crowds as we go.

I try not to think about the fact that I only have this one last night with her. We haven't talked about when we'll be able to see each other again, only that we want to see where this goes. My chest aches and I pull Zoe a little closer, dropping a kiss on top of her head. She wraps her arm around me, sneaking her hand under my shirt. She laughs when her cold hand causes me to sharply inhale.

"Oops, I didn't mean to freeze you, I just needed to feel you," she says, smiling up at me.

"Does that mean I need to help you warm up?" I ask, my voice betraying my hope.

"Absolutely," she nods, quickening her pace.

Fireworks boom behind us on the beach, tourists and locals not ready to end their night. We bypass my truck in the parking lot and hurry down the street toward her rental. We are at the door within minutes.

"I have a surprise for you," she says, bouncing on her feet a little as we step inside.

I give her a questioning look. She tugs on my hand and I manage to lock the door and drop the blanket on the couch as she pulls me to the bedroom. In the middle of the bed is a small gift, wrapped in what looks like a brown paper bag, tied with string.

She got me a present. I can't think of the last time someone wrapped a gift for me when it wasn't Christmas. Not even my birthday. Gramps, Nancy, and I celebrate by going out to dinner together. I can't even say thank you, I have to swallow down the rush of emotions caught in my throat before they choke me.

"Well, open it!" Zoe says when I don't move. She takes my phone and keys from my hand and puts them on the nightstand, motioning for me to sit down.

She sits on the edge of the bed next to me as I carefully unwrap the present. Three books are stacked on top of one another in a small pyramid.

A Man Called Ove.

The Friend Zone.

The Night Agent.

"I thought we could read together," she explains hesitatingly. "I know we don't always have the same taste in books but I thought it'd be a way we could share something when we're apart?"

I kiss her. I don't know what else to do so I just kiss her.

She's been thinking about ways to make this work while I've only managed to low-key panic.

"Great idea. I love it. Which is first?" I ask, slowly pulling away.

"Well, A Man Called Ove made me think of Henry when I read the back cover, and the author wrote one of my very favorite series so I had to buy it. I think it's also a movie, or maybe two? The second book is my favorite romance author, she's hilarious. I know romance isn't a guy thing, but I thought it'd be fun. I already have both of those books on my kindle. And The Night Agent, I didn't even realize it was a book. I saw a preview for the series on some streaming service the other day so when I saw it at the book sale on Sunday, I grabbed it. Books are always better anyway. But I don't have my own copy of that one yet."

"Books are always better," I agree. "Zoe, this is really thoughtful. You're amazing. I don't deserve this. You. Us."

She takes the books from my hand and sets them on the small nightstand next to my keys and phone. Then she climbs into my lap, wrapping her legs around me, and leans her forehead on mine. My hands automatically wrap around her hips, steadying her.

"You deserve everything. You're amazing. I was a little nervous when I decided to come surprise you, but I've had such a good weekend. So thank *you*, Luke."

"I still can't believe you showed up," I say, shaking my head. How the hell did I get so lucky?

"Yeah, I can't really believe that either," she says, her cheeks turning pink. "Maybe not my best idea, throwing myself at you like that."

"Absolutely the best idea," I tell her, tightening my grip and pulling her flush against me.

"Well, I got you in my bed, so it did work out quite nicely," she says, wiggling her hips into mine. "And it seems like at least part of you is happy about that." She grinds into me again to prove her point.

"All of me is happy about that." I slide my hands up her back, anchoring her to me as I lean back and then roll so we're laying face to face. I cup her cheek and pull her in for a long, slow kiss.

She hooks her leg over my hip and pulls herself into me until there's no space between us. I run my hand down her side and slip it under her shirt, relishing the feel of her soft skin. We don't share any words, we don't need to. There's no rushing, no frantic undressing, no urgency tonight. Instead, we slowly undress each other, kissing endlessly between each piece of discarded clothing, as if the slower we go, the longer we take, the more time we'll have.

When I have her completely naked beneath me, it takes every ounce of my willpower not to sink into her heat. Instead, I lick and kiss my way down her body, remembering every single spot that made her writhe beneath me last night. I nearly lose myself watching her come undone. When I do lose myself to her, her eyes are on mine, my hands are in her hair, and my heart is hers.

She crawls back up my body slowly, her hands and lips still exploring, like she just can't get enough of me, and I don't think there's a way I can leave this bed tonight. When her hand finds my jaw and her vanilla lips find mine, I know I can't.

"Can I stay?" I whisper.

"Are you sure?" she asks, pulling back to look me in the eye.

"I'll sneak out early, go home to get ready for work," I reassure her, knowing she's worried about Gramps.

"Am I selfish if I say I want you to stay?" she murmurs, burying her face in my neck.

"Am I selfish because I want to stay?" I counter.

"Please stay," she whispers.

130

At my nod, she pulls the sheets over us and snuggles in beside me. I wrap myself around her, tucking her slender body into my chest, wishing once again she wasn't leaving in the morning. She pushes herself into my embrace even more, as if she's trying to burrow into me. If only this was more than just tonight, more than a stolen visit.

"Set your alarm," she murmurs sleepily, reaching for my phone on the nightstand in front of her and handing it to me.

I quickly set the alarm for just a few hours from now and shove my phone under my pillow. I pull Zoe tight against me and despite the distant boom of fireworks, her breaths even out quickly. I try to roll away, give her space so she can sleep, but she reaches for me as soon as I move. I smile in the darkness, tucking her into me once again, before falling asleep to the scent of her shampoo.

***

Selfish or not, waking up with Zoe still pressed against me is worth the 5 a.m. alarm. I silently groan that I have to leave this warm bed and this naked woman wrapped around me. I want to stay in this moment forever, but real life beckons. I breathe her in one last time before I carefully slide from bed without waking her. After I've brushed my teeth using my finger and stolen toothpaste, I see her eyes blink open as I pull my jeans on.

"Good morning," I tell her, crossing the room to gently kiss her lips as she smiles sleepily at me. I want to climb back in bed with her, pour my heart out and beg her to stay.

"Mmm, give me a minute and I'll walk you out," she says. She snags my worn hoodie off the floor as she pads to the bathroom.

"I mean, watching you cross the room naked was amazing, but I also like this look," I tell her, tugging gently on the end of her messy braid, when she walks back out wearing my hoodie.

She's absolutely dwarfed in it and I'm about ninety-seven percent certain she's completely naked underneath, since I didn't see her grab any other clothing on her way to the bathroom. Her eyes are still sleepy and she has a line on her cheek from the pillow. She's beautiful, as usual.

"Can I keep it?" she asks. "Until next time?" She looks up at me hopefully.

131

"There's a tiny part of me that wants to say no, just so you have to take it off and I get to see what, if anything, is underneath," I say, pulling her in. "And I can't wait until next time." I slide my hand down to the hem, which hits mid thigh, and run my hand up her leg. Naked. I groan and grip her waist.

"Well, it was a rhetorical question," she says with a sly smile. "I'm keeping it."

"Didn't take you for a thief, Zoe Last Name Campbell," I tease.

She reaches up and wraps her hands around my neck, standing on her tiptoes to close the distance between us. She has minty breath and vanilla lips. I think I might be addicted to her chapstick at this point. When I reach my other hand under her, well, my, hoodie and run my hands up her ribs, she swipes her tongue across my lower lip. I gladly allow her access and our tongues tangle together. I'm gently pushing her toward the bed without even realizing it.

"Lucas Henry Stark," she says when the backs of her legs make contact with the bed. "Don't make me kick you out." She pushes against my chest and glares at me, trying and failing to hide her smile.

"I'll kick myself out," I tell her. "You should get more sleep."

Of course she doesn't listen and instead threads her fingers through mine. I pick up my books and keys from the nightstand and look around the room. I want to stall. I want to take her back to bed. I want to ask when I can see her again. Instead, we walk to the front door, my feet feeling heavier with each step. I cup her cheek and kiss her lips. I don't say goodbye and she doesn't either. It feels too final. With one last kiss, I gently close the door behind me. She's too good to be true.

Chapter Sixteen
Zoe

"You can't tell me you eat cinnamon rolls and look like that. Bitch."

"I thought you were about health, this looks like a one way ticket to diabetes."

"No wonder why that last pic showed fat rolls."

"Unfollow."

"Oh good, you're not pregnant, just fat."

The internet can be a dark place and at this point, I'm unsure why I came back to my real life. One funny cinnamon roll reel (thanks to Kelsey, who I had coffee with before leaving) with my happy dance, and these are the notifications I have when I get home. Plus a frantic text from Kelsey, apologizing. After reassuring her that this is, unfortunately, par for the course, I vent to Abby.

Zoe:
people can suck it

Abs:
the internet is hungover this morning after the 4th. hangovers make people mean

Zoe:
(pic) look at the sweet message lucas left on the box though

Abs:

casey and i are home, come over?

"Guys, I'm in deep," I declare as I burst in through their apartment door. "I love his grandpa, I love how they have a little chosen family that all help each other, and I love how hard Lucas works. I freaking love the Team Merc girls even more than I did before and I love their little town."

"Are you still on a cinnamon roll sugar high or is he that good in bed?" Casey asks, eyes widening at my energy.

"Yes. Both." I fling myself on their couch and cover my face with my hands. "But mainly the bed thing. And everything else about him."

"Um, okay Miss I'm-Not-Going-To-Sleep-With-Him," Abby says. If my hands weren't covering my face I'm sure I'd see her roll her eyes.

I sit up and point my finger back and forth between them. "In my defense, I didn't have sex with him."

"But?" Casey asks.

"But I was very well taken care of," I say, wiggling my eyebrows.

Abby cracks up and throws a pillow at me. "I knew it! I knew you couldn't keep your hands off him."

"But really you guys, what do I do now?" I moan, leaning my head back against the back of the couch.

"Uh, go back and see him again?" Casey looks bewildered at my question.

"But I like him. *Like* like him. A lot." Understatement of the century.

It scares me a little, maybe a lot, how much I like him. How easily I slipped into his life. Didn't I do this with Aiden? Jump in too fast?

I need to stop comparing the two of them, they couldn't be more different.

"I don't understand the question," Casey replies, frowning in confusion.

134

"Yeah, you teach a lot of classes but you can also shift your schedule around. It's not like you *need* to teach," Abby tells me. "Have you even talked to your accountant lately?"

I love teaching, I really do. My regular classes pay basically nothing, especially compared to my "brand" and "influencer" jobs, but it's the part I love the most. Abby does bring up a good point though. I've made a shit ton of money. No lie. My yoga and smoothies pretty quickly turned into an audience of half creepy old men wanting to see a bendy eighteen-year-old and half supportive females looking for inspiration in their own health journey.

I was already well known when Covid hit, thanks creepers, but then we took things to a whole new level. Abby, Casey, Kristen and I were bored to tears, sitting in our four-bedroom apartment, so we hit it hard. Any and all social media platforms. Yoga (thank you, mom, for letting me tag along to your yoga classes starting at age nine and helping me become an instructor), a living room strength series, even mental health interviews over Zoom with medical professionals. We did it all.

Enter Aiden, master manipulator but also very good at building business relationships. The last four years have been crazy, nothing I could have imagined. And Abby's right, even after paying everyone their percentages, I don't *have* to teach.

"Teaching is honestly my favorite part of this," I tell her. "I'm not ready to walk away from teaching."

I don't tell her that I'm ready to walk away from other parts. I mean, I make videos with my best friend, I cannot complain. But…maybe I do need to think about what Nancy and Gramps said.

"So when are you going to see him again?" Casey asks.

I'm about to answer when my phone buzzes in my waistband.

LucasHenryStark:
I just looked at our album and had to excuse myself to the back room. Damn.

"You are blushing! What did he say?!" Casey exclaims.
"You are so red, Zoe!" Abby adds.

LucasHenryStark:
How did you spend all weekend here and I didn't see you in that bikini once?

Zoe Last Name Campbell:
but you saw me out of it

LucasHenryStark:
A vision that will be in my brain forever.

***

"Zoe! Who even are you right now?!" Casey says as Abby tries to steal my phone.

I don't freaking know. Definitely not who I've been recently. That's the real Zoe answer.

***

To say I'm distracted over the next few days is an understatement. I teach classes, make videos, stare at fabrics for the new leggings line I'm supposed to be designing with my brand partner, teach an entire yoga class a TikTok dance, and ponder the meaning of life. Or at least what to do with my life.

Why am I doing what I do? Do I care about leggings? I mean, yes, a good pair of leggings can make or break a workout, but is this what I want to do with my life? If I didn't do this, what would I be doing? Can I do more? Should I do less? Why is Nancy all the way in Rock Beach when I could really use her deep questions and heartfelt advice right now?

Instead, I try my mom. It backfires spectacularly.

"That's not helpful," I whine, sprawled on my bed as Egg glares at me from his perch on the windowsill.

"I literally just told you that you should do what makes you happy," Mom says. "How is that not helpful?"

"I need step-by-step instructions," I tell her.

"On being happy?"

"On what to do!"

"Oh, honey, that's like grade A, top-shelf parenting, I'm just a mediocre parent, like the participation trophy of parents," she says. I can

136

picture her shaking her head. "Maybe just get another tattoo? Or run away. Oh! On a motorcycle! Climb a mountain. You should get kicked out of a bar. Buy a horse. Wait, you're scared of horses. Ooooh! Cold plunge, that's all the rage, isn't it? Try that. A cult? No, no, that's too extreme. Don't do that."

"Not. Helpful."

"Zoe McKay Campbell, you have a very unique opportunity here. Not many people have the ability to do whatever they want. You have that. Literally, whatever you want. Live a little. Go do stupid shit," she says.

"Mother, when I turned sixteen, you gave me a keychain that actually said 'don't do stupid shit' and now you're telling me to go do just that?" I ask, laughing. I still have the keychain on my keyring.

"I'm sure your dad would be the voice of reason but he's in his office. You're twenty-four, you spent your college years locked away during Covid, then that predator got his claws in you," she says. Not quite true, but a partial truth I guess. Also, guess who never liked Aiden and saw right through him? "I know you feel obligated to keep going with ZoeSays, to keep Abby on the payroll, but you need to do what you want to do. Otherwise, we're going to revisit this conversation often. And my advice won't improve over time. That I can guarantee."

"So you're telling me to just go do dumb shit?"

"Yes."

"Well, thanks, I guess?" I should have called the Rock Beach Library and asked for Nancy.

I can hear my little sister, Tatum, saying something in the background.

"Tate says to stop taking calculated risks and take a real risk," Mom says. "So, she's on my team."

"Of course you're ganging up on me," I mutter. Those two are two peas in a pod. If only Dad was out of his office, he really would be a voice of reason. "Ugh. Well, thank you both for the mediocre advice."

"You're welcome. You've got this, Zoe. You'll figure it out. That's like the one thing I'm certain of in life, that you and Tate will be awesome humans doing awesome things, despite my mediocre parenting," Mom says confidently.

"Your parenting, while questionable at times, is at least slightly above average," I tell her. "Thank you."

"You're welcome. Now, go do stupid shit!" She laughs and hangs up on me.

I shake my head. My mom is weird. Maybe that comes from being a young mom, and maybe knowing she had me at twenty-two is what's making me question my own life. At my age, she was already making cloth diapers and blending organic baby food. She kept a whole baby alive at my age. I just killed off another houseplant and my cat hates me.

Zoe Last Name Campbell:
any chance you have a motorcycle?

LucasHenryStark:
No. I'm a little scared to ask any follow up questions.

Zoe Last Name Campbell:
i guess i'm getting kicked out of a bar

LucasHenryStark:
And you need a motorcycle for that?

Zoe Last Name Campbell:
i asked my mom what to do with my life

Zoe Last Name Campbell:
her best ideas were ride a motorcycle, the bar thing, or climb a mountain

LucasHenryStark:
Since I don't have a motorcycle, I vote mountain.

Zoe Last Name Campbell:
think i'm gonna go cult, that was the last one thrown out there

LucasHenryStark:
Well take your book with you because I'm invested now.

Zoe Last Name Campbell:
told you she's a good author.

Maybe not cult, but I'm at least going to start shifting some things around in my life. If only mom's suggestions had included finding a cute dimpled boy that reads romance books with me and gives me life-altering orgasms.

Chapter Seventeen
Luke

"Lucas? Lucas!" Tex waves her hand in front of my face.

"Oh, sorry, boss," I say, shaking my head. I'd try to clear my thoughts but there's no chance of clearing Zoe from my mind. How do you miss a person this much when you've only spent a handful of days with them? "What do you need?"

"Is your grandpa okay?" Tex asks, looking concerned. "Is that, this?" She waves her hand up and down from my head to my feet.

"He's doing great, actually. I'm just tired," I half-lie. Gramps *is* doing great and I *am* tired, but that's not the cause of my distraction.

"I was going to go clean The Glass House, our guests checked out and since it's Saturday of course we have another couple showing up in a few hours. Want to trade?" she asks. "No customers to ignore there." She grins at me so I know she's not mad.

She's been giving me weird looks since the book sale, I'm pretty sure she saw how close Zoe and I were all day. She's definitely spotted the romance book Zoe and I have been reading together. Her only comment was to let her borrow it after I was done.

Luckily Tex doesn't question me further, she just hands me the keys to the locked closet where the cleaning supplies are kept. Like the distracted fool I am, I check Zoe's Instagram as I walk to the rental. All that's new is a single picture on her story, her muddy hiking boots with "unfortunately my photographer isn't with me, just a girl in nature" text over the top.

LucasHenryStark:

If an influencer hikes in the woods without a photographer, does she even hike in the woods?

I'm rewarded with an incoming call.

"Professional Date Dane doesn't double as a photographer?" I answer her call with a question.

"Shouldn't you be working instead of stalking people on the internet?" she asks. I can hear the laughter in her voice, making me miss her even more.

"I've been sent to clean The Glass House; I'm walking over," I explain. "For some reason I've been a little distracted the last few days and Tex has banished me from the store."

"Probably because you text your girlfriend all day." She's never used the word 'girlfriend' before. She's called herself my girl, but girlfriend hits different. I like it. I like it a fucking lot.

"That is absolutely not true, I only text her when I'm in the back," I protest. "I am a good employee, just a little distracted."

"I've been distracted, too," she admits. "Which is why I'm hiking. Want to see?"

"Of course," I tell her. I'm silently wondering why she's hiking solo when she's so well known around Portland. Her fame still makes me uncomfortable for a lot of reasons, this being one of them.

A picture comes through and she's making a funny face, tall trees and a calm, glassy river in the background. A guy that probably spends more time in the gym than out of it stands behind her, flexing. He's not Jake, but he could probably give him a run for his money. My worry immediately washes away. I've never met the man, but I've seen pictures and heard a lot about him.

"Professional Date Dane is actually here," she says, then she raises her voice. "Too bad he sucks at photography!"

"Honey, I'm good at everything," a male voice calls back.

"Oh, babe, the confidence in you," another male voice says.

"This confidence is earned," the first voice replies.

"Children, play nice," Zoe scolds them. "Sorry, Dane's better half is here as well. They bicker more than an old married couple."

I like these little glimpses into her real life but they make me wish our real lives were closer together, more entwined.

"I'll let you get back to your hike. I reward Colt for good behavior with those little individual chocolate shells at the store, maybe try bribing the bickering couple?" My reward is her laugh.

"Ooh, good tip, I'll try that." She raises her voice again. "Hey guys, Lucas says if you're nice to each other the rest of the hike, I have to buy you iced coffee."

"You're my favorite, Lucas!" calls one of the voices.

"Ouch, I thought I was your favorite," says the other.

"And here I thought I was your favorite," Zoe chimes in. "Sorry Lucas, just wanted to hear your voice for a minute. Grocery and book date later?"

"Can't wait," I say, just as I hear "Oh my god, Zoe, get a room!" in the background.

I'm smiling as I hang up, even though I'm about to scrub toilets.

***

"I can hear your sigh from here, just go see her," barks Gramps from the living room. "Remember what I said about putting in the effort? Effort means she's a priority. Is she a priority?"

"I mean, yeah, but I have a lot of priorities, and some of them have due dates, like this stack of bills," I call back.

I sigh again and drop the power bill on the dining room table. I lean back in my chair and rub my face with my hands. This thing with Zoe is so far-fetched, it's not even funny. She consumes my thoughts but these bills consume my life. I'm taken back to our conversation on the Fourth. There's so much more out there for her, but for me, this is it. Juggling bills, shuttling Gramps to the library, remembering to fix the goddamn screen door.

"Those bills will still be there tomorrow, the girl finally has an afternoon off on the same day as you. Go see her," Gramps says. I can hear him getting out of his chair.

"Wait, how do you know she has an afternoon off?" I suddenly ask. "I never told you that."

143

"Just ask the girl," he says, placing his hand on my shoulder and putting his phone in front of me.

"Hi," Zoe says, smiling at me from his screen. My heart stutters. God, she's beautiful. "To avoid you getting bullied by a grumpy senior citizen any more, I'll ask you. Lucas Henry Stark, would you like to have dinner with me in McMinnville tonight? It's close-ish to halfway."

"I'm not bullying the boy, I'm giving him guidance," Gramps grumps from over my shoulder.

"You are absolutely bullying him," Zoe admonishes.

"You really did teach him to FaceTime," I say, laughing at the absurdity of this situation.

"Don't just leave me hanging," she says, smiling at my laughter.

"I'd love to, Zoe," I tell her. I immediately feel lighter, knowing I get to see her.

"And for your meddling, Henry, you have to come, too," Zoe says. "I'm bringing you a friend. So clean up nice."

She gives both of us a challenging look and I look over my shoulder. "You're the one that got us into this, guess you better do what she says."

He shuffles down the hall to get ready while Zoe laughs as she watches him retreat.

"Who's the friend?" I ask curiously.

"You'll see!" she sings. She looks quite pleased with herself. "We already had plans when Henry FaceTimed me earlier this afternoon. I didn't want to miss the chance to see you but I also didn't want to ditch my original plans, so this is perfect. And you don't have to worry about Henry while you're gone. Win-win."

Any chance to see her is a win.

***

It doesn't seem like a win when I pull into the Evergreen Aviation Museum parking lot a couple hours later and see that it's closing though. I park next to Zoe's red 4Runner and step out. She bounces out of her car and right into my arms. She beams up at me and gives me a chaste kiss. There's no one with her.

"Uh, Zoe, you had us meet you at a closed museum."

"Yep! Where's Henry?" she asks, looking toward my truck.

144

"I told him not to get out, since, you know, the museum is closing," I tell her.

"Well, hurry up, our ride is almost here," she replies, pushing me around the front of my truck as a golf cart approaches.

I open the passenger door and help Gramps step down. Zoe gives him a hug, still bouncy and beaming.

"Ready for a private tour before dinner?" she asks us with a grin.

Gramps and I look at each other. Does she know that Gramps always wanted to be a pilot? A far-fetched dream for a poor boy from the coast with a family to help support. Instead, he worked the docks from the age of fourteen until he was drafted into the army, then returned right back to the docks.

"Your chariot awaits." A man who could only be Professional Date Dane steps off the golf cart and bows.

"If he's your competition, you might as well give up now," Gramps says loudly, looking the muscular man up and down. Zoe giggles and squeezes Dane's bicep.

"You must be Henry, Zoe talks about you nonstop," Dane says, reaching his hand out toward Gramps. "And Lucas, nice to meet you."

I shake Dane's hand. "You pulled this off in less than two hours?" I ask, nodding toward the building.

"I wasn't about to let this opportunity go by," Dane says enthusiastically. "I love this place."

He helps Gramps into the front seat of the golf cart and Zoe links her hand with mine once we're settled in the back.

"His uncle is a big deal here. Actually, most places now that I think about it," Zoe quietly explains while Dane engages Gramps in conversation. "Nancy told me about Henry's love of airplanes and you've mentioned Top Gun, so I had already thought about bringing him here. I had plans with Dane tonight, then Henry pulled his FaceTime stunt and Dane got really excited. I can't believe you guys didn't hear him in the background earlier. He was like a little kid."

"This is amazing, Zoe, thank you," I whisper, kissing her temple.

We are treated to a full, behind-the-scenes tour by Dane's uncle, who flew here in his personal helicopter. Because that's normal. Bruce is some sort of banking wizard that wishes he was a real pilot, Dane's words. Bruce good-naturedly laughs and points out that Dane is only half the pilot he is. Something about fixed wing versus rotary.

This is a much bigger glimpse into Zoe's real life and I love it. She's obviously met Bruce before, he pulled her into a big hug the second he saw her. He gave me a quick handshake and then turned his attention to Gramps. I cannot believe the pep in Gramps's step as he walks between Dane and Bruce. Zoe and I are trailing behind the aviation nerds like little kids on a field trip.

The fact that she pulled this together so quickly for me, for both Gramps and I actually, makes my heart swell. With all the things she can do with her life, all the opportunity in front of her, she chooses this. Why? Because she likes my dimple? She should be the one on the receiving end of gifts like these, not the one doling them out.

"Hey, come back," she whispers, squeezing my hand. She tugs me around the corner, hiding us from view. "What're you overthinking about?"

"It's just, you did all this, in like two hours, for me," I say, shrugging. I can't meet her eyes, even as she peers up at me. "You have all this at your fingertips, opportunities like this, and earlier I was sitting at the table, wondering how to pay the fucking bills on time. You deserve so much more. This isn't what you want." I shake my head.

"I only wanted this opportunity because I'd be with you," she says. She reaches up and tips my chin so I'm looking at her. "Luke, I like you. I like spending time with you. I like your grandpa, even when he's a bully. I would have come all the way to you, spent the afternoon paying bills with you, if I would have known you had the day off."

I blow out a steadying breath. "Okay." I don't know what else to say. But I promised on our hike to be honest. "It's just hard, seeing what you'd be missing, if instead you were at home with me, paying bills and fixing the screen door."

"Um, my original plans were to paint my toenails and do a face mask with Dane on my couch while Chase was busy memorizing lines for some community play he's in," Zoe says with a snort.

I chuckle at the thought of Dane with a face mask. He really is almost as big as Jake.

146

"So, if I show up this weekend, will you have time to spend with me? Or should I just get bullied by Henry?"

"I'd love to do face masks with you, but I draw the line at painted toes," I say. I pull her into my chest, and wrap my arms around her. "How did you know I was overthinking?"

She returns my hug, squeezing my waist and keeping her face buried in my shirt. "You stopped rubbing your thumb over mine and your eyes were sad." Her voice is muffled.

"I'm sorry," I tell her and she finally looks up at me, her chin against my chest.

"Nope, apology unnecessary," she says, then her dark eyes turn playful. "Now, we have about two more minutes before Dane comes to find us, so please use that time wisely." She bites her lip.

"Hmm, what do you mean?" I ask, leaning down but stopping just short of her lips.

She winds her hands around my neck and pulls me the rest of the way down. She melts into me as our lips crash together, her body fitting perfectly with mine. I let her kiss my doubts away until a slow clap starts at the end of the hallway.

Zoe pulls back and rests her forehead on mine. "Please tell me that's just Dane, not Henry and Bruce," she whispers. The clapping grows faster.

"If we ignore him, will he go away?" I ask, glancing down the hall.

"No," she sighs.

"Dinner is here!" Dane calls, laughter in his voice. "Just, you know, whenever you're ready."

"Dinner? Here?" I ask.

"Bruce's magic," she replies with a shrug. "I don't question it."

Spaghetti and meatballs, Gramps's favorite, is catered to the museum. Because this is Zoe's normal life and she's sharing it with us. I shake my head and dig in, still overwhelmed. Zoe's hand finds my thigh under the table and she gives me a sweet smile as she squeezes my leg, reassuring me once again.

"For this, I'd probably let you paint my toenails," I whisper.

147

Chapter Eighteen
Zoe

"Oh my god, how much weight is that? You must be so strong!" I say in an extra-perky voice, sneaking up behind Jake as he loads plates onto his barbell.

"Hey...oh," Jake's face falls when he turns and realizes it's me. "It's just you."

"Nice to see you too, Jakey," I say. That earns me a glare.

"Really? Jakey? You, too?" he groans. "Where's Lucas? Does he know you're in town?"

"He's at work, so I'm doing a little work," I tell him. "I just met Lauren, the owner."

"What kind of work?" he asks curiously. "Give me a spot?"

I move around the end of the bench and position myself to spot him as he lays back under the bar.

"How many reps?" I ask.

"Sets of eight," he says, settling onto the bench. He easily reps out his set, then sits up, looking at me expectantly.

"I just wanted to see what the fitness community is like here," I tell him. "Expanding my horizons, all that." I add tens to one side of his bar as he loads the other side.

"Bullshit."

"You don't even know me, I don't think you can call bullshit on me like that," I scoff and roll my eyes.

"I've done yoga with you, that means I know you," he states. I snort and he holds up a finger, silently telling me to not discount him so quickly. "You're outgoing, but more than that, you like to actually connect with people in a meaningful way. You trust your gut, but you second-guess yourself too often when you have time to think, well, overthink. You're protective of those you care about but you care too much about those who don't care enough about you. You're stubborn and don't give up easily, which can be a good thing but can also mean you don't walk away when you should. And, you really, really like my friend."

"Okay, okay, stop." Apparently Officer Jake should be promoted to detective. "Do your next set." I nod to the bench, giving myself time to avoid his questions.

Jake easily reps out another eight and we add weight without speaking. Before I can break the silence, two teenage boys approach. Jake gives them a wide smile.

"Hey, guys!" He fist bumps them in greeting.

Their eyes dart between Jake and I.

"Hi, I'm Zoe," I say, giving them a little wave.

"Zoe, this is Cayden and Mason, they live in the same neighborhood as Henry," Jake says. "They help me out from time to time when I can't swing by to check on him."

"Nice to meet you guys," I say while they shuffle awkwardly, avoiding eye contact with me.

"Are you the fitness girl?" Cayden blurts out. His eyes widen like he didn't mean to say it out loud and Mason feeds an elbow to his ribs.

"I am the fitness girl. I'm just here visiting. Officer Jake and I are friends," I say and then give Jake a smirk. "We do yoga together."

"Yoga?" Mason asks, frowning as he looks at Jake's boulder-like shoulders.

"He's a work in progress," I tell them. "But everyone has to start somewhere."

They snicker at that and finally meet my eyes.

"I'll venmo you for the lawn," Jake tells them. "Hit leg day hard, boys."

With another set of fist bumps, the guys head over to a squat rack. I raise my eyebrows at Jake. He shrugs.

"They got into a little trouble, instead of coming down hard, I asked them to help me out. I pay them to mow Henry's little yard and check on him, but don't you dare tell Lucas," Jake tells me. "I also got them gym memberships and made sure they knew how to properly lift. They were just bored. Their mom isn't home much."

"You're a softie, Jake," I say with a smile. I need to stop and pay a few months of their memberships on my way out.

"Yeah, well, now you know me. And I know you. So. Bullshit. What are you doing at my gym?" Jake and I are in a full standoff now, arms crossed, glaring at each other. It reminds me of the first time I met him, standing on Henry's porch.

"Well, first of all, it's Lauren's gym, not yours. And she's a badass. I really did just want to introduce myself, in case I'm around a little more. I signed up for a membership, so I guess we're workout partners now," I say, shrugging.

"You signed up and paid for a membership when basically any gym in America would beg you to workout there?" he asks.

"Yep." I don't mention that Lauren offered to let me workout for free.

"And?" He's like a dog with a bone.

"And I might have said I'll teach yoga now and then. Do a little promo." I didn't mean to, I really did just want to get a workout in, but after talking to Lauren for a few minutes, hearing her passion for building a fitness community, not just a gym, I offered.

"You really, *really* like my friend," he says with a grin. He ducks back under his bar to avoid my glare.

"Can we just work out in silence now?" I ask.

"You think you can handle my workout?" he asks.

And that's how I end up working out with Officer Hot Cop Jakey, the big softie, who makes me lift heavy weights, which I haven't done in ages.

***

"I've been thinking a lot about our conversation at the library," I tell Nancy as we chop veggies in her bright kitchen. She invited Henry, Lucas, and I over for dinner when I stopped in at the library earlier to say hello before checking into my hotel. "About what I want to do, how I can make changes."

"I'm glad our conversation meant something to you," she replies.

"It really did. I've started mentally cataloging some random things that jump out at me, that somehow feel like they could mean something," I tell her. "From the things I do that make me happy, like teaching and hiking, to the things others do that I'd like to help with."

"Such as?"

"The after-school program I volunteer with, doing living room yoga with Henry, someone donating gym memberships to teenagers that can't afford their own, the yoga series I did for kids. I just don't really know where I'm going with all of this, but I think I'm getting closer." I shrug. "My sister Tatum told me that I always take very calculated risks which don't count as real risks. And she's right. Maybe I need to take a big risk, just once."

"You do have a lot of options, that's for sure," Nancy tells me, topping the salad with the carrots, cucumber, and radishes we just sliced. "And I have no doubt you'll find your way." She picks up the bowl and carries it toward the dining room.

"At least one of us has confidence," I mumble, grabbing the bread basket and following her. She gives me a gentle smile over her shoulder so I know she heard me.

While I'm still lacking confidence in what I'm going to do, I am confident that change is coming. And I have a really good feeling that these people I'm surrounded with at this little dinner table will be a big part of it.

Gramps asked to do yoga earlier, which led to me researching senior citizen activities in Rock Beach. There aren't many, but a new inclusive park is being built, part of a bigger state-wide initiative to bring outdoor spaces to all ability levels. While I immediately pictured kids with walkers or wheelchairs, a representative for the local assisted living center is quoted in the article and I realized this is great for seniors who aren't as steady on their feet. That hadn't even crossed my mind.

Nancy's library was having a science day for tweens and teens earlier and when a couple of the older girls recognized me, I sat with them and learned more about their lives outside of school. What they enjoy, what they wish they had more access to. I saw Nancy taking notes so after sneaking a peek over her shoulder, I made an anonymous donation for a teen art program on my way back out the door.

And Lucas. Abandoned by his parents but raised with love, he didn't think twice about leaving his dreams behind to care for Henry. Dreams that, based on the pictures he took on our hike, would be well within his reach.

I don't think I have a dream to leave behind. Or even work toward. Jake was right, I do second-guess myself too often, but he was also right that I trust my gut. And my gut is telling me that I'm on the right path, I'm just not there yet.

***

"So what do you want to do on your day off?" I ask Luke as I tuck the blanket tighter around us. We're back at the beach for sunset after taking Henry home. There's a cold breeze and I'm wishing I had grabbed another layer.

"Well, unfortunately what I want to do and what I need to do are very different," Luke says, his voice vibrating against my back as I lean into his chest, stealing his body heat. "I *need* to finally fix the screen door, swap out propane tanks on the grill, fix the leak under the sink, and change the oil in the truck. The sheets need to be changed and I really owe Jake a couple hours of work over at his new place. We're almost out of groceries and I should really figure out some better lunches for both of us. But I really *want* to take you to hike Drift Falls and have a picnic before spending the rest of the day on the beach. I'd love to treat you to a nice dinner and then get lost in you all night. But that's not an option, for a lot of reasons."

"Hmmm, well I've always wanted to learn how to fix a screen door. I also did a whole series on learning how to grill, aimed at young women, so I call dibs on propane and making us a nice dinner. And if you do sexy, manly things like changing the oil in your truck, I guarantee you'll be lost in me all night," I tell him. He huffs a small laugh, slips a hand under my shirt and his thumb starts rubbing lazy circles on my skin.

Picturing sweet, laid-back Lucas sliding out from under his old, beat-up truck that I adore, oil on his hands, dirty jeans riding low, that's

153

something I need to see in real life. I move my hands to his thighs that I'm nestled between, and run my hands down his worn jeans.

"Zoe?" Luke says my name with a note of sadness in his voice.

"Mm hmm," I hum, leaning my head back on his shoulder.

"I wish I could give you the 'want' day," he whispers in my ear. "I wish I could give you so much more. You take time away to come out here, pay to stay in town, and then end up helping with Gramps."

"Sorry, what did you just say? I was lost in a really good daydream about you walking toward me after sliding out from under your truck, backwards hat, dirty hands on my skin," I say. His hand that's resting on my hip stills, then tightens. "Really Luke, I just want to spend time with you. The 'want' day sounds amazing, but the 'need' day sounds just as good to me. I promise."

It really, truly does. Aiden always wanted to take me out and the next thing I'd know, he'd be networking instead of talking to me, using me as a selling point, a real-life visual aid. He'd want to work out with me, only to tell me I shouldn't lift too heavy, I needed to stay thin, not get too muscular or bulky. A quick stop at the grocery store turned into a photo shoot at least half the time. The one hike I took him on, he spent the whole time mad that my outfit didn't show my abs for the pictures. It was cold and raining. "A waste of a day" is what he called it. A waste of a year of my life is what our relationship was. I was young and dumb, thinking he was just trying to help me. Looking back, I realize that he wanted ZoeSaysSoFitness, not Zoe. Having a regular day sounds like a really good time to me.

"In that case, I don't want to brag, but I've been changing the oil in my truck since I was fifteen," Luke says before he lightly kisses my neck.

I tilt my head to give him more access as a shiver runs down my spine. "Oh my god, why does that sound so hot?"

"I'm really good with plumbing," he says, dropping his voice.

I can't help but giggle. "If you keep going, you're going to have to take me back to my hotel and get tangled up in me right now," I tell him when I finally get my laughter under control.

"I went to Jake's cousin's ranch once, bucked hay all day. All. Day."

154

I jump out of his lap and start running to the small parking lot. I can hear him chase after me. He catches me right as I reach my 4Runner. He spins me and presses me up against the front bumper.

"Zoe, I built a fucking table last week at The Mercantile," he says, staring into my eyes, his hand continuing to press me into my car. I can feel my body responding, craving more of his touch.

"Mmm, tell me more," I whisper.

His voice deepens even further. "And three big, heavy shelving units."

"Yep, we gotta go, right now," I tell him, laughing once again.

He slowly pulls my keys from his pocket and makes a show of pressing the button to unlock my 4Runner, which I insisted he drive. Except he hits the alarm button instead. After shrieking in shock when the horn blares behind me, I dissolve back into giggles. Before I know what's happening, I'm upside down, thrown over his shoulder.

Lucas stalks around to the passenger side and opens the door, carefully depositing me on the seat so I'm sitting sideways. He stays standing between my legs. I hook my fingers into his belt loop to keep him from stepping away and look him in the eye.

"Luke," I say, keeping my eyes steady on his. "Will you take me to the hardware store tomorrow?"

"I thought you'd never ask," he says, cupping his hand behind my neck and tilting my chin up to steal a kiss.

"Luke," I say again. "Will you take me to my hotel room?"

"I thought you'd never ask," he repeats, his eyes darkening.

He gives me another soft, slow kiss that I desperately want to turn into more. His fingers softly trail down my throat and I wonder if he can feel my heartbeat hammering in my pulse point. He traces my collarbone before withdrawing his fingertips and I immediately want them back.

With one last kiss, he steps away and softly closes my door.

Chapter Nineteen
Luke

I can feel her eyes on me the whole drive to her hotel. Our hands are linked on the center console and her thumb is brushing mine. I glance over and catch her staring.

"What's that look?" I ask her, squeezing her hand in mine.

"I'm just really glad I met you," she says, making my heart beat a little louder in my chest.

"The feeling is mutual," I tell her, wishing I wasn't driving and that I could pull her into my lap. I need her closer.

Luckily the hotel is close and as soon as I park, I turn to her. I bring her hand that's clasped in mine up to my lips, kissing it softly. She smiles at me in the dim light before unbuckling her seatbelt and leaning over to press her lips to mine. She tugs her hand out of mine and opens her door, hopping down before I can make it around the hood.

"Ocean view," she says, pulling a key card from her waistband and holding it up with a grin.

The hotel is built into a cliff and we enter on the tenth floor. The entire back wall of the lobby is one giant window that looks out over the ocean. Zoe leads me to the elevator and as soon as we're inside, she pushes the button for the seventh floor, moving to stand between my legs as I lean against the wall. She wraps her arms around my waist and rests her head on my chest.

"Confession," she says quietly. "They're all ocean view rooms."

I laugh at her confession as the elevator door opens. She leads me down the hall nearly to the end before swiping the keycard at room 707. But it isn't just a hotel room, it's a suite. A large living space welcomes us and the waves sparkling in the moonlight beyond the floor-to-ceiling glass draw my eyes outside to a spacious balcony that runs the entire length of the room. It's the middle of peak summer season, a weekend no less, this must have cost a fortune.

"Want something to drink?" Zoe asks, walking toward the kitchen. Of course there's a kitchen. And of course it's bigger than my kitchen at home.

I've never been in a hotel this nice. I didn't even know this hotel existed in my own town, that's how far out of my league I am. My breaths come quicker, my chest tightens, and I feel like I'm about to start sweating. I rip my hoodie off over my head. This isn't real. This can't be real. What am I doing here?

Zoe notices my reaction and wordlessly takes my hand, leading me to the couch. She hands me a cold bottle of water and then climbs onto my lap, straddling me. She places her palm on my chest, right over my heart. I can feel her always-cold hand through my shirt and it somehow steadies me. The air doesn't feel quite so thin, I manage to take an even breath as I try to gather my thoughts into words.

"I thought we lived in different towns or cities, but we live in different worlds, Zoe," I say, shaking my head. I take a gulp of water before twisting the cap back on and setting the bottle on the couch next to me.

"Hey," she says, studying my expression. "It's just you and me, Luke, all this is just stuff." She takes her hand from my chest and waves it around to indicate the suite without taking her eyes from mine.

"I don't know what to say or what to do. You have friends that fly helicopters, you go to fundraisers and stay in fancy hotel suites. I'm just trying, and failing, I should add, to pay the bills," I tell her. "You have millions of people that follow your life, I wasn't even important enough for my own parents to stay in my life."

Why the fuck did I think this would work? I close my eyes and lean my head back.

158

"Luke," Zoe whispers. I feel her hand cup my jaw, her thumb gently rubbing my cheek. "Lucas, please look at me."

The hitch in her voice is what makes me open my eyes. She's smiling at me as tears fill her dark eyes. When my eyes land on hers, the tears spill over. My chest tightens all over again.

"Zoe, please don't cry," I whisper, reaching up to brush them away. "I'm sorry."

"Luke, this is just you and me. Whether we are in this stupid suite they gave me because someone recognized me in the lobby or in your home that I love, on the beach or in a museum or hiking in the woods, it's just us."

"I'm sorry, Zoe," I say miserably. I've ruined our night. We were having so much fun and now we aren't.

"I'm not," she says firmly, despite the tears still rolling down her freckled cheeks. I can't wipe them away fast enough. "This is all part of it, part of us. When I said I want to see where this goes, I really meant that I want to make it work. I want to put in the effort. I want to show you over and over again that you're an important part of my life. Because you are, Luke. You are important to me and so many other people. I'm lucky to know you, to get to call myself your girlfriend, and I'll reassure you over and over again. Every time."

Just hearing her call herself my girlfriend makes me smile. She's amazing and she's here, sitting in my lap, reassuring me, telling me exactly what I need to hear.

"Just you and me?" I say with a question in my voice.

She leans forward, her hair a dark curtain that closes us in, and gently kisses me. Her lips are soft, tasting of vanilla and salty tears, and they disappear from mine all too quickly.

"Will you still take me to the hardware store tomorrow?" Zoe whispers, resting her forehead on mine. "Please?"

"It's a date," I promise. I rub my hands up and down her thighs, absentmindedly tracing the seam of her leggings, trying to pull myself back into this moment.

"I can't wait," she says, kissing me again, this time lingering.

When my hands slide up to her waist, pulling her closer, Zoe sweeps her tongue across my lips, wanting more. Wanting me. She buries

159

her hands in my hair and shifts her hips forward, leaving no space between us. There's no way she can't feel my response to her, a fact that's proven when she arches her back to rub against me. She moves her mouth to my neck and her hands to the hem of my shirt.

"I need to feel you," she whispers, tugging my tee shirt up. Her hands find bare skin; I can feel her smile against my neck when my abs contract, reacting to her icy hands.

I slip my hands under her layers and she sits up. I pause and she smiles, biting her lip enticingly. Her hands retract from under my shirt and she slowly crosses her arms, plucking the hem of her sweater, slowly pulling it off over her head. My eyes drink her in. I love her confidence, the ease she has with herself, her body, how she draws my eyes to her soft curves as she subtly rolls her hips.

I grip her waist, pulling her closer to chase her vanilla lips. After another lingering kiss, she brings a finger to her swollen lips, then slowly leans back, tracing a line down her sternum, my eyes following her finger down her flimsy tank top. When she tugs her last layer up and over her head, I can't help but groan. Lace. Black lace. She smiles at my reaction before tilting her head, thighs gripping me tightly.

"You like?" she asks, bringing her hand to cup my jaw.

"Zoe," I groan. I sit forward and kiss a line along the swells of her breasts. "You're so goddamn sexy in your leggings and workout tops, but this feels like a secret just for me."

"It *is* just for you," she says, arching her back to push her breasts closer, wordlessly asking me to continue kissing and tasting them. "I went shopping especially for this weekend. Especially for you."

I've never seen her in anything but workout clothes. Even on the 4th of July she had on an athletic tee with her cut off jean shorts. She looks fucking amazing in anything and everything, but knowing that she wore this just for me? Fuck. I don't deserve her.

"And there's more," she whispers, threading her fingers in my hair and urging me to look up at her. Her lips are pink, her cheeks are red, her hair is falling in waves around her shoulders, and her eyes are locked on mine. She's fucking beautiful, and she's here with me.

"More?" My breaths are choppy as I tear my eyes from hers and let them wander downward.

She seductively rolls her hips as I lean back, her abs flexing and stretching. Until Zoe, I didn't know abs could make my mouth water. But fuck, I want to lick them. I settle for tracing them with a light touch, mesmerized by her movements. She covers my hands with hers, continuing to writhe and roll as she slowly moves my hands to her waist. She tucks our linked hands into her waistband until my pinkies encounter lace.

"More," she confirms with a wicked smile.

I've never gotten to strip panties off her body. I thought she was hot as fuck without underwear, but I cannot wait to see her with these. I stand up so fast I nearly drop her. She wraps her legs around my waist and laughs into my neck as I carry her to what I hope is the bedroom.

It is a bedroom, a huge king bed in the middle, piled high with white pillows. I gently lay her back on the bed and rip my shirt over my head.

"Impatient?" she asks with a smirk, her eyes dancing.

"You have no idea," I tell her, tugging at the waistband of her leggings, peeling them off her lean legs.

Finally, she lays before me, an absolute fucking vision in matching black lace, neither bra nor panties covering much. I tip my head back and take a deep breath, trying to slow myself down. It's not just the fact that she's spread out before me in tiny scraps of lace. It's that she picked them out just for me. That she's here. That she's *her*.

Despite having the world at her fingertips, she showed up here, for me, and once again immersed herself in my life. She sees my insecurities and doubts and obliterates them with her words, her actions, that look that she gives me, silently telling me that it's just us, just her and I.

But also, the tiny scraps of lace. Fuck.

When I bring my eyes back to her, it's a completely different look dancing in her eyes. It's hunger and lust, want and need as her eyes roam my bare chest. She's moving backwards toward the middle of the king-size bed, shoving the covers down as she goes. When she notices my eyes on her, she freezes. Her dark hair is fanned out over the white sheets and she gives me a slow smile. She reaches her arms over her head before arching her back off the bed and bringing one hand down to the

161

top of her breast. I watch, mesmerized, as she slowly trails her hand down her body, dipping it in the top of her panties.

Fire ignites in my veins the second she bites her lip and I rip the covers the rest of the way off the bed. With a gentle tug of her ankle, she's in front of me, hips at the edge of the bed, that taunting hand disappearing further into her panties.

I lean over her, one hand resting on the mattress, the other covering her wandering hand. "Now who's impatient?" I whisper.

"Me," she gasps as I move my lips to her earlobe. "I am."

"Hmmm," I hum, enjoying her squirming under me. "What are you impatient for?"

"You, I need you," she moans. "Luke, please."

"I fucking love watching your hands skim down your body, Zoe, but it's my turn." I take both of her hands and place them above her head. "Don't move."

"That commanding tone, why does that make me so hot?" Zoe pants as I inch my way down, enjoying the lace edge of her bra, kissing her through the thin fabric, watching her nipples pebble with my touch.

"Everything about you is hot," I murmur, kissing down her lickable abs.

I drop to my knees between her legs and lick a straight line up the black lace that's still covering her. Her hips buck and her legs shake.

"Luke," she breathes my name in a way I haven't heard. In a way I want to hear a hell of a lot more. "I want all of you."

I freeze.

"Luke." She brings her hands down from where I had placed them above her head and presses onto her elbows, looking down at me. "Come here."

I kiss over her center again before moving over her. She places one over my heart and the other behind my neck, gently pulling me in for a kiss.

"I *need* all of you," she whispers.

When I pull back, she watches me carefully. I want her so bad it hurts. But I also know that once this last barrier between us is gone, there's no going back. She gives me a small smile and I know I'm already past the point of no return with her. She's had me since day one.

162

I place another kiss on her lips and then move off the bed, fumbling for my wallet with shaky hands. I take a condom out and toss it on the sheets. Zoe watches as I unbutton my jeans and slide them down, taking my briefs with them. I see her breath hitch as her hungry gaze travels over me.

"Fuck, Zoe," I murmur. "When you look at me like that, fuck."

She just smiles and reaches for me, pulling me down on top of her, kissing my neck, biting my shoulder, whispering how bad she wants me, wants us, as my hands roam. It takes me no time to unclasp her bra and her lace panties follow it to the floor mere seconds later. My heart pounds in my chest as I sit up and tear the condom wrapper with my teeth. Zoe's lust-darkened eyes never leave mine.

"You and me," I whisper, lowering myself over her. I stroke her cheek with my thumb and give her a slow kiss.

"You and me," she whispers back, then hooks a leg around my hips to pull me in.

We both gasp as I sink inside her heat. Feeling her clench around me, I don't move, waiting, barely breathing. She releases a shaky breath, her eyes steady on mine. We simultaneously break the moment, unhurried but with a hint of desperation. Her hips come up to meet mine and she moves with me like she was made for me.

"You feel so good," she gasps, her fingernails digging into my back.

I'm lost, nearly drowning in the intensity of her gaze, of her touch, her rolling hips, her whispered pleas for more. My hands already know every inch of her body, every sensitive sliver of skin, each place that she wants and needs to be touched, kissed, worshipped.

"Luke," she moans, threading her fingers through my hair. "Please, I need-"

When she doesn't say more, I pull back. Her eyes are dark, desperate.

"I need you to kiss me," she nearly begs. "Please."

I feel her shudder as soon as my tongue finds hers. I can feel her building closer with every frantic kiss. She bites my lower lip and I slip my hand between us, urging her closer. Her entire body trembles and she

163

whispers my name as she finds her release, begging me to come with her. I follow her over the edge, breathless, spent.

Before I collapse on top of her, I roll us so we're facing each other.

"Holy shit," she whispers.

"Yeah," I agree, unable to say more.

It's never been like that before. Ever. The way her body knows mine, how she moves, how she feels, how her eyes lock on mine and I feel them in my fucking soul. She claimed I wrecked her the first time, whatever is beyond wrecked, that's what I am. But if I try to put that into words, I'm going to say something stupid, like I'm falling in love with her. Which I am.

"Yeah?" she asks, laughing.

"Zoe, that was…yeah." I kiss her nose and shake my head. "Holy shit covers it."

"It's never been like that," she whispers, cupping my jaw. "Sorry, I don't think I'm supposed to tell you how intense that felt, but Luke. Holy shit. I can't be anything other than yours after that."

I suck in a breath. "Thank god you felt that, too."

"Just you and me," she says with a smile. I press one more kiss to her vanilla lips and then head for the bathroom.

I climb back into bed after disposing of the condom and before I can pull her into me, Zoe is moving toward me, draping her body over mine. She rests her head on my chest and I play with the ends of her long hair.

"Zoe, you're amazing," I tell her, tightening my hold on her.

"I think that was us, together," she says, her hand on my chest tracing mindless circles on my skin.

"I want to stay," I tell her, unable to imagine leaving her here in this bed.

"I'm not kicking you out," she says, laughter in her voice. "But I know what you mean. Want to set an early alarm? I also understand if you need to go."

She gets up and heads for the bathroom, leaving me with my thoughts. I only feel a slight twinge of guilt as I fumble for my phone and set an alarm. Less sleep, more Zoe. Worth it every time, which is confirmed as she crosses the room toward me wearing only a smile.

"What's that look?" she asks as she climbs back in bed. I pull the covers over us and breathe her in as she moves even closer, hooking her leg over my thigh.

"It's the 'I can't believe that girl is mine' look," I tell her honestly.

"Guess I should have worn the lace last time," she says with a laugh.

"It's the girl, not the lace," I reply, trying to pull her even closer.

She huffs a small laugh. "It's the man, not the dimple. But god, that dimple."

I laugh at that and kiss her forehead. She sighs and I can feel her heartbeat slowing, her breaths evening out. All I can think as she falls asleep in my arms is that I hope she meant it, that she can't be anyone's but mine, because my heart already belongs to her. I think it has since the first cinnamon roll.

Sometime in the night she must drift away, because when I wake up, she's no longer sprawled on top of me. I reach for her and only find cold sheets. Confused, I stumble out of bed, drunk with sleep. I open the bedroom door and am nearly blinded by bright light shining into the room. Fuck, I missed my alarm to check on Gramps.

Chapter Twenty
Zoe

"Good morning, Miss Zoe," Henry says as I attempt to quietly sneak in the front door. "A little early for breaking and entering, isn't it?"

I freeze, caught in the act. What exactly was my plan here? I mean, no matter what time I showed up, it was going to be obvious Luke wasn't with me and that I had his keys, therefore it'd be a pretty easy assumption that we spent all night together. Or that I murdered him and stole his keys? Something nefarious, for sure.

"Coffee?" Henry asks, a twinkle in his eye.

"Yes, please," I squeak out.

"I don't offer very many felons coffee," Henry says, handing me a steaming coffee mug. He shuffles his way toward the back door so I follow, making sure to slide my phone in my pocket in case Luke calls.

"Thank you for making an exception," I tell him, settling into Luke's chair.

He just grunts in reply.

I pull my feet up and sit cross-legged. I stretch my spine and do some gentle neck circles, working through my morning routine that I skipped earlier in my haste to check on Henry. I do some deep breathing and when my coffee is cool enough, I take a sip.

"I wasn't born yesterday and I understand if you want to stay elsewhere, but I hope you know that you're welcome to stay here," Henry says without preamble.

I nearly spit out my coffee. Did he wait for me to take a sip? A little twitch of his upper lip tells me he did.

"Henry!" I exclaim, coughing. "A little warning, please." My cheeks flame and I fan my face.

"You come all this way because the stubborn boy won't leave me alone," Henry grouches. "Least we can do is show you some hospitality."

"Well, thank you, I appreciate that," I tell him. "I'm glad you didn't call the cops when I broke in or ask if I murdered your grandson. Which I didn't, by the way. I just thought he'd appreciate a day to sleep in."

"You're good for him," Henry says before pausing. I wait to take another drink of my coffee, just in case he says something else that would cause a spit take. "You're good for both of us."

My heart warms. Sweet, grumbly old man. "I'm glad you think so," I reply, sipping my coffee, this time without choking. "You guys are good for me, as well." Hashtag truth.

"So you didn't murder him?" he asks, smiling at me.

"No, you old grouch, I did not," I say, giving him a playful glare. "He has to teach me how to fix the screen door and the sink before I do that."

"This old grouch can teach you those things," Henry says.

I raise an eyebrow at him. "Oh, really?"

Henry slaps both hands on his knees and pushes to standing. "Welp, better bring your coffee," he says, nodding to my half-full mug. "I've got to-go cups in the cupboard."

***

"That was easier than I thought it'd be," I say, shimmying my way back out from under the sink.

Henry turns the faucet on and I hold my breath. No leaks!

"I did it!" I do my happy dance all around the little kitchen, making Henry chuckle.

"You didn't flood the place, so that's something," he begrudgingly admits. "But your pants are ringing."

I was so proud of myself that I didn't even feel my phone vibrating in my pocket, let alone hear the ring. When was the last time I had my ringer turned on? Never?

168

"Good morning, Lucas Henry Stark," I answer Luke's call, hoping he can hear the smile in my voice.

"Mmm, it would have been better if I woke up next to you," he says.

"I'm sorry, I thought you could use a little more sleep," I say.

"Since it's after ten in the morning, I'd say you were right," he replies. "I can't remember the last time I slept this late."

"Well, I can't remember a time I've ever fixed a sink or a screen door, so we're both having a big day," I say, smiling at Henry who gives me a pat on the shoulder.

"Wait, what?" Luke asks.

"Well, your grandpa offered to teach me, so we kinda went to the hardware store without you," I tell him, biting my lip, suddenly a little guilty. This was supposed to be our thing today. Shit.

"You fixed the sink and the screen door?" His voice tells me he's not mad, just perhaps a little shocked.

"Henry is a good foreman, great at bossing people around," I say, winking at Henry who smiles back. He motions me toward the door and hands me my keys. "He's also pushing me out the door, so I think I'm on my way to get you."

"I'm so confused," Luke says. I can hear him yawning.

"Henry, don't forget to move the sheets to the dryer!" I call as I walk down the steps.

"Even more confused now."

"Go back to bed, I'll be there in ten minutes," I tell him, opening my car door.

"That sounds amazing," he replies. "But-"

"Nope, go back to bed, I'll see you in ten minutes," I say, and hang up before he can argue.

Nine minutes later, I'm quietly opening the door to the suite. I start losing my clothes as soon as the door closes behind me.

"Holy shit," Luke says when I slip into the bedroom. "This is the best dream I've ever had."

He throws the covers off the bed as I cross the room toward him. I can feel his eyes on me but I'm too busy taking him in to think twice. He has an arm behind his head, making his bicep flex slightly, his other hand rests on his muscular chest, and I take a moment to appreciate his abs. And everything below.

I slowly crawl onto the bed and up his body, finally landing my eyes on his as I swing my leg over his hip, straddling him. The heated look he's giving me nearly does me in. I want to pull the covers over us and hide here with him forever. I start with a kiss, which escalates just as quickly as I hoped it would. There was a tiny part of me that wondered if things would be different this morning, but when Luke groans my name, that fear flies out the window.

"I can't believe you woke up early and fixed a sink for me," Luke whispers against my lips, pulling back just far enough to look in my eyes.

His hands continue roaming my naked body, making me ache for him in all sorts of ways. I've always been comfortable in my skin, but the way he looks at me, touches me, worships me makes me feel a whole new level of confidence.

"I don't want to brag, but I was really good at it, zero floods." Unable to resist, I sit up and run my fingers down his chest to his abs. I love the way they flex, moving with every touch as I trace down that ever-tempting V that points me in the direction I want this morning to take.

"Does that mean no hardware store date?" he asks, his hands gripping my thighs tightly as I rock gently against him.

"Oh, well, if that's what you want to do, we can do that I guess," I say, making a move like I'm going to climb off his hard body, which is absolutely not happening. I think I might die if I don't get to have my way with him this morning.

The next thing I know, I'm flipped over and pinned to the mattress. Luke is hovering over me, caging me in with his arms, pure lust combined with laughter in his bright green eyes. The best combination.

"So, is that a no on the hardware store?" I ask innocently.

Luke answers by capturing my mouth with his, his tongue searching for mine. I arch into him and he reaches a hand down to grasp my thigh, urging me to wrap my legs around his waist. I shift my hips and he groans, pressing into me.

"I need you, Zoe," he says, his eyes on mine.

170

"I need you right now," I pant, rotating my hips impatiently. "So bad, Luke. So fucking bad."

He loosens his hold and reaches sideways for his wallet. The tear of the condom wrapper is music to my ears. And when he puts both hands on my hips and pulls me to him, I gasp his name.

After, we share the oversized shower, where he trails soft kisses along my collarbone and gently soaps every inch of me. We barely make the check out time.

**

"You're kicking me out? I live here," Luke says, playfully glaring at both Henry and I after we eat the lunch from Mo's we picked up on the way back from the hotel.

"I hate to think the leg sets Jake will make me do the next time we workout if I don't," I tell him. "Go help Officer Hot Cop for a couple hours."

"Miss Zoe said she'd let me help with dinner," Henry tells him. "Skedaddle."

Luke throws his arms up in the air and stomps toward his truck, making both Henry and I laugh, which I'm sure was his goal. I chase after him and catch his hand just as he opens the truck door. He turns, raising his eyebrows at me, green eyes sparkling with laughter.

"Don't forget you have to change the oil in your truck later, because I have not forgotten that fantasy," I whisper, blatantly ogling him from head to toe. I even take his hat and turn it backwards on his head. God, he's hot.

"Great, now you're kicking me out with that on my mind," he says quietly, laughing and shaking his head at me.

"If I don't have your dirty handprints on me when I drive home tonight, I'm going to be quite disappointed," I say, licking my lips as I look up at him.

"Damnnit, Zoe," Luke says, reaching up to trace my bottom lip with the pad of his thumb. "Why are you so perfect?"

I glance behind me to make sure Henry has gone back inside. Once I'm sure the coast is clear, I reach my arms up around Luke's neck and kiss him hard.

"Not helping," he groans, pushing his hips into me so I can feel what I'm doing to him.

"I can't wait," I whisper, pulling away from him.

"Are you two done making out? We have chores to do!" Henry hollers from the doorway.

I dissolve into giggles as Luke leans his forehead on mine.

"Hey, before you go, you should know that Henry invited me to stay here the next time I visit. I want you to have time to think about it," I tell him when I get my laughter under control.

"You definitely should," he replies without missing a beat.

"Are you sure?" I ask.

"I'm sure," Luke says. "Now you better get back there before you get us both in trouble and your invitation gets rescinded."

That makes me laugh again, especially when Henry coughs pointedly from the doorway.

"Okay, okay!" I call up to him. "Goodbye, Lucas Henry Stark."

"Goodbye, Zoe Last Name Campbell," Luke says, pinching my side and sliding into the driver's seat.

I basically float back up to the house where Henry is waiting impatiently.

"I've made a decision," Henry declares as soon as I step back inside. I raise my eyebrows at his announcement. "I'm going to pull myself up by my old bootstraps and start doing more around here. And you're going to help me."

I don't know how to respond. I'd love to help him, and therefore Luke, but I don't know what he has in mind or if he can physically do more. The first time I met him, I showed up because he couldn't find his lunch in the fridge. Although today, he's doing laundry and bossing me around like a champ.

"Well, what do you have in mind?" I ask, unwilling to commit to anything without Luke's okay.

"You're already making me do laundry, why do you think I asked to help with dinner?" Henry counters.

"Because you don't trust my cooking," I deadpan.

172

That earns me a Henry harrumph. But then we sit at the table and come up with some easy, healthy meals that Henry would be able to start while Luke works.

"This should be doable, right? We can come up with a weekly grocery list for Luke, then everything will be on hand," I say, capping my pen. I look up to see Henry in another world. I give him time, not wanting to push.

"I just got lost after Elle passed away," Henry finally says, staring out the small window. "Then with Luke gone at school, I just didn't have it in me I guess. And now I'm weak, a burden."

I blink back the tears that fill my eyes and cover his hands with my own. "Henry, we all get a little lost sometimes. I'm a little lost right now, but you've become one of my anchors. And Luke does not see you as a burden, he cares so deeply about you. You've raised a good man. You are not a burden, don't you dare think that for one more second."

"Thank you, Miss Zoe," Henry whispers gruffly. He pulls one of his hands from mine and wipes a tear from his weathered cheek. "But it's time for me to live again and I need your help."

"I'm honored you want my help," I whisper through the tears that spill down my cheeks. I squeeze his hand.

"Well, that's enough of that," Henry says when he sees my tears. He quickly pulls his hand away.

"Sorry, geez, let a girl have a moment," I say, laugh-crying as I wipe my cheeks.

"What's first?" he asks, definitely *not* giving me a moment.

"First, I'm going to the store to get groceries and propane while you wash the bath towels, then, we're cooking dinner and prepping for the week," I tell him, pulling myself together.

"And then yoga?" he asks.

"And then yoga," I confirm.

***

"Yep, this is just as hot as I thought it'd be," I say when I walk outside after helping Henry with the dishes.

Luke laughs from under his truck. He came back from Jake's a hot, dirty, sweaty mess after building a new fence along the back property line. Did I mention hot? After dinner outside on the small front

173

stoop, Henry and I cleaned up while Luke started on his truck. I sit down on the front steps and let my mind wander as Luke finishes up the last chore of the day.

Henry and I did a lot today and he already bid me goodnight. I know he's tired and I chew my lip as I worry if it will carry over to tomorrow. I love that he's trying to do more, but I don't want him to *over*do anything.

"What are you sighing about up there," Luke calls.

"The fact that you're still under there, and I'm up here," I call back to him.

"Almost done, I know you have to go soon."

I hate that I have to go, but really, weekends here are worth the drive and the workload that's waiting for me in Portland. I'm hoping to get the entire six-week power series that we're launching soon filmed this week. Abby has two different studios booked so we should be able to get it done quickly. I mentally flip through my schedule for the week, hoping I can see Luke again.

"Hey," Luke startles me. He leans forward, placing his hands on the steps on either side of me, trapping me between them. He's sweaty, dirty, and I can't resist running my hands down his arms. He smiles, showing me his dimple. "What are you thinking about? You look so serious."

"Work schedule," I tell him, shrugging. "It's boring."

"Did you think about what Gramps said?" he asks, leaning in for a kiss.

"About what?" I ask. I don't think Henry has talked to Luke about 'living again' and I don't know how to handle this. I don't want to lie to Lucas but I also don't want to break Henry's trust.

"Staying here next time. I think you should, as long as you're comfortable with it," Luke says, watching me closely.

"I'd love to, especially if I get to see you all sweaty again," I reply, smiling up at him.

"Next weekend?" he asks, the hope in his eyes making my heart stutter.

"I should be able to do that, as long as Maia or Abby can take care of Egg again," I say, watching him light up. That dimple. It's not fair. I look down at my phone to see the time. I groan.

"I feel bad that you do all the driving," Luke says, misreading my groan.

"I don't mind the drive, I actually like driving. I just don't like leaving you," I tell him.

"How about I call you after I get cleaned up and I read you a few chapters from our book as you drive?" Luke asks.

"That sounds amazing," I tell him.

He's so sweet and funny, kind and thoughtful, I can't get enough. And that heat he hides, that comes out when he presses me against my car door to kiss me goodbye, leaving dirty handprints on the bare skin under my shirt, I can't get enough of that either.

Chapter Twenty-One
Zoe

"What is this attitude all about? Did Dimples break your heart?" Chase asks as we sit at our usual table after class. "Three, pencil skirt by the creamer."

Dane stands at the end of the counter waiting for our drinks as Chase and I play our usual game, counting how many times Dane gets checked out and/or hit on. Thanks to the gray tee shirt stretched tight across his chest, I have a feeling today's number is going to be higher than usual.

"Quarter-life crisis," I reply. "Four, guy in glasses walking out."

"Five, guy with airpods by the window. That seems dramatic, even for you," he says.

"Ugh, I know, I'll snap out of it, sorry."

The only thing I like about this week is the handful of yoga classes I teach. It's only Wednesday and I'm annoyed by everything else. I don't care that the bright, shiny new gym that everyone is talking about is requesting I attend their grand opening. They have silent partners and Bruce-type money behind them which makes me think of Lauren and what she's done with her little gym in Rock Beach. Which in turn makes me eager for Saturday morning when I can head to the beach.

"No one noticed in class, don't worry, we all have those days," Chase says, nudging my foot with mine. He tilts his head toward Dane, who is chatting with a woman in head-to-toe Lululemon. He's completely oblivious to her advances, even as she leans in and laughs, half a second away from putting her hand on his forearm. "Six."

We sit in comfortable silence until Dane brings our drinks. When he sets his hand on Chase's, Lulu woman's face falls. Chase and I exchange an amused glance.

"Okay, serious question," I say once Dane has settled onto the too-small chair. "That new gym wants me to attend their grand opening party and I don't want to."

"Hon, that's not a question," Dane says.

"I wasn't finished. My question is this: am I a fraud if I get paid to attend the party but I don't support the gym?"

"Yes," Chase says at the exact time Dane says "No."

"Wow, thanks guys," I deadpan.

"No, not a fraud. It's a job. Go to the thing, take the pictures, move on," Dane says with a shrug.

"It depends on *why* you don't support them. Are they doing something unethical? You should support the people and businesses you want to support, not necessarily because you're getting paid," Chase disagrees.

"What if I use that paycheck to pay gym memberships for teenagers that wouldn't be able to pay on their own, and maybe spend their gym time getting in trouble?" I ask.

"Why don't you just make that part of your contract?" Chase asks.

Dane snaps his fingers. "Yes, that. They have to hold a certain number of spots open. I don't know how they choose what kids, but that could work," he adds, nodding. "But they also have to pay you."

"Oh, well I was going to pay for kids at a different gym," I say, frowning. "But that's actually a good idea. Why didn't I think of that? One sec."

I quickly email Seth, the majority-owner that seems to be the most hands-on. He's the one that reached out to me.

"Why don't you bring Lucas to the grand opening?" Dane suddenly asks.

178

"Oh, well, Henry is why. Jake works a lot of weekends and nights so Lucas doesn't like asking him to stay over," I tell them. "If Seth agrees to my new contract, I'll go solo if I have to."

"Wow, I'm sitting right here," Dane says, shaking his head.

"I'm not dragging you along again, I'm sure you two have better things to do."

"Isn't the grand opening in like a week-and-a-half?" Chase asks. I nod. "I'm out of town. He's all yours. Please, entertain him so I don't have to get a sitter."

I laugh at that. "Maybe you and Lucas can share sitters," I suggest.

"Wait," Dane says, holding up a hand. "I think I have an idea. Yep. I have a brilliant idea." He grabs his phone off the table and walks outside to make a call.

Chase and I look at each other and shrug. It barely seems like a minute later when Dane bursts back in and nearly runs back to our table.

"I'm babysitting Henry," he announces loudly enough and with enough freaking Dane flair that half the coffee shop turns to look at him.

"What?" I ask. "No, you're not. I'm not asking you to do that."

"And I'm taking him flying," he adds, completely ignoring my interjection. "Bruce said I could take the little plane, there's an airstrip in town, I'll figure out ground transportation between now and then. He'll love it!"

"Dane, I'm sure he would, but you'd have to stay the night, make dinner, play checkers, be domestic..." I trail off.

"Sleepovers are awesome, I'll order pizza, I was on the chess team in high school, and I'm domestic as hell," Dane ticks off, making Chase scoff, I'm guessing at the domestic claim.

"Zoe, just let him do it, can't you see how excited he is?" Chase says. "And he doesn't shut up about Henry at home."

I glance between the two of them. Dane is nearly quivering with excitement and Chase only has eyes for Dane. This would definitely count toward Henry's "live again" goal.

"Okay, yeah, I'll run it by them," I say. "Seven."

"Really, you're playing that game again?" Dane groans, looking around the coffee shop for number seven.

"Oh, I just meant the way Chase is looking at you right now." I shrug. But really, they're madly in love and it's the best.

***

"Are you sure this is okay?" I whisper uncertainly when Luke walks out to my 4Runner to get my overnight bag. I left my apartment early this morning and managed to get here before Luke leaves for work.

"We both want you here but neither of us wants you to be uncomfortable," Luke replies.

I chew on my lip. Luke patiently waits until I give a nod, then he grabs my duffel from the backseat and slings it over his shoulder. He shoots me his dimpled smile, takes my hand with his free hand, and leads me up the steps.

I don't know what I was worried about. Watching Henry's face fall on my iPhone screen when I had said I'd be out later in the afternoon made my heart hurt, so of course I agreed to spend the day in town despite Luke's schedule.

I take Henry to an early lunch and we swing by the library to say hi to Nancy. We make a quick grocery store stop but then Henry pushes me back out the door, telling me that he's making dinner for the three of us.

Jake meets me at the gym for leg day and we run into Cayden and Mason again. After getting a subtle nod from Jake, I invite them to finish the workout with us. Even though I'm really trying to keep my time here quiet and away from ZoeSays, I pose for a few pictures with them, per their girlfriends' requests, and tell them I'd love to go for a hike one day with all of them. I guess I never realized how many teenage girls follow me.

"Jenna is gonna be so pumped!" Mason tells me. He shows me a picture of Jenna, who actually looks a little like Tatum.

"I'll let Jake know when I've got a little more time," I promise them.

"Bruh," Cayden says, punching Jake on the shoulder as they walk away.

"You know you didn't have to do any of that, right?" Jake asks. "Pictures or offering up time."

180

"Yeah, and you know you didn't have to set them up with gym memberships, right?" I ask, giving him a glare.

"You mean the memberships that have suddenly been paid well in advance?" Jake counters, also glaring.

I look away. "Ugh, go patrol the streets, Officer Jake," I grumble.

"Thanks for the workout, Lucas's Girl," he replies, grinning.

"Leg day every day," I say, knowing I'm going to be sore as shit tomorrow. Jake doesn't mess around.

"Hey Zoe, seriously, thanks for that," Jake tells me as we walk outside. "Not just for their memberships, but for taking the time to talk with them, connecting with them. They don't always get that from adults. In fact, they rarely do."

"Stop being nice to me, it's weird," I say, wrinkling my nose. "Go flex for tourists, Jakey."

On the drive back to Luke's, I again have a little inkling of an idea, like a blurry picture that my brain can't quite clear up. Unfortunately I don't have time to try to work it out, because Abby calls.

"I found another Asshole Aiden contract," she says flatly as soon as I answer.

"Okay," I blow out a breath. "Hit me with it."

"A fucking weight loss supplement," she says.

"Oh, fuck no," I say. "Fuck. No."

I think of Tatum, Kelsey, the teenage girls I sat with at the library those weeks ago, Mason's girlfriend Jenna, and all the other teenage girls that apparently follow me. I had enough crazy responses to posting a picture of a cinnamon roll. No way am I going down the awful, terrible, no good road of diet supplements. I will post smoothies all day every day because I love them, they're delicious and mostly healthy, but adding any weight loss supplement? Fuck. No.

"My thoughts exactly," Abby says. "Want me to handle it?"

"Nope, send me the contact and as soon as I park, they're going to hear from me directly," I tell her. I don't care that it's Saturday afternoon, this is getting dealt with immediately.

"Okay, I'm pretty sure they thought they were already hearing from you, Aiden pulled some real shady shit on this one," she warns.

181

"I've realized everything he did was real shady shit. I'm not going to rage at them, I'm just going to explain there's no way in hell I am fulfilling whatever he said I'd do," I tell her.

This is not how I wanted to spend my afternoon. I'm hoping the issue can be easily resolved. Luckily, and surprisingly, my call is answered quickly by a guy named Shane, who immediately forwards me everything he has, which is an exact copy of everything Abby just sent over as well.

"I'm one hundred percent not interested in any partnership," I tell Shane, trying to keep my voice pleasant. "I'm sorry that this might put you in a bad situation, but I was not included in any of the original contract, my signature was forged. That was all someone who is no longer on my team. We are still digging through the contracts he hid from us, I'm so sorry that your company was included in this."

I clench my jaw and close my eyes as Shane gives me a sales pitch despite my previous statement. I know he's just doing his job, but it's still nothing I want to hear. As Shane talks, Luke pulls in and parks his truck next to me. I'm sitting sideways in my seat, my car door open. He gives me a questioning look as he steps out of his truck and rounds the hood. I just shake my head and hold up a finger.

"I appreciate that, Shane, I'm sorry we won't be working together," I say when Shane agrees that we don't need to get attorneys involved. I'm pretty sure I do need to get an attorney involved with Aiden though. Shit.

"Everything okay?" Luke asks when I throw my phone onto the grass in frustration.

"Yep, just, ugh," I tell him. "Other than that, I had a great day." I reach out and grab his shirt, pulling him in for a kiss.

"Knowing you were here made my day better," he whispers as he steps back. He reaches down to retrieve my phone and I put it on Do Not Disturb before shoving it into my waistband.

It's impossible to let my frustrations linger as I walk in the house behind Luke though. Henry's proud exclamation that dinner is almost ready, followed by Luke's dimpled smile sent my way, washes it all away.

***

182

"Come with me to the grand opening next weekend?" I whisper. I wind myself around Lucas, enjoying the fact we woke up together. "Please?" I tuck my head under his chin, using his chest as my pillow. I fell asleep in this same position, Luke's chest vibrating under my cheek as he read another chapter from our book.

He playfully gasps. "But what about Professional Date Dane?"

"Well, he actually offered to come stay with Henry," I say. "He's sick of carting me all over town."

"Stay here? Does he know where we live?" I can feel the tension running through Luke's body.

"Dane isn't like that, he wouldn't care if you lived in a tent. He'd still order pizza and play checkers. I promise."

I let him have a minute to think it over, knowing he still struggles with our different lives at times. I run my hand over his bare chest and hook my leg over his. I can hear his heartbeat under my cheek and feel his chest rising and falling with each breath he takes. If there was a way, I'd wake up like this every morning. I am falling so fast for this man, it should be alarming. Instead, it just feels right.

"I'd love to go with you, let me talk to Gramps though," he finally replies.

"Can I ask him?"

"Of course." His hand rubs lazy circles on my hip.

I jump out of bed, unable to hold in my excitement. I can't wait to see his reaction. I might be falling fast for Luke but I've already fallen for Henry.

"Wait, where are you going?" Luke asks, watching in confusion as I fumble in the dim morning light for clothes.

"Well, I gotta go make coffee and talk to Henry," I say, pulling Luke's hoodie on and digging through my bag for clean leggings.

"Give me a sec," Luke says, stretching.

"Nope, you stay in bed," I tell him over my shoulder as I walk out. "I'll bring you coffee."

Henry is just shuffling into the kitchen as I scoop the grounds into the filter. I flip the switch and turn to face him.

"Just the man I wanted to see," I tell him, giving him a smile. I thought it would be awkward staying here, but instead it just feels like a second home, thanks to the two men who live here.

"Good morning, Miss Zoe, you're looking quite chipper," Henry says. He suddenly stops, seeming to realize how that sounded and his eyes dart toward the hallway that leads to Luke's room.

Oh. My. God. I take back the not awkward thing. I turn back to the coffee maker. I'm absolutely blushing and I can't turn back around to face him.

"She didn't look that happy when she left my room." Luke appears in my peripheral vision. He crosses the kitchen and kisses my temple. "I love when you blush like this." My cheeks flame hotter.

"Be a gentleman, that is not what I meant," Henry fires back. "Zoe, I just meant that you look more relaxed."

"Gramps, not better," Luke says, laughing.

"I take it back," I announce, turning around to face both of them. "I was going to invite this one," I tip my head toward Luke, "to an event next weekend, and I had Dane all set to fly out here in one of Bruce's planes, maybe even take you up in the air for a joyride, but if you two can't behave…."

Luke's jaw drops and Henry's eyes widen into saucers.

"Way to go, Luke." Henry turns on his grandson, hitting him across the chest.

"You started it!" Luke tosses back, throwing his hands up in the air.

"Zoe, I really just meant that when you show up, you're a little tense from your time in the city. A couple days out here and your smile is brighter," Henry tells me. "I like seeing that smile."

"And there's no way I would take away a flight day for you. Now, whether or not Luke is still invited to go with me is another story."

Chapter Twenty-Two
Luke

Zoe is absolutely blowing me away as she leads me through the grand opening party. Not only is she stunning in her little black dress, but for someone who claims she's uncomfortable in these kinds of social situations, you'd never know it by looking at her. She stops to chat with anyone who tries to get her attention, which is basically everyone, and introduces me as her boyfriend. She laughs freely, poses for pictures, and answers all questions thrown her way. The only indication I get that she's slightly uncomfortable is a tightened grip on my hand when she's approached by a new group. Every single time we excuse ourselves and continue on our way, I feel their eyes on me, judging if I'm good enough for their idol. I already know I'm not. I don't think anyone is.

"If she starts with the bad puns and dad jokes, no one will blame you if you leave her there," her little sister Tatum had told me during dinner, right after Zoe and her dad cracked up over a tomato joke. (Why did the tomato turn red? Because it saw the salad dressing.)

No jokes yet, but I wish there were; it's harder for me to read her here in her world. Everything is different here. Her childhood home is a five bedroom mansion compared to my trailer park life. They have a backyard pool. I have a hose bib leak that's about to form a pond off the back steps. Her mom cried when I showed her the pictures Dane sent of Gramps flying above Rock Beach. According to a hushed conversation I overheard as a kid, my mom didn't even shed a single tear when she left me behind and never looked back. Zoe lives in a two bedroom apartment with her best friends right across the parking lot. My best friends are senior citizens (sorry Jake).

"Hey, where'd you go?" Zoe asks, gently squeezing my hand.

We've finally made it across the large weight room and I can see the man she needs to talk to just a few feet away.

"Sorry, just…I'm not used to all of this, maybe you should have kept Dane as your date," I tell her.

"Hmm," she hums, tilting her head as she looks up at me through long eyelashes. "But then I wouldn't be able to do this." She tips her chin up and presses her vanilla lips to mine.

I huff a small laugh. "That might be a little awkward, you're right."

"Luke, this is the best I've ever felt at one of these and it's because you're here, holding my hand. Also, I'm really enjoying this casual sport coat look," she says, bringing one hand up to pat my chest. She gives me a devilish smile and leans closer. "Although I think it's going to look even better on my bedroom floor later."

"Zoe Last Name Campbell, that's presumptuous," I laugh. "And I can't wait."

"Well, you're going to have to wait a little longer because we need to go talk to Seth," she says with a slight nod at the man she pointed out earlier. "You okay?"

"Your weekends are just a lot different than mine." Understatement of the century. But, as usual, she calmly, easily reassured me without a second thought, and brought it back to just us.

Before she can reply, I squeeze her hand and lead her over to Seth, whose Rolex probably cost at least six months of my living expenses. I shake his hand and instead of dismissing me like many have tonight, he includes me in conversation and asks questions about growing up in a small town. I tell him about being raised by my grandparents, killing hours at the library, and how there's one hidden beach that us locals have managed to keep for ourselves.

"I would have gotten into even more trouble as a teenager than I did," Seth says, shaking his head with a rueful grin. "The third time the cops brought me home, my dad decided it was enough. He dragged me to the gym and introduced me to powerlifting. After that, instead of stealing shit from the 7-Eleven on the corner, I went to the gym."

"Is that why you liked my idea?" Zoe asks, suddenly speaking up. She's been very quiet since we started talking with Seth.

"Absolutely," Seth says. "That introduction to lifting weights probably saved my future and it's definitely why I invested in this gym. I love your idea."

I was following the conversation until now. What idea?

"I suggested that they offer scholarships to teenagers who can't afford a gym membership," Zoe tells me with an embarrassed smile when she sees my confusion. "And I should credit Lucas's friend Jake, a police officer in their town, for the idea. It seems he has similar ideas for some local kids as your dad did with you."

Pride hits me, not just because this amazing woman standing next to me keeps claiming me as her boyfriend, but because she and my best friend (sorry, senior citizens) did this together. Very quietly did this together, as I hadn't heard even a whisper of it from either of them.

"It was more a demand than a suggestion, which I appreciated. It made me take notice," Seth says with a laugh. "And now that you have the wheels turning, I think we could do something big with this. I'd *like* to do something big with this. Can we keep in touch?"

"Absolutely," Zoe nods enthusiastically and bounces slightly on her feet. "I'd love to help market the scholarship program, maybe connect you with the director of the after-school program I volunteer with once the school year starts back up."

"Molly's school?" Seth asks. "She's the one who suggested we invite you tonight. She and my wife were roommates in college."

Zoe lights up. "Yes! I love my time at her school."

They delve into conversation about the after-school program Zoe's a part of and I just stand back and admire my girlfriend and all that she is, all that she does. Watching her here, working an entire room as people clamber to meet her, it's amazing that she can go from this to doing yoga with my elderly grandfather in our tiny living room without missing a beat.

When we finally walk away from Seth, Zoe does her happy dance. It might not be a dad joke, but it's proof she's happy in this moment.

"You're incredible," I whisper in her ear.

She is. There's no doubt about it. At first, I thought her job was selfies and smoothies, yoga and more selfies. But I've learned over the last couple of weeks that she has small group trainings where she connects with a dozen people over a month's time to help them find ways to make their fitness goals a reality; she has an extensive YouTube channel with specialized yoga classes, cooking demonstrations, and a few different workout series that need limited equipment; she works with brands on visibility and marketing; she's even helping design a line of leggings with an up-and-coming local designer. That's all on top of guest teaching all over Portland and maintaining her regular class schedule.

Incredible doesn't even cover it.

***

I can see the tension in Zoe's shoulders from across the room. At first glance I thought it was Seth approaching her, but the man is too lanky. Seth is broad. I keep my eyes on her as I weave my way toward her from the locker room, the only bathroom I could find in this massive building.

"I see more companies are dropping you," the man's voice carries as I draw closer. "Can't say I'm surprised."

"I still have nothing to say to you, Aiden," Zoe replies, her voice barely giving away her anger. "My business is just that, mine." She returns her eyes to her phone.

So this is Aiden. Asshole Aiden, according to her friends that I met for the second time before dinner tonight. Abby quietly told me if I were to punch him in the dick she'd give me a thousand dollars. I had laughed, but now I'm considering it, not for the monetary prize.

"That's a load of bullshit, it's Abby that runs you like a puppet, especially now that I'm not there to help you," he says. "So really, your business is her business. And it's obviously going downhill. You should have broken up with her, not me."

I flash back to that call Zoe was on when she threw her phone. Shit. Was she losing deals because she was with me at the beach, not here for work? Zoe stays silent, still doing something on her phone. I pause,

188

waiting to see if she needs me. After watching her tonight, it's even more apparent that she's capable of handling herself.

"Let me guess, letting Abby decide what to post? Have you ever made a single decision on your own? Is any of this really yours? You started yoga because of your mom. You went to the same college as your dad, same program, same degree. Abby orchestrated your rise to fame. I brought in all those contracts last year," Aiden continues ranting, his eyes narrowed on Zoe's phone. "What's the new guy for? What's he telling you to do?"

Zoe doesn't move, but I can see a slight tremor and her jaw tics. I move closer, settling my palm on her back, silently letting her know I'm here. She tilts her phone toward me so I can see what she's studying. It's a picture that Abby took earlier. In the photo, I'm looking at the camera, but Zoe is gazing up at me, her cheeks flushed. New favorite photo.

"I like that one," I whisper, brushing my lips on her temple.

Zoe leans into me and takes a shallow breath. I can tell by the ways her eyes dart around the room that she doesn't want whatever this is to escalate any further.

"I'm Lucas, the new guy," I say, holding my hand out. I'm still tempted by Abby's offer but maybe if I'm non confrontational, he'll move on, which is obviously what Zoe wants.

Aiden looks me up and down, then slowly reaches out to shake my hand in a crushing handshake. When you've grown up around fisherman and dock workers, that trick doesn't work. My handshake is just as strong and just as steady.

"Aiden," Aiden says curtly, his eyes narrowing slightly when I don't pull back first.

Zoe's still tense beside me, unspeaking.

"For the record, Zoe, I'm telling you that you're smart, kind, funny, and beautiful. I'd never tell you what to do, and after talking to Seth earlier, hearing your ideas, I'm even more blown away by you and what you're already doing on your own and with Abby," I tell her, looking into her dark eyes as soon as they turn my way.

She wraps her arm around my waist and gives me a small smile.

Aiden isn't ready to let it go. "Of fucking course he knows Seth. Is that why he's here? Still using other people's connections? Using their ideas?" Zoe flinches and maybe I'm about to make a thousand dollars. I wonder how much Abby will pay out if I break his nose. My left hand stays steady on her back but my right hand clenches into a fist at my side. "You're not even included in her world, not a single picture. Scared of what they'll say about him, Zoe? What they'll say about you, after me?"

Zoe's head snaps back in his direction. Something in there pissed her off. Her dark eyes flash and she squares her shoulders. I wonder if Abby will pay that thousand dollars to Zoe.

"You know what Aiden? You're right. I don't always make my own decisions. I ask my friends and family for advice all the time. I respect their opinions and know they want what is best for me. Abby is really fucking good at the job I pay her to do, just like I paid you for the shitty contracts you guilted and manipulated me into," she says furiously. "For the record, those companies you said dropped me? I dropped them. Most of them because I didn't even know I was under contract with them. Thanks for that, by the way. I'm guessing the only way you could have found out is if they asked you to get me back for them. That will *not* happen. All that will happen is you'll be hearing from my attorney. And Lucas and I met Seth for the first time an hour ago. I would never use Luke, or anyone, like that, even though you spent a year using me. I should be a pro at it now, thanks to you."

"Z-" Adan cuts her off.

"No. I'm not finished. Before you, Aiden, those comments you were always so worried about? They never bothered me. It was your words that turned them into a monster in my mind. Your words that made me believe I had to be perfect, always on, always ZoeSays, never just Zoe. I keep Lucas off there because what we have is ours. Not anyone else's. Now, please, stay out of my business *and* my life."

Damn. I still want to punch him for making her flinch with his words, but also, damn. I think she needed that.

Zoe removes her hand from my waist and grabs my hand instead, gripping it tightly as she weaves us through the crowded room. I snag a sparkling water off one of the small bars set up inside the squat racks and hand it to her when she finally stops moving.

"Thank you," she says quietly, taking a sip, her eyes on the floor.

"Well, he wasn't my favorite person I've met tonight," I say, trying for a little humor. I hate how her shoulders are hunched forward and I hate the fact she won't look at me even more.

"You can say that again. I'm sorry you had to be part of that."

"I'm here for all the parts," I reply. "Even the not so fun ones. I mean, I do still owe you for fixing my sink."

"I'll bill you," she says, giving me a weak smile.

"You okay?" I run my thumb along her jawline and then tip her chin up slightly, stealing a quick kiss before I search her eyes.

"He's right though. Aiden is right. I don't make my own decisions. I've been struggling all summer, trying to figure out where to go from here, what to do, but I *can't*. Instead I just hide at the beach. I have these pieces of ideas floating around, but it's like my brain doesn't know how to make one single fucking decision," she whispers miserably. Her eyes fill with tears.

"You don't have to have it all figured out, Zoe," I tell her, using my thumb to wipe the tears that spill over.

"I should just take my mom's advice and run away and join a cult; don't cult leaders make all the decisions anyway?" Zoe asks, giving me a wobbly smile.

"I'm really glad your mom didn't give me any life advice at dinner earlier," I reply, wiping the last of her tears. "You want to go?"

She shifts her weight back and forth before nodding. As we make the rounds saying our goodbyes, Zoe once again gripping my hand tightly, I'm still stuck on one thing. It's not until Seth walks us out the door that I realize what it is.

"If I ever wander into your neck of the woods, I'd love to take you and your grandfather to dinner," Seth says as he claps my shoulder.

Wander. Gramps. Run away. Mrs. Campbell. Damnit. Zoe.

***

"Liquid courage," I say, sitting on the edge of Zoe's bed and handing her an americano from the coffee shop just down the street. I keep the cinnamon roll hidden behind my back.

"Uh, is there alcohol in this? What do I need courage for?" she asks, pushing her tangled hair back. I love sleepy, disheveled Zoe. Fuck, I think I love just Zoe. Which makes what I'm about to say even stupider.

191

"No, no alcohol, but I've seen what caffeine does to you," I tell her, watching her take her first sip. I lean forward and kiss her, unable to resist.

She wrinkles her nose at me. "I have morning breath, no kisses."

I kiss her again anyway then run my finger along the line her pillow left on her cheek. She leans into my touch and I can't say it yet. I need another minute. I need another eternity.

"You're about to have cinnamon roll breath," I say, pulling the box from behind my back. Zoe's face lights up. "If they're better than Marabelle's, please don't tell me, or her."

"Oh my god, Lucas Henry Stark, best boyfriend ever." Zoe opens the box and dips her finger in the frosting before slowly licking it off. "Definitely good, definitely not as good as Marabelle's."

Yep, I love her. I love her playfulness, I love her goofy happy dance. I love when full-names me, I love when she calls me "Luke." Why I'm about to ruin the best thing that's ever happened to me, I don't know. But I have to. I spent all night tossing and turning, trying to figure this out.

Around 3 a.m., something she said came back to me. It hit me like a truck, in fact, and I haven't slept since. She said she's been hiding at the beach with me instead of figuring out what to do with her job, her life. I don't necessarily think that's true, at least, I don't think she's been *using* me to hide, but I want her to be happy. Happy on her own, not just happy hiding with me, if that's what she insists on calling it.

After seeing how everyone in attendance gravitated toward her last night, listening to how she persuaded Seth to put a scholarship program into place, I'm more convinced than ever that she's set to do great things. But wherever she goes, whichever direction life takes her, it needs to be her choice. Her decision. Because all that will happen if she continues to hide at the beach like she said, is she'll realize that my life is in my small town, and that can't be enough for her.

Am I about to be a supportive boyfriend by gently encouraging her to spread her wings? Or am I the scared boyfriend, pushing her away before she even has a chance to leave me behind?

Obviously both.

"Zoe," I say, my voice betraying my emotions.

I can't get it out. I can't say it.

She starts to say something, but I cut her off.

Chapter Twenty-Three
Zoe

"Luke, I'm running away," I blurt out, unable to hold it in, especially when he looks at me like that, just as he says...what? "Wait, what did you just say?"

"You should go," he repeats.

"What? I live here."

"Wait, what did you say?"

"I'm running away."

We stare at each other. I can't read his expression. Is this because he had to put his own dream on hold? Or after last night maybe he's realized that my world is too much for him. He's not interested. This is his way out. Any and every dark thought that's run through my brain in the last few restless hours finds its way back to the forefront of my mind. He must see my hurt and confusion because he breaks the silence first.

"Zoe, you said that Gramps told you to wander your way to happiness. And I think you should. Wherever the road leads you, you should go. You said you've been trying to figure it out all summer, trying to find what makes you truly happy. So go do it. Take the opportunity you have. Don't hide from it. Explore, in whatever way feels right to you. Try new things, see new places, sign up for new classes, find a new job. Whatever it takes, you should do it. You need to be happy with yourself, with what you're doing, not hiding from your life with me."

Tears prick my eyes as I take a shuddering breath. Of course he's thinking of me. Of my happiness. He's always thinking of me, of everyone around him. Why would I ever run away from him?

"Why did you say you're running away?" Luke asks, cupping my cheek, his emerald eyes searching mine.

I spent all night tossing and turning, thinking this over. It pisses me off that Aiden was right, but he was. I don't make my own decisions. I mean, granted, two people suggested this new plan, but if I really do it, I'd have to make my own decisions. I'd have to figure my shit out. I wouldn't have a choice. Right? It's not on Luke, Abby, Mom, or anyone else to make me happy. This is my life, my job, my way forward, because the one thing I do know, that I'm absolutely certain of, is that I'm ready for change. Scared, yes, obviously. But ready.

"I just, I'm sorry Luke, but I think if two of the wisest people I know, and please never tell my mom I called her wise, but if they are both suggesting the same thing, maybe I should do it. Aiden was right, I don't make my own decisions. But I wasn't lying when I said I value the opinions of those supporting me, because I do. I know they want what's best for me." I shrug, not really sure what else to say. I just know that I need to do this. "So maybe I should just do it. Actually run away. And then when I'm out there, it's on me, sink or swim. Like you said, try new things, explore, see what makes sense to me."

Luke nods as he listens, a small, dimple-less smile on his face. "What's step one?"

"Well, I don't know. What do you think?"

Oh my god, I'm thirty seconds in and can't do it. How did I let this happen? Was it really Aiden?

It fucking was. From the second he walked into my life, flashing that fake, charming smile, he took over. I let him. I can try to place the blame on him, but I let him. And now here I am, asking my current boyfriend to tell me what to do.

I am broken.

"Zoe, I'm not going to tell you what to do," Lucas says gently. "But I'm happy to help you come up with some ideas, based on what *you* want though."

196

Why am I running away from this sweet, small town boy that only wants what is best for me? Who takes care of his grandpa, who draws maps on pastry boxes, who lit my body and soul on fire with our very first parking lot kiss?

I am an idiot.

"What's one thing you want, Zoe?" Luke prods as I sit frozen.

"I want to go for a hike. Alone." The words burst out of me. I don't think I've ever gone for a solo hike. Even just a short one. "I've always been too nervous, not even because of ZoeSays, hikers are literally the nicest people, but, I don't know. I just never have and I want to."

"I like that one," Luke says softly, smiling.

"I want to eat ice cream for breakfast."

I am ridiculous.

Lucas laughs at my declaration. But it's true, I want to eat ice cream for breakfast. I tell my clients and my followers that health is about balance, but before my newfound cinnamon roll obsession, there was no balance. Also, ice cream is delicious. But I know I need bigger goals as well. I could go for a quick solo hike, stop for ice cream, and be back before mid morning. That's not enough. I want more. I need more.

I chew on my lip. I close my eyes. And I see it.

"I want to see the kind of mountains that you picture when you close your eyes and think of mountains, the kind that make you want to cry because they're so beautiful," I tell Luke, without opening my eyes. "I want to do something I never thought I'd do, that never even crossed my mind as a possibility. I want to take a real risk for once in my life, not these little half-ass risks. A whole-ass risk. And I want to face a fear. Maybe two."

That escalated quickly. Maybe I've been holding onto those things longer than I thought. I open my eyes cautiously, like my entire bedroom might have changed with my declaration, the world might have somehow shifted. I'm not sure what Luke's reaction will be. I'm not sure what *my* reaction will be.

Instead, I open my eyes to the same bedroom, same perfect boyfriend, same Egg-cat who has now made himself comfortable on Luke's lap, glaring at me as usual. Everything is the same. But I'm different. Even with my eyes wide open inside my very plain, neutral apartment, I can see those mountains, their wild beauty against a big sky.

Decision made.

Luke gives me a smile, dimple included this time. While a trickle of excitement starts building in my veins, one smile and I just want to pull him back into bed with me and kiss him until I forget this crazy idea. Make running away mean running to the beach. Hiding in Luke's world. But that isn't what this is. I will not go back on this decision.

"But Luke, I'm scared that I'm going to end up doing this for you," I whisper, realizing it as I say it aloud. "You're too easy to get caught up in. I'll just want to come home to you."

I'm a stage five clinger.

"I get so lost in you, too, Zoe," he says quietly, wiping a tear from my cheek that I didn't even know was there. "Since day one."

Have I done to him what Aiden did to me? Has he even been taking pictures lately? What about his happiness, his dreams? Shit.

I am selfish.

"Will you do something?" I ask him.

"Of course," he immediately replies.

"Take pictures." He frowns. "Lucas Henry Stark, you are an amazing photographer. I know life threw you a curveball, but take some pictures, and not just for work. I've seen you behind the lens, I know that's where you're supposed to be."

"For you, Zoe, yes," he says. "I'll take some pictures."

I smile because I know he'd do nearly anything for me, but I also know that's not what this is supposed to be. I'm supposed to go out and find my own happy, just like I want him to rediscover his. Not for each other, for ourselves.

"Not for me, for you, Luke. Take pictures because it's what you love to do."

Luke nods silently, thoughtfully. "Okay, Zoe Last Name Campbell," he finally says. "You go wander, I'll take some pictures. Just you, just me. Separate. When we're ready, we find a way to show each other. See if we can be you and me."

198

I nod, both loving and hating what I'm agreeing to. Then, much to Egg's dismay, I pull Luke back into bed with me and kiss him until I'll never forget this feeling, no matter what mountains I'm staring at.

***

"You can't change your life trajectory for a boy, no matter how cute his dimple is," Abby states flatly. Egg glares at me from her lap like he's agreeing with her.

Her reaction to my announcement is unsurprising. As were all three of their reactions when I told them about what Asshole Aiden said. The only surprising thing is that, so far, they have agreed not to murder Aiden.

"While I agree, sometimes life has a funny way of taking you just where you need to be," Kristen says, looking at something on her phone, a soft smile playing on her lips.

"This isn't about you and your Hot Firefighter," Casey says from her spot, glancing at Kristen's phone.

"Wait, what?" I ask.

Kristen quickly flips her phone upside down and sets it on the coffee table.

"We're talking about Zoe, not me," she says, glaring at all three of us.

"Okay, I'm not going to lie. He's obviously had a big impact on my life in the last two months, but I was feeling this on *our* beach trip, standing there looking out over the ocean. I was so fucking annoyed with you Abs, when you had to take that video on the hike," I say. "And you were just doing your job! A job I hired you to do that you fucking kick ass at. It started then. No, before then. So don't blame Luke."

"I blame Aiden for everything, if that helps," Kristen interrupts quickly. "We saw it, we know." Abs and Casey nod their agreement.

"You guys, I need this. ZoeSays was just supposed to be for fun," I tell them. "And it was, we worked our asses off but we had so much fun building it up. Then Aiden showed up and I don't know what the fuck happened. He turned ZoeSays into something else entirely. He made it seem like it was my fault if some internet asshole made a sexist comment. He made me believe it was unacceptable to share anything less than perfection, anything that wasn't on brand, meeting a goal, making

199

money. You guys saw me change, I just didn't listen when you tried to talk sense into me. So now I'm trying to fight my way out of that mindset. I feel like so many of my decisions are based on other people, not what I actually want. I don't make decisions to begin with, and when I try to, they're not for myself. I need to live again, like Henry is doing. Live for myself, not for what I think internet strangers want to see. Or even what I think you guys, or Luke, or my family want to see me doing."

"So Aiden was right?" Kristen asks incredulously. "That seems wrong. But also, Zoe, I love you and I'm proud of you."

"He's right about the decision thing. He can go fuck himself about the rest," I say.

It feels good to say that. To realize everything he did. Everything I let him do.

"Am I fired?" Abby asks.

"What? No!" I say quickly. "I mean, do you want to be?"

"Well, no. But also, maybe this is good for both of us. Maybe it's time for me to take a step back." She drops her eyes. "Maybe I can try to reconnect with my sister."

Kristen, Casey, and I exchange worried glances. Erin is not our favorite person, but we really do try to understand that addiction is an illness. It just really, really sucks when we see Abby getting hurt time and time again.

"How's she doing?" Kristen asks timidly.

"Not great," Abby says, her eyes still on the floor. "It just feels like we're getting close to rock bottom."

"Abs," I say, moving to sit next to her.

"No, don't you dare," Abby says suddenly. I freeze. "No, I mean, yes, come sit next to me, but I mean, don't base your decision off Erin, or how I'm feeling about Erin. I have my family, these two, and obviously I'll have emotional support cat Egg."

I sink down next to Abs and emotional support traitor Egg jumps down. Jerk.

"I'll keep paying you," I tell her.

"Zoe, I have other clients, a lot of other clients, you do know that, right?" Abby asks. "I promise, this is a good thing. We can both explore new things, different jobs. But if you do need me to do anything, call. Or let Kelsey take a stab at it. It'd be huge for her."

Huh. There's an idea. Do I really want her to have to deal with assholes? No. But she could edit the hell out of whatever I choose to send her.

"I could be her backup," Kristen offers. "Obviously not on days when I have the kids, but Gabe is taking some time off so I won't be working much the next month."

Kelsey on edits, Kristen on comments. This could work, assuming I choose to share anything with my followers. Do I even want to take them along?

"What do you guys think?" I ask, looking around the room. "Should I do this?"

"Zoe, you said you want to make your own decisions, but you're sitting here basically asking us *if* you should do this, *how* to do this," Casey suddenly says after quietly listening to all of this. "Just fucking do it. We support you. Go do all the things. We'll be here when you get back. If you get back. Call us every day. Or don't call us. I mean, make sure someone knows you're safe, but Zoe. Go do the things."

Holy shit. This is happening. I'm going to go do stupid shit.

Chapter Twenty-Four
Zoe

"Hello internet friends and strangers," I begin, unsure where I'm going with this. When I decided to share this journey, I told myself to be authentic, so here goes nothing. "Zoe here, giving you a real life update. First, welcome to my home, also known as my car." I pan around, showing that I am, indeed, in my car. "Second, don't worry, Egg is being well cared for, he's moved in with Abby and Casey, who I'm pretty sure he likes better anyway. No, I'm certain he does. Third, I am so lucky to do what I do, especially since my best friend works with me. We've worked hard to build this community and I'm so thankful you've followed along on my journey. But today, I'm setting out on a different kind of voyage, and this is your official invitation to join me.

"I started ZoeSaysSoFitness as a fun way to document my life, a photo journal of my yoga evolution, a creative outlet, and it grew into what it is now. Abby and I, along with Kristen and Casey in the early days, worked our asses off to get us here, but I'm overwhelmed, to say the least.

"Don't get me wrong, there are so many parts of this that I absolutely love. I love teaching and sharing yoga with you, working with my small group clients, introducing people to new ways to look at fitness and health. I love connecting with you all in the real world, hearing your stories."

I stop. I do love those things. I stare blankly at the camera. What am I doing? I have an amazing job. Why did I think this was a good idea? I bring my hand up to run it through my hair and catch sight of my sunset tattoo and my bracelets from Mary and Luke. Two different trips, two different times I thought about what my job was and what I wanted it to become.

"But, I've let the bad parts grow, and, if this was a break up, it'd be the perfect time for me to tell you that it's not you, it's me. *I've* let this happen. I let myself get caught up in relationships and partnerships that were not healthy for me. I let myself believe that this, ZoeSaysSo, is the best part of me, maybe the only part of me that people like and want to see, and for some of you, that may be true. That's fine. But what it's done to me is not fine. I second-guess every decision I make, wondering what strangers on the internet will think. That's not okay. That's not the life I want to live. I've been making changes, changes that mean a lot to me, but it's time to go bigger. It's time for something real."

I blow out a breath and look out the windshield at my childhood home. I don't think I've ever been more than one hundred miles from this house without someone with me. No wonder why Mom told me to run away. It's well past time for me to spread my wings.

"I realize this sounds crazy, but when I asked my mom for advice, she actually told me to run away." I laugh and shake my head. "But I'm taking that advice. I have a little bit of a to-do list but my updates might be sporadic. They're also going to be a little messy, a little more like how this all started, just me, sharing my life. First on my list: wander, as a very smart man suggested, or perhaps run away, as my mom said. Yep, I'm getting on the open road, no real plan, so let's see where I end up. Until next time, friends." I blow a kiss to the camera and wave.

Before I can overthink it, I send the video to Kelsey, who very enthusiastically agreed to be my on-the-go editor, and take a deep breath.

This is it. Here I go.

Wait, do I have my second charger? Yes.

I'm doing this. Right now. Here I go.

Hold on, did I forget my, okay, Luke's hoodie? Nope, it's sitting right on the passenger seat.

Okay, *now* I mean it. Here I go.

A knock on the window scares the shit out of me. Tatum's grinning at me. I glare at her but roll down my window.

"Hey, Zoe, you've been sitting here for like twenty minutes, staring out the windshield like a weirdo," she says. "Just thought I'd come check on you."

"Okay, okay, I'm going. I really am," I tell her. I am. Here I go.

"Good, because if you wait too much longer, Mom's probably going to come out," Tate says. "And I hate to think what other advice she'd come up with."

"Fair point. Thanks, Little T."

"Love you, ZoeBear," she says. "Now please leave. I'm ready to be an only child."

"Love you, TatorTot." With that, I back out of the driveway.

Here I go.

Wander: check.

***

Turns out, when you wander, you get lost. And when you get lost, you contemplate sleeping in your car. When you contemplate sleeping in your car, you wonder if you're going to be kidnapped from the side of the dark highway.

"Fuck fuck fuckity fuck," I say, laying my forehead on the steering wheel. I think I've cursed more today than I have in the last year. If only that was on my to-do list.

Curse like a sailor: check.

This is fine. Everything is fine. Making my own decisions is going *really* well, thanks for asking. It's not like I've spent the entire drive overanalyzing every decision I've made in my life, up to and including pulling out of the driveway this morning.

Driving into the Columbia River Gorge was amazing. Tall trees along a winding road, I had an americano in my cup holder, The Chicks were singing about wide open spaces, and all four tires were still firmly planted in Oregon. As the trees gave way to the arid landscape of the eastern side of my home state, you know, actual wide open spaces, nerves settled in. Washington is where I really started questioning my ability to find my way, in life and on this stupid roadtrip. There was really only one way to go when I hit Spokane, east, and Idaho came and went before I knew it. When I hit the Montana border, that's when the real panic set in.

I take one more look at the setting sun behind me and my hand goes to my necklace. I swallow the lump in my throat and take a deep breath.

This. Is. Fine.

Make. A. Fucking. Decision.

I have just enough cell service to pull up my AirBnb app. I'll let Airbnb decide for me. Cheating? Maybe.

Montana Glamping Outfitters. Cute lakeside guest cabin or your choice of luxury "glamping" tents. Mountain views, instant book, available tonight. I'm sold. I can drive two more hours.

Two hours and multiple near-suicidal deer later, I pull into the driveway of a more-rural-than-I-thought cabin, knuckles white as I grip the steering wheel. Perhaps dark highway car camping was actually the better option. I can see a few large "glamp-sites" further down the meadow, a campfire glowing between two of them, so at least there are other humans within the vicinity.

This is ridiculous. I am being ridiculous. I'm a grownass adult doing grownass adult things. I grab my backpack from the front seat, double check that I have the door entry code, and march my scared ass up to the front door. With shaking fingers, I key in the code. Nothing happens.

Fuck fuck fuckity fuck.

I try again. The lock clicks open and I feel like an idiot. I swing the door open and then hastily shut it (and lock it) behind me. Safe.

I shake my head, laughing at myself for being so ridiculous. I fumble for the hall lightswitch and warm light fills the cozy cabin. I can't wait until morning when the lake is more than an inky black expanse stretching toward the dark, moonlit mountains. First thing on my list is definitely lakeside coffee and yo-

I choke as my heart leaps into my throat, a scream somehow still working its way out, echoing around the small space. I taste blood in my mouth and stumble backwards into the door.

Holy fucking shit. A bear is staring at me from the living room.

Note to self: look at AirBnb pictures more closely so as not to be startled by taxidermied predators.

When I've stopped maniacally laughing and my heart moves from my throat back to my chest, I take a quick tour of my home for the next two nights. The bitter taste of adrenaline is slowly waning as I sink onto the couch farthest from the snarling bear. You know, just in case.

Now what? I have the overwhelming urge to check my social media. My fingers actually itch. What kind of messed up addiction is this?

On a whim, I delete Instagram, SnapChat, TikTok, and YouTube from my phone. Yes, I still want to document this weird trip, whatever it ends up being, but no, I don't want or need to see the comments. I don't want to be influenced by anyone else, friend or foe, real life or internet stranger. I don't need their validation. I just need to remind myself of that on a very regular basis.

What I do want and maybe need is to return to what makes me happy: photo and video journaling. I want this for me. To look back on and remember the highway meltdowns and taxidermied bear attacks. To show my weird mom, Tate and Dad, Abby and the girls, Dane and Chase, Henry and, I hope, Luke.

Just thinking about Luke hurts. I wonder how many pictures he took today. I wonder how Henry's day went at the library. Which recipe did they try? I want to tell Luke about my day, like I usually do, hear his laugh when I tell him about the bear incident. But I can't. This is for me.

I can start on my own journal though. I set my phone on a bookshelf instead of braving the dark to dig my tripod out of the car and hit the little red circle.

"Hey, Luke, it's Day One and I'm feeling a little like I'm failing. Wait, why did I just say Luke?"

I manage to start my first video diary as awkwardly as possible. Why didn't I just say "Day One" at the very start? I close my eyes and sigh. Why does everything feel foreign right now? I make videos for a living and suddenly I can't even do that? Oh, great, I didn't even stop recording. I guess this is going to be a very real video diary. Well, wasn't that the goal? Real decisions, real experiences, real story telling? I blow out a breath and look back at my phone.

"Hi, wow, I'm a little bit of a mess right now. Day one. I'm near Flathead Lake in Montana, at an AirBnb I booked a few hours ago as I was having a meltdown on the side of a deserted highway at sunset, which I thought was going to be the low point of the day. Instead, the low point was, well, wait, a visual aid is helpful."

I pick up my phone and turn so the giant snarling bear is over my shoulder.

"The low point was when I saw my new roommate and screamed bloody murder. Not joking. I'm honestly surprised no one called 911. So you could say things are going great. But I'm doing this. What this is, I don't know. But I'm doing it."

Chapter Twenty-Five
Zoe

"Come on babe, we're going out," Jules, my AirBnb host, calls. "No one at The Dive will realize who you are, and if they do and they make it weird, the bartender will kick their ass."

I should have known something like this was going to happen. Jules caught me teary-eyed as I stared at the mountains across the lake this morning and decided to save me from myself. By teary-eyed I mean crying. Ugly crying. Borderline sobbing.

Cry-worthy mountains: check.

I thought she was done saving me after her sales pitch on hiking Glacier National Park, which, by the way, I was easily sold on. I was also easily sold on the bear spray canister one of the "glampers" asked if I wanted, since they were headed to the airport after a week in the area. I forgot to ask if it will work on my taxidermied living room predator. I'm guessing not.

I have another internal debate on whether all of this counts as someone else making decisions for me, then I say fuck it, and pull off Luke's hoodie. I grab one of the few non-athletic tops I packed and glance in the mirror. Can you tell I'm an emotional train wreck that cohabitates with a dead bear? Maybe.

"Put this on," Jules says when she catches sight of my tank top. She hands me a leather jacket and ushers me out the door before I can ask any questions.

I shrug the jacket over my shoulders and burst into laughter when I see what adventure awaits. I take a quick picture of the Harley before strapping on the helmet Jules hands me. I can't decide if this feeling that has my stomach rolling is overwhelming excitement or sheer terror. When Jules accelerates onto the highway, I realize it's absolutely the latter and I curse my mom for her terrible advice.

By the time Jules parks in front of The Dive On Inn Bar and Grill, I'm wishing we could keep riding. My mom is a genius. I guess I should have added her "stupid shit" to my list.

Ride a motorcycle: check.

"That was amazing!" I exclaim as I pull my helmet off, adrenaline still pumping through my veins.

Jules laughs at my wild expression, or maybe my wild helmet hair because she reaches out and tries to tame it for me before leading me into the bar. It's a small town, so a lot of heads swivel our way as we walk in, but only a few do the nudge-and-whisper thing that I usually take to mean they recognize me. Although this time I think it's Jules they're looking at as a few raise their hands in greeting or call out her name.

"Hey Jules, who's your friend?" A petite blonde bartender greets us when we belly up to the curved, copper bar.

"Katy, this is Zoe, my current AirBnb guest, who is kinda a hot mess. Zoe, meet my favorite bartender, Katy-with-a-Y." Jules doesn't mince words in her introduction but she's not wrong.

"What can I get you?" Katy asks.

Jules turns to me expectantly. Normally I'd order a vodka soda and only have one or stick with sparkling water with lime. Hashtag fitness. What do normal people order at a bar?

Now I can't even decide what to drink, great. Jules and Katy look at each other.

"Just my usual," Jules says. I watch as Katy fills a large glass with ice and then adds…Coke? Jules turns to me and shrugs. "I don't drink. Which means I can drive you home, assuming you can still hold on, so maybe let loose for once. I get the feeling you don't really do that."

"And?" Katy looks at me again.

"Beer," I blurt out. "Something local?"

When is the last time I had a beer? Have I ever had a beer? Like a real beer, not a Michelob Ultra that I drink half of before tossing.

I'm pretty sure Katy-with-a-Y sighs. She gives me a hard look before pouring me a Bonsai Pretty in Pink. I feel like she's giving me a test that I really want to pass.

"Good choice," the guy next to me says, looking at my pink tank under my borrowed leather jacket.

I take a small sip. Katy read me right. I close my eyes and take another drink, enjoying the crisp, hoppy taste, the noise from the rowdy crowd near the pool tables, and the adrenaline that's still buzzing through my veins from the ride over.

"Nope, nice try, Stan," Jules says and I open my eyes to find the guy next to me watching me very, very closely. "Zoe, you any good at darts?"

I give the man a polite smile and then trail after Jules to the back corner of the bar. I lead our team to a massive loss against two of Jules's friends, Hope, who runs the glamping side of their business, and Morgan, a river guide. Turns out, I am not good at darts. In fact, I'm terrible.

"It's a bar game, you just need another beer," Morgan says, nodding with conviction.

"Seems like solid advice," I tell her. "Another round? On me?"

They all nod so I find a spot at the end of the bar and wait for Katy or one of the other bartenders to make their way down the line.

"So, Zoe, you are Zoe, right?" The guy from the bar, Stan, I think, is back. I guess, technically, I'm back at the bar, but he was not here when I stepped up to get Katy's attention.

He waves his phone at me. I can tell which picture he has pulled up, just based on the flash of color in my peripheral vision. He went *way* back to find that picture. Years. That's commitment to scrolling.

"I am Zoe, nice to meet you," I say politely.

Katy makes eye contact from halfway down the bar and I hold my glass up and motion for a round of three. She nods, understanding my hand signals, and shoots a glare at Stan, but he's back to staring at teenage-me on his phone. It's really hard not to cringe.

"Why don't you let me get this round for you," Stan says, looking back up at present-day-me, somehow moving even further into my personal space despite the barstool I put between us.

"Oh, that's really nice, but no thank you," I say, holding my ground.

"Come on, Zoe, let me be a nice guy," Stan says, leaning on the bar, making me feel trapped between him and the pillar behind me. "One drink. Get to know the locals."

"I have a boyf-" I start before getting cut off.

"Nope. Stop right there. Full stop," Katy says loudly, setting three beers on the bar in front of me. I freeze at her tone. When Jules said the bartender would kick anyone's ass, I assumed she meant the burly guy that's serving an older couple at the end. Now I realize she meant this petite blonde badass in bright pink stilettos. "She said no. It doesn't matter if she has a boyfriend or not. You offered. She said no. That's the end."

It hits me that I *don't* know if I have a boyfriend or not and my breath hitches. Luke, with his green eyes, easy dimpled smile, and the hidden heat that hides behind his steadiness. I can almost feel him, pressing me into the pillar, playful smile on his lips.

Instead, I have Stan, who throws his hands into the air. "Oh, come on, Katy. You know me, I'm just trying to be a nice guy, welcome her into town. See if she wants to stay a while."

"Don't give me that shit, Stan," Katy says. "For that, you're buying this nice girl a drink and then keeping your ass on that barstool. One step in her direction, or anyone else's for that matter, and you're out."

"Bu-" Stan argues.

"No." She turns to me. "Coke for Jules?" I bet Katy never had an issue making her own decisions.

"Oh, yeah, thanks," I reply, watching as she quickly grabs another glass and fills it with ice. Stan shifts next to me.

"Ass on the stool, Stan," Katy says, her eyes never leaving the glass that's filling with soda. She barely gives me a nod when she sets the glass of Coke next to my three beers, doesn't spare a glance at Stan who is sulking on his barstool, and moves to the next person trying to get her attention.

I drop the beers and Jules's Coke at the table and duck into the hallway to find the bathroom. I need a minute. When I step back out, shaking my hands in the air thanks to a broken hand dryer, I run into Stan. Like actually run into him, wet bathroom hands directly on his chest and everything.

"Zoe, fancy meeting you here," he says, putting his hands out to catch me as I stumble. He leaves a hand on my hip as he leans against the wall, keeping the hallway partially blocked.

I take a large step back, out of his grasp. I don't even think of putting on my ZoeSays smile and dealing with him that way. Instead, I channel my inner Bartender Katy-with-a-Y.

"Stan, I have no interest and you're making me uncomfortable. Back up, now," I say, my voice only slightly shaky. He doesn't move closer but he doesn't let me pass either. He just keeps his eyes on me, waiting to see what I do.

"Stan, you have half a second to get out of my bar." Katy's voice is not shaky. She's petite enough that she's hidden from my view by Stan, but that's definitely her.

"Well, my night just got twice-" Stan starts, shifting so he stands between us, looking Katy up and down appreciatively.

"Time's up," Katy says flatly.

"Oh, come on, Monty," Stan protests, as the huge bartender materializes behind Katy.

Monty levels Stan with a murderous look that would make anyone think twice. Stan throws his hands up and storms down the hallway. Katy stalks after him on hot pink heels. Stan's abrupt departure elicits cheers from at least half of the females in the place.

"You okay?" Jules asks when I return. She hands me my beer.

"Honestly?" I ask her. She nods. "I think I'm in love with the bartender. One sec."

I make my way over to the bar. Monty raises an eyebrow at me. "Next round, for every female in here, is on me."

My cover is quickly blown when Katy tells me I have to announce it to the bar, but I happily pose for pictures before paying my

213

tab, with a very large tip included, and Monty walks us out. The ride home is zero terror, all exhilaration. Just before we pull in the driveway, I realize that maybe I didn't get kicked out of a bar like my mom suggested, but someone did. I'm counting it. I don't know if I want to remember what else was on her list.

Kicked out of a bar: check.

I sit on the front porch of my cabin for a few minutes, smiling as I look at the pictures from tonight on my phone. This is how ZoeSays started, pictures of my life. I should have just started scrapbooking with Aunt Eileen. Although then I wouldn't have met so many of the people in my life, Lucas and Henry included.

I laugh when I see the picture that Monty took of Jules and I on her motorcycle outside the bar. I start a new album and label it Life Changes, deciding to keep track of the moments along this journey that help guide me on my way. Before I come down off this high, I record my video diary.

"Hey Luke, Day Two. And I guess that means I'm just starting all videos that way. Which makes sense, because I miss talking to you every night. Still in Montana. Had my second meltdown of the trip, but this one was about how beautiful the mountains are. Checked that off my list. I'm heading to Glacier National Park tomorrow, probably going to cry at more mountains, hopefully solo hike. I've somehow ended up checking things off my mom's crazy list. Motorcycle, check. Kicked out of a bar, check." I laugh. I can't believe both of those things happened. I shake my head. "I don't know, despite this not going at all how I envisioned it would, I think I'm on the right road. I just, I just miss you."

I really, really do. But I'm still doing this. One day at a time. And today was pretty rad, meltdowns, motorcycles, and all.

After a quick shower, I curl up in bed with the second book Luke and I were supposed to read together, A Man Called Ove. I remember the selfie I sent Lucas when reading at the beach and snap another. I add it to our shared album, wondering if he will see it. I go back and add the two videos as well. Then I start reading about a grumpy old man and wish I would have FaceTimed Henry earlier. I settle for sending him the picture Jules took of me sitting on her Harley. He'll get a kick out of that one.

**

214

Iceberg Lake is even more beautiful than I had imagined after hearing Jules's description. Calm, turquoise waters with a backdrop of towering cliffs. I can't catch my breath and it has nothing to do with the hike (which was challenging and every single noise sounded like an impending grizzly attack, not of the taxidermied nature). I stand and stare in wonder, unable to look away. Then I drop my pack and my bear spray next to a large, flat rock and climb up, sitting cross-legged, dropping my hands to my knees.

Even with other hikers enjoying the lake, it's so incredibly peaceful. I let my eyes close as I focus on my breathing. Inhale, hold, exhale. Over and over. It feels like my heart is pumping a double dose of adrenaline, still on a high from my solo hike up, my breaths fighting to calm the exhilaration thrumming through my veins. The clash of emotions makes my measured breathing falter and my eyes fill with tears. I let them fall, I let myself feel it all. I tip my head back and just breathe.

Solo hike: check.

When I finally climb down from my rock, I feel empowered, un-fucking-stoppable. I leave my pack and walk to the water's edge. I untie my hiking boots and toe them off, pulling my socks off one at a time. I dip my toes in and gasp. Obviously I expected Iceberg Lake to be icy cold, but holy shit, that's cold. Maybe I am stoppable.

I slip on my boots, retreat to my pack, and dig out a granola bar and my phone. I take a few pictures of the lake and then shove my phone back in the front pocket of my pack.

"Excuse me," a woman's voice interrupts my thoughts.

I look up and a woman about my mom's age is giving me a tentative smile. She's holding her phone toward me.

"Hi," I say cautiously. I'm still having a little bit of a moment but I don't want to be rude.

"Not to be weird, but I noticed you were alone, and I love taking pictures, so I snapped a few when you were meditating. It looked like an important moment for you. Can I AirDrop them to you before I delete them?" she asks.

"Oh, wow, thanks," I say. It *was* an important moment. I pull my phone back out. "Hi, I'm Zoe."

"Nice to meet you, I'm Emily," the woman says. She hands me her phone. "Here, just do the technology for me so my teenagers don't make fun of me. Then you can delete them."

I laugh, thinking of Tatum and how frustrated she gets with our parents and their tech questions, half of which I'm pretty sure they ask just to make her mad. I zoom in on a couple of the pictures Emily got and damn, I love them. She got one from the back, my messy braid running down my tall spine, the perfect Sukhasana yoga pose, but the lake and cliffs in the background are the real show stopper. This is the exact picture Abby would have set up if she was here.

"I didn't realize what a moment it might have been, so when I saw that," she nods to the one I'm looking at now, where you can see a trail of tears making their way down my cheek, "I stopped. It was just a mom instinct to take the pictures, sorry if this is weird."

I love this picture. This is the photo that Luke would have taken, the one that makes you feel the emotions I was breathing through. I close my eyes and see what he would have done differently. He would have waited another half second, until I tilted my head toward the sky, showing my slight smile as I soaked in the moment.

"No, honestly, thank you, Emily. I think you just saved me," I say, opening my eyes again. She looks slightly alarmed. "No, no, I just mean that it *was* a moment, then I chickened out on the *next* moment. But now, I'm going to do it. So, thank you." I finish AirDropping myself the pictures and hand her phone back to her.

Emily returns to her teenage daughters who both look a little embarrassed, as teenagers tend to be by most things their moms do, and I return to the water's edge with newfound determination. I pull my tank top over my head and kick my boots off, sliding my phone inside one, which I immediately regret, knowing how sweaty my feet were. And then I stand there. And stand. And stand some more. I close my eyes, fighting tears. Of all the things to get me, really?

"Let's do it," a voice next to me says.

"We got this," another voice says from my other side.

Emily's daughters are standing on either side of me, matching determined glints in their eyes.

"Okay," I tell the girls. I take a deep breath and reach my hands out, grasping theirs tightly.

The graceful, serene entrance that I had pictured turns out to be stumbling over rocks, shrieking and laughing with the two girls, before finally ducking under the crystal clear water. The water is so cold it takes my breath away. I laugh at the blank slate feeling that washes over me. These cold plunge people might be onto something.

Cold plunge: check.

"Oh my god, I just swam in a lake in the middle of freaking Montana with ZoeSaysSo," the younger sister says, collapsing on the rocks next to me after we stagger our way back out of the lake. Luckily the sun has warmed the rocks; I stretch out like a lizard seeking heat, goosebumps covering my entire body.

"What is ZoeSaysSo?" the older sister asks, looking around.

"Oh, that's me," I say sheepishly. "Hi, I'm Zoe."

"Ugh, I cannot believe you still don't do social media. Strava doesn't count," the younger one says. "Hi, I'm Mia. And that's Reese."

"Strava counts, I mean, if you want it to count," I tell Reese.

Reese laughs as her sister sputters. Emily walks over, smiling at her two girls. She hands her phone to me and the girls and we scroll through the pictures and videos she just took. Once again, she really caught some good ones. You can see our muscles tense as we make our way into the water, our shocked expressions as we resurface sends all three of us into fits of laughter, but what I love the most is the looks on our faces as we collapsed on the rocks.

Suddenly Mia freezes. "Oh my god, am I going to be in one of your TikToks?" she asks, her eyes alight with hope.

"Well, that's probably up to your mom, but if she says it's okay, then definitely," I tell her.

Mia gives a very Kelsey-esque squeal and falls back on the rocks dramatically, her hand over her heart. Reese rolls her eyes.

"Did I break her?" I ask Reese.

"She's been broken for a while," Reese stage whispers, shaking her head.

"Mom, this is Zoe, and she's like super famous. Can I be on the internet with her? You know, the World Wide Web? The Googles?" Mia asks her mom, still lying with her hand over her heart.

Emily laughs and nods, Mia fist pumps the sky. I AirDrop myself a few of the pictures, the one of the girls and I holding hands as we stumble into the water goes directly into the Life Changes album as does the one of us successful and shivering.

"How long are you guys here for?" I ask, trying to prolong this conversation, not quite ready to end my time with the three of them.

"We're heading to Yellowstone tomorrow, we're camping there for like a week," Reese says.

"I have actually never been camping," I tell them. "It wasn't really my family's thing, and I never thought to give it a try on my own. Or even with my friends."

"We have two sites booked and the other family can't come anymore," Mia tells me excitedly. "You should camp with us!"

"Okay, Mia, I'm sure Zoe has plans," Emily breaks in, mouthing "sorry" to me.

"I mean, technically, I don't. But I can't just crash your family trip," I tell the cute trio. "As I'm sure Mia knows, I'm just on a bit of an extended wander, seeing where life takes me."

"I love that, good for you," Emily says, sounding very mom-ish, but normal-mom-ish not *my* mom-ish. "And really, the extra tent site can be yours if you want it. They just canceled on us yesterday. So, if you wander to Yellowstone any time in the next week, come find us. I'll let the girls set their tent up but we can easily move it if you wander our way."

"I'll DM you!" Mia helpfully suggests, sounding hopeful.

"Oh, I actually deleted those apps for this trip," I tell her. She gapes at me like I've grown a second and possibly third head. Reese gives her sister a smirk. "But I'm due to check in with Kelsey, so I'll make sure she gets the videos and pictures your mom took. And I'll give you my number."

"Old school," Mia breathes, her eyes wide.

I exchange numbers with Emily and thank her profusely for the offer. I retreat back to my rock and let my leggings and sports bra dry as I stretch out in the sun, soaking up the view. I have another snack before I pack up and head down the trail. I keep my bear spray handy, but I don't spend the whole hike back convinced a bear is going to eat me. Instead, I contemplate where I should wander next. Maybe I *should* try camping.

Chapter Twenty-Six
Luke

That motivation, inspiration, whatever it was that I felt driving home from Zoe's? That was short-lived. I haven't taken a single picture since getting home. Not one. Not even for work, I've pushed those off on Kelsey. Instead, I fixed the porch steps like Gramps asked, worked extra hours since Tex is sick, and sat in the corner of the library, glaring at the travel section as Gramps happily perused the stacks.

"Can you just take the fucking picture?" Jake asks impatiently.

We're at the end of the trail on Cascade Head and I'm trying to set up the perfect shot. All I can think about is that this is the hike that Zoe did just before walking into The Mercantile. Into my life. If I close my eyes, I can see the video of her spinning in a circle, arms outstretched, happy smile, hair flying in the wind, endless ocean waves as her backdrop.

"Just give me a minute," I tell him, eyeing the cloud cover. The light isn't right. This isn't going to work.

"It's been twenty minutes and you haven't taken a single picture," Jake says.

Fuck. I thought it had been five minutes, max. I think I've lost it. Whatever *it* is. The thing that guides my shot.

"Fuck it, it's not working," I say and shove my camera back in its bag. "Let's go."

I stomp off down the trail, back toward my beat up truck that I'll drive to my beat up trailer that I can barely pay the bills on. What a joke, thinking I'd ever be able to do this. That my pictures could lure my girlfriend back. My girlfriend, who is destined for so much more, which she's probably realizing at this exact moment. I hike faster, avoiding eye contact with the few hikers I pass, not even giving them a "hello," and ignoring Jake behind me. The quicker I get off this trail, the better.

It takes me at least five minutes to realize Jake isn't behind me. I slow down, then stop, waiting to hear him coming down the trail. Shit. Did he somehow get hurt? Did the do-gooder stop to help someone else? I hurry back toward the meadow.

"What the fuck, man?" I ask, when I find him sitting on the same goddamn rock.

"Just waiting for you to take a single picture," he retorts, leaning back on his pack, like he has all the time in the world. He even checks his watch and stretches his legs out.

"I can't," I tell him.

He watches me evenly, not moving a muscle. Just waiting. I rub the back of my neck.

"Bullshit. You can take a picture. Just take one single picture, even if it's a shitty one," he says, a bored expression on his face, like this is a normal day, not the day Zoe realizes she's better off without me.

I just stare at him. What else is there to do? We're in two different realities. All he's losing is a workout partner, which for him, I'm sure they're a dime a dozen. I'm losing Zoe. *Zoe.* The person who FaceTimes Gramps just to make him smile. Whose dark eyes see more of me than anyone has before. Who fits so perfectly in every part of my life.

"You really gonna make me give you a motivational speech?" Jake asks. "Should I go with 'the first step is the hardest' or more of a tough love approach? I'm better at tough love, this is a good chance to work on the supportive way I guess."

Why did I invite him along? I should have left him at the gym. Wait, he invited me. Shit.

"Lucas, it's always the fi-" he starts.

He's really going to do it? Asshole.

"No, stop. I'll take a fucking picture." I set my pack back down and fumble with the zipper.

222

"What are you scared of? It's not even about the picture," Jake continues. "She doesn't actually care about the pictures, I mean, she does, but she cares about *you*, man. Just you."

I pretend not to hear him, like his words aren't piercing daggers into my heart. He doesn't understand, it *is* about the pictures. This is the way to get her back, the only way, assuming she even comes back to begin with. I yank my camera bag from my pack and stalk away from him before he can say more. Before I snap back that he's right, I am scared.

I'm scared of wanting to dream again. I can't walk away from Gramps so where would my dreams lead? It's just a dead-end road.

I'm scared of Gramps ending up in a retirement home. I'm scared of Gramps *needing* a retirement home and not being able to afford his care.

I'm scared of Zoe leaving for good, realizing she's meant for so much more. Realizing I'm not worth staying for, just like my parents realized twenty years ago.

I'm scared of not being good enough. For Zoe or for my dream.

I just hope he's right about the other part, too.

I know he is. Zoe cares about everyone. I just don't know if I deserve her. I can't even take one picture.

I set up my shot and half-heartedly snap a handful of pictures looking south over the Salmon River estuary. The same picture that nearly everyone takes at the end of this trail. I pause. I remember hiking Silver Falls with Zoe. How she made it fun. How I wanted to find a unique shot for her. How the light filtered through the trees, shining down on her. Her smile, her laughter.

I started falling in love with her that day. And then I told her to leave.

"Let's go, asshole," I tell Jake as I storm past him.

"Well, that backfired," Jake mutters.

Our hike back down to the truck is silent.

***

"Don't leave your muddy boots there, we have guests coming," Gramps barks as soon as I step in the door.

"Jake doesn't count as a guest," I tell him.

223

"Ouch, man," Jake says, shoving me. He steps back outside and moves our boots under the chairs, well out of the way.

I pause. "What's that smell?"

"The roast will be done in an hour, our guests should be here any time," Gramps says, calmly folding laundry as he sits on the couch, stacking folded shirts on the coffee table in front of him.

"Smells great!" Jake chimes in. "I'll work on the salad." He steps into the kitchen and I can hear him wash his hands.

"Gramps, what is going on?" I ask.

"Just thought we should have a nice dinner if we have friends coming," Gramps says. "There, go put yours away." He nods to the stack of laundry that's mine.

I grab the small stack of shirts and stalk down the hallway. Something catches my eye when I set the laundry on my dresser. A Man Called Ove. The next book Zoe and I were going to read together. I know it was not on my bed before. What is Gramps up to?

"I know you had a hand in this," I tell Jake when I pull my shit together and return to the kitchen.

"Can't a guy just ask his good friend to go on a hike on a specific day for a specific amount of time?" Jake replies, grinning like the asshole he is. He dumps cucumbers on top of the salad and puts the bowl in the refrigerator before washing the cutting board.

I lean against the counter as Jake starts to slice the french bread. Is it her? It can't be. She's only been gone a few days. I hear a car in the driveway and my heart manages to hope that it's her laugh I'll hear at the door.

Male voices filter through to the small kitchen. I hear Gramps laugh and welcome his guests to our "humble abode." I sigh and start toward the living room, Jake following me out of the kitchen. Might as well get whatever this is out of the way.

"Lucas! Are you coming with us tomorrow?" Dane asks, pulling me in for a bro-hug as soon as I step into the room.

"Hey man, I didn't know you were coming," I say, clapping his back, genuinely happy to see him. "You must be Chase, nice to meet you in person." I offer my hand to the tall, dark-haired man in glasses that I've only seen in pictures and heard over the phone.

"I've heard a lot about you," Chase says, shaking my hand. He turns to Jake. "Hi, I'm Chase. The guy staring at your much bigger and much more masculine biceps is my worse half, Dane."

"Jake. Nice to meet you both," Jake says, laughing and shaking their hands. Dane really is staring at Jake's massive arms. Seeing them next to each other, it's no wonder Zoe easily befriended Jake, he's just a bigger, blonder Dane.

"Dinner is almost ready, why don't you boys go sit out back while I finish up?" Gramps says. "Grab a beer, relax."

"I'll help you with dinner," Chase volunteers.

I stand frozen on the spot, unsure what is happening. Gramps cooks? Does laundry? Invites people that aren't Nancy and Jake over? He's definitely up to something, I just can't tell what.

Jake grabs a few beers from the fridge, shoves me toward the back door, and motions for Dane to follow. They sink into the chairs and twist the tops off their beers, clinking the bottles together before taking long pulls. I lean against the doorframe, trying not to be amused by how similar their mannerisms are.

"So, are you guys coming with us tomorrow? Bruce is bringing the bigger plane," Dane says. "We've got a couple extra seats."

"I honestly have no fucking clue what's going on. I didn't even know you were coming," I tell him, confused as hell. Did Zoe set this up?

"Oh, well, Henry and I were chatting the other day and he mentioned how Zoe's pictures made him wish he had traveled more, so, we're going exploring," Dane says with a shrug. Because flying in a private plane on a whim is normal for him. I didn't even realize Gramps and Dane talked.

"She's sending him pictures?" Jake asks. "I can't even get a text back."

"Same," Dane says, shaking his head. "But that Instagram reel is amazing. It's so Zoe."

Jake nods in agreement. "Glad she-"

"Where are you taking Gramps?" I interrupt, not wanting to go down the path this conversation seems to be taking.

"Just a day trip," Dane tells me, misreading my interruption as concern. "He says he's never been to Astoria and you used to watch The Goonies all the time. Bruce knows a guy so we'll have a car."

"It seems like Bruce knows a guy everywhere," I mutter.

"Oh, he absolutely does," Dane replies cheerfully, ignoring my piss-poor attitude. "It's best if you just roll with it."

"Well, I have to work," Jake says. "So I'm out."

What can my excuse be? That I just don't want to? The door behind me opens.

"Luke is coming," Gramps announces. "And dinner is ready."

I guess I'm going flying.

***

"Do you have your camera?" Gramps asks. "I want to make sure I have pictures to show Zoe."

I flinch at her name. After hearing she's been sending Gramps pictures, I had to see her Instagram updates for myself. I watched the reel from Iceberg Lake a dozen times. She didn't hide behind her ZoeSaysSo smile at all, it was Real Zoe through and through. It was honest, raw, and her tears gutted me. Her beaming smile at the end was somehow even more painful.

I watched it again and again, then tossed my phone across the room. It was a reminder that she's out there doing what I hoped she'd do, slipping farther away, while I'm here, failing to find my own way.

"I've got my camera," I reassure Gramps, patting the bag.

I didn't want to bring it. I didn't want another reminder that I'm failing. That I'm not good enough. That even my dream abandoned me.

As soon as we reach the airfield though, I'm glad I have my camera. When Gramps stares at Bruce's airplane as he brings it in for landing, I capture the awe in his expression. I catch how he runs his fingers over the control panel when Dane helps him into the small cockpit, his head tilted as Bruce patiently explains what every button and lever does. When his knuckles turn white from gripping the armrest tightly during takeoff, I cover his weathered hand with my own and take a left-handed picture that will probably be blurry. I'm willing to bet my next paycheck that it will be my favorite though.

226

I see our entire day through my camera lens. Even when my camera is tucked safely in its bag, I still see it in frames. Bruce, head thrown back, roaring with laughter. Chase, watching Dane as he helps Gramps out of the plane, tenderness in his eyes. Our waitress giving Dane a flirty wink, Chase laughing in the background. Gramps smiling. Gramps laughing. Gramps with tears in his eyes. I see all of these moments as pictures. This hasn't happened in years, not even on my hike with Zoe.

"You ever coming back out?" Gramps asks, poking his head in my room as I upload the pictures to decide which to edit.

"Yeah, give me a few minutes," I say distractedly.

"Get any good ones?" Gramps asks. "Can you show me?"

I turn to the doorway where he stands. His expression is hopeful but I can see his exhaustion. It's barely 8 p.m. but I'm sure he's going to bed soon. I quickly choose a dozen or so shots that look promising before unplugging my laptop and following him back to the living room.

I chose well, the pictures are even better than I hoped. I study them with a critical eye, choosing the ones I like best to edit first. I angle my laptop so Gramps can see my screen from his spot next to me on the couch.

"This expression, this is what's been missing," Gramps says suddenly as I work on the picture of his laughter in the cockpit.

"Laughter?" I ask.

"Not the picture Luke, you," Gramps says. His tone of voice pulls me from my editing tunnel vision. I turn to face him on the couch. "Your expression right now, your joy behind the camera earlier today. It wasn't there when you came home from school. I saw flashes of it whenever Miss Zoe was here, I saw it all day today, and I see it right now."

I really thought I had been doing a better job of hiding my stress. My what-the-fuck-am-I-going-to-do feelings. It hits me like a ton of bricks. Both Gramps and I have been living this in-between. I've been trying to pay the bills and convince myself I don't have a dream of my own while Gramps has been grieving and trying to find his footing, his new normal, without Grandma. It took Zoe to bring both of us out of our stupor and now that she's gone, we're sinking. Or at least I am. Gramps seems to be rising.

"Well, I've seen expressions from you in the last few weeks that I haven't seen in quite a while either," I counter.

"I told Miss Zoe that I was ready to move forward, start living again," Gramps says quietly. "And I want you to do the same."

"What?" I ask. What does he mean?

"I'm sorry, Luke," Gramps continues, his voice hoarse with emotion. "After Elle, I got lost. And I brought you down. That stops now. We're pulling ourselves up."

"I don't think you brought me down, Gramps, I think we both just got overwhelmed with reality, with grief, with life," I tell him. "But I don't really know what I can do about it."

"What *we* can do, Luke," Gramps says stubbornly. "We can both start living again."

"I don't think I know what that looks like," I say, mentally calculating what I have in the bank versus what I think he means by living again.

If he thinks we can wander like Zoe, he's sorely mistaken. I don't know how to tell him that though. Maybe, if he keeps his energy up like he has the last couple weeks, I can work some extra hours. Except it's nearly fall, summer tourist season is almost over. Even with Kelsey off to college, I doubt I'll be needed as much at The Mercantile. Fall does mean lower prices though, so maybe I can scrape something together.

"It doesn't mean huge changes, Luke," Gramps says. "I want you to hike more, or take day trips, travel with your camera and your dream, see where you end up."

"I thought this was about both of us," I remind him. "Does that mean you're coming with me?"

"Only if we can share our journey to living again with the world," Gramps says, looking at me evenly over his glasses.

"I don't know what that means," I say.

"It means I want to use your pictures for my Instagram," Gramps tells me.

That's one way to leave me speechless.

228

Chapter Twenty-Seven
Zoe

"I want to go camping," I boldly tell the long-haired salesman at Montana Camp Supply.

"So, are you here for gear?" he asks, brow furrowing in confusion.

"I mean, do you think I can camp?" I backtrack hastily.

"Everyone can camp!" he responds enthusiastically. "But gear definitely helps. What do you have so far?"

"Uh, a newfound interest in camping, dirty hiking boots, and that's honestly it," I tell him. "Wait, my favorite pillow is in my car. So I have that. And a small cooler."

He gives me a laugh and dives into selling me what feels like half the store. I manage to slow him down and he gets me set up with a small tent that he swears is easy to set up, a something-degree-cold-rated sleeping bag and small sleep pad, a camp chair, a lantern, and a headlamp. He walks me through camp stove options but I don't know if I'm ready for that yet.

"Don't most national parks have restaurants and other grocery options?" I ask.

"And already-booked campsites? Yes," he tells me.

"Shit," I whisper.

I don't know how to camp, I don't even know how to find a campsite, and I don't really even know where I think I'm going. But at least I have my favorite pillow? I should have tried Hope's "glamping" option instead.

"You might get lucky in the next few weeks as kids go back to school," my salesman says. He's probably worried he's about to lose the sale he just spent almost an hour on. "Or jump from campground to campground, sometimes there will be sites that have a night here or there, which is a pain, but if you're sticking to minimalist gear, it wouldn't be too bad, and you get to see more of the parks."

"I'm on the 'wing it' plan anyway, so let's do this," I tell him. He looks relieved to have not lost me altogether.

An hour later, I'm back in my hotel room checking in with my mom, talking through my AirPods as I try to set up my new tent.

"So, you're really doing my list?" my mom asks. "I mean, you've run away, ridden a motorcycle, gotten someone kicked out of a bar, and done a cold plunge. What other fabulous ideas did I give you?"

"Those things just kinda happened, it wasn't planned," I protest. "Shit, why isn't this working? And your ideas included joining a cult, so I think 'fabulous' maybe isn't the best description. Goddamnit, I'll call you another day. I have to figure out this stupid tent."

It takes another ten minutes of fighting, but I think the tent is set up correctly. I watch as it leans sideways as soon as the fan kicks on. Definitely not set up correctly.

I flop onto the bed. This is supposed to be a solo trip, but here I am, ready to crash another family's vacation because I can't set up my own tent. I send Emily a text, including a picture of my sad-looking tent inside my hotel room, and she immediately texts back with a campground name and campsite number. I guess I'm going camping.

***

"I freaking did it," I whisper to myself, standing back to admire my handiwork.

"You freaking did it!"

I jump a mile and turn to find Mia, Reese, and Emily all smiling at me. I was so focused on my tent that I didn't hear a thing other than the curse words running through my head and my heavy breathing. All three of them are in dusty hiking boots with sunglasses perched on their hats, pack straps across their chests, looking like an REI advertisement. Somehow my tent battle made me the sweatiest and most disheveled of the group.

"Hi, you guys, thanks for letting me move in next door," I tell them, relieved to see friendly faces. Getting my tent set up was a start, but I am so far out of my comfort zone it's not the least bit funny.

"Absolutely," Emily says. "We're glad to be part of your first camping experience. We'll let you finish getting set up, let me know if you need anything though."

Do I need anything? I don't even know. I toss my sleeping pad, sleeping bag, and favorite pillow inside my expertly constructed tent and then look around. Now what? What do you do when you camp?

I pull my new camp chair out of the back of my 4Runner and set it up facing my tent so I can relish my woman-versus-tent victory. I sink into the chair, phone in hand, and open the National Park Services app. Thank god this campground has service because, looking at these maps, I am not prepared at all. Shocking, right? After making a list of what I think should be a full day exploring for tomorrow, I sit and stare at my tent. Now what?

There's a flash of movement out of the corner of my eye and I immediately think "bear!" Of course I don't have my bear spray within reach. The dark shape moves behind my tent and I'm slightly reassured that it's much smaller than the taxidermied beast from Jules's cabin. Although, if it's a bear cub, I'm probably about to get eaten by a mama bear. I haven't even lasted a single night camping.

"Oh, hi there, little guy," I hear Emily say in a soothing voice. "Where's your mama?"

Of course the solo mom, camping extraordinaire, road tripping thousands of miles with her teenage daughters is going to save a bear cub. I hear footsteps running my way. What should I do? Why didn't my camping gear salesman prepare me for this?

"Oh no! Sorry, he likes climbing!" a panicky voice calls. "I'm so sorry!"

"He's okay!" Emily calls back.

I stand up to investigate. My bear cub is actually a young boy, maybe about Colt's age, who is currently scaling the ladder on the side of Emily's Land Rover Defender.

"I'm so sorry, he doesn't understand," the flustered mom says, trying to grab her son who clambers onto the roof of the SUV and well out of her reach.

"I mean, that's what the ladder and rack are there for," Emily says with a shrug. "I just don't want him to fall."

"Hi cutie," Mia says to the boy, craning her neck to peer up at him.

"He's nonverbal," the mom says, tears pooling in her eyes. "I'm so sorry."

"Does he sign?" Reese asks. "It's my language class for school."

Her hands move gracefully as she signs to the boy. The little boy stops moving and stares at Reese. Her fingers fly again but he just climbs further back on the roof rack.

"He signs a little, but he's been in the car all day and just wants to run and climb," the mom says. "I'm sorry."

"Please don't apologize, there's absolutely nothing to be sorry about," Emily reassures the overwhelmed mom. "I'm Emily, and these are my two daughters, Reese and Mia. And this is our friend Zoe."

"I'm Tiffanie, this is my son, Jay." Her tears spill over and she takes a gulping breath, waving her hands in front of her face, the movement causing the messy bun on top of her head to tip sideways.

Reese signs something to Jay but he just watches her with serious, deep brown eyes, his head tilted to the left.

"Mia, go to the other side in case he tries to climb down over there, I'm going up," Reese says quietly as Emily consoles Tiffanie and I stand frozen, feeling helpless and incompetent.

Mia skirts around the back of the Defender as Reese slowly climbs up to join the adorable, dark-haired boy. He observes her from the corner of his eye but she doesn't crowd his space so he remains still. They sit at opposite ends of the roof rack, eyeing each other.

"He won't come down until he's ready," Tiffanie says, hiccupping. "He's a good climber, he won't fall."

Mia peeks her head around the SUV and at Tiffanie and Emily's nods, returns to her spot at the picnic table.

"Well, I guess we have time to sit and relax then," Emily tells her. She motions to the chairs. "Is there anyone that's going to be looking for you that Mia should go find so they don't worry?"

"My parents took my sister and her family to the general store. I thought it would be good for Jay and I to go for a walk before dinner, exercise usually helps both of us."

"Me, too," I say at the same time Reese does from her perch atop the SUV. She shoots me a grin.

"His school has a partnership with a yoga studio so he gets to do that nearly every morning before school starts," Tiffanie says. "We kept it up this summer but this morning we were in a rush to get here to meet my sister and I guess this is my consequence."

"That sounds like an incredible school," Emily says enthusiastically, offering Tiffanie a bottle of water.

"It is, it's one of the reasons we moved back to Wyoming," Tiffanie replies, smiling through watery eyes. "They also have an equine therapy program."

"Does he like yoga enough that he'd climb down if we do yoga?" I ask. Emily catches my eye and slowly nods. "And I'd love to hear more about equine therapy."

Horses scare the shit out of me but I've heard a little bit about a program outside of Portland, it's supposed to be amazing. I've wanted to visit for ages. Aiden said it wasn't in line with my brand so it wasn't worth my time.

"Maybe some partner yoga, I used to do that with the girls when they were little, they always climbed all over me," Emily adds.

"I mean, we can try, but I don't know much about his class. I work full-time," Tiffanie replies, tears spilling over once again.

"Mom guilt is the worst. But that's why they say raising kids takes a village," Emily says with a smile. "And yours just expanded to include a yoga instructor, an experienced mom, and two of the coolest teenagers this side of Boise."

"Ew, Mom, don't say I'm cool," Mia huffs, throwing a towel at Emily, who catches it and lays it out like a yoga mat.

That pries a smile from Tiffanie, who wipes her tears before thanking us quietly as she lays out the towel that Mia offers. Equine therapy might not be my brand, but yoga definitely is.

Twenty minutes later, Jay is sitting on top of Mia as she holds a plank and I have the name and number for the equine therapy program director.

***

"Hey Luke, day seven. I survived a whole night camping in a tent! Zero freak-outs. Well, maybe one. Or two. But I woke up with the sun, snuck in a little yoga right here at my campsite, then did all the touristy things.

"I hiked up above a geyser then to a waterfall. I saw bison and a real freaking bear! Of course I had to stop at Old Faithful. It was *all* amazing, but the thing that was the *most* amazing? I didn't realize how much of Yellowstone is accessible to *everyone*, all ages, all abilities. A lot of the geysers and pools have boardwalks that can accommodate wheelchairs or even just someone who isn't as steady on their feet. Obviously there's tons of hiking, too, I just didn't expect to see so many non-hikers I guess.

"I talked to an elderly man on the boardwalk around Old Faithful, he was taking a video on his flip phone and he reminded me so much of Henry I almost cried. Okay, I did cry. I helped him send some pictures to his granddaughters. We tried to FaceTime them with my phone but I didn't have enough service.

"Then tonight I saw Tiffanie and Jay again. I had wondered how their day would be since he likes to bolt, it seems like a lot of the geysers and stuff would be hard to navigate, but she said they went to Jenny Lake in Grand Teton and he loved the boat ride. The boat captains were super nice to him, and then they splashed in the lake. I might meet them there tomorrow. I just love how many people can enjoy the parks. I wish you were here to enjoy them with me."

Chapter Twenty-Eight
Luke

"Like this?" Gramps asks, holding his phone toward me.

"I think so," I tell him. "Hold on."

I have never posted a single thing on Instagram and now Gramps wants me to help him learn how to use the app. I wasn't lying when I told Zoe I set up an account just to support her. But I do know someone that uses it like crazy.

Lucas:
Can you do me a huge favor?

Kelsey:
maybe

Lucas:
Will you help my tech-unsavvy, elderly grandfather learn to use Instagram?

Kelsey:
is this like asking for a friend when really it's for you?

Lucas:
No. Gramps actually wants to start Instagramming.

A new notification pops up. "KelseyLove3R requested to follow you."

Lucas:
How did you already find me on here?

Kelsey:
maybe we should just set a time that i can show both of you...

Kelsey:
omg your gramps is the cutest

"I have my first follower!" Gramps says excitedly. "Kelsey Love requested to follow me. Who is that? A stranger from the internet?"

Lucas:
He just called you a stranger from the internet.

Kelsey:
bring him to work tmw. insta help and he can meet team merc and help with the new little library avery is going to have you build for the front of the store

That's not a bad idea.

"It's the Kelsey that I work with, Gramps," I tell him, trying to hide my smile at his excited expression.

"No, that's Kelsey Griffen," he replies, shaking his head.

"Gramps, you can use any name you want on here, it's like her nickname."

"Is that why I can't find Zoe?"

I swallow hard and show him how to find Zoe. He's transfixed by her current story, which is filled with wild animals, her dusty hiking boots, waterfalls, and smiling selfies.

"That one is for me!" Gramps exclaims, when he sees a selfie of Zoe, her hand held up with her middle and ring fingers tucked down. "I showed her that. Elle used to do that. It means 'I love you.' She takes

236

those just for me." Of course she does. I push the emotions welling up inside me far, far down and keep my focus on Gramps.

He gasps when the picture moves to the next, and I show him how to tap to the left to bring it back, then hold a finger on it. He gazes down at Zoe, who is sitting cross-legged on a rock, mountains behind her. My breath catches when a tear splashes on Gramps's phone. I never thought of social media as a way for Gramps to feel more connected to the people he loves. His world. Hell, the world in general.

Grandma used to have friends over for dinner all the time, but over the last handful of years, even before Grandma passed away, more and more of their friends transitioned into assisted care, moved in with extended family, or passed away. Gramps isn't just missing Grandma, he's missing his friends, his community. How did I not realize this before? He was so happy when Zoe would stay for dinner, or even just Jake and Nancy, who we see on a regular basis. The night when Dane and Chase showed up? I absolutely should have realized it then. But this should be an easy fix. If I've learned one thing from the women of Team Merc, it's that they value community over business.

"Gramps, want to come to Three Rocks with me tomorrow?" I ask. "Kelsey can show you how to use Instagram and you can help me build a little free library for the store."

Gramps tears his gaze away from smiling Zoe flashing their sign, and looks up at me, his eyes still shining with tears. "I'd like that, Luke."

***

"I'm going with this young man," Gramps tells me as I tighten the last screw on the hinge, opening and closing the glass door of the little library to make sure it swings smoothly.

I glance up. Gramps and Colt are standing in the doorway, Colt's little hand dwarfed by Gramps's weathered palm. They wear matching grins.

"We have to water the flowers," Colt says seriously. "Mom said so."

On the one hand, I should have brought Gramps here on my very first day. He didn't help with the library at all, instead he was fed cinnamon rolls and coffee while Kelsey patiently taught him everything there is to know about Instagram. I heard them discussing Zoe's fame as

237

well as the various Team Merc accounts that Kelsey oversees. She showed him travel accounts, whatever "bookstagram" is, and an account dedicated to vegetable gardens. Since then, there's been a steady stream of locals stopping by to chat with him. Based on the wink Kelsey gave me, she's behind this sudden Three Rocks fame that has Gramps smiling nearly as much as he did on both of his flight days.

On the other hand, Gramps is going to be exhausted tonight. Especially if he walks to The Green Door Garden and back. I can't let five-year-old Colt be in charge of making sure Gramps is okay and I can't leave my job.

"I'm meeting them there in West's truck," Jessie whispers behind me. "I'll keep an eye on him."

"Have fun!" I tell Gramps and Colt.

"I think I owe your grandpa babysitting money," Jessie tells me as we watch the duo walk toward the bridge. "He just talked to Colt for nearly an hour about airplanes while I completely redid the front planters."

"Oh, well, in that case, I think I owe Colt babysitting money. I ran out of airplane facts a decade ago."

Jessie laughs and nudges my elbow. "That'd be a pretty cute picture, the two of them on the bridge."

I don't have my camera, but I pull my phone from my pocket and jog after them. Colt, who usually skips or runs everywhere, still has his little hand in Gramps's grip as they walk slowly down the street. I catch the moment when Colt looks up at Gramps, adoration in his eyes.

"That's more than cute," Jessie tells me when I show her the picture. "Colt doesn't have grandparents on either side, today means a lot to him. Thanks, Lucas."

"If Gramps starts telling me he wants great-grandkids, I'm going to need to borrow Colt," I reply, sending her the pic before I pocket my phone.

Instead of great-grandkids, Gramps wants more pictures for his Instagram.

***

I can't wait much longer or I'm going to be late. I drum my fingers on the counter, debating what to do. I know Gramps must be exhausted, but

238

I'm still worried. Not only does he have his library days, but he's tagged along with me to work two more times, plus Jessie and Colt took him out to dinner last night.

I pace the kitchen before grabbing my keys and wallet. I can't be late, not after all Avery and Tex have done for me, for us, the last week, let alone all summer. I don't even make it off the front stoop before I turn around.

"Gramps?" I knock on his bedroom door.

Nothing. Silence.

My hand shakes as I reach up to knock again. A metallic taste fills my mouth and I struggle to inhale. Instead of knocking, I burst into Gramps's bedroom, adrenaline rushing through my veins, and trip over his slippers.

"Luke?"

Thank fuck. I refuse to put into words what just ran through my mind.

Gramps sits on the edge of his bed, eyes wide in confusion as he takes me in. I sink to the floor, leaning my back against the wall for support, and duck my head between my knees.

"You slept in," I finally say, raising my head. I can still feel my heart pounding against my ribcage and I struggle to keep my voice steady.

I don't miss how his eyes soften, probably knowing exactly what I thought. I also don't miss how his hands shake in his lap.

"I'm just tired, Luke," Gramps says quietly. "Some mornings it's just hard without her here."

We've had a different relationship since our conversation about living again, but this is the first time he's acknowledged his grief in this way. My heart breaks for him. I have a sudden flashback to the two of them dancing in the living room, him dog-tired from work, Gram with her flowered apron on, me doing homework at the table, rolling my eyes at their swaying. What I wouldn't give to see that one more time.

"I know, Gramps," I tell him. "I know."

We sit in silence, both of us staring at our hands, pretending our eyes aren't filled with tears as we think of the same woman. I don't know how long it takes, but eventually I realize that yes, his hands are shaking,

239

but he's also rolling something between his thumb and pointer finger. Gramps silently holds his hand out. When I offer my palm, he gently drops the small, lightweight object onto it.

A gold band. Grandma's wedding ring. Delicate, simple, just like her. Dainty, petite, and slight, yet never fragile. Modest, unadorned, but never plain. Steady in her love, unwavering always.

I have to blink away the sudden onslaught of images that flood my mind. Zoe laughing, cheeks tinged red, hand on her necklace. Zoe tucked to my front, staring in wonder as the sun sinks into the horizon. Playful Zoe, teasing Zoe, reassuring Zoe.

"She wore it for fifty-five years, and now it sits here, waiting," Gramps says.

I rub the gold ring between my fingers, feeling its warmth. I wonder how long Gramps has been sitting here this morning, this ring in his hand, lost in his memories. Their memories.

"Remember when it went down the garbage disposal?" Gramps asks, a smile slowly spreading across his face.

"Of course I do, I was the one that hit the switch," I reply, turning the ring to find the scratch that caused me to cry for hours.

"You were more upset than Elle."

"I was six! I thought the garbage disposal had eaten it!"

"She was only upset because you were upset," Gramps remembers.

"I didn't use the sink for a week!" I rub my finger over the scratch on the ring, smiling at Gramps's chuckle.

"Go to work, Luke," Gramps finally says. "I need a day here. I'm tired, but I'm just fine."

"Are you sure?" I hate leaving him when he's upset in any way. At his nod, I stand, holding out the ring.

"Keep it, Lucas. It's been sitting here waiting, but not for me," Gramps says gruffly. Then he gives me a half-smile. "But I think you already know who it's waiting for."

The ring is suddenly heavy in my hand.

***

"You're going to lose that," Marabelle says, startling me, which of course makes me drop the ring on the counter. She shakes her head. "Put it on this."

I eye the gold chain she's holding. I am not a necklace person. I wasn't a bracelet person either though, until Colt and I made matching friendship bracelets.

"Just do it, Lucas," she says impatiently. "I already bought it."

"Need a refresher on returns?" I counter, pointedly looking at the iPad that works as our register. She just glares at me. "Fine."

I slip Grandma's ring on the chain and feel its weight against my chest. At least this should prevent any garbage disposal incidents.

"Want to talk about it?" Marabelle asks.

"Talk about what?"

"The fact that you've been playing with that ring for five hours now, looking like a kicked puppy." I am shocked by her words.

"It was my grandma's," I tell her stiffly. "Of course I look sad."

"Sure," she scoffs.

I gape at her. Mar has never been anything but kind.

"No, no, sorry. I mean, yes, of course it hits hard, but I don't think that's what *this* is about." She waves her hand in my direction.

What does she think *this* is about then? Of course Zoe's dark eyes flit through my mind. Her laugh. Her head tilt. Her blush.

"Yeah, that," Marabelle says, easily reading my expression.

I just sigh. There's no denying it. This ring is a reminder that the woman I love, who I can easily picture living room dancing with decades from now, is far away, in so many ways.

"I'm in love with her," I admit. "But she's meant for more than me, which I'm sure she's realizing every second of every day."

"Lucas, there's never been a question in anyone's eyes, hers included, if you're good enough for her. So you can stop that right this second." Mar's eyes hold mine, challenging me, daring me to disagree. "Now, you ready to do something about it?"

"So I just call her up and tell her that she should come back?" There's no way that's what I'm going to do, but I'm trying to make my point.

"Absolutely not. She'll find her way back here when she's ready. I saw how she looked at you. But just because she'll find her way here, that doesn't mean you shouldn't give her a roadmap, or a sign or two. Sometimes it's easy to get lost."

It's like she's been talking to Gramps, that effort speech he likes to give. But she's right, just like he is. It's only when Kelsey breezes in, staying just long enough to restock the welcome basket for Breakers Bliss, posting pictures of it on the rental accounts, that I realize what kind of effort might show Zoe that I'm ready, I'm waiting.

It just might be a little weird when I ask my elderly grandfather for help using Instagram.

Chapter Twenty-Nine
Zoe

"You're Zoe, right?" a teenage girl asks when I lead Potato, one of the dozen or so therapy horses, down the aisle. Her tone makes it feel more like an accusation than a question.

I spent the morning with Hannah, the equine director of the program, and Chris, the on-staff therapist, filming a short interview and trying to stay a safe distance from the horses. They invited me to stay, without my camera, and volunteer for the afternoon. There's a group of ten female teenage athletes that have been here all week for a retreat and Hannah is leading them on their last trail ride of the session.

When Chris mentioned quite a few of the girls struggle with disordered eating and body dysmorphia, I wasn't sure my presence would help. Isn't social media to blame for a lot of impossible standards nowadays? Am I to blame? Chris gave me a hard look when I asked if she was sure, tucked her vibrant copper braid over her shoulder, and posed a single question.

"Are you willing to be honest and vulnerable with them?"

I thought of Tatum, Kelsey, Mia and Reese, the girls from the Rock Beach Library, and every other teenage girl I've spent time with, whether thirty seconds for a selfie, or an hour of yoga, and immediately agreed. Now I just have to get over this whole fear of horses.

"I am Zoe, it's nice to meet you," I tell the teenager that's currently giving me A Look from underneath the riding helmet she's wearing. "Want to help me put Potato in the cross ties? Because I'm not

243

totally sure what that means. Hannah put too much faith in me." And also, Potato is terrifying.

The standoffish girl helps me guide Potato into what she says is a wash rack, and then shows me how to clip the cross ties to the sides of his halter. She lets Potato snuffle her neck as she gives him a hug and speaks quietly to him as other volunteers and teenagers bring in the rest of the horses from the pasture.

"Hey Josie, since you have a lot of horse experience, can you help Zoe with Potato? I'll bring Lightning in for you to ride," Hannah says as she passes by down the aisle.

Sullen Josie just nods and grabs two brushes from the shelf and wordlessly hands me one. I take a few calming breaths before following her lead, softly brushing Potato's neck, trying to keep my toes as far away from his heavy hooves as possible, wondering why in the world Hannah thinks I'm the one that should hang out with this girl. The other volunteers seem to be happily chatting with the girls as they all work together to get the horses ready.

"So, I guess you know why I'm here, do I get to know why you're here?" Josie asks, giving me a glare over Potato's back.

"That's a long story," I say. "Should I assume, since you knew my name without an introduction, that you've seen me on social media?"

Josie nods. "Yep." She pops the "p" sound, reminding me of Tate.

"I'm guessing you saw my video from when I left Portland, and probably the Iceberg Lake plunge. Maybe even some random pictures from my hikes the last few days," I say, watching her nod. "Well, even though there were tears at Iceberg, that's just the highlights of my last ten days. I have a feeling Hannah somehow knew the lows."

I still haven't logged into my accounts, instead sending Kelsey pictures every night, but I did watch the reel she put together from Iceberg Lake. It's the most real, honest thing we've ever posted and I love it. Kels did an amazing job. I have no idea how my followers reacted and I'm a little scared to ask.

Josie scoffs. I watch as she throws a rectangular padded blanket and then a saddle over Potato's back, patting his shoulder before she tightens the band around his belly.

"I couldn't even make it through the first day without having a full-on breakdown on the side of a highway," I tell Josie, who barely looks my way. "Like snot everywhere, sailor-cursing meltdown. I realized right then that I should have packed a lot more Kleenex."

"So you cried and then went hiking," Josie says, unimpressed.

"Well, I mean, yeah," I say. Teenagers, dang, they're ruthless. "Which, for a lot of people, apparently like you, isn't a big deal. But for the last year or two, especially the time when I was dating Aiden, who you probably saw a lot of if you follow me, my life was planned for me. I barely made a single decision by or for myself. I just really let things get away from me." I pause, unsure where I'm going with this. I watch as Josie puts what I think is a bridle on Potato and starts buckling a variety of straps. "I guess, I just realized that everything was about ZoeSays, not Zoe. Which, saying it out loud, especially to a teenager, sounds really dumb."

"It sounds dumb," Josie confirms. "But having someone else dictate your life in any way sucks."

"Yeah," I say, thinking we're getting somewhere.

"Mounting blocks!" Hannah calls down the aisle.

Panic takes hold as Josie shoves a helmet at me and hands me Potato's reins without another word. She stalks off toward Hannah, who is leading two horses toward the doors at the end of the aisle. Josie takes the reins of the gray horse and swings into the saddle as soon as they step outside.

On shaky legs, I maneuver Potato down the aisle after the others and watch as they line up by the two mounting blocks, which are really just a few steps that I'm supposed to climb up before getting on the back of this 2,000-pound animal. Potato nudges my arm as we wait our turn and I nearly jump out of my skin. When I turn to face him, he just watches me, head lowered so his dark eyes are even with mine. I tentatively pet his nose, surprised at how soft it is. When it's our turn, I stand frozen at the mounting block, Potato waiting patiently for me to climb into his saddle.

"Are you coming?" Josie asks impatiently.

"Uh, maybe?"

Luckily getting everyone else mounted is taking a few minutes, so I have time for a thirty second freak out followed by thirty seconds of breathing. I convince myself to put my left foot in the stirrup and swing my right leg over Potato's back. He doesn't budge as I settle into the saddle, gripping the reins tightly.

Face a fear: check.

"Let's go!" Hannah calls, turning her horse to take the lead through an open gate.

"Take care of me, Potato," I whisper to him as we start down the trail. I try to move with his rocking gait, but I'm definitely not doing it right. I've done yoga every day for a decade, my body control is well above average, but this is not natural. At all.

"Loosen your grip on his reins," Josie says from beside me. I startle when I realize she's riding next to me but obediently loosen my death grip. "Yeah, like that."

We ride in silence, side-by-side, Josie confident and me...not.

"Look up, not down," Josie finally says.

I look up, sucking in a breath when we come around a corner and the trail opens into a meadow. The Grand Tetons tower in front of us, just as breathtaking as the first time I saw them.

"When you're distracted by the mountains, you're a better rider," Josie tells me. "You relax into the saddle more instead of fighting against his movements."

"Thanks," I reply, still staring at the mountains. They're still cry-worthy, even after seeing them daily for the last five days.

I try to let myself feel Potato's gentle stride under me but it still feels awkward. Much like my non-conversation with Josie.

"My mom planned my running career. When I ran in middle school and she saw how fast I was, she saw this big, huge plan," Josie says when the trail narrows and we're side by side once again. "She said it was my way out of town. I loved running, so I went along with it."

I glance at her when she falls silent and I can see her chewing on her lip, thinking. I don't say anything, just let her have a moment.

"Once I hit high school, I was expected to run forty miles a week," she finally continues. "My freshman year, I won the mile in the Nevada state meet by thirty-three seconds. Summer training came and it

246

was fifty miles a week. I was told again and again that I needed to be the best, make it out of town, run in college and beyond. I kept winning, but I was overtrained. I started breaking down. I was unhappy, stressed all the time, I didn't eat enough, I just wasn't hungry. I didn't eat enough so I got injured. So here I am. Sixteen and broken and hating running."

"I'm sorry," I tell her honestly. I don't know what else to say.

She fidgets with Lightning's reins. "Having other people plan your life sucks. Having them take something that was yours and make it something else entirely also sucks."

A-freaking-men to that.

I don't really know what to say, what advice to give. If only Nancy was here. What would she say? What did she say to me all those weeks ago? I close my eyes and hear her voice.

"What does the real you want to do? I understand not wanting to let people down, especially your best friend, but happy counts."

"Without thinking about your mom or your coaches or anyone else, how would you want to plan your life?" I ask Josie. "What would you want to do? Just for you?"

"Well, the good thing about getting injured is that I was encouraged to cross train, so I swam and hiked and it was amazing," Josie says. "I was getting stronger, healthier, and I had this hike planned. Mt. Wheeler, it's really close to where I live in Nevada, but then I was sent here."

"I mean, there are worse places to be sent," I say, trying for humor.

"Yeah, there are," she agrees, leaning down to pat Lightning's neck. "But I really wanted to hike that stupid mountain. It's not even that hard of a hike or that cool of a mountain, but it's *my* mountain. My town. My recovery."

Now I see why she was pissed that my sob story was that I cried and went hiking.

"Well, are you going to hike it when you get home?" I ask her. "Don't you leave tomorrow?"

"Yeah, first thing I do," she says with a determined smile.

"I hope you do, maybe someday you'll climb lots of mountains. I know someone that runs trail races all over the world," I tell her, suddenly remembering Tatum's old gymnastics coach. "Maybe I'll see your name alongside hers in the future."

"Maybe," she says quietly. She's chewing her lip again, so I let her think. "I know there's a lot I can do with my talent, and there's more out there than my little town, but, I don't know. I like my little town. I like being able to ride my horse every day if I want to, I like knowing everyone helps each other out, I like the old guys down at the feed store who don't care that I run, they only care if I load my own grain. I don't know why my mom thinks I have to go run for Oregon." She wrinkles her nose. Another mark against me, I'm an Oregonian.

"Well, the University of Oregon has an amazing running program and the state of Oregon is pretty awesome, too," I tell her. "So if you do end up in Oregon, running or not, I think you'd like it. Might need to invest in a rain jacket if you're from the desert, though."

"Thanks, Zoe. If you're ever in Ely, Nevada, I hope you hike my mountain, maybe even without crying. But, fair warning, there's nothing to do in Ely besides…well, we've got a prison and a national park and honestly that's about it. But I love it anyway."

"I've recently learned that small towns with nothing to do are actually pretty great places with even better people, and happy counts for a lot," I tell her. "So I think that might be in my future."

"Hiking my mountain or a small town with nothing to do?"

"Both?"

***

"Hey Luke, day ten. I bought a horse today! Technically I sponsored the purchase of another therapy horse for the program, but still. I'm counting it. Buy a horse, check! Hannah, the equine director, was so passionate when we were talking this morning, I can't wait to see what Kelsey comes up with. I sent her so much footage she must be a little overwhelmed. I did a little research last night about equine therapy, but reading about it and being there, experiencing it, is completely different. Hannah invited me to stay for the afternoon and she partnered me with a surly teen, like picture the exact opposite of Kelsey and Tatum, and it took a while, but we got through to each other. I wasn't sure why I was there, how I could help, but I really think I did help her, and she

248

definitely helped me. Plus, bonus, we went for a trail ride at the base of the freaking Tetons. It was amazing."

Chapter Thirty
Zoe

When I wake up to find picture after picture of Henry, Bruce, Dane, and Chase waiting on my phone from Henry, my heart cracks. Luke's been taking pictures. He's been taking amazing pictures. Why hasn't he shown me?

The texts accompanying the pictures make me smile though.

Henry:
Miss Zoe why did not these pictures send?

Henry:
I will ask Nancy to make the letters bigger.

Henry and his determination to learn to use his iPhone. I love that this simple technology is expanding his world. Simple to me, not as simple to Henry. I know Nancy will be able to help him. I should have thought to change the text size on his phone last time I was there. Actually, I have a better idea. A surprise. But it will take a few days.

Miss Zoe:
I got the pictures! Looks like a great day.

It really does look like they had a great day. I knew Bruce and Dane were already fast friends with Henry, but it's the picture of Henry and Chase, heads bent together, that makes my heart twinge. The way that Luke captured their expressions, I feel like I'm both included in their conversation but also that I'm trespassing upon their moment. Tears burn my eyes and I haven't even looked at the mountains today.

I step outside to the front porch of my Airbnb cabin, my mind scattered all over, and cry until I'm hiccuping. Then I cry some more. I cry until the tears run out. My heart aches and I don't really know why. When I finally calm myself down, I start my gentle morning yoga routine. It doesn't work. All I really want to do is run until my lungs are on fire and my legs collapse. Is that what I need today? This is why I came on this trip, why I've been wandering. To find what it is I want and need. I need to run.

I check my watch. I calculate the distance. I have time.

I was surprised when West texted me, asking me to coffee near downtown Portland. I told him that I could get coffee, but over FaceTime only. He's going to get a very sweaty, disheveled FaceTime call but I don't care. I shove my phone into the back of my sports bra, lace up my shoes, and take off like a bat out of hell. This is not a morning to warm up, this is a morning to *run*.

Thanks to the elevation of this mountain town and perhaps my fragile mental state, it does not take long for my lungs to catch fire. I run angry. I pound the pavement, cursing every decision Aiden manipulated me into agreeing with. Every hurtful internet rage troll comment that I let cross my mind more than once. Fake contracts. Fake smiles. They can all go right to hell. There will be no more of that in my life.

My hamstrings tighten but I just run faster. I outpace the rage that's been simmering just below the surface that finally bubbles over when I think about how I let myself lose my way. For not trusting myself. And then, when I think my lungs are caving in and my hamstrings might actually snap, I let go. I just stop. My legs stop moving, my chest heaves, and I collapse in a heap on the sidewalk.

I let go of *everything*. I let go of my anger, of the heavy disappointment in myself that I've carried along this journey, and I find more tears to cry. It feels good. I was hiding, trying to escape in Lucas, in everything that comes along with him. I needed to hide. Then I ran away. I did it on my own. I explored, I pushed myself. I needed to run.

252

And now this. It feels like this is what I needed. This moment. I needed to break. But now I'm ready to rebuild.

***

I take advantage of the patio with the stunning views and slowly sip my americano. I eyed the cinnamon rolls but just couldn't do it; luckily this huckleberry donut is a good second choice. Maybe I should become a pastry reviewer, because, damn. While I wait for Abby to call, I browse through my "Life Changes" album.

Picture after picture, memory after memory. Jules and her motorcycle. Katy-with-a-Y standing on the bar. Mia and Reese pulling me into the lake. Emily and Tiffanie with Jay between them, my perfectly-constructed tent in the background. Mr. Flip Phone and I in front of Old Faithful Lodge. Hannah leading Potato toward me. Josie rolling her eyes as I laugh, both of us on horseback, the stunning, cry-worthy Tetons behind us. I should rename the album "Life Changers" because, looking back, it's been the people I've met that have had the biggest impact on me.

I started this trip to wander, make my own decisions, but the best days have been thanks to the people I've encountered along the way. I loved my days hiking and exploring on my own but doing yoga with Jay climbing all over me, Josie rolling her eyes at me from atop Lightning, and Mia's excited shrieks over....well, anything and everything, those are my favorite moments. Even the brief encounters with people that recognized me, taking pictures for families so everyone could be included, chatting with employees that came from all over the world to work at our national parks, those have been my Life Changers.

The same is true over the last few months. Meeting the Team Merc girls, Lucas and Henry, Jake and his wayward teenage workout partners, Seth and his enthusiasm for giving back, Nancy and her library programs, and Marabelle with her quiet way of watching over everyone. It's *always* been the people. I started ZoeSays to share my life with others, to connect with them, to build my own little village that enjoys the same things I do. It's why I teach. Why I work with small group clients. Community. I've found the final puzzle piece.

I wish I could tell Lucas. I do the next best thing.

253

"Hey Luke, day twelve. I'm in a coffee shop, I ran here, had a full-on meltdown along the way, but I think I just had an epiphany. Like, I'm sure I did. This trip for me hasn't been about the places I've been, but about the people I've met. They've changed me. Just like you did. Anyway, I just wanted you to be the first person I told. I know what I'm going to do, I know where I'm going to go. And I can't wait to really tell you about it. I miss you."

I'm buzzing with excitement, which could be endorphins from my run or might be a caffeine rush thanks to the americano sitting in front of me. Definitely not a sugar rush from the donut. I should probably have another.

But I've really got it. Abby better be sitting down when I talk to her. She's going to kill me, isn't she?

"I've called three times, what the heck?" Abby says when I finally realize my phone is vibrating. I quickly pop my AirPods in and move to a table at the corner of the outdoor seating area, not wanting to disturb any of the other people enjoying their coffee with a view.

"Abs, I think I have it," I say. "No, I know I have it."

"Okay?" she says with a question in her voice.

"It wasn't the wandering I needed, it's the people," I say. "And, I guess the horses, because I bought a horse."

"You bought a horse," Abby deadpans. "Jesus Christ. You're scared of horses. Did you tell your mom? That was on her list, wasn't it?"

"Buy a horse, check!"

"So, you have it…as in, you have a horse?"

"No, I don't have the horse, I donated the funds for a new therapy horse," I tell her proudly.

"Well, that's really cool, but I'm still confused as shit," Abby says.

"I'm a people person," I tell her.

"Did it really take you getting pulled into a cold-ass lake and buying a horse to realize this? Zoe, I've known this since I met you," Abby laughs.

"That's fair, but no. I'm a people person. It's the people, that's the part of ZoeSays that makes me happy. The part that's always made

254

me happy. I mean, I like the pictures and the digital scrapbooking aspect to it. But it's the people. I lost sight of that when Aiden made it seem like they were just an audience, just commenters, viewers, numbers. But that's my happy part. And now I know that I love working with the people that tend to get passed over. Seniors, eye-rolling teenagers, kids like Jay. Did I tell you about Jay? I want to work with Nancy on a program to introduce yoga to seniors in the community, and maybe a kids' class that encourages all abilities. I want to help Jake expand his work with obnoxious teenagers, maybe connect him and Lauren with Seth. I want to highlight other programs that are doing similar work. It's still coming together in my head and I'm not sure how to make a living at it, but I'm going to figure it out," I say excitedly, still seeing the pieces coming together in my head.

"I love seeing you, well, hearing you, excited about work again," Abby says after a pause. I can picture her smile and miss my best friend.

"Are you excited about work again? How's Erin? How are you?" I ask her.

"Remember that non-profit gym I told you about? The one that hosts the sober workout group? I'm doing some work for them, and it's been really helpful for me," Abby says, somehow making my brain work even faster. "Especially since Erin is still struggling."

"Abs, I'm so sorry about Erin, but that's amazing about your work! I think that'd be a great direction to take your amazing marketing skills," I tell her enthusiastically. Another small idea forms. "Hey, West, AKA Hot Lumberjack, is supposed to call me in a few. The job he wants me to do sounds like it's perfect for you. Colt's dad is an alcoholic and really screwed some things up. West needs some PR work, I'm going to refer him to you, is that okay?"

"Definitely," Abby says, just like I knew she would. "Thanks, Zoe. I'm so happy to hear your voice. You sound refreshed. I think *your* new direction is perfect."

"Also, I'm moving to the beach, okay, West is calling, bye!" I say quickly and hang up.

Of course she immediately calls me back but I decline her call. West isn't calling, we still have ten minutes until our scheduled meeting time, but I don't need anyone to make me second-guess this. The first decision I made this summer, the one that was just for me, was when I decided to go to Three Rocks for the Fourth. I didn't ask a single person what to do, not even Luke, I just went because I wanted to, because it made me happy. I need a breather from city life, something Henry tried telling me weeks ago, and the beach is where I've felt most inspired. Where I feel I can have the most impact, do the most good.

To stop myself from being the one to make me second-guess this decision, I call West a few minutes early. His expression when he answers my call and sees where I'm sitting cracks me up.

"I needed a change of scenery," I say with a shrug, hiding my grin. "But I still wanted to turn down your offer face-to-face."

"Well, thanks, I guess?" he says, giving me his trademark half-smile.

"I think you should talk to my friend Abby though, she does at least half of the work for ZoeSays and her sister is an alcoholic, so she has more knowledge than me," I tell him. "She'll smooth over your sudden closure as well as handle anything that comes up if Liam joins you at the shop. I'll text you her number. Call her."

"Thanks, Zoe. And I have to say, you look like you're enjoying your change in scenery," he says, making me smile. "Is it a permanent change?"

"It's an extended trip but I'll be back," I tell him, looking out at the mountains. "I'm hoping to find a house there someday soon."

"Interesting," he says slowly. "I might know of one coming up for sale."

"Seriously?" I ask, shocked. Is this some sign? Is fate smacking me in the face?

I gulp when I see the details. That's a lot of money. Money I very fortunately have, but it's a good chunk of change. Is this one of Tatum's real risks? I think it might be.

Real risk: check.

I sit at the coffee shop for a long time. A really long time. But when I stand, I've made a lot of really big decisions.

First up? Climbing a mountain.

256

Chapter Thirty-One
Zoe

"Hey Luke, it's day fifteen and I'm at the top of a mountain. Climb a mountain, check! It's absolutely beautiful, but not in the way I pictured the top of a mountain to be. It feels barren, stripped down. Also, really windy. I felt like I was going to get blown off the trail. If all of that's not a metaphor for this trip, I don't know what is. I set off thinking it was going to be one thing, and now here I am." I shake my head and laugh, because if that ain't the truth.

"But I'm here. At the top of a mountain. Holy shit. Look at this view." I pan the camera around and the two couples that hiked the last mile with me wave when I circle around to them. "That's Beth and Michelle and their husbands who, I have to admit, I can't remember their names. Oops." I sink back down, partially hidden behind the stack of rocks that create a windbreak.

"But yesterday I set up my tent in record time. Zero tent-related catastrophes. Or really any of any kind. A great near-end to this whole trip. I have two more stops before I pack up my Portland life. Who would have thought I'd ever say Portland wasn't home anymore? I think I felt it that first trip out though, my girls' trip, I just didn't listen to myself. Didn't trust myself. I can't wait to see you. God, I miss you so much it hurts. But first, I need to go for a run with a surly teenager here in the middle of the desert, then I owe Abby one thing. I mean, I owe her a lot, but this one thing really means a lot."

***

"I freaking love it, thank you," I tell Brendan, turning sideways to look in the mirror. "Last thing to do is join a cult, any suggestions?"

"I mean, didn't you do that this morning?" he asks, shaking his head with a chuckle as I do my happy dance in his mirror.

"What? We worked out," I tell him, frowning in confusion. I twist in the mirror, trying to figure out how to get a better picture.

"Here, give it to me," he says, holding his hand out for my phone. "A lot of people call CrossFit a cult, that's what we did this morning, so maybe that counts."

I freeze at his words. My morning was spent with Brendan and two of his friends at the gym that hosts the nonprofit Abby has started working with. I had called Abby as soon as I had enough service after summiting Mt. Wheeler and asked her to meet me on the other side of Nevada. This visit is for her, for everything she's done for me, which is an extensive list if we were to actually be keeping track. Luckily we aren't. But this is for her.

Brendan, just over five years sober, was my partner and personal cheerleader for the workout. I might have been hiking almost daily, but he had his work cut out for him getting me through that workout. Jake and Dane would be ashamed at the weights I used. As we laid on the gym floor next to each other, exhausted after the timer went off to signal the end of the workout, Brendan asked about my tattoo. Between gasping breaths, I told him about my plan to add cry-worthy mountains to my rib cage.

The idea came to me that first morning in Montana, tears streaking my face as I moved through my morning yoga, the imposing mountains casting dark shadows that stretched across the lake before me. With every tear shed since, from the happy tears I cried when Jay signed 'hello' after seeing me at Jenny Lake to the sidewalk sobbing meltdown on my way to eat a donut, I've felt nearly every emotion pulled from my body over the last weeks, mountains always in sight. Now, they'll always be with me, no matter what kind of tears I'm crying.

"I know a guy," Brendan told me. That guy was him. And now here we are.

Brendan takes advantage of my frozen state and takes a few pictures of my ribcage. He hands my phone back and, big shocker, tears

258

fill my eyes when I see the close-up of my new tattoo. Brendan used my necklace from Lucas as a starting point, then altered it very slightly to mimic the outline of Wheeler Peak, which he says he climbed a year after getting sober. Of course he did, it's like one more way life is telling me I'm on the right path.

Tattoo: check.

"Maybe it does count," I say slowly, pondering this fitness cult idea. "But I didn't join the gym. What if I could though?"

"You're moving here?" Brendan asks, his brow furrowed in confusion.

"No, but what if I took the cult home?" I ask quietly, more to myself. I turn back to Brendan with a smile. "Brendan, I think you're a genius."

"Well, Zoe, please tell that to my mother, who thinks I'm a moron for many reasons," he replies with a wry grin.

"Give me her number and I will, right after I call a friend about starting a cult," I tell him. "But first, can I get a picture with you? And then as soon as Abby is here, let's talk recovery."

I'm going to highlight Brendan's gym as my second project on this new path. I figured if I could survive riding a horse, I could survive a CrossFit workout. It was a close call, I'm really glad Brendan was my partner.

One of the other artists takes a few pictures of Brendan and I flexing and laughing before he covers my mountains with clear wrap. I add our picture to my Life Changers album, pay him for his work, and run out of the building. I plow directly into Abby who is waving to her Uber driver.

"Hey! Whoa, what's happening?" Abby asks, catching me before I faceplant. Her backpack falls to the ground with a thud.

"Hi!" I squeal and pull her in for a hug. "I've missed you so much! But I gotta make a call, I'll be right back. Sorry! Just go in and ask for Brendan."

"Wow, hi! I've missed you, too!" She squeezes me tight but then releases me to pick up her bag. She pulls open the heavy door and disappears inside as I frantically search through my contacts.

259

"Jake," I say as soon as he answers. "I have an idea and I know you're at the gym, because you're always at the gym right now, so is Lauren there?"

"Uh, hi?" Jake replies. "You could have just called Lauren or the gym, you didn't have to call me."

"I suppose, but you're in this, too," I tell him. "Please, is Lauren there? Can you spare me five minutes?"

He huffs in annoyance but the clanging of weights in the background gets quieter as I pace the tattoo parlor parking lot. There's a jumble of muffled voices then a door clicking shut.

"Hi Zoe, you're on speakerphone with both of us now," Lauren's cheerful voice comes through the phone. "One of us is much more pleasant today than the other."

Jake just grunts.

"You guys, I want to start a nonprofit gym and I need your help," I tell them. "I'll handle the funding. It's like an expansion of Jake's not-so-secret teenage membership program, combined with this sober CrossFit class I took."

"But you don't do CrossFit," Jake interrupts.

"I did this morning, and you will, too," I tell him.

"Bullshit," he says. "But if it expands my very-secret teenage membership program, I'm willing to listen."

"You-"

"Uh, I do CrossFit," Lauren interrupts what's sure to be an epic bickering session. "I used to do a lot of CrossFit. I'm in. Whenever you get home, whatever idea you have, I'm in."

Home. I'm ready to be home. But first, Abby. After giving Lauren and Jake a brief outline of my idea, we set a virtual meeting time for next week that I'm really hoping will be in-person. Then I go in search of Abby. I find her inside with Brendan, the two of them sitting in chairs by his table, heads bent together, talking quietly.

"I want to go home," I tell her.

"Like now? I just got here. What about our interviews tomorrow?" Abby's looking at me like I've lost my mind.

"I'll absolutely stay, but I think this project is yours and it will have so much more meaning for you to be the face of it. It's not ZoeSays,

260

it's both of us, and it has been for a longass time. I want this to be yours. For Erin. For you."

Abby gives me a hard look, assessing me in the way that only she knows how. I don't waver. Yes, I want to get home to Lucas, but this really is for her. Just like I want Jake to be the lead on our gym project, I want Abby to take this as hers. I've spent years as the face of ZoeSays, I'm ready to be the support crew behind these new projects. She cuts a quick glance at Brendan, who is looking at his phone, probably trying to make sure he's not pulled into our silent standoff.

"Fly home, I'll drop you at the airport right now," she says, surprising the shit out of me. "We can trade keys, my car is PDX. I'll drive yours home after I'm done here. Do it, Zoe."

"Are you sure?" I ask. Who is this and what happened to my best friend? "It's like a twelve hour drive."

"I think I was wrong," she says. "You can alter your life trajectory for a boy, as long as it's the right boy. Aiden was not, but I think Lucas is. I want you to be happy Zoe, no matter what that means. If it blows up, I'll still be here, just like you'd be for me."

"Uh, okay?" Who is this and what has she done with my best friend?

"So, am I taking you to the airport or what?" Abby asks.

"Wait! I gotta FaceTime Henry first!" I remember, looking at my watch. Shit. "I can't call him from the airport, he'll know. I want to surprise Lucas."

"There's a great deli with an amazing view of Mt. Rose, I'd be happy to take both of you, then drop you at the airport. Abby and I can come back and get your car after," Brendan volunteers, having silently sat through this entire exchange. "You'll have plenty of time to FaceTime while we eat and the airport isn't too far. There's not a flight out to PDX for like four hours anyway." He holds up his phone to show some travel airfare app.

"Get your ass in the car," Abby says.

Holy shit. This is happening.

Chapter Thirty-Two
Luke

"Gramps, what's this?" I call, picking up an iPad that's sitting on the entry table.

"That's my iPad," he replies with no further explanation.

"You have an iPad," I repeat back to him.

"You're holding it." We aren't getting anywhere.

"Where did you get an iPad?" I ask.

"I learned how to use it at the library," he non-answers.

We don't have any extra money, I budget everything, where in the hell did he get an iPad? I've been doing money math like crazy, trying to find ways to help Gramps with his quest to live again. He's still floating on our small adventure days and, despite what it will mean to our debt, I'm taking him for an overnight trip along the southern Oregon coast tomorrow. But this iPad might have been our overnight fund.

"Is that how you read the news now?" I ask him, pulling up my banking app. Our savings account isn't in danger of growing, that's for sure.

"Don't be ridiculous, I read the news in the newspaper. I do my yoga class with it."

Am I on drugs? A quick scroll of our checking account shows no unexpected charges, so I honestly have no idea how he got an iPad.

"Oh, and the groceries for our trip will be delivered in the next half an hour so why don't you just sit down and relax?"

He takes what is apparently his iPad from my hands and walks to sit in his recliner. I continue to stand frozen in the entryway.

"Oh, there she is! Right on time!" Gramps says eagerly, fiddling with the adjustable cover to prop it up on the table next to him. "Hi there, beautiful!" He beams at the screen.

I'm definitely on drugs, there's no other explanation. Did he get a credit card?

"Luke just walked in. No, he's just standing there all confused-like." He turns to me. "Well, are you going to come say hello or not?"

I blink a few times and Gramps harrumphs and turns the iPad toward me. Zoe's smiling face is looking back at me. My heart lurches, my breath catches. My hand moves to my chest, where Grandma's ring hangs on its chain, hidden beneath my shirt. On the screen, Zoe's hand mimics mine.

She's still wearing her necklace.

"Well, at least say hello to the girl!"

I finally remember how my feet work and cross the room.

"Hey, that's mine," Gramps grumbles when I pick up the iPad.

"Surprise?" Zoe says, her bright smile fading as Gramps disappears from her view. I walk into the kitchen, trying to find a little privacy.

"You did this for him?" I ask, drinking in the sight of her.

The second I see her dark eyes and scattered freckles, I regret everything. Why would I ever tell her to leave? Why wouldn't I have told her sooner how I feel?

"He's helping me with a few things and I got sick of arguing about how little the words on his iPhone are," she says with a light laugh. "I saw your pictures, Luke, they're amazing."

She's sitting at a table, maybe a cafe, and I'm certain she's not in the same state as me. There's sunshine, sage brush, and unfamiliar mountains in the background. Meanwhile, it's gray here, a real reflection of my mood. It's like Mother Nature is reminding me that we're always worlds apart.

"Zoe," I start, then stop. What am I supposed to say? If she's seen my pictures, she's seen it all. But she hasn't called me. She doesn't

264

want me. I have to remind myself to breathe. Gramps comes first, always. "Thank you. Thank you for doing this for him."

"Of course, Henry is one of my favorite people," she says, her smile gutting me. She's out there doing exactly what I had hoped she'd do.

"You look really happy, Zoe," I tell her, swallowing the lump in my throat. "And that makes me happy. I'll give you back to Gramps, now."

"I am happy," she tells me. "Really happy. And, what I said in the last video, it's true. Portland isn't home anymore, but I -"

My heart actually stops beating. She's not coming back? She's not coming back. I won't even have a chance to try again.

"I'm glad you figured it out," I say quietly, interrupting her. I quickly turn the iPad away from me, so she can't see my face.

Gramps happily holds out his hands when I cross the room, waiting for me to hand Zoe back over.

As Gramps beams at her once more, I pause. What video? I quickly pull up Instagram, but her page has nothing new. I can't sit here and listen to her and Gramps laugh together, so I stalk back to my small bedroom.

***

It finally hits me, when I'm laying on my bed, staring at the ceiling, where her video might be. I nearly roll off my bed trying to find my phone in the covers. This is it, it has to be. My finger hovers over our shared album. Once I click, there's no going back. There's no way I don't watch whatever it is. Heart pounding, I click the album open.

***

"Hey, Luke, it's Day One and I'm feeling a little like I'm failing. Wait, why did I just say Luke?"

Zoe pauses and I can see she's been crying. I want to pull her into my chest, run my hand down her back, and tuck her under my chin.

"Hi, wow, I'm a little bit of a mess right now. Day one. I'm near Flathead Lake in Montana, at an AirBnb I booked a few hours ago as I was having a meltdown on the side of a deserted highway at sunset, which I thought was going to be the low point of the day. Instead, the low point was, well, wait, a visual aid is helpful."

265

The camera pans around the room and I laugh when I see a snarling bear in the corner of a small living room, standing to its full height.

"The low point was when I saw my new roommate and screamed bloody murder. I'm honestly surprised no one called 911. So you could say things are going great. But I'm doing this. What this is, I don't know. But I'm doing it."

The determined glint is back in her eye. I desperately want to skip ahead, find the video where she tells me she's moving, but I don't.

***

"Hey Luke, Day Two. And I guess that means I'm just starting all videos that way. Which makes sense, because I miss talking to you every night. Still in Montana. Had my second meltdown of the trip, but this one was about how beautiful the mountains are. Checked that off my list. I'm heading to Glacier National Park tomorrow, probably going to cry at more mountains, hopefully solo hike. I've somehow ended up checking things off my mom's crazy list. Motorcycle, check. Kicked out of a bar, check."

No fucking way Zoe got kicked out of a bar. I laugh at the absurdity. I want the real story.

"I don't know, despite this not going at all how I envisioned it would, I think I'm on the right road. I just, I just miss you."

I hate the sadness I hear in her voice, but I'm selfishly glad to hear she misses me. Or at least she did back on day two.

***

"Hi Luke, day three. Hotel for the night before I solo hike tomorrow. I'm nervous, but excited. But did I mention nervous? And excited. Okay, I need to get to sleep, big day tomorrow!"

I can see the excitement in her expression. I wonder if she got any sleep that night. I'm guessing not.

***

"Hey Luke, Day Four. I don't know if you'll watch the reel from today, but oh my god, I did it. I hiked through bear country by myself, ending at the most amazing lake. It took some tears and a couple teenagers, but I jumped in the damn lake. And none of us got hypothermia, so that was a nice bonus. Also, the girls made me consider going camping. I don't

266

camp. I hike and do outdoorsy things and then go back home and sleep in my cozy bed after a hot shower. But maybe that's what's supposed to be next? I mean, this hotel I'm in is making me a little crazy, so maybe it's a sign to sleep in the great outdoors. Where the bears live. Sounds scary. So I should probably do it."

I switch to Instagram and re-watch the reel. Her tears, her smile. Fuck. I'm so in love with her. This is torture, not knowing where this is going. Do I even want to watch the rest of these? I have to.

***

"Hey Luke, Day Five. I'm going to do it. I'm going to camp. Outside."

She makes wide-eyes at me. Well, the camera. Then she bites her lip and I'm unsure I can continue watching.

"Out. Side. Camping. Of course, this is all dependent upon being able to set up my tent. The trial run in my hotel room did not go so well. So, wish me luck!"

***

"Hey Luke, Day Six. Holy shit, this is it. I'm camping."

I laugh, she's whispering, huddled in a sleeping bag in a tent.

"I don't think I'm supposed to be on my phone, isn't that like anti-camping, anti-nature? I had such a fun evening with my camp neighbors. I want to tell you about Tiffanie and Jay, but this feels anti-camping, so goodnight."

She blows a kiss and snuggles further down into her sleeping bag, making me wish I was there with her.

***

"Hey Luke, day seven. I survived a whole night camping in a tent! Zero freak-outs. Well, maybe one. Or two. But I woke up with the sun, snuck in a little yoga right here at my campsite, then did all the touristy things.

"I hiked up above a geyser then to a waterfall. I saw bison and a real freaking bear! Of course I had to stop at Old Faithful. It was *all* amazing, but the thing that was the *most* amazing? I didn't realize how much of Yellowstone is accessible to *everyone*, all ages, all abilities. A lot of the geysers and pools have boardwalks that can accommodate wheelchairs or even just someone who isn't as steady on their feet. Obviously there's tons of hiking, too, I just didn't expect to see so many non-hikers I guess.

267

"I talked to an elderly man on the boardwalk around Old Faithful, he was taking a video on his flip phone and he reminded me so much of Henry I almost cried. Okay, I did cry. I helped him send some pictures to his granddaughters. We tried to FaceTime them with my phone but I didn't have enough service."

Of course she thought of Gramps and of course she made friends with another elderly man. That's so Zoe.

"Then tonight I saw Tiffanie and Jay again. I had wondered how their day would be since he likes to bolt, it seems like a lot of the geysers and stuff would be hard to navigate, but she said they went to Jenny Lake in Grand Teton and he loved the boat ride. The boat captains were super nice to him, and then they splashed in the lake. I might meet them there tomorrow. I just love how many people can enjoy the parks. I wish you were here to enjoy them with me."

Me, too.

***

"Hey Luke, Day Eight. Wow, over a week. I feel like I'm on the right path, it's just a little winding. And I'm easily distracted. I spent the morning at the lake with Tiffanie and Jay, he signed with me! I cried. Tiffanie cried. But we just played and threw rocks and it felt a little like spending time at the beach with Colt. I miss that little race cheat. It's my last night camping, I gotta go, I'm having s'mores with some new friends. I still miss you."

Her cheeks are pink and she's happy, which makes me happy, but also it feels like a lead weight has moved onto my chest. Is she staying there? In Wyoming? Fuck, that's far away.

***

"Hey Luke, Day Nine. I'm in a hotel and I think I miss my tent."

Zoe loves her bed. And my bed. Any bed. It makes me laugh that she misses a tent.

***

"Hey Luke, day ten. I bought a horse today! Technically I sponsored the purchase of another therapy horse for the program, but still. I'm counting it. Buy a horse, check! Hannah, the equine director, was so passionate when we were talking this morning, I can't wait to see what Kelsey comes up with. I sent her so much footage she must be a little

268

overwhelmed. I did a little research last night about equine therapy, but reading about it and being there, experiencing it, is completely different. Hannah invited me to stay for the afternoon and she partnered me with a surly teen, like picture the exact opposite of Kelsey and Tatum, and it took a while, but we got through to each other. I wasn't sure why I was there, how I could help, but I really think I did help her, and she definitely helped me. Plus, bonus, we went for a trail ride at the base of the freaking Tetons. It was amazing."

She's finding her way, I can see it in her expression and hear it in her voice. Maybe she really is staying in Wyoming. Fuck.

***

"Lucas Henry Stark, it's Day Eleven and I miss you. I wish you were watching this sunset with me."

The camera pans around to show the sky's brilliant colors as the sun sinks behind the mountains. Then Zoe's smiling face fills my screen again.

"I know we said that we were doing these things on our own, but you've been with me the whole time."

She gives a little shrug and looks past the camera at the sunset, pulling a blanket around her shoulders with one hand. I can see her sigh, her shoulders rising and falling, then she gives me another smile.

"Thank you, Luke, for everything."

The weight gets heavier on my chest. Why does this sound like goodbye?

***

"Hey Luke, day twelve. I'm in a coffee shop, I ran here, had a full-on meltdown along the way, but I think I just had an epiphany. Like, I'm sure I did. This trip for me hasn't been about the places I've been, but about the people I've met. They've changed me. Just like you did. Anyway, I just wanted you to be the first person I told. I know what I'm going to do, I know where I'm going to go. And I can't wait to really tell you about it. I miss you."

The excitement in her voice, the shine in her eyes, it all just makes me miss her.

***

"Hi Luke, Day Thirteen. It feels like I'm packing up to go home, even though I still have things I need to do. Shit, there goes..."

The video doesn't stop and instead the camera rocks as Zoe takes off running, chasing, well, I'm not quite sure what.

"Got it, sorry, the wind is crazy and littering is bad. Oh! Wait. Did you know littering is a massive problem in National Parks? If only it had been picked up sooner. Get it? Litter? Picked up? I can just picture your half-amused smile at that. Gotta go before I make Mother Nature mad!"

The bad joke tells me she's happy, but where is she going? Where is home?

**

"Hi Lucas, Day Fourteen is coming to you live from the side of The Loneliest Road in America, where I just changed a tire! By myself! Don't worry, Rod watched to make sure I did it right. Here he is, say hi, Rod!"

She flips the camera and an older man with what is obviously a knife sticking out of his pocket is leaning up against a semi truck. He tips his hat. Of course Zoe made friends with a knife-wielding trucker.

"There was a solid seven seconds when I thought it was the beginning of a horror movie, I looked up and he was stalking toward me. Turns out, super nice guy. He stopped because he has a daughter about my age. Then, instead of taking over or mansplaining, he just made sure I was doing it right. And I was! Okay, gotta go, bye!"

Rod or no Rod, I hate the thought of Zoe stranded on the side of a lonely highway. But I'm also impressed that my city girl did that on her own. My girl. Where is the loneliest road? Is that the real name? No matter what, I don't think it's in Oregon.

**

"Hey Luke, it's day fifteen and I'm at the top of a mountain. Climb a mountain, check! It's absolutely beautiful, but not in the way I pictured the top of a mountain to be. It feels barren, stripped down. Also, really windy. I felt like I was going to get blown off the trail. If all of that's not a metaphor for this trip, I don't know what is. I set off thinking it was going to be one thing, and now here I am."

She shakes her head and laughs. Her cheeks are red and windburnt, she has tears in her eyes but she's still smiling.

"But I'm here. At the top of a mountain. Holy shit. Look at this view."

She slowly spins the camera, and it's desert and mountains as far as the eye can see. A group of four people wave.

"That's Beth and Michelle and their husbands who, I have to admit, I can't remember their names. Oops."

She sits back down and the wind gets quieter.

"But yesterday I set up my tent in record time. Zero tent-related catastrophes. Or really any of any kind. A great near-end to this whole trip. I have two more stops before I pack up my Portland life. Who would have thought I'd ever say Portland wasn't home anymore? I think I felt it that first trip out though, my girls' trip, I just didn't listen to myself. Didn't trust myself. I can't wait to see you. God, I miss you so much it hurts. But first, I need to go for a run with a surly teenager here in the middle of the desert, then I owe Abby one thing. I mean, I owe her a lot, but this one thing really means a lot."

Wait. What did she just say? Pack up her Portland life, but then she says something about her girls' trip. The one here? Does she mean she's moving here? Or to Three Rocks? Is that what she meant by home in the other video? My heart is racing, I can't help but hope.

***

"Hey Luke, Day Sixteen. I'm not on a mountain anymore, check out this probably-haunted hotel I'm at in Ely. I went for a run with Josie today, she kicked my butt, even after months of being unable to run. It was really good to see her and meet her mom. But all I can think about now is getting home. Home to you. Home to you and me."

Home to me. That sounds perfect. She just told me that she saw my pictures, why does she look a little nervous? There's no way she'd miss the captions. Her job is Instagram, how did she miss it? Where is she? What day is today?

***

"Lucas Henry Stark, day seventeen. I drove across the Loneliest Road in America again today. It's pretty lonely, but the towns out there, they're full of good people. I can't wait to get home to *my* people though,

271

Driving really gives you time to think, huh? Too much time, sometimes. But now I'm waiting on Abby, I'll see her tomorrow. Then I'll see you in a few days. I hope."

She hopes? Of course she will. Why did she say she saw my pictures? Between these videos and the five seconds on FaceTime, I don't think she did. I frantically count the days since she's been gone. Eighteen. This last one was yesterday.

I call her. Straight to voicemail. Text won't deliver. Shit.

"Gramps!" I burst into the living room but he's no longer on his iPad. He's in the kitchen, stirring something on the stove. "Where's Zoe?"

"Well, I think she said she and Abby were in California, she had to hang up," he answers. "They're doing something for work, some new job that I don't understand."

The doorbell rings and even though Zoe was just on FaceTime, obviously not anywhere near here, apparently taking a job in California, my heart still skips a beat.

It's just groceries.

***

"Hi Zoe, Day Eighteen. I just watched every single one of your videos. Gramps and I have been busy, but something tells me you haven't seen any of it. I just want you to know…well, just know I'm here, finally seeing these, and that I miss you more than anything."

Chapter Thirty-Three
Zoe

My leg bounces as I sit at the gate, waiting for my flight to board. What was that expression he gave as soon as he saw me? Playful Lucas with the dimple wasn't there. It was like the light faded from his eyes as soon as he saw me. And he completely avoided my comment on his pictures. Did he not want Henry to send them?

After Lucas practically threw the iPad back to Henry, I quickly schooled my expression and put on my ZoeSays smile to listen as Henry exclaimed over his new iPad. He told me about having lunch with two of the other senior yoga participants that Nancy recruited for our pilot program and how Mason from next door helped him order groceries. He was going to find the crossword game that Marabelle told him about next. But nothing about why his grandson can't look at me.

I finally rushed him off the phone, telling him Abby and I needed to get started on our new project. Instead, I had turned my phone off and shoved it to the bottom of my bag while Abby gave me a concerned look.

This is a huge mistake. Maybe I can just live out of my car, never set foot in Oregon again. Bum around from town to town, chasing nonprofits around the country, highlighting them for the internet world to see.

Actually, that's not a bad idea.

"Now boarding group G!" the gate attendant announces.

I am in group G. By the looks of this waiting area, I am the only passenger in group G. I stay sitting in my chair and tap my paper boarding pass on my leg. I couldn't even look at my phone long enough to use my electronic boarding pass, instead, I went to the counter, not even a self-check terminal. Hashtag boomer.

"Last call, Reno to Portland, all boarding groups, please board now." The gate attendant is looking directly at me, a single eyebrow raised.

I stand, swallow the lump in my throat, and board my plane, bound for heartbreak.

I give my seatmates an apologetic look as I take my spot between them, shoving my backpack under the seat in front of me, keeping my book clutched in hand. I need a distraction.

"Oh my gosh, I love that book!" The woman sitting in the window seat gestures at A Man Called Ove. She smiles brightly at me. Any other day I'd strike up a conversation, but not today. I just give her a brief smile.

"Me, too!" chimes in the woman on my other side.

"Did you see, hold on, let me find it," Window Seat scrolls on her phone, types, and scrolls again. "This!" She triumphantly holds up her phone, an Instagram profile on the screen. "He reminds me of Ove."

Aisle Seat leans forward and Window Seat hands the phone across my lap. I declared myself a people person a few days ago, but right now, I just want to sulk and read my book. Can't a girl just have an emotional breakdown over a cute boy in the middle seat of a packed airplane?

"Henry Stark lives again," Aisle Seat says, looking at the phone. "Oh my god, he is the cutest!"

God, I hope the plane door closes soon. Let's get this over with. I take a deep breath and lean my head back, closing my eyes.

No. Henry Stark. My eyes fly open.

"What did you just say?" I demand.

"Uh, that this old man on Instagram is the cutest?" Aisle Seat says bewilderingly.

"Can I see that?" I ask, motioning to Window Seat's phone in Aisle Seat's hand. Wow, I'm not a people person, I'm just your average asshole. "Sorry, I think I know him. Hi, I'm Zoe!"

"Oh my god, you're Fitness Zoe," Window Seat breathes. "And Zoe-Zoe. Fitness Zoe is Zoe-Zoe. Give her the phone. Quick!"

What is going on right now? I fumble with the phone when Aisle Seat passes it off to me.

HenryStarkLivesAgain: a grumbly old man

My heart explodes. Picture after picture of Henry, all with thousands of comments.

Henry holding a paper bag of groceries on the tiny porch. Henry and Kelsey on the porch of The Town Mercantile. Henry on a dock, a bridge high above him in the background. Henry and Colt, having a thumb war in a restaurant booth. Henry dwarfed by Jake as they chop vegetables in Henry's cozy kitchen, backs to the camera. Colt and Henry, hand in hand, walking across the Three Rocks bridge. Nancy and Henry on the steps in front of the library. Henry and Bruce, heads thrown back in laughter. Henry in the cockpit of an airplane with Dane. Henry leaning against Lucas's old truck, a brilliant sunset behind him. Henry and Lucas playing checkers. The wedding picture I saw the first time I was in their house.

Did Lucas do this? Was I supposed to see this?

I start at the beginning, clicking on the wedding picture. *"My Love, my Elle. I was lost without you, but now I am choosing to live my life the way you would want me to. With joy."* I wipe a tear and sniffle. Window Seat silently hands me a tissue.

I'm guessing Lucas took most of these pictures, but this is Henry breaking my heart. I touch the screen, wishing I could give the old grouch a hug. Another tissue is held out for me.

Lucas and Henry playing checkers. *"My grandson, my proudest accomplishment in this life."* More tears.

Henry by the truck. *"For Zoe."* His hand isn't waving like I thought at first glance, he's signing 'I love you' for me. My tears might never stop.

I vaguely hear a flight attendant making an announcement and almost miss the last part of the caption.

"One of many photos by @LucasHenryStark."

I click on his name, heart in my throat.

There's photos. So many photos. This is the missing piece. I can feel it. I close my eyes and take a deep breath.

I scroll and start at the bottom, the beginning.

"The day I stood on this cliff overlooking the ocean, I was uninspired."

I recognize the hike, it's the one I did the morning that I met Luke. It's a beautiful photo of a beautiful place, but if he hadn't posted it, I wouldn't have known he was behind the camera.

I laugh when I see Jake's comment. "You weren't just uninspired, you were also an asshole."

"But then your professional date and his better half showed up with an entire airplane and pilot in tow."

A collection from the day Bruce took them flying. Some that Henry sent me, but some I haven't seen. The way he caught Chase's expression as he watched Dane laugh with Gramps, I can *feel* Luke behind the lens.

This time it's Dane's comment that makes me laugh. "God, obsessed much, @chasingthelaughsPDX?"

"We started exploring."

A day in Newport. The picture I glanced at on Henry's account, the one on the dock, really should be in a magazine. Henry's scarred hands and stooped shoulders combined with his expression, that little sparkle in his eye that he gets every time he looks at his grandson, as he stands with the fishing boats, the huge bay bridge above him, tells the story of decades of work, resilience, and love.

"And trying new things."

I'm nearly hyperventilating with laughter at Henry's various expressions as he tries sushi. It appears he was not a fan.

"I found my inspiration, but I still missed you like crazy."

A single photo. Sunset. The kind of sunset you feel deep in your soul. My breath catches and tears start to fall once again.

"And I saw you everywhere."

His truck, door open, my speaker sitting in my seat. A gooey cinnamon roll that makes my mouth water. The Green Door Garden rental, flowers of every color in full bloom. An orange kitten in a window, a little baby Egg-cat. A yoga studio. The hardware store. A coffee cup with The Town Mercantile logo on the front.

"I love you."

These aren't Luke's pictures. They're *our* pictures. My favorite selfie from Silver Falls, my cheeks pink and blushing. Henry and I laughing together doing living room yoga. And our first sunset pic, from that little beach down the street, my eyes shining with happy tears, my head tilted toward his, his arms wrapped tightly around me. I want to climb through this stranger's phone back into that moment.

A tissue appears in front of me and I messily wipe my tears. No wonder why Luke looked so stricken, he thought I had seen this and not said a word. He put himself and his photos out there for the world to see, for me. And for Henry.

I want to get home.

I need to get home.

"Hi there folks, this is your captain speaking, unfortunately we have some bad news."

***

I jog up the steps to The Town Mercantile and fling open the door. It's completely empty. I spin in a circle. I step back out onto the porch and realize that there are zero cars in the parking lot. Why is the door unlocked if no one is here?

After our very delayed flight, I knew I couldn't stay awake for the drive out here. Instead, I set my alarm for 5 a.m., hoping to get here before Lucas. I slept right through it. And my second, backup alarm. It was Kristen who woke me up.

"Zoe, they love this," she said, sitting on my bed, waving her phone at me. "This, you, Kelsey's reels, how very not-ZoeSaysSo you've been, all of it. They. Love. It."

"What?" Nothing made sense, it was the kind of sleep where you wake up and don't know what year it is. Nap sleep is what I usually call it.

"One follower pointed out that it was a return to the real Zoe, the happy Zoe that started it all. Someone else even had screenshots of

277

Aiden's bullshit. I went down a rabbit hole following that up, but Zoe, wherever you take this, they're with you. We all are."

"What?" I couldn't even remember where my phone was.

"Oh my god, you need caffeine." Kristen laughed and shook her head. "And maybe a shower."

"I'm moving to the beach," I blurted out.

"Good. I've been trying to reach you for days, to make sure you saw Insta, saw what he did for you. Go get him. You're happier there," she said. "But shower first. And don't forget your cat, he's been terrorizing Casey."

I showered, Kristen made coffee. I drank coffee, Kristen repeated herself.

"Your followers, they're with you. Your plan, the nonprofits, I love it, they'll love it. Now, go get him."

Attempt One, Operation: Go Get Him.

FAIL. Seriously, where is everyone?

"Zoe? Zoe!"

"Oh my god, Kelsey! Hi! I missed you!" I yank her into a hug. "Thank you for everything, you did amazing!"

I still haven't logged back in, but Kristen quickly showed me everything Kelsey had put together. I hadn't looked at much since she sent me the Iceberg Lake reel, instead just sending her random pictures and giving her free rein. Not only was everything absolutely how I would have done it, but my followers loved it. Loved *me*, real Zoe, not perfect ZoeSays. My eyes are probably still red from the tears I cried over their support.

"Are you okay? I said your name like seven times," Kelsey says when I finally release her.

"Sorry, I had a one track mind," I tell her. "What's happening? Why is the store empty?"

"Team meeting of sorts," Kelsey tells me, stepping sideways so I can see behind her. Tex, Avery, and Jessie are all sitting around one of the small tables on the porch. "Join us?"

"Uh, yeah," I say, still trying to figure out why Luke isn't at work.

278

"Welcome back," Jessie tells me, smiling and using her foot to push a chair out for me. "Colt's going to be excited to see you."

"Hi, Zoe," Avery says, her voice subdued. I look around the table. Something is wrong.

"Tex, are you okay?" I ask, suddenly very, very concerned. Tex is in tears, holding….a spoon?

"Are you here for Lucas?" she replies, answering my question with a question.

I'm starting to freak out. What has happened since I've been gone? Is it Gramps? Is that why Luke isn't here and they're all like this? No, I just talked to him yesterday.

"Um, well," I stammer. "Wait. Is that ice cream?"

"It's dairy-free, but almost ice cream. I can share," Tex says, pushing the carton toward me. "I only have real ice cream when it's Tillamook Vanilla Bean, just because I can't resist. A few spoonfuls, worth the stomachache every time."

"Oh my god, my last thing," I say, my eyes widening. "If this isn't a freaking sign, I don't know what is." How I didn't do this one immediately is beyond me. I guess I was too busy crying at mountains and screaming at dead predators.

Ice cream for breakfast, check.

Marabelle appears like magic, handing me a spoon and a large coffee cup. "Sorry, hon, I was in the back when you walked in. You girls enjoy your time together." She gives my shoulder a squeeze and walks back inside the store.

"You guys are all freaking me out, what's going on?" I ask, digging my spoon into Tex's fake chocolate ice cream. It's delicious. I close my eyes and sigh.

"I'm moving to college this afternoon!" Kelsey says, smiling and doing something on her phone, screen tilted away from the table. Then she looks around the table at all of us and deflates just a little. "But I'm going to miss my pretend sisters." She leans over and digs her spoon into the carton.

"Colt saw his dad for the first time in months last night; it went really well but it was a lot," Jessie says, reaching her spoon across the table. "And he starts kindergarten in three days."

279

Now I really want to see Colt and let the little cheat beat me at a race. I remember the first time I met him, thinking what a carefree beach life he was living. Little did I know what was really happening beyond the flying sand and beach races.

"Cooper, a boy I never thought I'd see again, who I spent a single week with as a teenager and then measured every other guy against, was at the bonfire last night. Oh, and showed up on my run this morning. Did I mention that he's now an insanely attractive man and bought the property next to mine?" Avery's turn for ice cream. Honestly that all seems like a good thing to me but based on the amount of ice cream piled on her spoon, I'm not so sure.

"I'm pregnant, so I'm probably going to throw this up before long," Tex says, taking the entire carton back. I guess that explains ice cream breakfast.

"Holy shit you guys, I hope there's more ice cream inside," I say. "This is a lot. Pregnant?! That's amazing, congrats! I'm so happy for you!"

My mind is reeling with all of their updates. Of course Kelsey is going to have an amazing time at college, she'll have so much fun that even Officer Hot Cop couldn't drag her home. And Tex, pregnant? Unsurprised. She and West are goals. I bet Colt will be ecstatic to have a little cousin.

"Your turn." Tex shoves her ice cream back to me.

"I cried and went hiking," I say, quoting Josie. I give a little shrug as I take another spoonful of fake ice cream. I glance up and laugh at everyone's expressions. "Okay, okay. And then I realized that I want a job in the real world, helping real people. So I'm buying West's house, working with Lauren who owns the gym in Rock Beach to start a program for teenagers, helping Nancy at the library start yoga for seniors, and I probably need like a real-real job, at least for a bit."

"Of course you're moving here when I'm leaving!" Kelsey says, playfully pushing my spoon out of the way.

"Did I mention that Officer Hot Cop is helping with the gym program?" I ask her, shimmying my shoulders her way.

Tex and Avery burst into hysterical laughter, startling Jessie, who looks between them with wide eyes. With a huff, Kelsey grabs the entire carton of ice cream and stomps toward the door.

"You're all the worst, except Jessie!" Kelsey calls over her shoulder as she disappears into the store.

"She'll be back," Avery says confidently.

She and Tex attempt to explain to Jessie how Kelsey's small-town-romance binge reading led to an Officer Hot Cop fantasy, which led to whatever the heck happened in The Merc after our hike, which led to this. I sit back and sip my americano. It's delicious, but it'd be a lot better if Luke had made it for me.

"I take it back, I'm not going to miss you guys," Kelsey announces, returning with two cartons of ice cream, one labeled dairy-free.

"My favorite," Tex moans, immediately ripping the lid off of the dairy-free cookie dough carton. "And, Zoe? What else?"

"And I fell in love with Lucas. I thought he'd be at work this morning, so here I am," I tell them.

"I knew it!" Tex gloats. "The second you called him 'Luke' back during the Fourth weekend, I knew."

"I'm in deep, you guys," I admit. "So, can someone please tell me where he is? I thought I was going to get to surprise him, just walk in and order my americano and a cinnamon roll like the first day."

"He took Gramps on an overnight trip," Kelsey says, pushing her phone toward me.

She has Henry's Instagram pulled up, his story shows a picture of two backpacks in the middle seat of their old truck, my bluetooth speaker nestled on top, Luke driving with one hand on the wheel, the other out the open window, a smile that I know shows his dimple spread across his face.

My turn to cry. Avery pushes the chocolate ice cream my way. "I'm so happy for them," I try to say through a mouthful of ice cream. And I am. But I also ache to see both of them. "These are happy tears, I swear!"

"Well, you look super happy," Kelsey deadpans, waving her spoon in a circular motion around my face, which I'm sure is splotchy and red.

"What kind of real-real job are you looking for?" Avery asks, raising an eyebrow at me.

Tex glances at her best friend and nods slowly before getting another spoonful of her non-dairy ice cream.

"Uh, I guess the kind that helps pay some bills, because I'm still working through how to run these programs and not go broke," I say.

Holy shit. Bills. Adult stuff. I'm paying cash for the house, like the entitled social media influencer I am, but there's still a ton that I barely skimmed over with my financial advisor. He said I'm "doing just fine" but I should have paid a lot more attention to what that really means.

I snatch the ice cream away from Tex, who protests weakly, and dig my spoon back in. I don't think ice cream will solve everything, but it's worth a shot.

God, I just want to see Luke.

"But probably part-time, while you work on these new programs, right?" Jessie asks, glancing between Avery and Tex. Has she learned how to read their BFF telepathy?

I nod, mouth full of ice cream, brain freeze imminent.

"Want to join Team Merc?" Avery asks.

"Hell yes!" I do my seated happy dance despite the brain freeze. I don't even know what the job entails, nor do I care, I just know I want to be a part of their girl gang.

"Let's start your training," Kelsey says, standing up abruptly. "Right now. Bring your spoons."

She reaches to the middle of the table and takes the tub of ice cream away from Tex, who immediately protests. Kelsey holds the door open as we stay seated. She gives Tex a look and shakes the ice cream tub at her.

"Okay, okay," Tex grumbles. "Let's go, girls. She's obviously up to something, we might as well get it over with."

Jessie, Avery, and I stand and follow Tex toward the front door. I take one last look at the parking lot, hoping to see a beat-up old pickup truck pulling it. The lot stays empty.

Chapter Thirty-Four
Luke

"Are you sure you're okay?" I ask Gramps. He's been talking about our overnight trip all week, but if he's not up for it, we shouldn't be going anywhere, even if it means losing the hotel money.

"I'm an old man, I just move a little slow some mornings," he snaps. "Stop rushing me."

Okay then. I take our empty coffee mugs inside and wash them out while Gramps glares at his iPad. I knew this burst of activity over the last few weeks would catch up to him at some point, I guess today is that day.

"Why aren't you ready yet?" Gramps calls. I can hear him open the front door and I shake my head when I see him trying to shoulder both of our backpacks.

"Gramps, I got those." The last thing we need is for him to fall.

"Hrmph," is the only reply I get. He refuses to let go of my camera bag and stomps down the steps to the truck while I lock up.

This might be a longer day than I anticipated. Sitting in the truck won't be too much different than sitting in his chair, so I don't really see any harm in still making the trek south. I can get great shots of him staring stoically at the ocean from the passenger seat.

"Ready?" I ask, climbing into the driver's seat.

No response.

I look over at my grouchy grandfather who might be more addicted to his phone than Kelsey. He's methodically tapping out a message but quickly angles his phone away from me when he sees me looking.

I shake my head and start the truck. One more glance tells me he's still buried in his phone. Is this what parents of teenagers feel like? I barely make it out of our driveway before music fills the truck.

This fucking song. I will never hear Cole Swindell and not think of Zoe.

"Gramps, who taught you to use Zoe's speaker?" I ask, gritting my teeth. Her speaker, which I haven't charged in weeks, her song, my heartache.

"Mason, when he helped me order groceries after Jake sent him over to mow," Gramps replies. "Showed me how to charge it and everything. Isn't this the song you're always humming when you do dishes?"

First, Jake swore he'd stop doing that. Second, yes, yes it is.

"Take a right," Gramps demands when I reach the highway.

"We're going south though," I tell him, my heart sinking a little more.

"You remember what I said?" Gramps levels me with a glare when I glance at him.

I stay at the stop sign at the end of the street, thankful no one is behind me. I turn and look at Gramps, trying to assess what the hell is going on. I've never encountered this side of him, ever. Grouchy, sure. But this? No. He ate breakfast and physically he seems just fine, but he's never been this irritable. Isn't irritability an early sign of dementia?

"What you said about what?" I am exhausted and we haven't even turned onto 101 yet.

"You need to put in effort if she's the one, make her a priority," Gramps barks.

"Gramps, Zoe isn't here," I say gently. "And right now, you're my priority, our trip is my priority. When she is here, if she comes back like I hope she does, I will do everything I can to show her she's a priority. I promise."

"Will you take her on a trip like this when she's here?" Gramps asks aggressively.

286

I don't know where this is coming from, but I do know the hospital is to the right, and at this point I'm concerned enough to consider an expensive-as-fuck emergency room trip because of his behavior. I put my turn signal on and wait for a logging truck to pass before pulling out.

"She's here," Gramps says. He's holding his phone up but, with a logging truck in front of me, I'm not about to take my eyes off the road. "Zoe's in Three Rocks. Right now."

I turn and gape at him. For half a second. Then my eyes are back on the road. I think he was trying to show me a picture of The Mercantile, but honestly, the Final Destination 2 scene has me keeping my eyes glued to the truck ahead.

"She's here, Luke, let's go get her," Gramps says with a nod. He slowly cranks his window down and turns up the music.

I shake my head, still unwilling to believe him. But, even as I think that I'll be right back at the hospital we're passing by, I can't help but hope. And Gramps really seems to believe it, so I roll my window down, too, and laugh as he tries to sing along to the next song.

***

There's no red 4Runner in The Town Mercantile parking lot. My heart sinks like a fucking rock. Now, not only is the girl I love still hundreds of miles away, but I have to take Gramps to the emergency room instead of on this trip he's been so excited about. I pull into a parking spot, figuring I might as well get the man a cinnamon roll and maybe Marabelle can give me a read on how Gramps seems to her.

Gramps is already out of the truck and walking toward the steps, so I scramble out after him. The man is on a mission. He even pulls the door open before I can get there, holding it open and ushering me inside. Not even ushering, pushing.

"Good morning."

Zoe.

My heart leaps in my chest and I can't breathe.

Zoe is here.

There is no air. I can't move.

Zoe with her dark eyes and flushed cheeks and beaming smile is here.

I suck in a breath and drink her in. Her eyes shine with tears and she laughs as they spill over.

"Can I help you?" she asks, leaning on the counter that's the reason she's not already in my arms.

"Are the cinnamon rolls as amazing as they look?" I parrot the first words she ever spoke to me back to her as I gently wipe her tears.

And then she's climbing over the counter and into my arms. She wraps her legs around me and I step back from the counter, gripping under her thighs, holding her as close as possible to me. As soon as her mouth is on mine, I'm lost. The weeks apart slip away and it's just us.

It's her vanilla lips, her fingers in my hair, her tongue sliding against mine as she tightens her legs around my waist. It's the vice grip she's had on my heart since day one, the way she fills my chest with hope, the rush of genuine happiness that flooded my veins the moment I saw her. It's Zoe.

"Lucas Henry Stark," she whispers against my lips. "You're going to get me fired on my first day."

I hear clapping, and, keeping her in my arms, turn around. Gramps, Avery, Tex, Jessie, Kelsey, and Marabelle are all clapping. A few bewildered tourists join in as well. Zoe buries her face in my neck and I can feel her shaking with laughter.

"Was this you?" Zoe demands, pointing at Gramps after wiggling her way out of my grasp and back to the ground.

He starts to shake his head until Marabelle loudly clears her throat and Kelsey throws her hands in the air in exasperation. He just shrugs with a smile, his twinkling eyes trained on Zoe.

"I love surprises," Zoe tells him, then gently pulls him in for a hug.

"Well, your real surprise is a trip down to Florence," Gramps tells her, looking over her head at me.

How long did he know she was coming home? Did he plan tonight for Zoe and I all along?

"Henry James Stark, this is your trip, not mine," Zoe scolds. "I am here to stay, so take your trip and enjoy every second of it."

Stay.

I like the sound of that.

288

Zoe moves to hug Kelsey and Marabelle, who I'm assuming are Gramps's co-conspirators. Tex starts crying for what must be the four hundredth time in the last few days. I hold my arm out and she steps into me, hugging me tight. She's never hugged me. I'm pretty sure she doesn't like hugs in the first place.

"It's the hormones, I swear," she whispers, sniffling before continuing. "It's not Kelsey leaving, it's not Zoe staying, it's not your cute grandpa, and it's not your stupid love story. It's the hormones."

"Okay, boss," I tell her.

West is going to murder me for making her cry, so I have that to look forward to. I shift my feet but she doesn't release her grip so I just clumsily pat her back while Avery smirks at me. A throat clears behind us and I'm sure it's West. It's been a good life, at least I got one last kiss from Zoe.

"Well, this is awkward, I could swear it was Zoe you were a goddamn mess over," Jake says loudly.

"My ride's here," Gramps announces.

Zoe squeals and hugs Jake.

"You're in on this, too?" I ask Jake, rubbing Tex's back because honestly I'm not sure what else to do with her.

"I'm just his ride home." He gives me a smirk that rivals Avery's.

"Jake, this is Avery, who owns the store, and my new boss," Zoe starts the introductions. "Tex is the one crying into Luke's shirt. Marabelle makes the amazing cinnamon rolls that shouldn't go near your abs, and this is Jessie, whose son Colt cheats at races. Kelsey was here a second ago, I don't know where she went. Guys, this is Officer Hot Cop."

That gets Tex to stop crying. She goes from soaking my shirt with tears straight into fits of laughter with Zoe, finally releasing me. Avery laughs and shakes Jake's hand, as do Jessie and Marabelle. Jake just shakes his head at me, smiling at Zoe and Tex, who are unsuccessfully trying to pull themselves together.

"Nice to meet all of you, but I need to go before Brian or any of his firefighters show up. They have a field day with that one," Jake says. "Put the station's cinnamon rolls on me today though."

289

He drops cash onto the counter before ushering Gramps outside.

"So, you want to go on an overnight road trip with me, Zoe Last Name Campbell? Just you and me?"

"Only if you bring your camera, Lucas Henry Stark," Zoe replies, standing on her toes to kiss me again.

"Yes, please take the making out elsewhere," Kelsey says, walking in through the door that leads to the kitchen.

"Hiding from anyone in particular?" Zoe asks innocently.

"Oh my god, please leave!" Kelsey moans as the girls all crack up.

"I can't leave! I'm at work!" Zoe says.

"Wait, you're really working here?" I look between Zoe, Tex, and Avery.

"Start when you get back," Avery says with a laugh. "Or when you move, or whenever you can."

"You're really moving here?" I whisper.

"You guys have a lot to catch up on, get out of here," Tex says, pushing us toward the door.

I take her words to heart and tug Zoe out the front door and toward the parking lot.

"Wait!" she cries, bolting back inside.

I see her pulling Kelsey in for another hug, then she's running back down the steps toward me. She pulls a backpack from a car I now recognize as Abby's and tosses it onto the middle seat of my truck. Before she can climb up, I press her against the side of the truck with my hand on her hip.

"Parking lot make out?" she asks, sliding her hand under my shirt.

I laugh, loving the smile she's giving me, the way she's looking at me, even loving her cold hands. I love the way she melts into me.

"Zoe," I whisper, lost in her eyes. Lost in her.

I can't believe she's here. I can't believe she's mine. I can't believe I haven't told her. I can't go another second without telling her.

"Mmm," she hums, tugging me down, her fingers in my hair, her lips on mine. Okay, I can go a few more seconds.

"Zoe, I-"

"I love you," she whispers, cutting me off, which is so perfectly Zoe that I can't even be mad that she stole the words from me.

I catch her lips again, unable to resist. "I love you, Zoe Last Name Campbell."

"I should have told you weeks ago. I love you, Lucas Henry Stark," she says between kisses. "You and me."

"Just you and me," I whisper.

Chapter Thirty-Five
Zoe

The wind whips my hair as I stand in the meadow at the end of the trail, looking out over the endless whitecaps of the Pacific Ocean. There is no knot of tension, no social media video needing to be filmed, only Luke's arms wrapped around me. I inhale the salty sea air and close my eyes, leaning back into him, listening to the waves crashing against the cliff far below. This is the very definition of a full-circle moment. I'm so glad Lucas suggested we make the hike before heading south.

"Zoe?" Luke whispers in my ear before kissing my neck.

"Hmm?" I tilt my head, giving him more access, shivering as soon as he finds the spot below my ear.

"I brought you a surprise," he says softly, pulling back just enough to turn me in his arms.

He's holding his hand out, a nervous flicker in his green eyes. I gasp when I see what lays in his palm.

"Lucas Henry Stark," I breathe. "That's…is that…?"

Before the words finish leaving my mouth, I know the answer. I've seen that ring before, in pictures and sitting on Henry's bedside table. I think of the wedding picture, the framed version in their home and the caption Henry used on Instagram. Tears prick my eyes.

"This has been waiting for you, Zoe," Lucas says quietly. "Gramps said that he wanted to live like Grandma would want him to, with joy, and the joy you bring to both of us, to everyone around you, is unmatched. As soon as he set this in my hand, I knew. I knew it was yours."

My tears fall fast. There's no stopping them. "I love it. I love you. But, Luke, I...are you sure?" I tentatively reach out and touch the slender gold band with a single fingertip.

"I know it's a ring, I know what that usually means, and I do want to marry you, more than anything, but for now, this necklace is yours. Until you're ready, we're ready." His green eyes are steady on mine, telling me everything I need to know.

There is no other end to our story, other than this. It doesn't even feel like a decision, it's just us.

"Lucas Henry Stark, I love you and I want to marry you. I'd marry you right now, I'd marry you in twenty years. I want just you and me forever. But that is a very special ring, a wedding ring, and-"

His warm lips are on mine before I can even finish what I'm saying. His hand closes around the ring, taking mine with it, our palms holding the ring safe between them. His other arm wraps around my back, pulling me flush against him. He kisses me like he might never kiss me again.

"Marry me, Zoe," he says when he finally pulls away, resting his forehead on mine.

My heart lurches. It beats wildly against my chest, trying to escape my body, like it's clawing its way toward the man who has held its fate in his hand since that very first dimpled smile.

"Is that a question or a demand?" I kiss him between each word.

"Zoe McKay Campbell, will you marry me?"

***

"I, Lucas, take you, Zoe, to be my wife. To have and to hold, from this day forward, for better or worse, richer or poorer, in sickness and in health, forsaking all others, to love and to cherish, until death do us part," Lucas says, only looking down to read from the phone screen once.

"I, Zoe, take you, Lucas, to be my husband. To have and to hold, from this day forward, for better or worse, richer or poorer, in sickness and in health, forsaking all others, to love and to cherish, until death do us part," I repeat, my voice catching at the end.

"With this necklace, I thee wed," Lucas says, gently clasping the necklace around my neck. Elle's ring sits beside my mountain sunset. I automatically move my hand, covering both of them for a split second, as I look into Luke's bright green eyes.

When we decided this is what we wanted, just us, on the beach, we also decided we didn't want to wait. *At all.* I don't care that it's not legally binding, to me, I think it means even more. I've lived a lot of my life over the last years in front of other people, that's not what Lucas and I are, what we've ever been. The only thing I wanted was to marry the sweet, dimpled, small-town boy that makes me the happiest I've ever been. I do want to talk to Henry before I wear the ring, so for now, it sits on the same delicate chain as my mountain sunset.

"With this ring, I thee wed," I whisper. My hand shakes as I slide the gold band we stopped to purchase on our way here. I suddenly ache to wear mine on my finger, but it means too much to me, to Henry.

"I don't know what's next," Luke whispers.

"I vote kiss," I say, smiling up at him.

"Good idea, wife," Luke says, tugging me closer. I love the sound of 'wife' almost as much as I love the look he's giving me.

I let him give me a soft, gentle kiss, the kind that he'd give me if this was a real wedding, instead of us standing on the beach, wind whipping and waves crashing, only a few people in the distance, making things up as we go along.

"I love you," I whisper, cupping his jaw, when he pulls away.

"I love you," he replies, giving me the dimpled smile that I've missed so much these last weeks.

Without warning, he dips me back low, kissing me through my surprised gasp.

"Lucas!" I laugh when he pulls me upright, shaking my head at him. I have loved his playfulness since the very first day. As if he can read my mind, he throws me over his shoulder and starts up the beach toward our hotel.

"Wait!" I cry.

Lucas immediately stops but doesn't let me down. His hand stays firmly planted on the back of my thighs.

"I need a picture!"

He slowly slides me down his front, then steals my phone from my waistband. After a handful of selfies, he hauls me over his shoulder again.

"Okay, wife, you needed a picture, but now I need you."

***

"Your tattoo," Luke says, his eyes catching on the ink as he pulls my shirt over my head. Our frantic kisses come to a screeching halt as he stares at the mountains on my ribcage.

"Cry-worthy mountains," I tell him, shivering under his gaze. I need him. Now.

"It's perfect," he says, gently running his fingers below the mountains. "You're perfect."

"Luke, I want you so bad," I whisper. It's been weeks without his touch and this is my breaking point. "Please."

"I only get to have one first night with my wife," he replies, skating his fingers from my ribs to my waistband before pausing to give me a dimpled smirk. "And I'm going to take *all* night."

"Well, it's afternoon," I tell him, watching as he peels my black leggings off, finally ridding me of my last article of clothing.

He sits back on his heels and drops them to the floor. I'm suddenly very thankful it's afternoon, the sun is spilling through our hotel room window and a beam of light hits his rippling abs, sending a jolt of need through me all over again.

"That just means I get even more time with you," he says with a smile, dropping a condom onto the bed next to me. "I've spent every night dreaming about you, wishing you were here. And now you are. Fuck. You're my real life dream, now my real life wife."

His ring flashes as he tosses his wallet to the floor and I can't breathe. My need for him is so intense, I don't know which way is up. I am drowning. He is my air.

"Luke," I whisper. "I need you to kiss me."

Immediately, he's hovering over me, licking into my mouth, one hand cupping my jaw, thumb rubbing my cheek gently. I wrap my legs around him, needing him closer.

"Hey, hey, what's wrong?" he whispers, pulling back when I take a shuddering breath between urgent kisses.

296

"I love you," I tell him, feeling my eyes fill with tears for the thousandth time in the last few weeks.

"I love you," he immediately replies. He wipes the single tear that escapes the corner of my eye. "So much."

He peppers my face with little kisses, making me laugh. Making me love him even more.

"It's just so much, this overwhelming rush of emotions, this need I feel for you," I try to explain. "I just need my husband."

I think 'husband' is the magic word. There's always been heat behind his kisses, in nearly every touch between us, but this is an inferno that feels like it will rage out of control. The clenching deep in my core feels like it's going to shatter my soul. I am frantic, reaching for his belt, pleading with him as he kicks out of his jeans. When he's finally above me, reaching for the condom that is lost in this tangle of sheets, I can't.

"Just you and me," I tell him, tugging him back down toward me. "Nothing between us."

And then he's sliding inside me, his mouth on mine, his whispered words in my ear, every part of him completing every part of me.

***

"Zoe and Lucas, day one," I say with a smile, leaning back into my husband's chest as I try to hold my phone at an angle to capture both of us without spilling the champagne that's in my other hand. "Day one of marriage. Holy shit. Yesterday I was in Nevada, waiting on an airplane, and now..."

I trail off, looking beyond my phone to the sunset. There really aren't words. But I've never been more sure of myself. Of where I am or where I'm going. What I'm going to do. Everything feels right.

"Now you're Zoe Last Name Stark?" Lucas supplies when I don't continue.

"I didn't even think of that, but I do like the sound of it," I murmur.

"Me, too," he whispers. He takes the phone from me as I falter, overwhelmed once again.

"To us," I say, lifting my plain white hotel room coffee mug of champagne up in a toast toward the camera.

"Just you and me," Lucas toasts, tapping his matching mug to mine. He rests his chin on my shoulder after taking a sip, a quick recreation of our very first sunset picture, then turns the camera off and tucks my phone into my waistband for me. We sink down into the sand, my back to his chest, and watch as our first day of marriage fades into the horizon.

Epilogue
One and a half years later

"Hi, Mrs. Stark," I whisper, sliding my arm around Zoe, who's standing with Kelsey's mom.

"Hi, Husband," she says, grinning up at me. "I thought Kelsey might be the lure Gramps needed."

All three of us watch as Gramps makes a beeline for Kelsey, who is dancing around the room with Pearl, the wild child that is West and Tex's baby girl.

"You really don't want a real wedding?" Mrs. G asks Zoe, for the hundredth time. "You don't think Henry would like to shuffle around a wedding dance floor?"

As I knew he would be, Gramps was ecstatic when Zoe and I came home and told him about our beach non-wedding wedding.

"All that matters is your promises to each other," he told us with a nod, like his word was final. And apparently it was, because Zoe grabbed him in a hug and cried until I slid Grandma's ring onto her finger.

"Oh, Mrs. G, I love you, but you gotta give it up," Zoe says laughing. "Ours was perfect. I live too much of my life with spectators."

"I just love love," Mrs. G sighs as Zoe nestles into me. "You two are perfect for each other."

Zoe slips back out of my grasp and hugs Mrs. G, who has become an extension of our family. She was the first person to show up on our doorstep when the three of us moved into West's house, a platter of cookies in one hand and a game of checkers in the other, plus a ball of yarn hidden in her purse for Egg. I quickly learned that if I thought the Team Merc girls took their commitment to community to heart, they had nothing on Mrs. G. She's the glue that holds Three Rocks together during those cold, dark, rainy winter months.

"We really did get married, though," I whisper as Zoe widens her eyes at me. I shrug. "At the courthouse, and she really did take my name." It's not really a secret, we just didn't tell anyone besides Gramps and Zoe's family. It's more an ongoing joke at this point, seeing how many times people ask us. (It's a LOT.)

A joke I will happily give up because seeing Mrs. G's eyes light up makes me smile. She and Zoe do a happy dance because, of course, Zoe has half the town doing it these days. I shake my head, plant a kiss on my wife's cheek, and head to the crowded kitchen to grab a drink.

"Hey Nate," Oliver, one of the new firefighters says in a low voice as I walk in. "Not only did the kid steal your girl, but now Gramps got a dance."

I glance back, watching as Kelsey laughs before saying something that makes Gramps's cheeks turn red. I remind myself to thank Kelsey once again for adopting Gramps as her own. Despite Kelsey moving to Corvallis, they've kept in touch ever since that first Instagram lesson at The Town Mercantile. The number of reels they send to each other on a daily basis is ridiculous. She even invited him to Grandparents Weekend at Oregon State.

"Even Zoe can't make him smile like that," I tell the group. "He told me he was too tired to come, but when Zoe sent him a pic of Kelsey dancing with the kids, he was putting his shoes on and demanding I drive him over."

"Can't say I blame him," Jake mutters under his breath. I raise my eyebrows.

"What was that?" Zoe asks, stepping into the kitchen.

"Nothing," Jake mumbles.

Pearl comes toddling around the corner and runs directly into Jake's legs.

"Uh!" the wild-haired girl demands, reaching her hands up.

Jake looks around the room in a panic. I can feel Zoe shaking with laughter, waiting to see how this plays out.

"Uh!" she demands again.

Jake reaches down cautiously like he's about to be bit by a rabid dog. Having spent a good amount of time with the kid, that's fair.

"Wow, you calmed the tiny tornado," Zoe says as Pearl leans into Jake's chest.

"Hi, Pearl," I say, offering a fist. She bumps her little hand to mine. I swear, this kid came out of the womb running. She'll be a year old in another week or so, but she's already a loose cannon.

Pearl points her little finger toward the couch. Jake looks at me and I shrug. He sighs and crosses the room as commanded.

"You need to take him hiking soon," Zoe says, watching as Pearl settles herself into Jake's lap. "The only time he's not a grouch is when he's at the gym. I swear those angsty teenagers are wearing off on him."

Before I can reply, she's pulled away by Tex, who starts teaching her the two-step. I lean against the counter and watch her laugh with Tex, thankful as always that she walked into The Mercantile that day.

She was the one that Gramps asked for in the emergency room the day he fell, the one that took him to physical therapy every week as he slowly recovered. She's the one that has given a voice to so many of our friends and neighbors, helping Nancy push for expanded library classes, highlighting the new all-abilities park with Abby and Gramps, and bringing Seth in to build upon her, Lauren, and Jake's gym program. She's recruited other content creators to join ZoeSaysDonate in featuring local nonprofits and the response is overwhelming, to say the least.

"Pretty glad I pushed you out there that morning?" Marabelle asks, appearing beside me.

"You have no idea," I tell her. Zoe catches my eye from across the room and gives me her beaming smile. "I knew those cinnamon rolls were magic from the beginning."

"I think your friend just might be next," Mar says, nodding toward Jake.

I frown in confusion. He has Pearl passed out on his chest, one hand protectively covering her back. His eyes are on Zoe, who is now laughing with Kelsey and Colt. She can't really think Jake's after my wife.

"Just wait," Marabelle adds.

301

When Zoe and Colt head for the kitchen, Jake's eyes don't follow them, they stay planted on Kelsey.

Oh, this is going to be good.

Afterword

Wow, look at us, right back here, you holding my book, me on the couch with a foster puppy.

I hope you enjoyed Gramps's story. I mean, Lucas and Zoe's story.

As usual, I did things a little out of order. Oops.

While the epilogue teased something different, the next book, the third in the series, is (finally) Avery's story.

I'm so glad you gave a new author like me a chance. Thank you.

Love it? Hate it? Find me on Instagram and let me know! My favorite part about being an author? Connecting with readers. Seriously. Look me up.

Acknowledgement

Thank you, as always, to my husband, for so many things. Mainly for claiming to hate social media as you show me reels you think are funny. About half are.

Thank you to my editor who only told me thirteen times to stop changing that one chapter before I listened. Also, thanks for always being my adventure buddy, even when those adventures involve tent camping in below-freezing weather.

Thank you to my cover photographer for trying to limit your exasperated sighs. I'm sorry you couldn't have chapstick in the tent but I didn't want you to be eaten by a bear.

A special note of thanks to Chris Clarke, the volunteer manager at High Hopes Therapeutic Riding, who helped me fine-tune pieces of Zoe's story, including her visit to the fictional equine program in Wyoming. While Chris's job title in the book and Zoe's entire visit are fictional, therapeutic horseback riding is very real.

Therapeutic horseback riding is perhaps the best-known aspect of equine-assisted services. Equine-assisted services help individuals with a wide range of special needs by allowing them to connect with horses through riding, driving, or ground-based horsemanship. These services can truly be life-changing for individuals with disabilities, improving balance, flexibility, muscle strength, coordination, confidence, and self-esteem.
There are over 760 centers providing equine assisted services in the US and Canada, largely supported by volunteers and funded by generous

donors. If you are interested in learning more or getting involved, you can find more information at https://pathintl.org/

Finally, thank you to every reader that took the time to reach out, even the ones that just asked if a character was named after them, as connecting with y'all is still my favorite part of this. Just not in a Zoe way. Because I'm not bubbly, I'm an introvert.

About The Author

Wesley Harper Wesley Harper is an amateur author, semi-professional coffee drinker, and advanced overthinker.

After thirty-nine-and-three-quarters years not writing books, she decided to write a book before her fortieth birthday.

And then another.

When not making random goals and accidentally writing books, she enjoys working out in her garage gym, fostering puppies, and embarrassing her nearly adult offspring. And maybe sometimes running away to the Oregon Coast.

www.ingramcontent.com/pod-product-compliance
Lightning Source LLC
Chambersburg PA
CBHW010533100726
47903CB00011B/2990